Ray Crowther was born in London and now l
He is married and has two daughters.

He read Cybernetics and Mathematics a
worked in systems development jobs in Engl
his own company specializing in human resources software.

During his systems career he had technical papers published and wrote more reference manuals than he can remember. He maintains that the exacting discipline of technical authoring prepared him well for a creative change into fiction writing. He cites Robert Goddard as his favourite author and biggest influence on his own writing style.

Ray's first novel entitled *The Nearest FarAway Place* (ISBN: 0954111001) was completed in November 1999 and published in 2001. This novel *Panglossian* was originally published in 2002 and awarded a Golgonooza Medal of Merit.

After a writing gap during which he sold his company, retired to the countryside and remarried, he completed this novel, *Schoolfrenz* (ISBN: 0954111036), in March 2005. Ray also regularly writes articles for motor sport publications.

When he is not writing, Ray can be found competing in motor rallies, jogging his local lanes and footpaths (where most of his fiction ideas evolve), organizing table-top rallies and pegularities, designing websites, developing payroll software and farming chickens.

He connects the achievements in his life to running: running a successful company; running around after his two daughters, Caroline and Rebecca; and running the London Marathon.

Panglossian

Ray Crowther

Published by Panglossian Books

Panglossian

Published by Panglossian Books

ISBN: 0-9541110-1-X

Cover photograph by Ray Crowther
Cover Design by Peter Rymill

Third edition – December 2005
(Second edition – April 2002)
(First edition – March 2002)

Printed and bound by Antony Rowe Limited, Eastbourne

Panglossian Books
Longfield, Tudwick Road, Tolleshunt Major, Maldon, CM9 8LP, England

ACKNOWLEDGEMENTS

To my proofreaders: Christine Grover, Diane Hernaman, Pam Rymill, Dave Keable, Steve Tumbridge and Angela Tumbridge.

To the homeless people I lived with during Christmas 1999, for inspiring many of the characters.

To Pete Rymill for cover artwork.

To Rob Gimes – my model for Robin Forest.

To Christine for her tolerance and patience while this novel was being written.

And to fill up the page, a list of friends, colleagues and heroes, who have surely influenced my life and provided novel inspirations:

George Hendry, Adrian Cull, Roger Lofting, Chris Farley, Alan Carter, Pete Smith, Alex Lane, Andy Brook, Tom Hood, Anna Villani, Tony Morris, Barry Harris, Bill Bannister, Bob DeAngelis, Joseph Kent, Richard Bird, Michael Grundy, Raymond Mayers, Kathleen Oliver, Brenda Moore, Gilllian Fellick, Emma Towers, Pat Secker, Brenda Smith, Frances Carey, Hettie Dixon, Christine Matthews, Jennifer Gold, Clare Pettitt, Clive Baty, Dave Pooley, David Potter, David Storey, Debbie Harrison, Don Grunbaum, Doreen Murphy, Emma Jay, Terry Tremlett, Emma Pemberton, Bob Pamplin, Grahame Points, Chris Larkin, Alan Huggins, Geoff White, Graham Roper, Heather Carnera, Paul Hernaman, Steve Lobb, Brian Smith, John Hobcraft, Jeremy Ceh, Kate Faithfull, Robin Hernaman, Keith Edgley, Keith Francis, Mike Dunion, Ken Allen, Jim Mullarkey, Sandra Stops, Roy Caselton, Hayley Gilmour, Ken Larking, Tony Woodhouse, Roger Clark, Kevin Dixon, Doug Coleman, Steve Rapley, Leslie Barnes, Lisa Robertson, Valerie Saywell, Terry Underwood, Tony Briley, Trevor Martin, Chris Fincham, Audrey Richardson, Jimmy Smith, Joseph Gillam, Michael Pizer, John Matthews, Mandi Garnham-Taylor, Mfanelo Bhebhe, John Lennon, Mike Alston, Graham Hill, Fred Dawson, Joanne Howard, John Stowell, Damon Hill, April Barclay, Jenny Keable, Mike Alston, Miles Henderson, Dave Herring, Ron Laver, Nadia Cane, Kay San Soen, Steve Thomas, Nicky Derbyshire, Nigel Booth, Sue Potter, Paul Leach, Peter Hayes, Jane Barnes, Chris Knighton, Stuart Peacock, Tim Morris, Christine Hayes, Tony Cook, Richard Baker, John Harmer, Terry Willingham, Terry Reid, Jacqui Hearn, Gordon Bird, John Kirvan, Ian Chambers, Eddie Crowther, Robin Morgan, Rhys Roberts, Lisa Halil, Ron Crowther, Richard Barnes, Les Long, Richard Strawson, Robert Boardman, Robyn Mitchell, Roger Dowgill, Rowland Costin, John Richardson, Sam Morgan, Sandra Beckerleg, Robert Wyness, Peter Webb, Julia White, Anne Morris, Paul Dodge, Mick Lee, Jennifer Bull, Dave Beckerleg, Sarah Gore, John Porter, Carol Guth-Hayden, Josephine Lyne, Ellis Chinn, Frank Porter, Brian Wilson, Pete Higgins, Agnetha Faltskog, Tony Pook, Sarah Cohen, Phil Chambers, Louise Towers, Wendy Grunbaum, Amy Derbyshire, David Galley, Geraldine Churchill, Anna King, Peggy Crowther, Roger Carpenter, Michelle Deacon, Keith Nicholls, Steve Tate, Sheena Mackenzie, Andy Llewellyn, Derek Corps, Brian Dunleavy, Stuart Adams, Peter Kaufmann, Sue Laver, Clive Selby, Suzanne Welton, Tim Moore, Simon Barnes, Tony Overland, Steven King, Laurie Murphy, Velma Barnes, Trish Cumbers, Pablo Contreras, Janice Herring, Duke, Bob Gray, Kevin Dixon, Patrick Bennett, Jan Blackhall, Susanne Chumbley, Cathy Boniface, Geoffrey Edler, Tony Frewer, Tony Rowberry, Jeffrey Green, Linda Towers, Jeffrey Keller, Elizabeth Livings, Joan Martin, Jim Hurley, Christine Shepherd, Lesley Worts, Anna Hine, Pamela Wright, Edie Allen, Sally Hendry, Robert Goddard, Michael Barclay, Gunther Schoemans, Jim Hair, Neville Skeet, John Grant, Geoff Lobb, Lyulph Hesling, Rod Cattini, David Barsby, Victoria Hazael, Charles Golding, Tony Gibbs, Neil Brett, Graham Love, John Dixon, Tony Thorne, Mark Longhurst, Paul Carlier, Malcolm Heymer, Peter Barnes, Margaret Richardson, Chris Rees, Dave Watkinson, Roy Johnson, Christine Crowther, Pete Goodwin, Tony Beesley, John Ringwood, Sabrina Achilleos, Nigel Derbyshire, Cathy Logan, Nick Duarte, Philip Frogg, Alan Warne, Susan Kipping, Norman Lewis, Robert Curry, Wally Greaves, Julie Banfield, Grace Potter, Marion Muspratt, Teresa Harrison, Chris Towers, Janice Wells, Mick Linsell, Jim Macintosh, Kathleen Kent, Bernice Dunn, Susan Baldwin, Susan Evans, Dave Hughes, to name but a few.

For Mum and Dad, Caroline and Rebecca

Indeed, history is nothing more than a tableau of crimes and misfortunes.
Voltaire, L'Ingénu, Chapter 10

Prologue

I still have flashbacks and dreams about those prefatory days.

The flashbacks can arrive at any time without consideration for my safety or peace of mind. What triggers them, I cannot say. I have been crossing the road, turning a steering wheel, showering, even making love, when a slight pressure inside my head announces a flow of memories is on its way. They come as a trickle – a brief opening of a tap – and show in real time, a few seconds of my normally inaccessible life. There is no pain and thankfully only a short lapse in concentration while I separate the past and present. I have now grown used to, and can handle, such ad-hoc intrusions in my new life.

When the manifestations of memories come in a dream, the trickle develops into an uncontrollable flood, and I am swamped with minutes or hours of personal history. When I wake, I am exhausted and emotionally confused, but I have learnt to deal with that too.

The recollections have become repetitive and unstimulating, and rarely do I glean any new fragments of information. I have wondered recently whether my perceived decline in images is real, or just my mind automatically discarding redundant material.

However, it does seem cruel and strange that my innocent past is denied me, yet the traumatic few days leading to this story have been continuously exposed in unrelenting detail.

My school and university days appear to be lost forever and most of my early working life too. Of course, the knowledge gained from distant lessons continues to be employed sub-consciously in my daily routine. It's the when, where and who that are missing, not the how and what. Time, place and person evade me. For example, I know how a petrol engine works, but not when I acquired the facts, or from where or whom. Does it really matter if Mr. Johnson (the Physics master?) taught me the principles of internal combustion in the third year of my secondary school education? Not to me; I have adjusted to the vacuum of my first twenty-five years.

Friends and family are willing and able to fill some of the gaps but I choose not to enlist their help.

Like me, perhaps your present is dominated by thoughts of the future rather than the past. I know in making decisions I could be disadvantaged, since I cannot consult experiences of old, yet I console myself that I approach each new problem with a mind clear of earlier prejudices.

The doctors hypothesize the earlier memories remain – since my brain is complete and physically undamaged – so there can only be subconscious reasons why they cannot, or will not, be accessed.

I have allowed my mind to be manipulated by hypnosis and drugs in order to satisfy the medical profession's curiosity, but each attempt has failed, and the highly-rewarded consultants have worried about me, only – cynical person that I am – until the next fee-paying appointment.

However, there will be no more appointments. Whatever the residual psychological or physiological reasons, the past no longer matters; I have a future to look forward to.

Chapter 1

FIRST FRIDAY – 3:30 p.m.

After my six-hour drive back from convalescence, it is a spur of the moment decision to visit the local library. I had borrowed a stack of books on French political history – a particular passion of mine – two weeks earlier. I haven't read them all and there is a week remaining on the loan period, but I am passing the library so I call in. I am eager to cram my head with more knowledge of 18th century Gallic constitutional thought in the remaining two days before I go back to work, so I browse the shelves for more reading material. I am attracted to two volumes by Voltaire, so I settle at a table and go through my ritual of scanning random pages to ensure my selections are relevant to my studies. Satisfied, I head for the checkout counter and noisily place two piles of books and my library card in front of the dozing middle-aged female librarian.

'Two to take out and these to return,' I say loudly, pointing to the separate heaps.

She visibly starts, and without looking up, swipes the barcode on the card with an electronic wand. The connected terminal beeps with satisfaction. She is about to swipe the first book when her attention moves from the display screen to me. Her look is blank and as if to mind read my observation she says, 'It's blank.'

'What's blank?' I ask innocently.

'Your library record of course,' she replies in a sleep-disturbed patronizing way. 'There's no name or address!'

'This happens often, does it?' I say, trying to echo her disdainful tone.

She chooses not to respond to my question but instead asks in the manner of a police officer confronting a suspect, 'I need to know who you are. What ID do you have with you? Passport? Driving Licence?'

'No, No,' I say with certainty and thrust my hand in my trouser back pocket searching for something with my name on it. I offer my plastic Visa card. 'How about a credit card?' I say triumphantly.

'Does it have your address on it?' my inquisitress demands.

'No, of course not; but then neither would my passport.'

That stalls her aggression. She looks bewildered for a moment then she bounces back. 'You'll have to come back with proof of address. You can't take these books out.'

'Then presumably as I don't exist, I can't return these books to you either?' I say argumentatively, placing my hand on the larger pile.

She taps a few keys on her keyboard, harder than seems necessary. She regards the screen, me, the books and then the screen again.

'You don't...' she begins and then realizing she is about to donate some books to me, she snatches them away. Reflexively I withdraw my hand as though snapped at by a dog, although bitch would have been a better analogy.

'Aren't you going to log them back in again?'

'I can't since they aren't booked out to you.'

It is now my turn to be officious. 'I'll need a receipt for them.'

The receipt dilemma leads to the summoning of the chief librarian – a large, balding, ruddy faced, casually dressed gentleman who I assess could be the prototypal pub landlord. His nature is more forgiving and, courtesy of his customer relations training, he apologetically resolves the quandary in my favour, the scapegoat emerging temporarily as the defenceless, and inanimate computer system without regard to its human programming or operation. I discern though – by the accusatory glance from male to female librarian – that the matter will receive further scrutiny once I have departed.

Unfazed by the time-wasting experience in the library I leave the building in high spirits. Suddenly the Voltairean adjective I had spied earlier, Panglossian – pertaining to a person who is optimistic regardless of the circumstances – appears unannounced in my head; like an omen. I consider its predictive nature and dismiss it. Despite my mysterious disappearance from the library records, I have no pessimism. Indeed, I believe I have much to look forward to: my scar is almost healed; I have two days of leisure ahead, one of which will be spent with Julie; and on Monday I return to a job I enjoy and which has great prospects.

Chapter 2

FIRST TUESDAY – 10:00 a.m.

I first noticed the smell: an antiseptic aroma, which reminded me of the oily liquid that the nurse at school used to administer for cuts and bruises. I felt nauseous and was initially uncertain whether the reason was the pervasive odour, or the searing pain over my eyes whenever I tried to move my head. I could hear distant voices speaking in hushed tones, and tinny music close by, reminiscent of the sound that escapes from the earphones of a Walkman. Occasionally, there was a hacking cough from someone to my right. The ambient noises had a familiarity about them, which I had experienced recently.

Quite how these sensations related to my most recent memories of a public library were beyond me.

I fluttered my eyelids open and briefly saw a slightly blurred white expanse before the increase in pain level initiated a reflex action to shut them again. At least three of my senses – smell, hearing and sight – appeared to be intact so I diverted my attention to taste. I moved my tongue gently from side to side in my mouth and immediately experienced a new pain from the swollen fleshy lump as it glanced against a newly discovered jagged edge. Then the taste buds kicked in as the coppery tang of blood registered in my brain.

Now for the final sense of touch. I started with my arms climbing the scales of achievement from finger twitching to wrist shakes, elbow bends and shoulder stretches, first the right arm and then the left. The right passed with flying colours: no twinges, no soreness, and no restriction of movement – so far so good. On the left, I detected a pliable material from the shoulder to just below the elbow – a bandage not a cast. Any shift in this area brought forth a pain, which drew beads of perspiration on my brow. I rested before examining my legs, working from toes to ankles, knee and hip. Again the right side felt intact and unharmed. Then the left; toes – okay; ankles – okay; knee – some discomfort; hip ...

Chapter 3

FIRST TUESDAY – 12:00 p.m.

After my earlier painful shock, when I had undoubtedly passed out, I had become wise to my situation. I laid still and once more in my self-imposed darkness, I concentrated on building a picture of my surroundings gleaned only from sounds. I heard careful footsteps approach and stop close to me. After a few seconds of silence a young woman's softly spoken voice said, 'No Inspector, I think I may have misled you earlier. I thought I'd seen him stirring just before I called, but he's been still ever since.'

'Now that I am here, I may as well stay for a short while. Would that be okay nurse?' the Inspector asked. His voice offered no clue to his appearance: foreign London accent, polite, well spoken.

I heard a chair scrape across the floor and settle near the bed head. Then I had the distinct feeling of someone leaning over me: a subtle change in the light permeating my closed eyelids, a temperature variance from a body nearby or maybe breathing sounds louder than my own. I opened my eyes and saw a receding shadow in my peripheral vision, and at the same time heard a gasp of surprise.

'Gawd. You frightened the life out of me son. How do you feel?' said the Inspector. He didn't wait for an answer – not that I was capable of giving one – before he called out, 'Nurse, nurse, he's awake.'

I focused on a white background again, but this time I could detect a clinically smooth high ceiling. Then I felt a soft hand gently grasp my right wrist and I glanced towards the attention. A blue uniformed staff nurse with a rosy face was beaming at me in satisfaction while she took my pulse. She moved her free hand towards my face. 'Watch my hand,' she commanded. I blinked, and then dutifully let my eyes follow her hand as she drew a figure of eight in the air. She hummed non-commitally, giving no indication as to whether I had passed the test.

From my prone state, I saw her nod at the black shape hovering on the other side of the bed, the small suggestion being enough for the ebony outline to leave and allow the nurse to draw curtains around my rectangular recovery area. I was puzzling about the secretive behaviour when my carer gently peeled back the bed covers and I felt a chill as my cocooned, almost naked body was exposed to the atmosphere. She regarded me thoughtfully. I was convinced she was staring at the exposed region between my legs, but my body seemed too medically suppressed to detect a flush of embarrassment.

She raised her eyes from my groin and said, 'Can you speak yet?'

What a stupid question I first thought, but when I came to answer, my bulbous tongue reminded me that she spoke from prior knowledge. I dribbled a painfully feeble garbled reply of 'Yeth, og corth'.

She laughed sympathetically, but I consciously withheld joining in her amusement for fear of a further testimony to my agonizing predicament.

'I'll give you a pain killer to ease the discomfort,' she said. She moved to the bed head and cranked a handle, which elevated my head and shoulders a few degrees into a more visually advantageous position. She stepped out through a gap in the curtains and I took the opportunity to examine my body and surroundings. I recalled my earlier physical reconnaissance and needed to confirm the source of my painful experiences. I craned my neck to its threshold of pain and carefully raised my left arm and there was indeed a white bandage covering the upper half. The area above my wrist was strapped too, and a clear plastic tube emerged and disappeared somewhere above my left shoulder, just beyond the comfort zone of my head rotation and vision. I couldn't see any dressing on my apparently injured left leg although the top looked dark in comparison to the whiteness of my stomach. It could have been a trick of the light so I decided to conduct an examination with my left hand. I started at the knee and gradually edged higher. At the top of the thigh my fingers detected a smooth tautness to the skin; I pressed lightly but it felt as though the World's strongest man was pushing a steel rod into my leg. With clenched teeth I continued my exploration and discovered the hypersensitive patch extended to a depth of six inches, and of a width from close to my groin to my left buttock. Most distressing was the area closest to my hipbone.

I was beginning to wonder how I had sustained such injuries, when the nurse reappeared with a white-coated man in tow, who stopped at the end of the bed and bent down to retrieve a clipboard. The nurse went to the cabinet to my right and I heard her pour a glass of water. She cranked the bed higher and then placed her left hand behind my head for support. Two small pink pills were waved in front of my mouth and I responded by producing a gap large enough for her to place them on my tongue. Awkwardly she picked up the prepared glass, rested it against my lower lip and tilted slowly until the liquid flowed into my mouth. I swallowed the pills, but not without a small cascade of water escaping via my chin to my bare chest. A tissue was quickly produced to avert a pool appearing in my navel. Despite the throb I licked my lips and my plea for more water was acknowledged, and this time administered and absorbed without spillage.

The nurse stood back and the doctor shuffled into her place. He was short with an untidy head of grey hair. There was matching stubble on his chin and the bright green tie beneath his white coat was slewed to one side. He had heavy bags under his eyes, which were magnified by the thickness of the large wire framed spectacles, which were balanced precariously on the end of his long nose. The friendly roundness of his face seemed at odds with the rest of his appearance, which I had associated with that of a mad professor who had emerged from an all night session of splitting atoms.

He held his hands behind his back and leaned over me scanning quickly over my body. Then he shuffled, probably limped, to the other side of the bed. There he deliberated longer, scrutinizing close up, but never touching, the part of me I had diagnosed was the most severe of my injuries. Disconcertingly he kept shaking his head from side to side and making short sucking noises. This continued for a minute before he straightened up and pulled the bedclothes up to my chest.

'Yes, his leg is a nice shade of blue. I believe it is healing well. He is looking much better after his ordeal. He has colour in his cheeks, don't you think so?'

He was looking at me but his comments were clearly directed to the nurse. There was a distant hint of an eastern European accent and for a moment, from his words, I harboured the thought I was the guinea pig of a bizarre experiment, contradicting my assumption that I was in a general hospital.

'Yes doctor, he can speak too,' said the nurse.

'Excellent. Tell us your story my young patient,' the doctor expressed excitedly and pulled up a chair to sit down. He sighed as though he was relieved to take the weight off his aged feet.

I swilled saliva in my mouth for lubrication and detected that the pink pills were already doing their job. My tongue felt almost normal, and my eyes were wider now the throbbing over my eyes had lessened. I opened my mouth to speak, but the nurse interrupted.

'Wait,' she said, 'the Inspector will need to hear this too.' She stuck her head through the curtains and whispered to the policeman to join us. The plain-clothed officer entered and sat in a chair that he positioned on the opposite side of the bed to the doctor. He was a large black man – probably in his forties – who immediately produced a notebook and held a pen poised as if ready to take dictation.

Suddenly a feeling of helplessness came over me. Until then, I hadn't been concerned with who I was, where I was or why I was here, I had been too concerned with the pain and my injuries. I searched my brain for answers but none came. Instead, questions began to form in my mind. The doctor must have been worried by the probable troubled look on my face and broke the silence reassuringly.

'You are in safe hands. I'm Doctor Boromin and I've been looking after you with nurse Rapley.' He nodded towards the nurse who was guarding the gap in the curtains. 'The officer here ...' he paused and pointed across the bed; on cue the big man said, 'Bradley, sir, Detective Inspector Bradley', '... is here to take a statement about what happened to you.

'Where am I?' I asked with a diction that was levels above my previous attempt at speaking.

I was looking straight ahead to the nurse at the end of the bed – the most comfortable position for my head. The nurse assumed I was addressing her.

'The Wellington Ward at the Royal London hospital, in Whitechapel ... East London,' she said.

The East London qualification wasn't necessary. I didn't know who I was, but my London geography appeared to be intact.

With difficulty I leaned to my left to face the doctor. 'Why ... am ... I ... here?' I stuttered and realized immediately it was a stupid question and action as a red-hot poker was plunged into my thigh and recoiled me back to my safe location. I quickly posed a more appropriate question as the doctor jumped up to attend me. 'What ... what's wrong with me?'

The doctor leaned over me and offered his clinical explanation. 'You have sustained several injuries to the left side of your body. A gash above your left eye extending to the crown has had ten stitches. Your upper left arm is severely bruised and there were multiple lacerations along the length of your arm. Your left leg suffered in much the same way, but the most troublesome is a grade two strain of your rectus femoris – that's a muscle stretching from your upper thigh to the knee area. The physical prognosis is excellent; I believe you will be mobile in about a week, albeit with some residual stiffness and soreness which will take longer to abate.'

The revelations came as no surprise; the only puzzlement was the lack of injuries to my right side.

'What happened to me?' I said to no one in particular.

It was the Inspector's turn to stand so that he was within my constrained view.

'You've had an accident. You were found unconscious at the side of the road in Hanbury Street two nights ago. We've been trying to discover how you got there and who you are,' Bradley said.

That was a statement I had been expecting and dreading. I was conscious and aware of my predicament and surroundings and I believed, though I wasn't sure why, that my knowledge of language and social customs was intact, but I was buggered if I knew any more.

9

'You'll have to help me there Inspector, I haven't the faintest idea. The most distant memory I have at the moment is from no more than a few hours ago when I first woke up in this bed.'

Bradley looked across to Boromin, his furrowed brow seeking an explanation.

Boromin ran his fingers through his hair and pondered. 'The most obvious conclusion is a temporary amnesia because of the blow to his head. That would usually account for the loss of memory for the time just before and just after his accident. Not remembering anything before then is more worrying.'

Nurse Rapley had joined the doctor and was leaning over me too; I felt like a specimen under a microscope.

'Can you recall anything about your state of mind before the accident?' Boromin asked.

I was tired and wanted to sleep. The diagnosis and scrutiny was beginning to take its toll on me. I had already given my fullest and frankest answer, and speaking had become a major effort. I considered shaking my head in response, but my short-term memory reminded me this might be too painful. Instead I mustered strength and uttered a weak, 'No'.

'Why is that relevant doctor?' Bradley asked.

'If my patient here ... let's call him Alan for want of a name; if Alan had previously been suffering emotional stress or had an overwhelming problem, this most recent event may have initiated retrograde hysterical amnesia. Sub-consciously Alan's mind is shutting out the past because it can't face the reality of his situation. It's only a theory. I've never encountered such a case before.'

As my eyes closed with fatigue, the voices continued above me, but had diminished to a level beyond the amplification powers of my fading consciousness. My last memory was an annoyance at being referred to as Alan; perhaps my past was already coming back to me – I was sure that wasn't my name.

Chapter 4

FIRST TUESDAY – 7:30 p.m.

I sensed someone nearby and confirmation came when I heard the tinkle of glass against glass close by. I opened my eyes and knew it was evening. The curtains were closed except for a gap a few feet wide in front of me. Through it I could see the other side of the ward – a couple of occupied beds and a window between them. From the blackness of the panes and a recall that earlier they had revealed daylight, I realized night had fallen. I must have stirred because the shape near me appeared as nurse Rapley.

'I have some medication for you,' she said as she popped another brace of pink pills into my mouth. She placed a hand gently behind my head and tilted me forward offering a glass of water with the other hand.

I swallowed the pills and studied her in detail for the first time. She looked about mid-twenties, and her round face and bob hairstyle gave her a chubby appearance, although the shape of her uniform showed that her facial plumpness had not been inherited in her body shape. But it was her bonny, rosy complexion and bright, clear, blue eyes that made me feel comfortable when she was in attendance.

'Could you do me a favour?' I asked.

She smiled suggestively. 'Scratch an awkward place?'

I smiled back. 'No, a mirror. Could you get me a mirror? I don't even know what I look like.' It was an obvious idea prompted by studying her face. Viewing myself in a mirror could initiate the crucial trigger I needed to discover my identity.

She disappeared briefly and returned with a double-sided shaving mirror. I swung it round to the unmagnified side and held it a foot from my face. I recognized my normal face immediately: the medium length, dark brown hair; blue eyes; clean shaven – except for signs of stubble growth from the last few (?) days; high cheek bones, on an otherwise undistinguished white face. There were unwanted additions: swollen lip; bruised forehead; stitches above my left eye; and using the magnifying side of the mirror, I located one broken tooth. It was certainly me, but still a nameless me.

'Can you put a name to the face?' the nurse asked.

'No, not yet,' I said positively. 'What's *your* name?'

'Nurse Rapley, but you already know unless your short-term memory is playing tricks too.'

'No, your first name.'

'Sam,' she said, pointing to the small badge on her uniform.

'As in Samantha?' I queried.

'No, as in Samedi, my mother is French and guess what day I was born.' She smiled quizzically as if to test my linguistic capability.

'C'est facile. Il est bon, que vous n'ayez pas été soutenus Dimanche, autrement que vous vous appelleriez Dim,' I replied and she laughed.

'Merde, vous parlez français très bien. Êtes-vous nés en France?'

The question stunned my Gallic flow. Like a nervous orator at a crucial moment in his discourse my mind froze, my body too. I shivered as I struggled to reach beyond the impenetrable barrier that guarded my past.

'I ... I ... don't know,' I stammered, reverting to English.

'Doctor Boromin predicted this would happen.' she said. 'As time passes there will be events, which will give you clues to your identity. I'll wager a few hours ago you didn't even know you could speak French. Our conversation seems to have triggered a recollection of part of your history.'

'Yes ... but now it's gone. For a moment I know I was thinking in French. Now the language knowledge ... I believe it's still in my head ... but I can't get at it.' The cold I felt conflicted with the beads of perspiration forming on my forehead. Sam reacted to my distress and perched on the edge of the bed. She took my hand and stroked it in an attempt to relieve my obvious tension.

'Apparently your experience is normal. You'll have infrequent, short visits to your hidden memories, but the frequency will increase and the visits will become longer. Eventually the only fact you will forget is that you ever forgot anything. If that makes sense?'

I must have looked sceptical because she patted my arm and continued. 'Don't worry. Doctor Boromin will be along presently and he will explain it to you in such highfalutin medical terms you'll be convinced. Believe me.'

I did worry though. I likened my head to a dam holding back an irresistible force. I could feel the pressure, not as a physical sensation but as a form of mental uncertainty, nonetheless it made my head throb. A small hole had appeared in the embankment wall and then something had come along to repair the opening. Such small leakages did not bother me, except collectively they might conspire to release a sudden devastating flood of background information. I had to assume my brain could handle the volume, but could my psyche deal with the content? From my limited experiences so far, my persona had slipped into a comfort zone of security. My outer consciousness was content to believe I was a man who was veracious and law-abiding and had been the unfortunate victim of an accident. If the dormant revelations were to dictate otherwise, then maybe I didn't want to revisit my past. Nonetheless, I had a compulsion to seek the truth and maybe Sam could act as a further catalyst.

'I'm feeling much better. May I sit up?'

'Of course.' Sam said. She reached down to open a cupboard next to the bed to extract a bolster, which she secured behind the existing soft pillow. Then she raised the bed head and I moved slowly until my back was almost vertical, relieved that the red-hot pokers of a few hours ago had been doused.

I needed to raise one element of the story that had been bothering me. 'Why have the police been involved in my accident?'

'Well, finding a trussed-up, unconscious body in the gutter is not an everyday occurrence so it needed investigating. You were loosely bound by the feet and wrists and had packaging tape strapped over your mouth. With the nature of your injuries, the police concluded you were probably thrown from a vehicle. In some ways it was lucky you were trussed, otherwise with flailing arms and legs you might have broken a few limbs.'

I thought for a moment. 'Thrown from the passenger seat of a car, for example?'

'That was their best guess. The circumstances were too elaborate for you to have been mugged. They reckon you were perhaps the victim of a gangland argument, and will want to speak to you again now that you are on the mend.'

'In my present state I'm not sure how I could help them. When I was brought in, didn't I have any identification on me: driving licence, credit cards, letters?'

'No. I undressed you when you first arrived. I searched all your clothes and looked for nametags. Nothing. There was one distinguishing mark on your body. The fresh scar on your lower abdomen suggests you had an operation for an appendectomy within the last few weeks.'

I tried to peel back the bed covers and lean forward to examine my scar, but the effort was beyond me.

Recognizing my problem, Sam said: 'Give me your hand,' and guided it to the telltale ridge on my body.

'So you know my body quite well then?' I really was better; it was my first post-accident attempt at humour.

Her reply suggested she took my flippant comment seriously.

'I was only doing my job,' she said, but an unmistakable blush made her cheeks even brighter.

'Is there any chance I could have some real food instead of this substitute stuff in my arm?' I said, waving the intravenous drip in my left arm in the air, 'I'm feeling very hungry.'

'Unfortunately you slept through dinner, though I'm sure I could arrange some soup for you if the doctor agrees.'

'And how long will it be before he gets here?' My pointed question was interrupted as the mad professor Boromin bounced into my cubicle. He appeared to have gone through a transformation: combed hair, shaved chin, no limp and a more conservative tie; either he had been home to freshen up, or perhaps I was seeing him in a different light now that I was more aware of my surroundings.

'Well Alan, you are in a more spirited mood. Has nurse Rapley been attending to your needs?'

Sam looked embarrassed and his statement surprised me. I assumed the sexual innuendo was unintentional and born of his relative inexperience with the nuances of the English language.

'My name isn't Alan,' I insisted disrespectfully.

'Excellent, excellent,' he said, dismissing my rudeness. 'Your memory comes back. How should I address you?'

'I don't know doctor, except I'm sure my name is not Alan,' I replied more humbly.

'He speaks French fluently,' Sam contributed.

'Ah, then it will be my colleague's task to discover your bête noire,' Boromin said triumphantly.

'I don't understand,' I said. 'Not the French but your statement,' I quickly qualified.

'I have asked Doctor Westcott to visit you tomorrow. He is a psychotherapist who will endeavour to destroy the barrier preventing you reaching your past.'

'Destroy sounds rather extreme. Will he beat the past out of me with a big stick?' Another attempt at wit from me, the subtlety of which was unappreciated by my foreign physician.

'No, no, Alan. He never uses physical violence,' he said seriously. 'He is strictly a mind doctor. Hypnotism and truth drugs such as sodium amibarbital are not in his portfolio of treatments. He may use a mild sedation to relax you and then he will explore various avenues of questioning with the hope that one of them will reveal insight to your identity.'

For the next fifteen minutes Boromin conducted various tests and examination of my injuries. Blood pressure and heart rate were normal, and the strength-sapping, infection-combative fever I had suffered earlier was almost out of my system. The abrasions were scabbing and the bruises were darkening. The clour on my head had subsided but the stitches were still sensitive to touch. Doctor Boromin's major worry was the hip muscle, which would need careful and precise tending over the coming weeks. He was satisfied there was no more he could do to promote my recovery. Nature was now the principal player in determining how quickly I could return to a normal mobile life. More importantly, he approved the intake of solid foods and before "lights out" my immediate wish was almost granted with a not so solid helping of tasteless warm soup.

Chapter 5

FIRST WEDNESDAY – 8:30 a.m.

The next morning a different, less talkative nurse removed my drip and allowed me a dry biscuit and a cup of tea. She also opened the curtains and for the first time I looked upon the rest of the ward. Over my simple breakfast, one that brought custom back into my life, I observed and tried to diagnose the ailments of my fellow patients by their posture or eating actions. My spirit was lifting and I was beginning to feel more in tune with the world, until the arrival of Doctor Westcott.

He appeared at my bedside as, with a moistened finger, I was harvesting the residual crumbs from my biscuit for a final taste of breakfast. You could have guessed he was a mind doctor; the huge square forehead was the giveaway. Otherwise, he was an ordinary looking stereotypical doctor: white coated, average height, average build and average brown hair of average length. Average age (meaning forty to me) for a doctor, facially not striking but above the eyes, you would have bet he had come from a Frankenstein monster look-alike contest. I had to double check his neck to make sure there wasn't a bolt through it. Moreover, when he spoke his voice was similar to one that could have been synthetically created by a computer.

'Good Morning, my name is Gordon Westcott. I'm sorry to interrupt your breakfast Alan, but I was asked to be here for nine o'clock.'

I must have looked very stupid. My eyes were transfixed on his forehead and my right index finger was firmly stuck in my mouth. I absorbed his words slowly and snapped out of the trance when I reached the word Alan.

'Look, I don't wish to be rude,' I started gently but reached a crescendo with, 'but I'm getting mighty pissed off being called Alan.'

Westcott looked hurt to begin with and then a smile gradually spread on his face. 'There, we are making progress already. The strong reaction to the name Alan suggests such a person may be a significant contributory factor to your present amnesia. So we'll start there, after I've explained the procedures,' he said calmly as he drew the curtains and sat down in a chair next to the bed.

I gasped audibly and forecast that my counselling session with this modern Prometheus substitute would be a complete waste of time. My prediction was correct, but reflecting on how my story unfolded, his opening diagnosis was strangely prophetic.

His methodology was simple. He would probe my mind by conversation and confrontation; the former would be casual questioning to promote a comfortable atmosphere and the latter involved an occasional provocative statement or enquiry to illicit an emotional reaction, which he hoped would reveal or provide direction to my suppressed background. I had to lie back and try to relax; if I couldn't, then before subsequent consultations I would be given a mild sedative.

I suffered his obtuse questioning for an hour. The dialogue was false and stilted, like meeting an inquisitive and obnoxious person at a party for the first time; someone who was keen to know you, yet you gave vague answers in the hope your disinterest would be detected, and they found someone else to annoy. The difference was that I could not provide *any* answers let alone vague ones.

As for the confrontational cues, they were hardly disguised, thereby diminishing their effectiveness. Westcott's face was a picture of conviviality during our mundane exchanges, but I could detect controversy brewing when his huge forehead wrinkled and his plastic smile abated. Then came a supposedly prickly question, which elicited from me not a disclosure, but an even more helpless expression. How was I expected to react to out of the blue questions like "Why did you hate your father?" when earlier ones had established I had no recollection of my father? I was amazed at his persistence though, since to all but my psychotherapist it would have been obvious that the interview had no direction and no likelihood of success.

It was a relief when he came to his closing remarks and his final recommendation was to read the daily newspapers. His mind-jogging theory was that news stories are stimulating to varying degrees, and I might encounter one that might provide a hint to my past. A sports page might even provoke a memory reaction, if for example, I supported a particular football team and I read it had lost an important match.

As soon as he had gone, the quiet nurse appeared to clear away the remains of breakfast. She made sympathetic sounds to my plea for more food and drink, but her haste suggested she was far too busy to go through the procedures apparently necessary to conjure extraordinary sustenance from the catering staff. I would probably have to wait until lunchtime – still two hours away. She made to open the curtains around my bed and I began to harbour thoughts of approaching my immediate bed-ridden neighbours for a sample of their visitor-supplied food stores when the dark shape of DI Bradley halted proceedings.

'Is it a convenient time to speak to your patient?' he said to the nurse.

'My word, you're popular today,' she said, turning to me and indirectly answering the officer's question. 'Can I fetch you a cup of tea, Inspector?' she continued. He accepted politely and the nurse must have sensed the frustration boiling inside me. 'I'll get one for you *too*,' she said to me and smiled, '*and* I'll try to find a biscuit.'

As she walked away, Bradley said, 'I couldn't help overhearing your food plea; I might be able to help you out there,' and he patted the large black briefcase he was carrying.

With my puzzled look he continued, 'Once a week my wife gives me asparagus sandwiches for lunch because they're supposed to be good for me, but I can't stand them. I always end up giving or throwing them away. Would you like them?'

Now I liked asparagus as a vegetable, but in sandwiches? A whole microsecond must have passed before I eagerly accepted the kind offer. Bradley looked pleased with himself as he extracted the foil-wrapped package and exposed the soggy mass. Frankly, they could have been jam and horseradish, and my mouth would have watered in exactly the same fashion. I wanted to snatch the sandwiches from him but my unknown upbringing waited politely until they were presented to me. I took them casually before losing my composure, and launched them hungrily towards my mouth. I wasn't the slightest bit self-conscious as green juice dribbled down my chin onto the bed sheets. Bradley just laughed, a genuine laugh. It struck me he was a happy man despite his wife's misguided lunch offering. I studied him as I ate. He must have been well over six feet tall and was strongly built. He wore a good quality dark brown suit, but the jacket was tight over his broad arms and chest. His hair was jet black and closely cropped, and his slight accent I guessed to be of West Indian origin.

He watched me, fascinated for a while, and then said: 'If my wife knew, I'm sure she would be glad my discards had gone to a good home.' He was in no hurry to pursue the reason for his visit and continued to study me until the nurse returned with the tea, just as I was popping the final sodden piece of bread into my mouth.

'What do you think you are doing?' she said with a look of shock. 'I'm supposed to monitor your intake of food. You'll get me into trouble.'

I had no answer to her admonishment but Bradley came to my defence with a calming voice. 'No harm done. It's not as if he's suffering from an internal complaint, he only has surface injuries. Keep mum and I won't report you.' It did the trick; I think the nurse was too taken aback with his cheek and quiet assertiveness to argue. She merely shook her head, deposited the steaming teacups and a plate of biscuits, and departed with a final shrug of her shoulders.

'I think I had better get down to business,' Bradley said, now with an air of authority. 'A woman has come forward who apparently witnessed your accident. She saw a white Ford Sierra driving erratically down Hanbury Street and thought the driver was drunk. The car slowed down suddenly, the passenger door flew open and a body – presumably you – fell or was thrown out and bounced a few times before lying still in the gutter; then the car accelerated wildly away. Ring any bells?'

I closed my eyes and prayed for one of those moments when the information might trigger a flashback. I registered several keywords: White, Sierra, Bounce, Gutter and waited for a hit; but the cerebral database to search was empty and my brain responded with "Not Found". Eventually I said, 'Nothing. Was it your witness who called an ambulance?'

'No. Based upon her recollection of the time and when you were picked up, you were lying there for about 20 minutes. So much for public concern,' he said shaking his head. 'Now I have to come to the tricky bit. The witness thought the Sierra had a stripe down the side and a noisy exhaust. Those facts were recognized by one of my colleagues; such a car belongs to Ronnie Kent, one of the local, never-been-able-to-pin-anything-on-him villains. He's thought to be at the root of much evil in the East End, particularly if it's anything to do with drugs.'

Bradley was scrutinizing me for any sense of recognition in my face; when he detected none he continued. 'We've paid him a visit. He says he was with his mother watching telly for at least the two hours either side of the incident. His mother has confirmed his statement.'

'You don't believe him?' I asked.

'No. His mother has frequently provided him with an alibi for a number of suspected crimes over the last few years. Furthermore he has a number of known associates who *are* on our files and ... ,' he paused, averting my eyes for a moment.

Suddenly it became obvious to me what he wanted to say, so I finished his sentence, '... you think I might be one of them?'

He shrugged his shoulders, which I took to be an accusation.

'I am *not* a criminal, Inspector,' I said indignantly.

'With respect sir, you have said you do not know what or who you are, unless of course your amnesia is just a pretence. A deception perhaps with a view to avoiding prosecution for ... something you now regret?'

I closed my eyes again, this time in despair of my situation and how defenceless I was to combat such accusations. Yet, for the briefest of moments, I felt a tiny shiver of recognition. Had I recently been in trouble with the police? There was an inkling of a memory, but no thoughts of guilt bothered my conscience. Perhaps my short-term memory was merely recalling yesterday's visit from Bradley.

'All I can say Inspector is that I don't *feel* like a criminal. I'm sure I have nothing to hide,' I said, which at the time was about as truthful as I could be.

'In which case, perhaps we might be able to help each other. Would you mind if I took your fingerprints and a mouth swab? It would be purely voluntary from your point of view,' Bradley assured me.

'I'm hardly in a position to *accompany you to the station* at the moment. Do you mean when I am discharged from here?'

'No, sir. I have brought the necessary materials with me.'

'In other words you don't trust me to attend for the tests. And if I refuse?'

'That's entirely your choice, sir. I can only insist if you have been convicted of, or charged with, a criminal offence. To my knowledge that's not the situation ...'

I interrupted, ' ... but it would help if you knew, particularly as I have possibly been seen with a group of known criminals.'

Bradley looked genuinely offended. 'On the contrary, my main concern is to help you discover your identity.'

I still wasn't convinced of his motives and said: 'How convenient that it's only convicted criminals you can help in this way, since only they have fingerprints and DNA codes on file.'

'I'm sorry you feel that way, sir.' Bradley stood up. 'I have no further reason to take up any more of your time.'

'Sit down, Inspector,' I said. 'I suppose I have nothing to lose. Do what you came for.'

And he did; a little too eagerly I thought, which added to my suspicion the exercise was more for police benefit than mine. Fifteen minutes later, he had efficiently taken ten prints, scrubbed my fingertips clean with an alcohol-based solution and stored in a test-tube a kind of pipe cleaner I had sucked. I signed a consent form and Bradley assured me the samples would be destroyed unless I was, or had already been, convicted of a recordable offence.

'You'll be back I presume, one way or the other?' I asked.

'Yes, sir. I'll have the results within a couple of days,' he said and departed with a disturbingly triumphant smirk on his face. Shortly afterwards, as I was reflecting on his visit, there was a moment when I regretted my co-operation. I had a distinctly déjà vu feeling about the fingerprinting; the procedure seemed familiar, but assured of my innocence of any crime I dismissed the thought as probably something recalled from a television programme.

Chapter 6

FIRST WEDNESDAY – 3:00 p.m.

I became a social beast that afternoon. The conversations I had with my fellow patients depressingly centred upon an exchange of intimate details about our respective ailments. As sore and incapacitated as I was, I counted myself as probably the luckiest on the ward. I had been told my physical problems would heal and leave no significant scars. I considered myself fortunate that, unlike my bedmates, I would leave the hospital with all of my innards intact, with no bodily disabilities or advice to take it easy because of a malfunctioning heart. During teatime the mobile patients, who were fascinated by my amnesia, surrounded my bed and a voluble interchange ensued to speculate upon my real name. Some viewed me as a "Robin", and "Nigel" was popular too; but after much debate, by consensus I was christened "Hugh" courtesy of one wag who thought "Hugh am I?" was most appropriate. I hated Hugh almost as much as Alan, but in deference to the amusement of my new friends, I let the name stick until I left their company, and then adopted the favoured selection of Robin.

As I had predicted, Doctor Westcott made no progress. Despite my scepticism, I don't believe I hindered his attempts, it's just in my non-professional's opinion, his psychoanalysis seemed textbook and unimaginative. I tried to be co-operative, even allowed myself to be sedated, but my history remained locked inside the vaults of my mind. I hoped it was only concealed and had not been permanently erased because of my mugging. At the end of the third abortive consultation, I tendered such a theory to the doctor and he agreed erasure was a possibility, though I concluded (for my own peace of mind) the response was an excuse for his failure, rather than a statement of fact. Nonetheless, he scheduled another meeting for three days later and although I didn't attend, I doubt whether he noticed.

I did look at newspapers over the next few days and my unexplained affinity to *The Times*, and therein the business financial pages, was undoubtedly a clue to my pre-mugged life; but despite reading each story avidly there were no sparks of recognition to qualify my interest. Such an intellectual pursuit did however provide me with another indicator that I was surely employed in a professional capacity, instead of a criminal one as implied by Inspector Bradley. And indeed, he confirmed that on his promised return two days later.

Chapter 7

SECOND FRIDAY – 10:15 a.m.

'The prints and DNA trace don't match anything in our records,' Bradley said resignedly, 'and I've checked the recent list of missing persons in the area. There's no one that matches your description.' He stood next to my bed holding a carrier bag and appeared to want to make the visit a brief one.

I smiled with relief and smugness at Bradley's disappointment. 'Are you sad for me, or sad for yourself, Inspector?' I asked.

'Truthfully sir, a little of both. I sympathize with your situation, but was hoping you might have provided the information with which to nail something on Ronnie Kent. I do hope your memory returns sufficiently well for us to talk again.' Bradley said and passed me his calling card. 'How much longer will you be in hospital?'

'Doctor Boromin reckons he will be able to discharge me tomorrow. I got up for the first time yesterday and walked, or rather hobbled, around the ward for an hour last night. I'm still full of aches, but I don't have muscle spasms any more and as long as I take it easy I should be walking normally within a couple of weeks.'

'I'm pleased to hear that, sir. Should we need to get in touch with you, where will you be staying?' he asked casually, but my suspicious mind thought it was a trick question.

'Oh, Buckingham Palace probably,' I offered sarcastically.

He formed a white-toothed knowing smile, 'I wasn't trying to catch you out. I wondered if you had arranged temporary accommodation.'

'I think that will be rather difficult since I have no money, no clothes and no ID.'

'There's a hostel in Jubilee Street – a converted library – about half a mile from here. You could stay there.'

I had to accept that soon I would be alone in the world, and would have to join the ranks of the homeless until my memory returned.

'What do I do, just turn up?'

'Normally there's a waiting list. I've routed a few drunks and druggies there before and I can put in a good word for you with the warden.'

'Well ... I ... suppose so,' I stuttered.

'Besides, if I know where you are then I can keep an eye on you.'

When I regarded him apprehensively, he added: 'Strictly from a welfare point of view, *only*.' I wasn't convinced of his apparent sincerity and thought of an excuse.

'I don't even know if I've a decent set of clothes to wear, let alone a spare set. Or a toothbrush, razor, wash things.'

'I think the hospital will be able to help you there. They have a voluntary support group, which can assist patients in difficulties. Speak to one of the nurses about it.'

I nodded my reluctant thanks.

'Have you chosen a temporary name yet?' he asked.

'The ward has voted that I look like a Robin.'

'And the surname? Not Hood, as in outlaw, is it?' Bradley said, chuckling.

'No, I haven't thought about one.'

'How about Forest? As in Nottingham Forest. Robin Forest has a decent ring to it.'

I agreed. 'It's as good as any other. Okay.'

'One more thing before I go. I've confessed at last to my wife that I don't like asparagus sandwiches. I was caught out the other night when I was telling her the story about you. She had some asparagus left and I mentioned I was seeing you again today.' He raised the carrier bag he was holding and placed it on the bed. 'So here's a little treat for you: two day's worth of sandwiches plus a few other titbits to keep you going for a while. I'll pass on your thanks to the missus.'

He left before I had time to offer my thanks. I think perhaps he was embarrassed by his own generosity; maybe I had misjudged his interest in me after all.

I examined the bag. Sure enough, there was a foil wrapped bundle a bit larger than a house brick, which from its mushy texture I assumed were the sandwiches. There was also a packet of chocolate digestive biscuits, three bananas, a small fruitcake, a packet of mini pretzels and a couple of muesli bars. A positive feast I thought and hastily returned it to the bag, nervous my sickly neighbours might come calling for handouts.

Chapter 8

SECOND FRIDAY – 3:00 p.m.

Later that day my favourite nurse – Sam – returned to the ward. I told her about Inspector Bradley's visit, and she seemed genuinely pleased I was (probably) not of the criminal kind. She joked that it would be impossible with an upright name like Robin Forest. She confirmed I would be free to leave the next day so long as I got up now and, without assistance, made my way to the day room in under a minute, so she could change the bedclothes. Her assumption was this would be good news. Medically it was, but the outlook of homelessness was rather scarier. I climbed out of bed feeling quite comfortable, but I pretended to be in pain and Sam watched me with interest. I began to shuffle awkwardly towards the end of the ward heading for the day room just beyond. I feigned the occasional twinge and then Sam appeared in front me with her hands on her hips.

'Robin Forest, if you think I'm going to fall for your little game …' She never finished her sentence because I had already given the deception away with a smile on my face, which had rapidly spread to both us laughing out loud. Other patients added to the bizarre behaviour by shouting out ribald comments.

I straightened my bent posture and said to Sam in a soft voice: 'Seriously Sam, could you join me in the day room, there's something I want to ask you?'

She replied, mimicking my secretive approach, 'I'll tell you now; I don't date patients or do bed baths.'

I laughed again and continued my walk, albeit with just a hip-induced limp on my left side.

Fortunately, the room was empty, and I eased myself into a hard-backed chair, fearful that slumping into one of the armchairs would make getting up a painful experience. Sam sat next to me in a similar chair.

'Is there some way I could stay here a bit longer?' I said immediately.

She thought for a moment, presumably analyzing my unusual request. 'Because you have nowhere to go?' she surmised.

'Not exactly. Inspector Bradley has recommended I try the hostel in Jubilee Street, but I'm sure I have a permanent home somewhere. It's just that ... well, I think there's a better chance of discovering who I am if I could stay here.'

'But I've heard that your sessions with Doctor Westcott haven't made any progress so far. Off the record, he believes he has little chance of success because you are purposely blocking his attempts to help you. Anyway, I don't wish to be unsympathetic, but there are far more needy people than you who would benefit from a hospital bed.'

'Off the record, Doctor Westcott is a theoretical egghead who has great respect for his art, but little for his patients. I wanted to stay here, not for his treatment, rather to remain in comfortable surroundings, which would be better for my recovery than having to endure the rigours of a homeless life. You are right though, I am being selfish.'

'You'll be okay at the Jubilee,' she said reassuringly. 'A neighbour of mine is a volunteer worker there and although it's not the Hilton, it's apparently comfortable and clean, and it has a good record of rehabilitation.'

I tried a different stalling tactic. 'But I don't have any clothes.'

'The clothes you arrived in are in the cabinet next to your bed. I took the liberty of having them cleaned as you had no visitors to arrange it for you, but they are in a sorry state because of your accident. However, following a request from Inspector Bradley I contacted the woman who runs the hospital support group. She will be here later and should have a surprise bundle for you.'

'I can't make my mind up about Bradley. One minute he's a hardnosed copper trying to discover if I'm a criminal and the next he's acting like a raving philanthropist.'

'I think he's just trying to be a model police officer – hard with the crooks, benevolent to the needy. Keep on the right side of the law and he could be a good friend to you one day. Still, that's enough chat. I'll be in trouble if I'm caught gossiping, and the other patients will concoct fantastic stories of what we've been up to. Give me ten minutes to change your bed and then you can come back to the ward if you want to.'

I didn't return to my bed for an hour. I followed Doctor Westcott's limited advice and browsed the daily newspapers, not to trigger memories, but to take my mind off the following day.

Chapter 9

SECOND FRIDAY – 4:30 p.m.

Miss Springtime looked about sixty years old based upon her iron-grey hair and wrinkles, but she strutted around the ward in a far more sprightly fashion than I could now. She wore a white coat and I watched her slight body as she went from bed to bed spending a minute or two with each patient. I assumed at first, she was an elderly doctor on her rounds, particularly when she merely nodded to me rather than stop to chat. As I was to leave tomorrow, I guessed that contact with me would be superfluous for someone in such a hurry, and when she left the ward, I felt snubbed. Yet moments later she came bounding back, carrying what looked like a large duffle bag, and headed straight towards me like she was a greyhound and I was the rabbit. She braked suddenly when she was alongside the bed.

'Mr. Forest, I am so sorry to hear about your dilemma. I managed to collect a few things for your journey,' she said. Reading from a slip of paper taken from the pocket of her coat, she proceeded to inventorize the contents of the bag. 'These are all clean, some are brand new: two pairs of thick socks; three T-shirts; a cotton sweater; a pair of grey trousers; two pairs of underpants; a light, waist length coat; toothbrush and toothpaste; four disposable razors; a pack of paper tissues; a bar of soap; a flannel; a hand towel and ...' she paused to reach inside her coat and produced a thin see-through plastic purse with straps, '... £20 in coins and notes in a waterproof money belt. You can check it if you like.'

I regarded my benefactor with amazement. I wasn't sure what to say. I felt dirty and inadequate, like a prisoner about to be released on the outside world; then the compassion of the gesture overwhelmed me. Before me was an aged Santa Claus presenting a wealth of presents which possibly doubled the value of the goods I currently possessed.

Seeing my gaping mouth, the eager Miss Springtime continued: 'I'm fairly sure the clothes will fit you. Sam Rapley described your body accurately to me.' At which point I blushed, but the worldly woman added. 'Though she couldn't be exact about your shoe size. What size do you take?'

It was a question from my past I assumed I couldn't answer but Pavlovianly I said, 'Size nine.'

'That shouldn't be a problem. I'll call back later with shoes and boots for you to try. Above all it's important your feet are comfortable.'

Return she did about an hour later, by which time I'd taken the opportunity to try on the clothes. They were a motley collection of colours and styles, but she was right, they did fit, but I wouldn't win any prizes at a fashion parade. I had been through this process mechanically, as though I might be selecting what clothes to take on holiday. Now everything was refolded and replaced in the bag, it dawned on me again that what lay before me was not a journey or holiday; it was a venture into the unknown, that past experiences couldn't be drawn upon to suggest if it would be an adventure or misadventure. My mind kept erring towards the latter and a depression was beginning to envelop me when the bouncy Miss Springtime reappeared with a large carrier bag.

'I have a selection of footwear for you to try,' she said, and proceeded to parade them on the bed. 'Slip your socks on and see which ones fit. Only one pair of shoes and boots mind, I've a few other clients to satisfy.'

"Clients" was a strange term to use, no doubt she was being polite avoiding the more appropriate terms of vagrant, hobo, homeless person or down and out.

My choice took no time at all. I settled on a pair of plain black rubber soled shoes, slip-ons because yet another minor anamnesis told me I hated lace-ups; and a pair of sturdy, brown, laced (was there any other kind?) hiking boots. Both were size ten and slightly oversize, but the thick socks and advice about swelling feet convinced me they were the right choice.

I suppose I moped for the rest of the day, avoiding contact with my fellow patients. Nor did I seek conversation with Sam; I felt embarrassed that I had selfishly tried to enlist her help to stay in the hospital. I ran through routines of stretching and manipulating my torn leg muscle, exercises demonstrated to me by a physiotherapist on Thursday. I interspersed the drilling with hobbles about the ward and corridors.

I picked unenthusiastically at my evening meal, but did finish it eventually, more from necessity than enjoyment. Then I lay in bed, listening to the radio through my bedside headset as a distraction from thoughts of what tomorrow would bring. The distraction lasted for an hour.

Chapter 10

SECOND SATURDAY – 6:00 a.m.

Is it really a wonder why I slept so badly on my last night in hospital? Thoughts of sleep were cast aside, as I made a last desperate attempt to focus my mind on an impenetrable past. The effort of it exhausted me, and I dozed fitfully each time that tiredness took control. I must have subconsciously called out many times, because the night staff regularly attended to check that I was in no pain; but I never recalled the reason for the outcries. Were they brought on by my impending isolation, a replay of my accident or something horrific from my pre-hospital life?

When daylight began to flow into the ward, I laid there fearful of sleep and how I would handle my first day alone.

Breakfast was normally served by the catering staff at seven-thirty, but at seven o'clock Sam smuggled in a tray with corn flakes, orange juice, toast and tea. She pulled up a chair by the bed, motioned to say something and then hesitated.

Through a mouthful of cornflakes, I gave her the prompt she obviously wanted, but I made light of the serious look she wore. 'What's up Sam …' I asked, '… you've discovered I'm a filthy rich pop icon, want to date me, but don't know how to ask?'

She forced the glimmer of a smile and then said, 'I'm sorry Robin, your bed is spoken for from eight o'clock.'

'The more needy person is about to arrive?'

'Yes. A heart transplant patient. I've only just heard,' she said in mitigation.

'It's not a problem, really. At least I'll be cast out on a full stomach and I packed my bag in readiness last night.'

She looked relieved and then troubled. 'You'll be alright won't you?'

'Who knows? I'm trying to fool myself into thinking I'm about to embark on an adventure; one that will eventually have a happy ending.'

She took a piece of paper from the breast pocket of her uniform and handed it to me. 'This is my phone number. If you ever need a friend, give me a call.'

Her eyes looked red and I thought she might cry. 'Thanks Sam … for nursing me.' I carried on eating my cornflakes as a diversionary tactic in case the emotion of the situation affected either of us.

More composed she said, 'You know how to find the Jubilee shelter?'

'Yes, Inspector Bradley gave me directions.'

'I have to attend a staff meeting in half an hour so I probably won't be here when you leave. Just let the nurse's station know you are going. Good luck, Robin.'

She left and I continued my breakfast, comforted that perhaps I had one friend in the world.

I suppose, due to nerves, I wasn't feeling hungry, but I ate everything on the tray, unsure when and where my next meal might be. I had stowed Bradley's food parcel in my bag and knew it would keep me sustained for a couple of days. I hoped the shelter would feed me, and I had £20, but I wanted that in reserve in case I needed money for phone calls or transport.

I fastened the money belt around my waist and I dressed in my original clothes. Despite the warning from Sam, I thought they were in reasonable condition and, ever hopeful, I wondered whether their familiarity might spark recognition of where I acquired them. I scrutinized each item as I put them on.

Underpants: Y-fronts; white; nondescript label; 32-inch waist.

Socks: light woollen, black.

Shirt: casual; long sleeved; light-grey; lower front, one button missing; black marks and a small tear at the top of the left arm; chest size 42; label which said "Croftwear".

Trousers: black; lightweight; cotton; brown stains, a couple of holes and a gaping flap about two inches square at the top left thigh; two side pockets, empty; 32-inch leg and waist.

Shoes: black; heavy duty; leather uppers; treaded rubber soles; Velcro flap fastening; slightly muddy.

Jacket: medium-grey; good quality; Burton label; pale blue lining; four side pockets, two with zips; hood built into collar; left sleeve, bad scuffing and shredded in a couple of places.

I gleaned little from the examination. From their casual nature, when I was wearing the clothes, I probably wasn't heading for work or a dinner party. The shoes gave the strongest clue; perhaps I had been walking or hiking to somewhere before I had been tossed unceremoniously from a car? The jacket was unusual too; maybe I had bought it locally?

Having quickly showered and shaved, I was ready to leave fifteen minutes before my deadline, according to the clock over the entrance to the ward. I had no watch of course, but I doubted knowledge of the time would be critical to my immediate survival. I slung the duffle bag over my shoulder conscious of the weight contribution of mainly boots and asparagus sandwiches, and headed towards the exit. Most of the other aware patients were pre-occupied with their breakfast and I was eager to slip out unnoticed; not that I wanted to be cold to them, more to avoid sad goodbyes and awkward questions that I probably couldn't answer. Despite my clothed appearance, a few recognized my limping gait and I heard calls directed my way – "Hugh's a pretty boy then?" being the most memorable. I had also brought forward my departure, hoping I could catch Sam before she went to her meeting, but instead the last person I spoke to in the hospital was a fresh-faced nurse I had previously seen on the ward. She barely acknowledged my existence, and then obliterated it permanently by erasing the word "Unknown", which had been written in red felt pen against my bed position on a whiteboard.

As I reached the automatic rotating doors of the hospital exit, I stopped abruptly, the word "Unknown" echoing around my head. Outside the sun was shining in a clear blue sky, but I was afraid to leave the comfort of that sterile building, which for the five days of my known life had been my home. Here I had been tagged as a member of the hospital patient community; once I had stepped through the door, I would be on my own, a non-person in a world demanding identity and caste.

Chapter 11

SECOND SATURDAY – 8:00 a.m.

Daunted by the prospect, I hesitated long enough for several people to regard me with concern, before I stepped into the warm sunshine and paused at the top of the brown stone steps that led from an archway to the street level of Whitechapel Road. I was immediately hit by the contrast in environments. From the quiet and antiseptic smell of the hospital I was thrust into the bedlam of city life and the fumes that went with it.

I first discovered the location of the hospital when one of my fellow patients had loaned me his copy of an A-Z map of London. I had studied the immediate area around the hospital and I found that I had a skill in memorizing the roads for a radius of almost a mile. This was helped no doubt by the fact that I seemed to be familiar with London in general and the East End in particular. Looking on to Whitechapel Road and the queue of morning traffic, I could picture myself in one of the cars. I was sure this wasn't just an empathetic projection towards the frustrated drivers, but a real memory. If true, then I had just learnt I could drive and that maybe I had lived or worked in this part of London at some time. Most encouraging was that perhaps Doctor Westcott's forecast was coming true; my memory would soon return once I became exposed to scenes and people from my past. I smiled at the thought. My homeless life was just starting, but the signs were this would only be a temporary distraction from my true future.

Ultimately I would head towards Jubilee library to secure my roof for the night. But buoyed by my latest train of thought I wanted to take the opportunity to explore the local neighbourhood, as if I was an inquisitive tourist on a short break before returning home. Opposite me was Whitechapel underground station. Train rides would have to wait until there was a purpose to such expenditure; now was the time to stretch my legs and exercise my defective rectus femoris.

There was a hive of activity on the other side of the road so I crossed at the pedestrian traffic lights, weaving my way through cars whose drivers had little respect for red, amber or green. Here there was a cosmopolitan array of shops and market stalls preparing for a day's trading. A multinational mixture of staff were busy raising security blinds, marking boards with special offers and unloading goods from double-parked trucks and vans, which were contributing to the traffic jams heading away from the City. None of the shops could be classed as up-market. Looking up, the underlying three or four storey properties were different styles and states of disrepair and probably built a century or more earlier and, to divert the eye from their façade, the street level premises were a spectrum of bright colours, bold adverts and bargain statements. Hopeful shopkeepers and stallholders were attempting to attract the constant stream of pedestrians to their goods with value-for-money broadcasts. I was immune to such retail opportunities and it occurred to me that my own appearance was rightly viewed to be below the necessary financial threshold. My scruffy attire and duffle bag probably projected a student image, albeit a mature one, and in another flash of déjà vu, this feeling of academic rejection was familiar to me. Of course, everyone has been a student at some time, but I sensed further education – a university maybe. Whether I was qualified to degree level I hoped might soon reveal itself. The idea suggested to me again that my background couldn't possibly be criminal. I trusted my previous lifestyle hadn't been coddled to the extent that a period of adversity would render me incapable of survival in my homeless existence.

The concoction of smells from the food stores and cafés was intoxicating. Too early for kebabs, burgers, or Indian or Chinese food, but my nose was attracted to the odours of an English cooked breakfast, hot bread and strong coffee, though hunger was not currently a pressing concern.

At the beginning of an alleyway adjacent to one of the cafés, I encountered what I thought at the time was a typical beggar. I paused to stare. In a sitting position, his head was tilted sideways and resting against the wall. He was old with a grey untidy beard and grey hair beneath a dirty brown bobble hat. His eyes were slitted and glazed, assisted presumably by the almost empty vodka bottle he clutched loosely in his right hand. The brown overcoat he wore almost concealed the remainder of his body, bar a protruding foot, which was covered with a worn and hole-riddled black boot. To his left was a bundle made from an old towel, which was knotted to a stick. His left hand was periodically shaking what looked like the base of a cigar box, which contained a few miserable-looking coins – no more than about 30p worth. As he shook the box he muttered something – clear to himself, but incoherent to anyone else – to draw attention to his pathetic state.

I had seen beggars before, though my feelings towards this sorry individual were more sympathetic than I imagined. Our respective situations were too similar for comfort. He was resigned to street life; I was just starting mine. I felt obliged to put money in his box since he was more needy than me, but what was the point? I doubted he would use the money other than to accelerate his alcoholic demise; besides, as yet I was unsure how lasting my own limited funds would be. I moved on and was glad that I had declined to be a benefactor, as clearly and loudly behind me the beggar said, 'Fucking nosy bastard'.

I continued my trek, amazed at the industry going on around me. The market area ended at a crossroads that marked the start of the Mile End Road. To my left was the Blind Beggar pub. I thought at first the word beggar had caused me to pause, but then I remembered an event that had made this particular pub notorious. Wasn't this where the infamous East End gangsters, the Kray brothers, used to hang out? And wasn't someone killed there once? The possible truth of the memory was disquieting, and I hoped the recollection was purely historical, instead of an indication I had a murky past. Either way it served as a reminder this area was one where I needed to be cautious about the people I might meet, or the activities I got involved in.

Further along the Mile End Road, I came to a small piece of waste ground, and parked on it was a dilapidated caravan converted to a makeshift café. The clientele were a motley collection of outwardly poorer individuals, presumably attracted by the crudely signed boards advertising cheap food and drink. I too was attracted to "Mug of Coffee – 30p" which was less than half the price of the equivalent I had spied in the cafés on route, and decided to make my first purchase of the day. It was indeed a cheap offering, steaming hot with a coffee taste. I wondered what germs I would inherit from the cracks and stained chips that adorned the mug. I sat on the crumbling wall that partly bounded the waste ground and observed the passers-by while I sipped the hot liquid.

I was envious of the people with purpose to their actions. I took pleasure in attempting to guess what their objectives were.

The dark-suited man carrying a briefcase, looking at his watch and striding quickly, but unnaturally, who was late for work or an appointment?

The hassled woman pushing a buggy containing a young child and dragging an older, reluctant child behind her.

A bleached blonde large breasted female, tartily dressed, who could be anything from a made-up 14-year-old playing truant, to a made-down 40-year-old secretary, who was employed for her cleavage rather than office skills.

A dishevelled man – dressed like the beggar down the road, but younger – who was pushing a rickety pram crammed full of the discarded paraphernalia of life. Periodically he stopped to examine something in the gutter, or rifle through the contents of a waste bin. He looked content enough as he hummed gently to himself, and nodded and smiled to the people that passed.

My detailed observations had been stimulating and as I rose to return my empty mug, I resolved what my second purchase would be: a pen and paper so that I could diarize or record my thoughts and experiences. This was something I felt capable of doing; maybe this time last week I had been earning my living as a journalist?

At Stepney Green underground station, I saw a more commercially organized beggar – a male youth sitting cross-legged outside the entranceway. He was well kempt, even the sprinkling of pubescent growth about his chin did not detract from his relatively wholesome appearance. Tunefully playing a mouth organ, he had before him an upturned baseball cap, which contained plenty of coins – mostly silver. Propped in front of his legs was a square of white cardboard with the words "Help my sick sister in hospital" neatly crafted in bold black ink. Of course, both ploys could have been deceptions: the money might have been a cash float, which he had seeded to illustrate the worth of his cause, and the cause itself might well have been bogus. Nonetheless, as I watched, two punters took pity on him and more coins were noisily added to his funds. He nodded his head slightly in thanks, and then held my gaze for a moment before dismissing me as a likely contributor.

By now my thigh was beginning to ache. I hadn't been conscious of walking with a limp, but as I turned south to head for my temporary refuge, I had to slow my pace to compensate for my stuttering stride and the occasional twinge that stabbed at my strained muscle. Fortunately, the hostel was less than half a mile away and, after a progressively agonizing ten minutes, I arrived at the hostel entrance in Jubilee Street.

Chapter 12

SECOND SATURDAY – 9:30 a.m.

The library – now hostel – was a two-storey redbrick building, which I believed typified public architecture of its age, and advertised by a carving of 1930 over the large arched main door. There were conflicting signs either side of the door. To the left: a professionally produced sign for "Terry's Snooker Club". To the right: a piece of wood, which only by close inspection revealed plastic lettering announcing "Jubilee Hostel". The puzzle was solved as I climbed stone steps and pushed open the heavy door – there were two inner doors. Another sign on the door to my left confirmed it led to the snooker club, with a taped paper addition advising: "Members Only. Strikly No Admittence To Hostel Users." – presumably spelling skills were not a prerequisite for membership. Out of curiosity, I pushed the door open and a stale smell of cigarette smoke greeted me. A staircase led upward and I could hear an occasional click from balls striking each other.

I turned my attention to the facing door that had a more welcoming sign on bright yellow card stating "Jubilee Hostel and Shelter. Please Enter", though in small print at the bottom a jester had written "At least we don't play with our balls all day". I turned the brass doorknob and with a strong shove the door creaked loudly and opened into a narrow entrance hall. To the right was a small room, accessed by a door marked "Keep locked at all times". Visual access was by a tall window above a wider counter, like a secure service point at a bank or post office. Prompted by the noisy door, a man hidden behind a newspaper, leapt up from his chair and presented himself at the counter window. He moved a latch and pushed the lower pane up, so there was just air between us. Behind him, I could see a matrix of wooden pigeonholes and, in a flash, they reminded me of a porter's lodge at the entrance to a university halls of residence, though the reason or connection was beyond me. The man was stockily built, perhaps in his forties, but his height was distorted since the floor in his room was about a foot below the hall floor. His head was level with my chest so he had to tilt it to look me in the eye. Perhaps it was this subservient position that made his greeting gruff and unfriendly.

'What d'ya want?' he asked.

'Hello. I'm Robin Forest. You may be expecting me?'

'I might be. Who sent you?' he queried.

'Inspector Bradley ... a local policeman.'

He eyed me suspiciously then ran his fingers through his greasy chestnut hair and wiped them on his green jumper. He reached up and unhooked a clipboard, which was affixed to the wall.

'You sound a bit posh to be here,' he remarked and before I could answer, he glanced at the board and continued, 'Bunk 12 in dormitory D. Any valuables?'

'Me? Valuables?'

'For the safe. Jewellery, cash, credit cards, sentimental objects?' he qualified.

'You have a safe?'

'Well, it's a big cupboard with a padlock actually. All our guests aren't so la-di-da as you. If you've anything worth nicking from a pair of clean underpants to a solid gold bar, either keep it with you or hand it over to me for safe keeping.'

'I'll risk the underpants, but I'm right out of gold bars at the moment,' I said jokingly.

'I'm not joking about gold bars. Last year we had a crazy old man who turned up and deposited a heavy, sealed biscuit tin. He died in his bunk a week later. Turned out to be Lord Craythorpe. When we opened the tin it contained three bars. Apparently he'd gone batty, sold his shares, converted the proceeds into solid gold and decided to become a tramp.'

'Well, I'm not sure who I am, but the most precious possession I have at the moment is asparagus sandwiches and I expect they'll be eaten by the end of the day. Anyway, how do I find dormitory D?'

'Hold your horses. There's paperwork to complete first.'

He then posed a series of questions to which I had little to offer. Name: Robin Forest (for the time being). Next of Kin: Unknown. Social Security Number: Unknown. Nationality: British (probably). Religion: Unknown. Current Employment: None. Valuables Deposited: None. Previous residence: Unknown. Length of Stay: Unknown (but the maximum I could stay was two weeks, although this could be extended for "acceptable behaviour"). Next residence: Unknown.

'I'll have to keep an eye on you as you've been so vague. Something to hide have you?'

'I don't know. Didn't Inspector Bradley explain my circumstances?' I asked.

He shook his head, so I brought my disbeliever up to date, but he was unconvinced.

'I'll still be watching you. We get some odd types here. Slightest bit of funny business and you'll be back on the street. Right, I'll ask Jasmine to take over reception and then I'll show you around. My name's Albert by the way.'

Albert slid his window shut, climbed a few steps from his sunken room and unlocked the door leading to his domain. A large bunch of keys dangled and jingled from his waist as he emerged and locked the door after him.

'Wait here,' he said and disappeared through the first door on the right, which stated "Women Residents Only".

While I waited I browsed the notices and brochures either side of the counter window; they made depressing reading. There were essentially three categories of information. Health: advice was on hand for every possible homeless related affliction and disease from head lice to AIDS; Substance Abuse: alcohol, resins and drugs; and Welfare: Samaritans, local charitable organizations and social security benefits. Currently I had no itches, cravings or philanthropic needs, so instead chose to study the rules of the hostel.

Raised voices brought me back to the present day as a very large black woman and Albert emerged from the women's quarters. No more than five-foot tall and possibly three feet wide, the woman in a bright orange dress and jet black braided hair was loudly berating Albert. The substance of her anger related to Albert's intrusion upon her morning break, despite his repeated reminder she was on call at all times to assist in the running of the hostel. The argument was silenced as their eyes fell upon me in the hallway. The woman regarded me disdainfully and, with a key from the set hung around her neck, she unlocked the reception room and slammed the door after her.

'Jazz gets touchy when I disturb her morning break, particularly if she hasn't finished her cup of tea and six Jaffa cakes,' Albert explained. 'Don't be put off by her appearance or display; she has a heart of gold when it comes to looking after the residents. She was a stray herself after her mother and father split up and abandoned her. She arrived here, became attached to the place and now she's the female warden.'

Albert led me down the corridor and pointed to the first door on the right.

'Women's quarters: Strictly out of bounds to men unless you want to be sat on by Jazz,' he joked.

Albert opened the second door and looked in. There were three people lazing in armchairs watching television. 'Morning. We have a new guest – Robin Forest. This is Charlotte, Keith and ... er ... Leslie.'

Charlotte was eating an apple and ignored the introduction. Leslie nodded her (or was it his?) head, but Keith stood up and came over to enthusiastically shake my hand. 'Nice to see you again,' he said, then lowered his voice and added, 'Pop in later for a chat about old times.'

'Er ... okay,' I stuttered as Albert grabbed my arm and led me away.

'That was the unisex common room. Only place you can mix with the women other than the kitchen. Charlotte's a junkie, supposedly in rehab, but I have my doubts. Keith's not long out of prison and will bore you to death with tales about his unfaithful wife. Don't be fooled by his statement that he knows you. That's just a ploy to get your attention. Leslie is a transvestite: a woman in a man's body, waiting for his sex change op so he can become a prostitute. It takes all sorts ... you seem normal by comparison.'

I whispered, 'Where does Leslie sleep? The men's or women's quarters?'

Not bothering about my quiet discretion, Albert replied laughing, 'While he's got a dick, the men's quarters.'

The last door on the right led to the men's quarters. As we entered, there was a smell of old books still lingering, which was mingled with sweat and burnt toast. Now in a long corridor, we passed the first four doors labelled A to D and took the next door on the left.

'This is the washing area,' Albert said.

It reminded me immediately of the changing rooms at a sports centre: communal showers, no baths, a stainless steel trough for a urinal, four toilet cubicles (two without doors), and seating along one wall constructed of sturdy wooden strips.

'How long has this been a hostel?' I asked.

'About ten years,' Albert said. 'Originally the ground floor space was two big rooms of the library. The remaining brick wall separates the male and female areas, the other rooms have been created by crude partitioning.' To illustrate his point he banged on one of the walls and it bowed slightly and made a hollow sound. 'It can be a bit noisy in D; the loos back on to the dormitory and the plumbing's rattly.'

The final door on the left of the corridor was another to be kept locked at all times. Albert told me to stay where I was, unlocked the door with a key from his set and went inside. Through the gap, I could see it was a kind of storeroom: different shaped boxes piled high and an industrial vacuum cleaner propped in a corner. Almost immediately he reappeared with a medium-sized towel and a small bar of soap, which he handed to me. 'Keep yourself and your clothes clean. Many of the minor ailments come from sores and bugs.'

Opposite the storeroom was a long narrow kitchen with wider L-shaped alcoves at either end. Each alcove contained a couple of tables and non-matching wooden chairs. A worktop ran the complete length of the left wall interrupted by two sinks, each of which faced a window looking out on to an alleyway. On the worktop were two electric kettles, a toaster and a first-generation microwave oven. Underneath I was introduced to a washing machine, tumble dryer, fridge, freezer and several cupboards. There were more cupboards at eye level. Albert said one of them was known as the lucky-dip cupboard by virtue of the supermarket-rejected dented and unlabelled cans (mostly soups apparently) that it contained. A door at the far end of the kitchen led to the women's quarters. The kitchen was a shared, or unisex (one of Albert's favourite words) facility.

'We used to have a gas cooker here,' Albert explained, 'but, a couple of years ago we had a serious fire when one of the solvent addicts tried to heat up his fix in a saucepan. Health and Safety weren't too impressed and said we had to make ventilation and fireproofing improvements before they would renew our fire certificate. It was cheaper to have the cooker removed, so hot water and toast are the cooking limits now. There's usually a supply of tea and coffee around, but the microwave's temperamental if you want to heat up a lucky-dip.'

'That's a shame,' I said, something triggering from the past. 'I think I'm a dab hand in the kitchen.'

'Well, even you might be defeated by the limits of a toaster. Besides, to cook you need ingredients, and you won't find many here. We get leftover and past-their-sell-by-date donations from the local shops, but usually we have to go to collect them, and Jazz or me don't always have the time. Morris, the Jewish baker, drops stuff in most days, though I wouldn't advise eating his mildewy bread or stale cream cakes until your stomach is desperate.'

I could hear bellows of laughter, which were coming from the room next to the kitchen. 'This place isn't how I imagined it. I expected everyone to be miserable and quiet,' I commented.

Albert smiled. 'There are two types of homeless people in my opinion. The ones that come here are mostly on the way up. They are seriously trying to give up their alcohol or drug habits. Many have jobs and are trying to earn enough money to start a new independent life. If they make real progress during their two-week probationary period with us, we let them stay longer and give them as much support as possible. Then there are the hopeless cases that have no interest in bettering themselves and prefer to be loners on the streets. Occasionally one of those gets through our filtering process, but either from choice they don't stay long or, to put it crudely, we make it difficult for them to remain. It sounds hard, but there's no point in chasing lost causes. There's a waiting list for a bed here. I let you jump the queue because Bradley recommended you. If you let me down, I've a dozen others waiting to take your place.'

'You've no worry there. I'll be a model inmate while I'm waiting to return to my earlier life,' I said.

Albert looked doubtful. 'We'll see,' he said. 'Let's go next door to the men's common room and meet Luther's card school.'

Chapter 13

SECOND SATURDAY – 10:00 a.m.

The laughter came to an abrupt halt as Albert pushed the common room door open. He sniffed the air in the windowless room and swept his gaze across the group of four who were seated around a low table. 'Okay, who's been smoking? You know the house rules, guys. You can smoke in the kitchen with the door closed and the window open, but nowhere else, and even that's going against the advice of the local fire department.'

Three of the men were my age or less and they looked towards the fourth for salvation. He was older, perhaps fifty, tall and strongly built, with a bald strip some four inches wide in the middle of his head. The group were casually dressed, but the younger ones were scruffy in comparison to the middle-ager, who was well groomed in quality trousers, shirt and shoes. He replied as spokesman: 'My dear Bert, my brothers and I ...', he said (presumably speaking in a trades' union rather than the relational sense), '... cannot be held responsible for the overwhelming fear you inflict on us when you walk through that door. So much so, young Danny here gets the shakes, and his wooden leg rubs vigorously against the table, which causes the slight burning smell you have detected.'

There was a moment of silence and I watched Albert's pink face become red and then purple, as the card-playing quartet collapsed in a heap of laughter. I held back my own reaction until Albert laughed too, infected by the contagious hysteria. But I gained the impression that deep down, he felt awkward being ridiculed in front of his newest boarder, and would have liked to have imposed his authority. Instead he chose a soft option.

'Alright, alright, very funny. Now calm down otherwise you'll give our new recruit the idea this is a slack operation. This is Robin Forest. I'll show him the dorms and then perhaps Luther, you could take him under your wing.'

Luther was obviously the older ringleader and responded with a wink and a hint of sarcasm, 'Sure boss. It'll be my pleasure.'

I crossed the corridor into room D with Albert and he closed the door behind us. The dormitory was a miserable looking place, the decor a flaky combination of yellow and green paintwork, which reminded me of *my primary school* (?). Other than a half dozen two-tiered metal-framed bunk beds – closely spaced – and a couple of plastic chairs, the room was devoid of comforts. Four of the beds were occupied and a variety of nocturnal sounds were coming from them. Storage space for residents' belongings amounted to whatever each person had with them; there were a variety of bags, rucksacks and crude suitcases littered on and around the beds. Now I understood Albert's reason for mentioning the safe. He must have noticed the dismayed look on my face.

'I know it doesn't look much, but it is clean, dry, cool in summer and warm in winter. The bedding is changed once a week or on request, and the radiator …' he said, pointing to the paint-flaked, metal monstrosity which ran the full the length of the window, '… is noisy but it does its job.'

Albert walked to the far right hand side of the room. 'This is your bunk, the bed on the top. It's a new one,' he added as if it were a privilege.

True. It looked newer than the others – a slightly different design and with all its paint intact. It rested tight against the wall.

'Looks like you've just squeezed this one in,' I said. 'How many inmates do you have here at the moment?'

'We don't call you inmates,' Albert said indignantly. 'We prefer the terms guest or resident, it's not a prison. But to answer your question we have 36 male beds and 12 female beds. Dorms A, B and C each have four double bunks. And you're right, we only squeezed another bunk in here last week otherwise we wouldn't have had room for you.'

'There aren't many *residents* around?' I asked pedantically.

'By this time of morning, most of the good guys have gone to work, gone to look for work or are trying to beg from the rush-hour traffic. Some have come back from their night shift working and are sleeping it off.' Albert waved his hand in the direction of the snoring sounds.

Suddenly there was a loud and disturbing retching sound coming from the washroom, only a thinly partitioned wall away.

'Then again,' Albert added with a sigh, 'there are those that have one fix too many and their bodies start complaining. I'd better check it out. When you're settled, pop and see Luther. He'll show you the ropes.'

Albert rushed away and it took me just five seconds to settle as I hung my bag over the end of my designated bunk and went in search of company.

'Ah, the rookie returns,' Luther said as I entered the common room.

This time there was cigarette smoke openly drifting through the air and there were now five occupants, the fifth was the youth I had seen begging outside of Stepney Green underground station. All the eyes studied me suspiciously.

'I'll be with you in a tick,' Luther continued and he refocused his attention on the beggar.

'... He was a big rozzer, about my height but twice my weight and age. He had a thin black moustache and a big bent nose, East End accent. Said he would book me if he saw me again,' related the beggar with a heavy Scouse accent.

Luther glanced at me then replied in a whispered, though still audible, voice. 'Okay, Rick, I'll sort it out. You've had a run in with Bill Haynes. He's the local beat bobby. If you'd said you were working for Luther, he would have left you alone. He's used to seeing Sniffy at that pitch and probably hasn't heard he's moved on because he's been recruited by Ronnie Kent's organization.' I moved closer to the conversation on hearing the name Ronnie Kent. 'I'll see Bill later and top up his extracurricular income. Take the rest of the day off and start again on Monday. Give me your takings.'

Rick reached into the inside pocket of his jacket and brought out his scrunched up baseball cap. Luther imitated him, but extracted a black drawstring bag. Rick unpeeled the cap and emptied the coins into the bag, then added a five-pound note from the back pocket of his trousers.

'£9.75 in total,' Rick said.

'Not bad for an hour's work,' Luther said. 'I told you it was a good earner.'

Luther looked at his watch and then at the group of three that hadn't spoken since I'd arrived. 'It's almost midday and time you were at work.' His words seemed innocent enough, but his three disciples jumped to their feet and without another word left the room.

Rick took the remote control from the table and aimed it at the portable TV resting on a high shelf in the corner of the room. He was content with the game show that appeared on the screen, collapsed into his chair and then pumped up the volume.

Luther gave Rick an icy stare then said to me: 'Let's go to the kitchen and get a cup of coffee. It'll be quieter there.'

'Voltaire,' I said in response to a question posed to a contestant on the TV programme.

'Do what?' Luther said, looking at me then the television. 'You're a bit of a smart arse, are you?'

'I don't think so,' I said humbly, 'the answer just came to me.'

Over the coffee making, Luther quizzed me about my background. Naturally there wasn't a lot to say other than to relate my immediate hospital history. I chose not to reveal the possible mutual acquaintance of Ronnie

Kent. A coincidence I was burning to declare, but I viewed it was premature to raise the subject without getting to know Luther better. Luther was philosophical and advisory about my amnesia.

'Best to not dig up the past, you never know what you might find. When I was dossing in Manchester, I met a guy with the same problem. He just turned up one day at the YMCA – not an accident like you – and couldn't remember beyond getting off a bus in Piccadilly. He was so confused and depressed he allowed himself to be dragged into a drug ring. He soon became an addict himself and was then gang raped.'

Luther paused to heap four spoonfuls of sugar into his coffee and stir it vigorously before continuing.

'Thereafter he was convinced he was gay and eventually caught AIDS. One night after a particularly bad trip, his memory came back and he recalled he lived in Oldham, was happily married with two kids, and had suffered a nervous breakdown due to work pressure. He couldn't face the outcome and two days later he was found floating in the Rochdale Canal – a presumed suicide. So believe me, start a new life, don't take drugs and don't bang your head. I'll help you on your way; I'm good at that.'

I took a swig of my black, unsweetened coffee. 'I'm certain there's nothing dodgy in my past, so in the meantime I intend to be a model refugee. I'm going to treat my exile as an exercise in survival. I shall be the eternal optimist – a true Panglossian,' I said and immediately there was a flicker in my brain, suggesting this unusual word had some meaning in my past. I struggled internally, trying to hang on to that tiny association in case it led somewhere.

'You've lost me there,' Luther said. 'Hey, are you okay? Your face just went white as a sheet.'

I came out of my daydream and Luther was shaking my arm.

'It's happening more regularly now.'

'What is?'

'Flashbacks. Well, not really flashbacks, but little insights into my previous life. I honestly believe I won't be here very long.'

'Don't rely on it. Anyway, how long is long? Even if it's only a couple of weeks, how will you feed yourself? If I were you, I would be a pessimist – assume this is your future. You seem a sensible and intelligent bloke. You should have a contingency plan and that's where I can help.'

I supposed Luther was right. My recollections to date hadn't exactly amounted to much. At their present rate of flow it could be years before I learnt enough about my history to have any chance of resuming my presumed rightful place in society.

Luther continued. 'Besides you are at a big disadvantage to most of the people here. You don't have an identity and until you do, you'll not be able to claim any Social Security benefits. The system is so tight these days even real people have to sweat blood to get money from the government.'

'I'm not sure I understand your own situation at Jubilee. Are you homeless? Do you have a job?'

'I'm not exactly homeless, though I do spend quite a few nights here. As for a job? Well, let's just say I am employed as a ... freelance social worker.'

He grinned and raised his eyebrows clandestinely. His action I assumed was meant to be reassuring; instead, it gave me the creeps. I wanted to ask him questions about his background, but I had the impression his answers would have been equally obscure. He was sounding me out and would be more forthcoming when I had gained his trust. I changed the subject.

'Who are the guys you were playing cards with?'

'Now there's an interesting story. They think they are the modern day Beatles: thick Rick, not much up top, guitar man; Jason, the athletic looking one, bass player; Danny, the guy with the mop top red hair, acknowledged leader of the band, plays keyboards; and Gringo, drums of course, and good-looking unlike his 60's counterpart. They are, or were, apparently popular in their hometown of Liverpool. The lads were talent spotted by a guy who promised he could book them some prestigious gigs in London. At the time, they were still at school and, with little money between them and a need to buy decent instruments and a van, they pooled their savings, stole the rest from their parents, bought their new kit and headed south. They spent their first night in London at a cheap hotel in Bow. When they got up the next morning they discovered their van, containing their instruments and spare clothes, had been stolen. The police think they were set up and there would be little chance of recovering their stuff. The gear wasn't insured; they couldn't go back home, so the hotel owner recommended they come here. That was a month ago and I'm helping them get back on their feet so they can start over.'

'What about Rick's sick sister?'

'Sick sister?'

'Yes. I saw him begging at Stepney Green underground station.'

I may have caught him off guard. He stared at me for a moment as though he was considering what answer he should give.

'You're not a copper are you? Or from the Social?' he said. They were rhetorical questions.

'I've told you my story. I might be, I don't know for sure, but I don't think so,' I said and shrugged.

He stood up and leaned his muscular body over me in a threatening way. I tried to be cool and took a nonchalant sip of coffee though my stomach was fluttering.

'You appear to be genuine enough. But I'll tell you now; if you ever cross me you'll be in big trouble. Play it straight with me and I'll guarantee you'll graduate from this place with honours.'

He straightened and looked at his watch. 'I have to go now. We'll continue this conversation later.'

'Yes, okay,' I said with hidden relief and Luther strode quickly from the kitchen.

I wasn't sure what to make of my meeting with Luther. His confident and astute behaviour was at odds with what I expected of an apparent destitute person. He had clearly been at the Jubilee for some time and his dominant influence over the Liverpudlians was disturbing. And he was obviously running a scam, otherwise why would he be anxious about the police or Social Security? He could be a serious ally to help me out of my dilemma or a man to be avoided at all costs. After such a brief encounter I chose not to make a judgement. Maybe a discreet chat about him with other residents might help me in the decision process. That could wait for now; I had more pressing activities to concern myself with.

Eating was priority one. I finished my coffee and returned to room D. The background snoring was louder now, enhanced by two more sleeping occupants, one of whom was cocooned in a brown blanket on the bed beneath mine. There was a strong smell of raw meat in the air. I noticed litter on the floor but ignored it as I reached for my bag (on the bed?). I felt sure I had hung it up earlier and as I rummaged in my less weighty bag for the asparagus sandwiches, I realized it had been raided. The sandwiches were gone and I took a quick inventory of the remaining items; the fruitcake was missing too. I bent down and saw the litter was a bread-crumbed piece of silver foil and a cake-crumbed cellophane wrapper. I shook the smelly object angrily. There was a disturbed snorting and from the blanket and an aged ugly head emerged: grey-haired, unshaven, pockmarked wrinkled face and gappy stained teeth.

'What the fuck you want?' he croaked.

'Did you steal my food?' I shouted.

The old man blinked and cowered. 'I ain't done nuffink. Don't hit me. I really ain't done nuffink.'

I had found my culprit – there were white and light brown crumbs in his wiry beard – but what was the point of pursuing my anger? I had been careless with my limited property and should have taken greater heed of Albert's earlier warning. The loss pained me most because someone who had genuine interest in my welfare had donated the food. Then again, given the choice, perhaps Mrs. Bradley would have given the feast to the more deserving wretch in front of me. It occurred to me that in this world of the sheltered homeless, perhaps food had become the new currency. With a roof over my head and clothes on my back maybe this had been an omen to set my priorities correctly. It would be a nuisance, but from now on I would either need to keep my bag with me all the time or deposit it in the "safe". I smiled at the thought of putting a few clothes and precious food under lock and key. The old man mistook my smile as aggression and cringed again.

'Forget it,' I said and grabbed my bag and headed to reception, hastening past the open door to the communal common room in case the garrulous Keith was waiting to pounce.

Albert was back in his closeted room talking to someone on the telephone. He acknowledged me, and held up two fingers that I assumed indicated he would be a couple of minutes rather than as a gesture of derision. I reached into my bag and selected my rationed lunch: the two muesli bars and a banana. I ate one of bars while I was waiting for Albert to finish.

'What's up?' he asked.

'Several things. First I'd like to deposit my bag with you while I go out.'

Albert regarded me questioningly so I told him about the food theft.

'So you've met "Gannet" then. Stinks a bit don't he? He works an early morning shift at Smithfields meat market as a porter. He may appear decrepit but he's as strong as an ox, cunning as a fox and has the appetite ... of a gannet, though I wouldn't class him as a thief.'

'Nonetheless, I'll not put temptation in his or anyone else's way.'

'Fill in these two labels then,' Albert said. 'Tie one to your bag and keep the other as a receipt.'

He passed me a biro, and I entered my name, the date and signed the labels. I attached a label and then hesitated as I passed the bag over the counter.

'Will I be able to collect my bag at any time?'

'This desk is always manned or ... personed,' said the politically correct and grinning Albert, who took the bag and checked the label.

'Next, where can I get some food? For free, that is.'

'Didn't Luther set you up with ... um ... an income stream?'

I didn't know what Albert meant but said, 'No. He had to go out before we finished our conversation.'

'Well, you can help yourself to anything you can find in the kitchen. Morris will be here this evening with his stale grub, but I assume you mean outside?'

I nodded.

'There's the Women's Institute soup kitchen in Little Lane. They serve soup – obviously – and sometimes other hot food, between midday and two on most days or until they run out. But the queue starts mid-morning and you'll be too late now. I take it you've no money?'

'Some, but I wanted to keep it for an emergency.'

'Every day on the streets is an emergency. You'll soon be spending money as quick as you can get it. I suggest you speak to Luther again; he'll have some ideas.'

'Okay. Finally, where's the nearest public library? A decent one.'

'What do you mean by decent? One that doesn't have porno books?'

It wasn't clear whether Albert was making fun – he didn't smile.

'No,' I said, 'One that keeps back issues of local and national newspapers.'

'There's the Bancroft Road library in Mile End – about a mile away, near Queen Mary College.'

So that's where I headed, though I was in no hurry. I chose a circuitous route visiting the residential districts of Stepney – many of which were low and high-rise blocks of flats – ever hopeful I might recognize a place from earlier times. I strode briskly at first to test my fitness. My thigh was improving; there was still a dull ache and I was still limping, but unlike this morning, the discomfort was not constantly playing on my mind. With that as an exception, I regarded myself as a fit person who probably exercised regularly. I was slim with toned muscles, but not a muscular build, so I doubted whether I worked out at a gym. There was nothing reachable in my mind about sporting preferences, so with the thought that my legs were the most developed part of my anatomy, I guessed at jogging, cycling or football. I presumed this wasn't my profession otherwise my identity would have been revealed; more likely any sport in my life was on an amateur or purely leisure basis.

Despite the coolness of the day I was soon warm with walking, so I slipped off my jacket and carried it over my arm. Besides I didn't want to become too hot or sweaty; there wouldn't be the luxury of stripping off and soaking in a bath when I returned, nor would there be a choice of fresh clean clothes from the wardrobe for the following day. I stopped for a moment with those thoughts. Had this been wishful thinking or another instance of an intrusion of the past? How was I supposed to distinguish between fantasy and reality? Were the snapshots so far merely my imagination seeking a better life than the one facing me? It was a depressing thought, so I dismissed it quickly and continued on my way.

The final part of my convoluted route took me past a gas works and through Mile End Park. The park provided a dramatic contrast to the earlier uninteresting housing estates and noxious industry, boasting unexpected flora and fauna, although the latter comprised only a few coughing sparrows, a rabbit and a half eaten rat.

From the park, it was a short journey west over the Regent's Canal and then right through the buildings of Queen Mary (and Westfield to be precise) College. I entered the Bancroft Library building shortly before two o'clock. I climbed the stairs to the first floor and as I saw the shelves of books, I had another strange feeling in my head; libraries suddenly seemed significant to me. Sure, the hostel was once a library too, but the connection was stronger than that. Somehow, I sensed the reason for Robin Forest existing, had started in a library; the whole notion was absurd at the time, and I rejected it without further consideration.

Chapter 14

SECOND SATURDAY – 2:00 p.m.

Shortly after enquiring at the counter of the Bancroft Library, I was sitting at a reading booth with a month's worth of the daily *East London Gazette* piled in front of me. My reckoning was this. Five days ago I was involved in an accident, which resulted in my hospitalization; before that, someone must have known me in a family, social, or employment situation. If so, by now I should have been registered as a missing person. According to Inspector Bradley, I wasn't on such a list, but I doubted whether the bureaucracy of the police force was efficient enough to ensure he had seen an up-to-date list. Soon I would seek out Bradley to check whether he had any new information, but in the meantime I had decided to consult the parochial press. Therein was the possibility someone might have reported an event, which either involved me or could act as a catalyst to nudge my memory. I knew the exercise could be seriously flawed for two reasons: First, I didn't know my real name, though I hoped a printed version of it might aid recognition; and second, I had no idea whether I was from this part of the world. On this latter point, I was gambling that since the immediate area was partly familiar to me, there was a chance I lived or worked nearby. The likelihood of success was slim, but I had to do something to keep my mind active.

Of course, there were other angles to pursue. A promising (albeit perhaps dangerous) one, was to track down who had dumped me from a car. Either they knew me, or I might obtain knowledge of where I was picked up. The Ronnie Kent connection via Luther might be fruitful though I would need to tread very carefully.

I could run an advertising campaign in the national and local papers. All I would need would be: my photograph; a catchy "Do you know this man" caption; contact details and thousands of pounds in advertising fees. With just under £20 in my pocket such a scheme would be a long way off. A cheaper, albeit ridiculous, alternative occurred to me using a sandwich board. Strap a couple of boards over my shoulders and parade myself endlessly around the local streets. I wondered whether I had the nerve to do such a self-conscious thing and I think I did, after all I had absolutely nothing to lose.

For the worth of these schemes, I may as well bang my head against a brick wall. I laughed aloud at the prospect of doing exactly that – another blow to my head was surely the best, albeit the most extreme, and potentially dangerous method of recovering my memory.

It was a slow process wading through the *Gazette*. At first I loitered on every page, reading everything from headline issues to the minutiae of local sports results. The most recent three issues took me an hour to study, and although time was a commodity I had in abundance, at my present rate, I would not be able to complete the backlog of local, regional and national newspapers I had intended to examine. I began to turn the pages quickly, scanning for headlines that caught my eye. Two booths away I noticed a man glowering at me. I ignored him at first and then I saw that he grimaced every time I noisily rustled the newspaper. Eventually he waved at me, then pointed to a sign on the wall – "Silence is Golden in this Library". I shook my head in acknowledgement and mimed the word sorry. I leaned back in my chair deciding to take a break and extracted the banana from my side pocket. I started to peel it and the man gesticulated again, this time indicating another sign – "Food may not be consumed on these premises". Resignedly I stood up and headed for the cover of bookshelves, where I could eat my banana in peace, hidden from the man's scrutiny.

I browsed the racks and unconsciously graduated to the section on French Literature. With my head cocked to the right, I studied the spines looking for inspiration. My gaze held upon the title *Candide*, but at the same time through a gap in the shelves, I spied someone I knew. There were tables set in a small alcove of the library that I hadn't visited. Sitting side on to me was a young woman, elbows on the table, head on her fists, intently studying a large volume in front of her. She occasionally scribbled notes as her eyes darted from page to page. My stomach fluttered with the knowledge I had found the link I had been seeking. Then the disappointment rapidly came; it was someone from the present not the past; the drug addict from the hostel – Charlotte. Not that she looked like a junkie in this environment; such was the studious expression upon her pretty face. I watched her secretively while I finished my banana and then stepped beyond the sanctuary of the shelves towards her table. I pretended to visit the shelves immediately behind and saw it was a section devoted to medicine. She didn't stir or glance up and I took the opportunity to study her more closely. She wore faded blue jeans and a white sleeveless T-shirt, which had the punch line '... so don't gimme any crap' inscribed on the back. Her hair was a consistent light blonde, neck length with a prominent parting down the middle. I guessed her height to be about five feet six and her build was slight, skinny maybe. I moved to view her arms; they were pale and smooth with no obvious signs of needle-induced scars. I decided on an introduction but it took two quiet "hellos" before she reacted. She visibly tensed but didn't turn around, so I moved to her side so she could observe my harmless intrusion. Slowly she raised her eyes to meet mine and leaned back. Her expression changed from neutral to worry and then her mouth creased slightly in relief. My eyes drifted to the front of her T-shirt. I was truly interested in the slogan but could not help noticing the swell of her breasts and the prominence of her nipples, which showed either side of "Life is shit already ...". I smirked as I remembered a favourite exaggerated simile of my brother "Nipples like thimbles".

'Do I know you?' she asked with a volume to show her annoyance at my gawping stare towards her chest, and promptly leant forward and crossed her arms.

'I have a brother,' I exclaimed, thoughtless that my loud statement might carry to the sign-pointing man.

'And I know your brother?'

I closed my eyes and tried to hold that moment. A brother. I could see him now: dark brown hair; bespectacled; same height as me, but heavier; older perhaps, but I couldn't grasp his name. Then the image faded and I opened my eyes again.

'And I know your brother?' she asked again.

'Oh, I wish you did. It could solve all my problems. Do you mind if I sit down?'

'It's a public place; I can't stop you. But if you carry on acting weird I'll scream and run.'

'I'm sorry.' I said. 'I didn't mean to frighten you. It's just that ... well ... I've just remembered I have a brother. It came as a bit of a shock.'

She looked puzzled for a moment and then she must have recalled our brief meeting three hours earlier. 'Aren't you the new guy at the Jubilee?'

'That's right,' I said smiling to put her at ease.

'What are you doing here?' we both said at the same time and then laughed at the coincidence.

Suddenly she stopped, 'You're not following me are you?'

'No. Of course not. *Are* you being followed?'

She frowned and said, 'I don't think I should say anymore,' and nodded in the direction of the man who had appeared behind me – the sign pointer.

I turned around and he stood with his arms behind his back and glared at me over his small round spectacles. His unsaid message was clear. I looked at Charlotte and whispered. 'Is he the man following you?'

'No. He's the chief librarian.'

'I think we have a lot to talk about and clearly this isn't the right place. Do you fancy a tea break?'

'Okay,' she said gathering her notes and coat. We both stood and made for the exit.

'Just a moment,' said the librarian, 'first you need to dispose of this.' He brandished the banana skin I must have left on the shelf when I was spying on Charlotte. I returned to retrieve it and smiled as I had a vision of a banana-eating monkey who was the chief librarian in a book I was certain I'd read not long ago – *Discworld*. 'And …' he continued in his officious tone, '… you both need to replace your borrowings from whence they came.'

Charlotte giggled at his manner, but then acceded to his wishes and returned her tome to the medicine shelves. I crossed the room to collect my newspapers and took them back to the reception desk. We met outside the front door.

'He's alright really,' Charlotte said, meaning the librarian, 'he's only doing his job. I like the quiet of the library. I complained about noisy people once before and he sorted them out for me.'

'You're a regular visitor then?'

'I've been every day for the last two weeks; I'm almost part of the furniture,' she joked.

'There's a little Greek café just around the corner in Mile End Road,' I said pointing back along my route to the library.

'No way,' she said sternly. 'I'm not paying £1 for a tiny cup of thick strong coffee. Follow me.'

She ventured in the same direction, but before we reached the main road, she turned right into one of the Queen Mary College buildings and then left through swing doors.

'Students' Union refectory – I'm a lapsed member,' she said triumphantly. 'Best value in the area. Trust me.'

'My treat. What will you have?' I said.

'Homeless people go Dutch – rule of the streets. Besides, I never accept gifts from strangers.'

We joined the queue and a few minutes later Charlotte was at the head.

'Hello Joe,' she said to the diminutive Oriental man serving at the drinks counter. 'The usual please.'

Joe selected a cup, placed it under a spout of a stainless steel urn and pressed a button. There was a hiss of steam and hot water then Charlotte tendered a five pence piece in exchange. I looked puzzled at her purchase.

'Coffee for me,' I said, and Joe went through the same ritual albeit via a different urn.

'25p. Help yourself to additives Guv,' Joe said – in a marked East London accent which contradicted his eastern appearance – and indicated a milk bottle and sugar bowl on the counter. I paid and ignored the extras.

Charlotte had moved away and I saw her open a small packet and then sprinkle the white powdery contents into her cup. I shuddered at what she was doing and looked away sipping my coffee until I thought she had completed her mixture. When I looked back she was waving at me to follow her. She led me to a far corner of the room and we sat down at an empty table. She took a drink from her cup and leaned back, closing her eyes.

'Ah, that tastes good. Told you it was cheap here.'

I was embarrassed with her action and sat stiffly upright wondering what to say.

'What's up,' she said, leaning forward and prodding my arm with her finger.

I glanced towards her. 'Does that really help?' I said nodding towards her cup.

She took another swig. 'Definitely. Usually I just have hot water, the caffeine in tea and coffee isn't good for you when you are on rations, but I needed my fix today. All that brainwork in the library can get tiring. Do you want a taste?'

'Um ... no thanks. What are you ... on?'

'What am I on? What do you mean?'

'The white powder.'

She looked at me strangely and then peered into her drink. 'It's a new designer drug – chicken flavour. Here. Try it yourself,' she said and wafted the cup under my nose.

It smelt like chicken, but having never taken drugs (which was either a revelation in itself or maybe a denial of my past) I didn't know what kind of odour to expect.

I shook my head disapprovingly.

'You idiot. You think I'm on drugs don't you? Is that what Albert told you?' she shouted.

I nodded.

She put the cup down on the table, reached into her coat pocket and pulled out a small packet and threw it into my lap. 'This is what I'm on,' she said angrily.

I turned the sachet over and read the label. Prominently displayed amongst a list of ingredients and the manufacturer's name were the words "Chicken Broth Cup-a-Soup".

'Chicken soup?'

'Supposedly. It does have a nice chickeny taste, though chicken isn't mentioned as one of the ingredients.'

'*Really* chicken soup?'

'Taste it.' An order not a request.

She picked up the cup and handed it to me. I took a sip; it tasted like chicken soup, good chicken soup. I returned the cup.

'Albert said you were a junkie in rehab,' I said to mitigate my mistake. 'I'm very sorry. My instincts did say otherwise, but I assumed Albert would know the truth.'

She smiled showing white, even teeth. 'It's not your fault. It's what you were meant to think. But please don't tell him to the contrary otherwise I'll be chucked out of the hostel.'

'I don't understand. Why do you want him to think you are a drug addict?'

'It's a long story and you look like someone I can trust. Are you in a rush to go anywhere?'

'Only to continue my research at the library, though I'm bored with that already.'

'Sounds as if Robin Forest has a story to tell too.'

I raised my eyebrows, surprised she had captured my name at the hostel.

'Yes, but it's not a long one.' A fly buzzing close by, distracted me, and I followed the sound to a waste bin near the table. This reminded me I was still carrying a sticky banana skin in my pocket. I reached in and extracted it and my spare muesli bar. I tossed the skin in the bin.

'Would you like to share my lunch?'

Her eyes lit up. 'Yes please, but I'll need to go on a diet when I've eaten that,' she said.

I took pleasure in studying her lithe shape to confirm she was joking. I then broke the bar into two halves and passed over her share. 'I thought you didn't accept gifts from strangers.'

She took the cereal bar eagerly. 'If we are about to exchange our life stories I don't think we are strangers anymore.' She rose from her chair and turned it towards an adjacent one. Then she stretched out with her feet up. 'I'm lying comfortably; you may begin.'

Isn't it amazing how easy it is to précis one's life? The four days since I woke up in hospital I managed to compress into a ten-minute monologue with little loss of significant detail. It saddened me to think so much of life was filled with trivia. Uninhibited, I laid bare my short known life to her, not merely the events but also my innermost thoughts and wishes. What did it matter? I had no secrets and I welcomed the freedom of speaking to someone who seemed genuinely interested in what I had to say. While I spoke Charlotte watched me like a child absorbing a bed-time story, prompting me with her eyes to hurry with the tale whenever I paused for breathe, or to remember. She didn't interrupt though and I was sure there were as many questions in her mind as there were in mine. Only once did she show any emotion – a slight frown – when I related Inspector Bradley's statement about Ronnie Kent and drugs. When the story was complete, she had finished her soup and consumed her muesli bar. My coffee had gone cold.

She looked thoughtful and I took the opportunity to eat my half of the solid lunch. 'And I thought I had problems,' she said eventually with a sigh. 'Does the recent knowledge about a brother help?'

That information had been gnawing in the back of my mind since we left the library. I spoke my thoughts aloud. 'It should do. If nothing else it narrows down my heritage by eliminating one-child families. I can picture him now, but that's all. I can't add a name, place or any background. The rest will come back I'm sure of it.'

'It may be a stupid question but how do you know the image was your brother? It could have been a work colleague or a friend? What triggered the flashback?'

I was afraid she would ask that question. I had no reason to lie, but decided to couch my answer in diluted language.

'My brother used to have a crude way of describing … protruding … nipples,' was my stuttered reply. Charlotte was leaning back with her arms propping her up, so I couldn't help my attention be drawn to her T-shirt again.

She looked down unembarrassed to check my observation, then leant forward to conceal the distraction. 'Are you being straight with me or are you just a voyeur?'

Again I felt compelled to tell the truth. 'Honestly, it's true,' I said ambiguously.

'About being straight or a voyeur?'

'Both.'

'No harm done. I suppose I'm flattered and I certainly admire your honesty. And I'm pleased my body has contributed to your memories …' she said calmly and added as an admonishment, '… so long as it doesn't happen again!'

She stood and shook her legs to encourage circulation after her prostrate position and sat normally this time. 'Your coffee's gone cold. Do you want a fresh cup?'

The truthful answer was yes, I hated cold coffee, but days of waste would have to be suspended in my current predicament, and the outlay would consume about one percent of my total wealth. A drink was a drink and I picked up the cup of black liquid, which already had a skin on the top. 'I'll manage with this thanks and now *I'm* sitting comfortably,' I said imitating her.

Chapter 15

SECOND SATURDAY – 3:00 p.m.

Charlotte rested her hands on the table and they became the focus of her attention.

'My name is Charlotte Rensberg and I'm twenty-two years old. I was born at a very early age ...'

I laughed at her ridiculous statement. For someone who was homeless she appeared confident with a strong sense of fun. This was uplifting but unnatural, and I wondered whether it was indicative of a fragile exterior.

'Seriously, I'll skip the early years otherwise we'll be here all day.'

I wanted to know all about her, but nodded in deference.

Her mood changed to a sombre one.

'Three years ago my parents were killed in a plane crash. You may recall – no, you won't of course – a charter holiday flight to Spain crashed in the Pyrennes Mountains, killing everyone on board. It was the summer before I started medical school in London. My sister, Kathy, who's a year older than me, had finished her first year of a Genetic Sciences degree at University College. A sad time for us both, but Kathy said we were reasonably provided for by a trust set up from the proceeds of our parent's estate. My sister was already sharing a rented student flat in Islington and I went to live with her. We were there for two years supporting each other in our grief and studies.

'Over the last year, Kathy's personality changed from the fun-loving person she was, to one that was secretive and moody. Until then we used to go everywhere together: the cinema, discos, parties and often co-studied in our rooms or one of our institutions' libraries, but Kathy began to come home late or go out in the evening on her own. She said the excessive demands for her final year project meant she had to spend long hours experimenting in the labs. I didn't query her reason; she was dedicated to her subject and aimed to excel in her final exams. However, she struggled to get her degree and by her standards, the lower second she achieved was as good as a failure.

'Nevertheless, by virtue of a research association the College had with a leading American biotech company, she was offered a lucrative job in Boston. By then the money we had inherited from our parents had been consumed in living expenses and study fees. To begin with, Kathy was excited about going to the States; it had been one of her dreams to work at the heart of genetic innovation; then she suddenly changed her mind. Her reasoning was she was reluctant to leave me alone in London, particularly as money was short, and she was anxious about the problems she envisaged in transferring funds to me from America. They were weak excuses, but she was adamant she would get a job in London and, with luck, might be able to pursue her job in America one year later, once I had qualified. I tried, but couldn't dissuade her from her plan and she eventually took a rather lowly lab assistant's job at a small pharmaceuticals company in Edmonton called BioRemedy.

'She had to give up her room in the flat and to minimize our outgoings she slept on the floor in my room, which was against my tenancy agreement, but my housemates understood our situation and kept the information to themselves. But the strain of sharing a cramped room, the odd hours she used to keep and her mood swings led to frequent disagreements between us and after a month Kathy said she might move out to live with her boyfriend. That news was a big shock. Although during our time together we both had a few casual relationships, nothing had ever developed to the extent of wanting to live with someone. Furthermore, this was the first I'd heard about a current boyfriend and I wondered whether this explained Kathy's recent behaviour.

'A couple of nights later she never came home and I assumed she had stopped over at her boyfriend's. She didn't call or leave a note so the next morning I telephoned BioRemedy, but she hadn't turned up for work. It was the same story on the following day. By now, I was frantic with worry. This was the first time for over three years when a day had gone by when I hadn't seen Kathy, so I had no option but to pass on my concerns to the police. They took Kathy's details and I gave them a recent photograph, but generally they were unsympathetic, saying that most missing persons turned up sooner or later.

'The next day I had a visit from a policewoman named Simone. I immediately feared the worst and although she had no news of Kathy's whereabouts, the information I was given shook me rigid.

'For over a year, Kathy had been under surveillance as a drug dealer. Apparently, a local villain with a codename of Ganja was suspected of importing pure cocaine from Columbia via Amsterdam and reprocessing it for distribution, but the police had never been able to find any incriminating evidence against him; instead, they embarked upon an undercover operation to trap his distribution agents. They discovered some of the pushers had been recruited from students at Kathy's college. Supposedly, this is common practice since many students are drug users, and the poorer ones are eager to supplement their income and fixes by selling to richer students. The police caught two students who were extremely co-operative about the details of their suppliers, but the hierarchy of distribution was so long and covert that the route to Ganja soon petered out. However, the testimony of a third student was more promising. She was closer to the source of the drug network and in her dealings had gathered useful facts about its organization. Eager to avoid publicity and ejection from college, and in exchange for immunity from prosecution, she agreed to act as snout for the police.'

I thought I could see where this was heading. 'Your sister?' I queried.

Charlotte looked sad and hung her head in shame. 'Yes, I'm afraid so.'

'But why on earth did Kathy get involved in this shit in the first place?'

'I said our parents had left us well provided for; that wasn't strictly true. They had left us some money, but it wasn't enough to see Kathy and I through our studies. Kathy being the eldest had been entrusted to look after the finances of our education. I often enquired about our financial state, but Kathy was always protective of the situation, merely saying we had no difficulties. Indeed, my college bills were always paid on time and whenever I needed money, Kathy provided it without question. I had no idea until later that our inherited funds had been inadequate. Kathy recognized this and her evenings away were not spent on her project, but doing various part-time jobs, mostly working in shady pubs and bars. Even then, the income from the jobs fell short of our requirements and she began to supplement it by distributing drugs, first via her workplaces and when that became difficult, as full-time evening work. During this time that she was arrested by the police.'

'Why didn't Kathy say anything to you? I've assumed you were close.'

'That's probably why she kept it to herself. She's always acted as the responsible big sister, ever protective and never wanting me to worry about anything. I assume she hoped that once she started work, our financial problems would be over and her drug-pushing days could be buried in the past.'

'Does this explain why she never took the job in the States?'

'Sort of. One of the conditions of being immune from prosecution was she had to surrender her passport to the police. I don't know, but I assume she tried to negotiate a release from her undercover operation once she graduated, though my guess is the police effectively blackmailed her into continuing to work for them. I accused them of this when they told me what had been going on, but according to them, Kathy's co-operation was purely on a voluntary basis. Furthermore, the company she joined in Edmonton was at the instigation of the police, because they had unsubstantiated evidence that suggested it housed the labs for freebasing the imported drugs into crack.'

'Incredible. The policewoman – Simone – told you all this?'

'Not when she first visited me; she had come to tell me the police were taking Kathy's disappearance seriously because of her undercover activity, and to enquire if there was any further information I could supply to help their enquiries. The rest came out a day later after they discovered Kathy's body.'

I was stunned into silence. Charlotte had been understandably downbeat in her story but I had no idea there would be such a tragic endpoint. She recognized my discomfort and attempted to qualify her statement.

'She's not dead. Well, not in the medical sense. She's in a coma and has been for more than three months.'

Her qualification did nothing to quell the deep sympathy I felt for Charlotte. I tried to speak. 'What ... ha ...'

'What happened? No one knows for sure. The coma was induced by a massive drug overdose of heroin. She was found unconscious in an alleyway in Camden Town. There were no witnesses to how she got there. Although Kathy had pedalled drugs, there was no reason to believe she took them. The police thought she was clean and I had never seen her take anything suspicious, nor seen her high except after a few vodka and tonics – yet there was a puncture hole on her arm. So, the police believe Kathy's overdose was not self-inflicted. Kathy hasn't spoken since, so the police have no leads – just a theory.

'Shortly before Kathy's body was discovered, she telephoned her police contact to say she had discovered a locked room at BioRemedy, which she had seen one of the technicians frequently visit. Nothing strange in that, as apparently most pharmaceutical companies have highly sensitive work which they try to keep secret, but Kathy was asked to try to find out more about the room. Two nights before her body was discovered, Kathy had arranged to work late with the objective of attempting to break into the room – she had described the lock to the police and had been given a crash course in lock breaking. A call from her was logged that night at ten o'clock but, according to the records, it wasn't significant. After Kathy's body had been found, the police visited BioRemedy ostensibly to make enquiries about Kathy's employment and background, but they took the opportunity to informally search the building and interview staff. They found a few locked doors, which were freely opened by senior staff. Some doors led to laboratories and manufacturing facilities, but nothing illegal was unearthed. So, the theory is that Kathy's collusion with the police was discovered and someone, somehow tried to make sure her knowledge never went any further. Then they cleaned up BioRemedy so that an inspection revealed nothing.'

'What about the boyfriend? Couldn't he help?'

'Maybe, if he exists, and could be found. In BioRemedy's records and according to those employees Kathy had confided in, she still lived with me in

Islington. That was the police's opinion too. I was the only person who had heard of a boyfriend.'

'When did all this happen?'

'About four months ago. I searched Kathy's belongings and discovered our family finances were in a dreadful state. Our joint bank account, over which Kathy had complete control, was £3,000 overdrawn. There was an authorized overdraft limit of only £2,000 and the bank had recently written seeking an urgent meeting to review the situation. The rent for the house hadn't been paid for three months, nor had my advance tuition fees for my final year. The last major outlay had been the settlement of outstanding fees for Kathy's degree course. If they hadn't been paid then Kathy would never have been awarded her degree. I immediately took part-time jobs: bar work in the evenings and cleaning early mornings, but the income wasn't enough, the bank were impatient and four weeks later I was homeless and an ex-student.'

'No aunts, uncles or other family to lend a hand?' I asked.

'Mother had been an only child; Dad's sister and parents live in Australia, but they are reclusive and didn't come to the funeral; my other grandparents are dead.'

'Couldn't your housemates or particularly the police help you out?'

'One of the students said I could secretly share her room, but the landlord became wise to the scheme – tipped off by another student I believe – so I had to leave.

'Officially the police have had to remain disassociated from any involvement with Kathy; unofficially they have been reasonably helpful. They arranged for me to stay at Jubilee hostel and they have ensured Kathy has had the best possible care in hospital. She's been examined by experts in narcotics and neurology, and is being continuously monitored by machines and medical staff.

'I visit her in hospital every day and occasionally a police inspector looks in to check on her progress. He often gives me money from the "snout fund", as he calls it.'

'Conscience money,' I said accusingly.

'Maybe, but I'm grateful for it. At least I don't have to beg or take a slave's job to survive. Anyway, I believe it actually comes from the inspector's own pocket. You might believe it too when you know I'm talking about the same benefactor – Inspector Bradley.'

'My Inspector Bradley?'

'It must be, based upon your description of him earlier, particularly since Kathy is under intensive care in the Helen Raphael ward at the Royal London hospital.'

I reflected on my own story and had expected from Charlotte's earlier reaction that Ronnie Kent would be the common denominator, not our philanthropic policeman Bradley and the Royal London.

'So now our pasts coincide as well as our present. Perhaps destiny will dictate the future does too?'

She smiled at my statement and I wondered whether she was humouring me or if she had had a similar thought. Charlotte sat back as though she had finished her story, but I still wanted to fill a few gaps.

'Why are you bothering to continue your studies now you've been thrown out?' I asked.

'I've spent over two years studying for my qualification and I'm a bright student. I'm not giving up just because I can't afford to finish my course. I'm sure I could get a day job and an evening job to fund my studies and better accommodation, but while I have a free roof over my head and enough money to eat, it allows my priorities to be elsewhere. My sister is my first concern and I want the freedom to visit her whenever I can. In between times, I try to take my mind off the situation by studying. It's no substitute for the real thing since I'm missing out on the practical work, but I have a copy of the theory syllabus and I'm slowly working through it. When Kathy is well again I will formally complete my course.'

I admired her approach and optimism. Of course I didn't know my own view on education. I'd had the sensation earlier that I had been at a university, though whether this was a visit (to see my brother?) or to attend, I desperately hoped I would find out soon. And had I been as close to my brother as Charlotte was to her sister? If I had, surely by now he would know I'd gone missing? Yet Bradley had checked the list of missing persons "in the area" he had said, but what area? Stepney Green? East London? London? South of Watford? In listening to Charlotte's story, I had detected a kind of brogue to her voice, which made me think she came from the West Country, Devon or Cornwall perhaps. I had an idea.

'Are you listening to me?' Charlotte said, prodding my leg with a finger.

'What kind of accent do I have?' I asked.

'English, but where did that question spring from?'

'I'm sorry Charlotte I was listening to you, but the talk about your sister made me think about my newly discovered brother. I know, well I think I'm English, British anyway, but what part of Britain does my accent come from?'

She thought for a moment, presumably analyzing our conversations.

'You're well spoken, probably well educated, English, Londonish from the occasional colloquialism. Not posh enough for West London; too smooth for South; close to North, nearer to East. In fact, your accent is quite similar – no, very similar – to a guy on the same course as me. He was from Essex; Epping I think.'

I wanted to flatter her linguistic abilities, her looks and intelligence, but with the pessimistic nature of our stories I thought it best not to be too informal.

'If you're right, it does narrow the search for my identity. I'll follow any leads at the moment.'

Now I'd lost her attention. She was looking around, spotted a nearby student and went to enquire after the time; she returned in a rush.

'I ought to be going. I always visit my sister at four o'clock and that's fifteen minutes away with a twenty-minute walk. Would you like to join me?'

It was a tempting offer; I'd certainly like to spend more time with Charlotte, but other matters were pressing.

'Having only left the hospital today I don't want to go back there so soon and I don't think I'm too comfortable in dealing with tragedies. Ask me another time and the answer will be yes. Right now I'd like to get back to the library to investigate my Essex roots.'

Charlotte looked disappointed as we made for the refectory exit. She shrugged. 'Okay, I'll see you later.'

'Before you go, you haven't answered my original question. Why are you telling the people at the hostel you are a reforming drug addict?'

'It's quite simple; the trustees of the hostel are sympathetic to drug addicts who are trying to kick the habit. Despite the police introduction, it was the only way I could guarantee a place to tide me over while I tended my sister. Anyway, I must dash,' she said and broke into a jog. I watched her until she disappeared around a corner.

Chapter 16

SECOND SATURDAY – 3:55 p.m.

Back at the library, I enquired about local newspapers for Essex and was amazed that every major town appeared to have its own weekly publication. The most general was the *Essex Weekly*, published every Friday, but the library only had last week's issue. The newspaper's main office was in Chelmsford and the helpful librarian (thankfully not the banana skin waving chief) telephoned to establish there was public access to a back issues department, Monday to Friday from 10:00 to 16:00. For regional daily newspapers, I consulted a writers' yearbook.

The nearest Essex-based daily was the *East Anglian Mail* whose head office was in Ipswich. This was a longer shot for my research; I doubted a Suffolk town would devote a great deal of reportage to a neighbouring county. Visits would have to wait until I had checked on the cheapest means of transport, besides I would want to go early one morning so that I could have a full day of newspaper scanning. I took the previous week's issue of the *Weekly* and settled at one of the tables. It was a weighty publication – 120 pages or more – and well thumbed by previous readers. Once I had discarded the housing, car sales and entertainment supplements, I was left with a more manageable 40 pages of news. I studied people, places, events, personal columns, even the occasional advert, waiting and wishing for the spark that would link me with the past, but it never came. I was bored too; although I had nothing better to do, I found the task onerous and unrewarding.

This was no way to spend my life, surely I would be more satisfied if I did what Charlotte was doing, keeping my mind active on a subject which could benefit my future? Yet what should I study? The odds of choosing an appropriate topic were stacked against me. If I were a computer scientist, chemistry wouldn't help. If I were a chemist, literature would be a waste of time. Maybe I should stick to something like current affairs or business matters, an up-to-date knowledge of those subjects could be generally useful. I was still dwelling on my dilemma when I had the decision process taken away from me. Now close to five o'clock – and closing time – banana skin man was on the prowl, unceremoniously ejecting the few people remaining. I rose to leave and noticed a small notebook and biro on an adjacent table. I moved towards it and casually looking around to check I wasn't being watched, I picked up the writing materials and, with a pounding heart, slid them into the inside pocket of my jacket. I recalled my emphatic statement to Inspector Bradley that I wasn't a criminal, yet with little conscience and a great deal of nervousness I had stolen. Admittedly the spoils of my theft weren't exactly earth shattering, but the temptation to circumvent the purchase of my basic priority one requirement had been too great. Maybe the acquisition had been seeded by the earlier attempt to recall my profession and the fact I had decided to cram my mind with current news – a reporter's notebook and pen would be high on a journalist's list of occupational tools. I argued in my head that taking something apparently discarded was not really stealing, merely a redeployment of unwanted goods. Nonetheless I felt extraordinarily self-conscious as I left the library with my writer's haul tapping against my chest from an inside pocket.

I emerged into a mild, overcast evening with no intention of hurrying back to the hostel and turned right to wander the streets around Bethnal Green. Frustratingly I observed the flow of people and traffic, jealous of the family welcome they might receive when they eventually arrived home. Instead of pondering my own problems, I replayed Charlotte's own story and I recalled Luther's advice about not attempting to discover what had gone before. Currently, I was in blissful ignorance and, if my immediate past was as troublesome as Charlotte's, perhaps it was best if I stayed that way.

Feeling hungry, I headed back to the hostel via Stepney Green station to ask about train times and fares to Chelmsford and Ipswich. I shuddered at the knowledge of how the necessary £8.80 and £19.70 respectively would dent or exceed my wealth, which I had computed as £19.45p. Next to the ticket kiosk there was a news and confectionary stand, in front of which was a small stall containing a limited selection of flowers and fruit. There were a number of people waiting to be served, who were delayed while a bunch of flowers were pedantically gift wrapped by an elderly saleswoman. What possessed me to take the next action I never did fathom. Was it the despondency of my limited funds; the hunger developing in my stomach; or the success of my recent introduction to undetected larceny?

I joined the disorderly queue at the end adjacent to the fruit stall and manoeuvred my left hand so that it was level with a tray of apples. I waited about fifteen seconds and then pretending to be frustrated by the queue's slowness, I turned quickly to the right shielding my hand from anyone viewing me from behind. In one swift movement, I grabbed an apple. In a flash it was buried with my hand in a jacket pocket, and I was heading for the station exit. My insides were churning and any moment I expected someone to call out or place a firm hand on my shoulder. I reached the pavement and began to stride quickly away from the scene of the crime. Two minutes later, having not dared to look behind, I slowed my walk and took deep breaths to reduce my heart rate. I paused to look in a shop window and glanced right to determine whether anyone had followed me. Nobody seemed to be paying me attention, the pedestrian flow focused on its homeward journeys – I had gotten away with it. I think my relief was not because of my successful steal – since I was truly ashamed of what I had done – rather that, despite my directionless existence, I had done something bold and positive in the day. Still, I vowed such proof would be inappropriate in the future; from now on, I would only express myself legitimately. I was determined that my light-fingered career was over, and indeed it was; however, I didn't know then a heavier variety was but a few days away.

Still fearful of being followed, I hastened my return to the hostel and didn't eat my apple until I was almost there. When I entered, Jazz was arguing with a scruffy looking woman who was carrying two bulging bin-liners. Jazz briefly paused to give me an unexpected friendly wave and smile and then continued her "Go away, we are full" tongue lashing of her visitor.

I peeked into the common meeting room hoping Charlotte had returned from the hospital. A group of six was watching television, but only one that I knew. Keith the ex-prisoner leapt up from the chair I had seen him occupying that morning and greeted me again like a long-lost friend. I wondered whether he'd been there all day.

'Have you come for our chat?' Keith said enthusiastically.

I hadn't, but the look on his face indicated he would be disappointed if I denied him. Also, I didn't know why he had been in prison. Did he bash people if they wouldn't chat with him? I looked at the others, but they kept avoiding my eyes, perhaps hopeful I was about to remove Keith from their presence.

'Sorry,' I said thinking quickly, 'I'm supposed to be meeting Charlotte. I thought she might be here. Have you seen her?'

'She doesn't usually get back from rehab until about seven-thirty,' said one of the women in the room.

'There …' Keith said looking at the wall clock, '… we could spend half an hour chatting.'

'Maybe later, I'm desperate to go to the loo,' I said and crossed my legs to emphasize my need.

Keith did look disappointed, but he was philosophical in his reply. 'Never mind. Calls of nature must come first. Destiny will eventually bring us together.'

I really did want the loo and hurried to pay a visit in the men's quarters. While there I could hear active noises coming from the kitchen and a few minutes later when I went to the source, dinnertime was in full swing. Dinner was perhaps an exaggeration; high tea would have been a better description. There was a brief silence as I entered while the occupants checked out my intrusion and then the conversations continued.

The pseudo fab-four from Liverpool were gathered around the nearest table and whispering to each other between mouthfuls of soup. Occasionally one of them tore a hunk of bread from a large misshapen loaf.

Leslie was arguing with the microwave; furiously pressing buttons, turning dials and banging it in frustration. He had changed his wig and frock since I last saw him; now he was blonde and wore men's flat shoes and a faded floral dress a couple of sizes too small for him; he looked ridiculous. For someone with an ambition to be a woman, his fashion sense was outrageous; and where did he get the money for his varied wardrobe?

At the other end of the kitchen there were two men and women, all perhaps a few years older than me. The men's voices were dominant, interrupted by an occasional nervous giggle from one of the women.

Sitting on a chair immediately in front of the washing machine and mesmerized by the spinning, swirling water was – I first thought – the beggar I had encountered that morning in the Mile End Road. It was an odd sight if I'd interpreted it correctly, this disarrayed man being concerned with cleaning his clothes.

I must have stared disbelievingly at this scene, because a voice said to me, 'They're not *his* clothes, he's doing that for Luther.'

Two men were sitting at a table behind the Liverpudlians. I took a double take at the first person I saw. He was a clone of the washing machine attendant – brown bobble hat, brown overcoat, black boots, grey hair and beard – except as I moved closer I noticed white smears on his beard from the cream cake he was stuffing greedily into his mouth.

The second man sitting near him continued speaking: 'You're the new guy, I presume; the one who's lost his memory?'

Of the kitchen assembly, he looked the most approachable and I had half an hour to kill before Charlotte returned.

'News travels fast. Mind if I join you?' I asked.

He nodded towards the chair next to him and placed the magazine he had been reading on the table. To me he looked like a schoolteacher. Aged about forty; sandy coloured and receding hair; clean shaven; thick spectacles; old brown tweed jacket with leather patches at the elbow; fawn trousers, but not true to type, blue and white trainers. I guessed he was a member of the hostel staff rather than a resident.

'You're too late for the mouldy rejects,' he said, 'the vultures have swooped already.' He nodded towards the beggar eating the cake. His hands and overcoat were now cream infested too and our eyes met briefly.

'Fucking nosy bastard,' he growled, showering the area in front him with small white dribbles. I had been wrong earlier, he was the beggar who had abused me before.

'Don't mind him. He's a Pole. That's the only bit of English he knows. My name's Adrian by the way, Adrian Perry.'

'Robin Forest,' I said and shook his hand. 'I'm puzzled ...' I continued quietly in case the Polish beggar could hear and knew more English than his expletive had suggested, '... I had the impression that the hostel policy was to shelter deserving and rehabilitative strays.'

Adrian recognized my caution and to indicate spoke louder than he had done before. 'The hostel, or library as it was, was purchased by a Polish businessman called Johann Sturtz. His father, Pieter, had come here during the war, fallen on hard times and spent a period himself in a hostel in East London. The two hobos before you, Gregor and Igor, were homeless at the same time as Pieter and they became, and stayed, good friends. Pieter vowed that if he could ever afford it, he would set up his own shelter for the homeless. Well, Pieter got lucky, worked hard and established an engineering company, which was reasonably successful, but he never became wealthy enough to realize his dream before he died. As a condition of inheriting the company from his father, Johann had to accept the legacy of founding a hostel as soon as finances allowed. He realized his father's dream ten years ago when he bought and refurbished this building. Then he transferred the property and a starting sum of money into a trust for subsequent administration. That wasn't the end of his involvement though; he is a trustee and is still active in fund raising activities. Out of choice Gregor and Igor have been homeless since the early days and through Pieter's and then Johann's insistence, have always been treated as special cases since the Jubilee opened.'

I had expected a short reply to my question, but Adrian appeared to like story telling and a captive audience. 'You're well informed. How do you know this? I assume neither Gregor nor Igor told you this.'

Adrian laughed. 'They may have done. Occasionally one of them will rabbit on for ages thinking you understand what he is saying. No, Johann told me. He visits here every couple of weeks to check the hostel and the "brothers Grim" are okay. We share a passion in aviation,' he said and nodded towards his magazine, whose pages were open at an evil-looking square-panelled fighter aeroplane.

Gregor (or was it Igor?) had finished his cake and was scooping errant cream from his beard. Oddly, he had been listening attentively to Adrian's discourse and was now eyeing me suspiciously.

Leslie had finally beaten the microwave into submission and joined us at the table bearing a bowl of steaming soup – minestrone by the smell and look

– and probably one of Morris's infamous bread rolls by the green colour round the edges.

'If my maths is correct then our friends here have been homeless for 50 odd years and must be at least 70 years old,' I exclaimed.

'56 and 74 respectively, to be exact,' Adrian replied.

'I haven't been homeless for a day yet and it's already driving me crazy. How could anyone survive for over fifty years?'

'Remember, homeless is a misnomer. We're not homeless, we are vulnerably accommodated. This place has been Gregor and Igor's home for the last ten years. Before that, according to Johann, they had homes in a number of other hostels. Their plight hasn't come from a lack of roof, more a lack of money. They refuse to work, sharing the opinion that after their experience under the Nazis, they would never again supplicate to a self-imposed superior. They beg their way through life, though how they manage with their manners and lack of English, heaven knows; though I suspect Johann makes sure they are never hungry and, somewhat against their principles, I think they do odd jobs for Luther.'

'Anyway, enough of my chat. What's your story?' Adrian said in a loud enough voice to attract attention.

Cake-man had been observing us intently throughout and looking to my left I noticed Leslie and washing machine-man had joined the scrutiny. The subdued chatter on the next table had also subsided and I heard a Scouse accent bid, 'Yeh, we all like a new story,' and then the rest of his group murmured their agreement.

And so for the second time that day I related my short life story. I reported the day's events too, but chose to ignore the details of my conversations with Charlotte. Although she hadn't stated as much, I felt sure that her background and recent events had been revealed to me in confidence.

Considering the diversity of my audience, they were politely attentive and did not interrupt. In contrast to my serious version to Charlotte, I tried to make light of my tale and inject humour where possible. They were receptive and gave generous laughter, the loudest response coming from the name of "Hugh" that my hospital colleagues wanted to give me. The two Polish tramps matched the timing and volume of the other's laughs, though whether this was an involuntary reaction, or as I suspected a true understanding of what I had said, I didn't discover until later.

With the tale complete I expected questions, but to my relief, none came. Either my storytelling power was compelling and thorough, the story plot was uninteresting or I had simply satisfied the curiosity of my colleagues, who now had better things to occupy them. Leslie excused itself, proudly announcing it had a date; with a final grunt Gregor (cake-man as I learned later) shuffled from the room; his Polish partner had completed his wash cycle and was now transferring his load to the tumble dryer; Rick and Co had resumed their secret whispers.

I assumed that a half hour had passed and with a lull in conversation, I decided to renew my search for Charlotte.

'Gannet died today,' Adrian said suddenly.

The news didn't register with me immediately.

'He usually snores like a trooper, so I investigated his silent body at lunchtime today, but he was dead as a dodo. Police and ambulance came to take him away. Apparently you had a fight with him this morning.'

Of course, the smelly character who stole my food. 'A verbal fight,' I said in defence, 'He stole my sandwiches and cake. What did he die from?'

'Nobody said. He was rather old and didn't exactly portray a picture of health. Heart attack, pneumonia, something like that I expect.'

I had no idea whether I had encountered death so close before and despite my initial anger at Gannet, I was truly saddened at his demise. I would have gladly suffered the smell and shared my food with him if I had known his ultimate fate. It worried me too that Adrian had mentioned the death merely in passing. Was this a regular occurrence amongst the strays of the street? Would I become a Gregor or Igor and spend the rest of my life in effective isolation from the rest of the world? My compatriots were so at ease and resigned to their state – so much for the hostel objectives of rehabilitating its residents. I wondered whether the dividing line between hope and despair was linked with family. No family – despair, with family – hope. If true, surely I was on the side of hope. I had a brother and the family connection, if not my resolve, would direct me away from this life.

I was desperate for convivial company and wanted to find Charlotte. I made my excuses to Adrian who went back to his magazine. I stood and moved towards the two "couples" at the far end of the kitchen. They had hovered in the background during my story and now appeared to be organizing a break for the unisex common room, their remarks concerned with which television programme to watch, and hope that Keith wouldn't be there.

'Hello,' I said to the group.

'Good story, old chap. Was it true?' said one of the men nudging his male colleague. One of the women giggled.

On closer inspection the men were both around forty but physically different. The accuser was medium height, stocky and prematurely bald. He wore a dark blue jumper and khaki trousers with multi-coloured paint smears down each thigh. The other man was over six feet in height; rake thin and with masses of curly blonde hair. He appeared to be wearing an identical jumper in colour and size which rode high above his waist and hung loose around his arms, almost covering his hands. His blue jeans were equally ill fitting, floating an inch or two above his ankles and made more noticeable by the holey black socks and absence of shoes.

'Yes,' I said in a tone, which must have sounded hurt.

'No offence chum; it's just that it's a bloody good ruse losing your memory, if you've been up to mischief and don't want to get traced. I did it myself once. Laid low for a few years then resurfaced when I'd been forgotten about.'

'Not purposely in my case,' I said, vexed by his tone and my need to move on.

I turned to the two women. Both were younger than my original assessment; body language and pose indicated an age akin to Charlotte's. They too were quite different in appearance. One was plain looking with shabby clothes and her weathered face aged her by several years. The other was dressed casually but smart, was good-looking with a nice figure, though top-heavy breasts. I noticed she wore a watch – gold coloured and expensive with a small face.

'Could you tell me the time?' I asked her.

Magically she answered without consciously looking at her watch, 'It's eight o'clock,' she replied.

'Would you do me a favour? Could you check whether Charlotte has come back yet?'

'The snooty blonde acid head?'

'Snooty – no; blonde – yes; I don't know about the acidhead,' I said protectively.

'What d'ya want with her?' asked the other woman? 'Fancy 'er, do ya?'

'I fancy her,' said the lamppost imitator.

'Shut up, Roger. You and Brian fancy anything with tits,' said the watch bearer.

'Yes, but Roger's got it so bad, we have to hide pictures of cows from him in case he gets too frisky,' said stocky Brian, and the group burst out laughing.

I didn't laugh. My empathy with my homeless brethren had not reached a level yet where I could join in with their humour, particularly those I hadn't been introduced to yet. 'Don't worry,' I said, 'I'll check at reception.'

'No, s'okay. I'll take a look. Can't stand in the way of love. My name's Georgie, by the way. Just in case you want somebody who's clean and fun loving.' She winked at me, and poked out her tongue in the direction of the men before disappearing into the women's quarters.

Not wishing to be left out, the other woman unsubtly introduced herself. 'And I'm Free,' she said. 'That's short for Freeda. I'm not free, but then I'm not expensive either,' she added in a tarty voice while simultaneously stroking her hair and wriggling her hips, in a manner that I could not decide was natural or acted.

I felt distinctly uncomfortable with the flirting from the women, which I knew was not for my benefit but to engender jealousy in their male companions. Roger thought the event was funny, but Brian was giving me an intimidating evil eye. Fortunately Georgie soon reappeared, just at the point I thought Brian was about to issue me with a "keep off" warning.

'She's not in the dorms, the loos or the common rooms,' Georgie said. Then sniggering she added, 'But Keith said if you are short of company, you could have your chat now.'

I thanked her for her help and easing myself carefully past Brian, who was making a stand by attempting to block my return path, I made my way via the men's quarters back to reception, vigilantly in case Keith waylaid me.

Jazz was still there and I went through the security procedure to retrieve my duffle bag. I rechecked with Jazz that Charlotte hadn't arrived and went outside.

Chapter 17

SECOND SATURDAY – 8:15 p.m.

The air was cool and fresh considering I was in London. I'd noticed earlier, most of the neighbouring streets were devoted to small businesses and warehousing, so traffic flow at this time of night was low, which must have had a positive effect on air quality. Opposite the hostel was a short stretch of waste ground, which now contained the rubble of a demolished building. Adjacent to the pavement was a low wall where I sat down and rummaged in my bag for something to eat. This was an habitual reaction. I hadn't eaten much that day and I didn't feel particularly hungry, yet nurse Rapley had advised I should have an adequate and nourishing diet. It was a key element to aid my recovery process; a good nootropic, she had said – whatever that meant. Thanks to poor Gannet, there was nothing that stirred my stomach juices: Pretzels and biscuits held no palatable attraction, and the remaining two bananas had blackened and might not survive another day, so I ate them and dropped the skins behind the wall.

The road was quiet but for the occasional visitor to and from the hostel entrance. In particular, I observed the arrivals and tried to guess if they were snooker players or homeless. My guess could be confirmed by watching whether they passed the window facing the road at the top of the stairs – a trivial game, with which I soon became bored. The homeless were easily distinguished by their purposeless gait and quality of dress. Of the twelve I counted in, I was wrong on one count: a slouching young man in a heavy overcoat and carrying a rucksack, whom I'd typed as homeless, headed for the snooker club instead.

While my observation of passers-by was mildly educational and time consuming, it concealed the real reasons for being outside, which came to the fore as the chilling air questioned my continued surveillance. For a start, I was uncomfortable with the atmosphere of the hostel. Its dark and depressing surroundings seemed foreign to my past. I didn't think claustrophobia was the cause of my discomfort, more a need to be in open space, so that I could focus my thoughts on the past, instead of being sucked into the despair of the present. I feared the longer I spent in the company of the unemployed and unemployable, the more I might be influenced to join their ranks. Surely, it was a good sign I wanted to get myself out of this dilemma, rather than being any form of aloofness? Maybe I was fooling myself; just one day into my plight I still felt positive, had clean clothes to call upon, and I wasn't starving. But things would undoubtedly get worse before they got better and I convinced myself that hope, above all, was a feeling I would have to preserve at all costs, lest I become absorbed into the culture of my current peers.

Then there was Gannet. His death had depressed me greatly and the thought of sleeping tonight in my upper bunk, knowing that hours before someone had died in the lower bunk, was a valid excuse to spend as much time as I could outside. But, attempting to be honest with myself, the major reason I was sitting on a wall in isolation was to await the arrival of Charlotte. Of the people I had met, she appeared to be the only one that had an achievable objective. Her resolve was merely in hibernation while she sat by her sister's side. We were kindred spirits, alone in the world waiting for a significant event to mould our futures. I had great respect and sympathy for her and, eager to align myself with positive influences only, I was desperate for her company. I felt privileged too that she had confided in me the true source of her homelessness. On the surface, we had a friendship and understanding that could benefit each other – well, benefit me. Her experiences to date led me to believe she had already achieved an independence, which I strove to attain.

I wondered why she hadn't returned from the hospital yet. By now it must be half past eight, an hour past her expected time if the information from the hostel had been correct. I wished I had accepted the offer to join her. On reflection I could have dealt with such a quick return to hospital and fact finding at the library could have suffered a day's delay. Maybe something had happened to Charlotte? It was sad there would be no one pacing up and down, worried she was late; presumably not even the hostel staff would call the police if she went missing. She would be regarded as merely another drug addict statistic, one that had failed rehab and drifted back to a chemical dependency for facing the troubles of life. Kathy couldn't fret for Charlotte's safety – her senses deprived of communication with the world. Perhaps Kathy's condition had changed; if it had, I prayed it had been for the better not the worse.

I had become accustomed to the chill, though my hands – thrust as deep into my jacket pockets as possible – were beginning to tingle with lack of movement. I looked behind and saw that at the rear of the waste ground there was an illuminated security light shining into the backyard of the adjacent premises. I moved towards it and noticed the plot was a builder's yard containing pallets of bricks, wooden planks and other building materials, surrounded by a sturdy looking wire fence. I perched on a pile of rubble in a position that afforded benefit of the light and was still an observation point for activity at the Jubilee. I extracted the notebook and biro I had acquired at the library and began to write my life history. I didn't set out to scribe a masterpiece of literature. Many of the events I précised into brief notes and headlines, ones I would be able to flesh out when I had more time, better surroundings and a dictionary to hand. I did however set out to express intimate thoughts about my plight and the feelings that went through my mind when I first discovered what a hopeless situation I had found myself in. With only five days to recall, the words flowed easily, helped no doubt by the recent recitals I had given to Charlotte and the hostel guests.

My jottings went further than my narrative, adding thoughts, which I had not shared with my audiences, and in one aspect, had not fully appreciated until I put pen to paper. My written feelings towards Charlotte went further than my conscious mind had allowed; I expressed a depth of affection that took me by surprise. Granted the purpose of my surveillance was to see Charlotte again and I convinced myself this premature flow of emotion was born of my frustration in spending an hour or more waiting for her return. I did consider heading towards the hospital, but my fear of what I might discover, and the avoidance of intrusion on her family matters, kept me rooted to my observation post.

Throughout my authoring, I was vigilant, looking up whenever I heard footsteps on the street, now ten metres distance from my vantage point. Human and vehicular traffic had subsided to an infrequent occurrence. Around ten o'clock (I guessed) there was a steady exodus of excited people from the snooker club and then the lights on the first floor were extinguished. Then I had one of those mini déjà vu experiences which told me that, in my youth, I had visited such a club which was not licenced to sell alcohol; hence, an early closure so that its patrons had time to visit a local pub before going home.

About half an hour later, with the cold beginning to bite and my backside exhausted of finding a comfortable position on the pile of rubble, I decided to give up on my vigil for Charlotte. Reluctantly, I would spend my first night in the hostel, if only to shelter from the cold enveloping me. I stood up, stretched, picked up my bag and threaded my way around the debris and into the shadows cast by the adjacent building. I saw someone appear at the entrance door to the old library and stopped to observe. It was one of the aspiring pop group, Jason – based upon his build. He stamped his feet and clapped his gloved hands together against the cold while looking furtively up and down the road. After a few minutes, during which he frequently consulted his watch, he moved a few yards down the road to shelter inside the doorway of the bicycle shop which was next to the hostel. I contemplated crossing the road to expose his hiding place when I heard distant footsteps approaching from the direction hidden from me. The steps quickened as they passed by on my side of the road and I saw a beckoning hand wave towards Jason, who looked suspiciously from side to side once more before crossing the road to join his summoner. From what I remembered of my morning encounter with Luther, it could have been him based upon build, clothes and lack of hair. Together they strode away speaking, but not loud enough to carry to my ears.

Of course, it was none of my business what they were up to at this time of night, but I had been curious about Luther, and to follow them was another reason to forestall the unproductiveness of bedtime. Tailing them was not easy: the streets were quiet and they frequently looked behind them, so I remained at a safe distance. I closed the gap as we neared the busier Mile End Road, in case I lost sight of them amongst the many pedestrians, increased no doubt by the proximity of pub closing time. They crossed the main road and continued to walk northwards, zigzagging through several blocks. When I turned a corner at a crossroads, they had vanished.

The street was a narrow one of terraced houses, made narrower by vehicles parked on one side. I looked up at the corner house and noticed the sign said Grace Street. Then I heard an engine start a short distance away and a blue Ford Transit van pulled out. I stepped away from the edge of the road and attempted to conceal myself behind a lamppost. The van paused briefly at the junction and then turned left and accelerated wildly away; Luther was driving and Jason was sitting next to him. For some reason, I made a mental note of the registration number, which suggested the van was no more than a couple of years old. I was mildly inquisitive by what I had seen. Why hadn't Luther picked Jason up from the hostel? And how come Luther could afford such a vehicle? It struck me as strange, albeit natural, that I was concerned with the oddities of other people's lives, since my own were not capable of being explained. Unenthusiastically I retraced my route back to the hostel.

It must have been a shift change when I arrived back, the reception clock was showing past eleven o'clock and Jazz was handing over keys to an old, but upright man, who was dressed in an army uniform much too large for him. Jazz appeared to be in a hurry and frustrated by the old gent's ceremonial approach to the transfer, as he counted and inspected each key. I waited until the ritual had finished and then hailed Jazz as she made a rush for the door.

'Jazz, did Charlotte get back?'

'Honey, I'm in a rush. No, she's AWOL, but don't worry she's a sensible girl. I doubt whether she's in trouble. I'll check around in the morning if she doesn't turn up,' she replied and waddled her chunky frame as fast as she could to the exit. She paused at the door and looked back: 'Don't get sweet on her child, she's been through hell and won't want you messing with her emotions,' she said in a motherly way.

Had Charlotte told Jazz her true story I wondered, or was Jazz referring to the bogus tale Charlotte had invented to secure her accommodation? Either way, her warning was unwarranted. I only wanted to help her if possible and receive her companionship in return – didn't I?

Up to now I hadn't felt sleepy, but as I trudged to room D a swamping tiredness enveloped me. Not that I had been particularly extended physically or mentally. Perhaps the hip pain – which had considerably subsided – had contributed to my fatigue, and I suppose my body was still recovering from its shock. Most likely, it was the nervous energy I had used in acclimatizing to my new life style.

The warmth, body smells and night-time noises as I entered the dormitory, suggested many of the bunks were already occupied. In the dim light shed from the windows I could verify over half the beds contained blanketed torsos. Were the remainder begging, drinking, and shooting up, or at their nocturnal jobs? In my tired state this was a question I couldn't be bothered to debate in my head. I trod carefully through the gloom to my designated bunk and saw that Gannet's had already been filled by a young man, fully clothed and with a multi-coloured bandanna tied around his forehead. His mouth was wide open and emitting a soft whistling sound – the most tuneful of the noises around. There was still a scent of blood and meat in the air and I wondered how long the presence of the departed Gannet would take to fade. I climbed the two-step ladder as quietly as possible and sat over the edge of the bunk to remove my shoes, then wedged them between the end rail of the bed and mattress. I took off my jacket and laid it over my shoes. The double blanket folded at the end of the bed smelt clean, but was coarse to the touch. I was too tired to remove the rest of my clothes, besides they would form a protective itch-free barrier against the blankets. I would shower and change in the morning. I propped my duffle bag under the skimpy pillow, put down my head and, despite the cacophony of noises around me and a review of the day evolving in my brain, I was asleep in minutes.

Chapter 18

SECOND SUNDAY – 5:30 a.m.

It was still dark when the coughing and wheezing started. I think I was already awake, drifting in that delirious time before full consciousness. From my nights at the hospital, I knew this was the period when I should try to concentrate my thoughts on dream revelations of my past, but I found the dormitory noise distracting. My only recollection was a conscious one that during the night, I had been awoken by the outline of Jason in the doorway, as he returned from his suspicious exploits.

I had no idea how long I had been asleep except I felt refreshed, albeit with an ache in my lower back from the solid mattress beneath me. I supposed that in the past I had been driven by the schedule of my life, because now I felt vulnerable to the vagueness of time imposed by daylights hours. For October, I knew that sunrise and sunset delimited my day between approximately 8:00 and 18:00. What did it matter? I had no appointments to keep, no trains to catch, no working hours, and mealtimes would not be categorized as breakfast, lunch and dinner, but as foraging snapshots whenever food could be purchased, stolen or accepted charitably.

No one else was stirring, and I recognized this as a quiet opportunity to use the washroom. After yesterday's experience of losing food I debated whether to take my duffle bag with me. Food was a precious commodity, but the pretzels and biscuits I had left weren't exactly a major gastronomic attraction, and everyone I'd seen so far – bar Gregor and Igor – were reasonably dressed. I looked around the dormitory and there were bags, cases and bundles in various insecure places so I assumed there was an implicit trust between the homeless and my bad experience of yesterday was a one-off. Nevertheless, rifling my crammed bag then would have undoubtedly disturbed my fellow billetees, so I slid silently from the bunk and took the bag with me to the washroom. Then I recalled how noise carried through the thin partition wall, but I was beyond consideration now, I was looking forward to clean clothes and a clean body to lift my spirits.

Previously I wanted to stay with my past clothes hoping they would spark a memory in me or someone else. The idea was only a day old, yet for the moment cleanliness took precedence over this unproven and remote notion. I rummaged through my bag and looked again at my total possessions; not a great deal of choice, but I was thankful for a choice at all. I selected the lace-up boots and a pair of thick green socks. I expected to be doing a lot of walking in the days ahead so I may as well break them in now. Shirt was easy – any one of three plain white T's; yellow underpants – who in their right mind would choose yellow underpants? Well I did – the other pair was lime green. That left Hobson's choice for the trousers – grey. I laid my choices on one of the wooden benches and stripped – bar my waterproof money belt – for the shower. There was soap and fresh towels, which was a plus, but the lack of hot water from the mixer tap was a body-shocking minus. I washed small areas at a time to lessen the impact of the cold water. Today I chose not to shave. Looking in the mirror, I decided that one day's stubble growth wasn't a visual hardship; perhaps I would grow a beard? As for the discarded clothes, they didn't smell and to defer my education on operating a washing machine they could be worn again later. After dressing and cleaning my teeth, I felt pretty good. The only small dent in my well being was hunger. I carefully repacked my bag, storing and separating the used clothes into the plastic carriers that were supplied with the new clothes.

I went back to the dorm and nobody had stirred. I placed my bag on the bed, took out the packet of pretzels I had left near the top, and crossed the corridor to the kitchen. It smelt of washing so I opened the window and cold dry air and traffic noises wafted in from the alleyway. The levels of light and noise suggested it was about six o'clock. I filled a kettle with water and set it to boil, and then inspected the lucky-dip cupboard. I shook a few anonymous tins and, based on sound and weight, selected one that promised a solid rather than a liquid meal. I opened it eagerly with the tin opener. Inside the tin were four sticks of a pale yellow vegetable immersed in salt water. I found a spoon and sampled something that had the consistency of boiled onions, but with a pleasant asparagus-type taste. I briefly considered heating them up in the microwave, but recalling Leslie's hassle with it, and eager to eat, I drained the water and emptied the contents of the tin into a bowl. This novel fare combined well with the mini pretzels, and I became so absorbed with my unusual breakfast I visibly started when a voice spoke behind me.

'You've struck lucky there. Celery hearts – the hostel favourite.'

I turned around and Luther was standing over me. He looked huge and imposing in the long grey overcoat he wore.

'Bloody hell, you frightened the life out of me. Were you trained in the SAS?'

'No, but silently and invisibly creeping up on someone is a skill which comes in handy sometimes. You obviously haven't mastered it yet.'

Was this an observation of my reaction or had he seen me last night? The answer came quickly as he leaned forward and spoke threateningly in my ear. 'Why were you following me last night?'

I told the truth – as sincerely as I could. 'I needed space while I waited for Charlotte. I got bored, saw Jason and was merely inquisitive about what he might be doing.'

'And what did you learn by your spying exercise?'

Now I lied. 'Nothing really. Jason met up with you; you walked a while and then drove off in a van. I presumed you were perhaps off to the pub for a drink. It's none of my business anyway.'

Luther was unconvinced. 'I still don't know what to make of you. You sound genuine enough, but I have a gut feeling you're bad news, particularly if you want to associate with that whore, Charlotte. I've offered to help her out, but she says she has a secured income. Sure she has, selling drugs, in which case she shouldn't be here at all.'

'I don't think you should pre-judge Charlotte. She's had a tough time and you might be surprised what she has to contend with.'

Luther burst out laughing. 'She hasn't conned you with the "sister-in-a-coma" story, has she?'

'She told you about that?'

'No, but I overheard her telling Jazz. She's a good actress alright, but it's a load of bollocks.'

Luther was surely lying. Perhaps he had a grudge against Charlotte because she wouldn't succumb to whatever scheme he had planned for her. The story Charlotte had told me was delivered emotionally and with such minute detail, it had to be true. Still, with Luther's aggressive attitude I wasn't inclined to disagree with him. The more I was exposed to Luther, the less I liked him, but now wasn't the time to tell him. I was accommodating with my reply: 'Well, the sneaky bitch. She certainly had me fooled.'

'You have a lot to learn about street people and street life. Trust nobody and don't sit back and wait for a lucky break. As an anonymous person, you'll not suddenly encounter a benefactor from friends or family. You need a campaign to get your own back on society – by fair means or foul. You can trust me and I can help you with your campaign.'

I gave him more encouragement. 'Really? You can get me out of this way of life?'

Luther unbuttoned his coat, took it off and placed it meticulously over one of the chairs before sitting down. 'Not personally, but I can direct your efforts so that you can achieve it yourself. So let's examine your starting point. You have a roof over your head and as long as you don't make yourself unwanted here, your short-term accommodation problem is solved. For everything else you'll need an income. A pucker job is the most legal way of getting money, but without any ID a regular, a well-paid job will be impossible to arrange. I can't even register you as a vendor of the Big Issue without ID, so you'll have to take on "no questions asked" casual work. That's where I can help.'

'Have you some contacts then?'

'If there's any black market work in the area then I'm the first to hear about it and I have first refusal for my clients. For the introduction I charge a commission of 25 percent per week.'

'Bloody hell, that's steep. The rate's negotiable I presume?'

'No. Take it or leave it.'

'Well … I don't suppose I have much choice. What's available at the moment?'

'That's your first problem. Nothing,' Luther smirked.

'What about Gannet's job?'

'Ah yes. Poor Gannet. His job has already been reassigned – to Rick.'

'You don't waste too much time, do you?'

'Time is money, for my clients and me. I'll put you on my list.' Luther said condescendingly. He reached to his coat and from one of the many inside pockets extracted a piece of card and studied it. 'Currently you'll be third in line. I presume you're not allergic to any form of work. Most of the jobs are manual labour and dirty – cleaning usually.'

'Anything will do. How long before something becomes available?'

'Could be tomorrow; could be a week or more. For a cash donation I could put you top of the list. How much money have you got?'

'I've about £20, but I might need most of that for bus and train fares – to carry out research into my true identity.'

'Twenty quid won't buy you any privileges or last you very long. In the meantime you'll have to do what most people do around here – go begging.'

'I'm not sure I could deal with that. I …'

Luther interrupted. 'Now look boy, basically you are in the shit and if you're going to survive, you'll have to swallow that upper class pride of yours and get your butt on the streets. Unless of course you want to consider alternative methods of earning money?'

'Such as?'

'A few opportunities come to mind. You're a clean, good-looking boy. I know wealthy men who would pay a premium if you co-operated with their needs.'

'Sex, you mean?'

Luther raised his eyebrows and nodded agreement.

'Christ. No way. I'd rather die first.'

'Your initial attitude is no different to a few young men who have passed through here and have soon realized what easy money it is. It's socially acceptable to be gay these days so what's the problem with a prick up your arse every now and again? The giver and receiver both benefit.'

So, as well as a generally disagreeable character, Luther was a pimp too. I was sickened at the thought of what he said and it must have showed on my face.

'Okay. I can tell you don't like that idea. So how about Robin Forest becoming Robin Hood? Rob the rich to give to the poor. Also socially acceptable; even the government try to do the same except they give it the fancy name of taxation. I have good outlets for redistributing wealth.'

Also a thief and a fence. 'I don't think I have the stomach for it. I stole an apple yesterday and I've been having nightmares and daymares ever since.'

Luther's mouth curled and he emitted a slow oscillating growl, which I took to be a laugh. 'The funniest thing is, for all you know of your past you could be the biggest gangster and bum bandit in the world.' He growled more quickly this time and looked pleased with himself.

'I may not know much about myself, but I'm convinced I'm a model citizen, and my reaction to pretty women tells me I am strictly heterosexual.' I had to be careful in what I said; I didn't want to project a total lack of interest in Luther's schemes. I wanted to cultivate his confidence in me so that I might probe his knowledge about Ronnie Kent, and anything he might know concerning the local drugs scene, which could bring Kathy's assailant to justice. I lowered my voice conspiratorially: 'What about drugs?'

'God help us, now the sweet and innocent boy wants to know about drugs? What, as a user or a pusher?'

'Distribution. I just wondered if there were any opportunities in that field; there's a lot of money to be made apparently.'

'I may be a rogue, but even I draw the line at drugs and violence. Drugs fuck up people's lives – big time. Not just the users but also the distributors. The drug barons are ruthless because of the big stakes, and with the slightest cock-up the next day you'll be floating in the Thames. I've never been involved in that scene and never intend to be. Big money – yes; but even bigger risks. I can live with arranging sex between consenting adults and keeping the insurance companies busy, but I'm a humanitarian at heart and wouldn't sanction any activity that physically hurt someone.' He leaned towards me again. 'If you do drugs, then I'll blow the whistle on you. Understand?'

'Yes, sure, I understand,' I said. Now I didn't know what to think about this conflictingly principled man. I thought it was best to ease my way back to a subject which wouldn't tax my or Luther's morals. 'I think I'd better stick to more legal ways of earning money. Looks like my only viable option is begging. How about a cup of coffee and then you can tell me all about it?'

While I cleared away my breakfast remains Luther prepared the coffee. When we sat down again, from a cavernous pocket of his coat he took a white paper bag and emptied two Danish pastries onto a plate. I eyed them enviously.

'Help yourself to one,' he said.

I checked his expression to make sure it wasn't a joke and grabbed one eagerly to taste. 'Delicious. Where did you get these?'

'I pass a bakery on the way here. Free … have you met Free?' Mouth full, I nodded. 'She helps with the early morning baking. The cakes are a perk I get for introducing her to the job,' Luther explained.

We finished our pastries in silence.

'You can't just beg anywhere,' Luther began, 'it's all a matter of supply and demand. Too many beggars on the street and a) you put punters off and b) each beggar's income gets diluted. So a few years ago, I conducted trials to identify the optimum number, location and returns for begging pitches within a mile radius of the hostel. I now have a list of them ranked in order of average daily income.'

'You mean there is a science to begging?'

'I wouldn't call it a science exactly, more the application of common sense with some maths to back it up. Besides, I do have a degree in Statistics, so I like to apply my knowledge occasionally even if it is on rather esoteric subjects.'

'If you have a degree, how did you come to be involved with the lives of the homeless?'

'No time for that now. We're talking about begging, right?'

He waited in case I contradicted him. I nodded, so he continued.

'I assign the begging pitches to the unemployed hostel residents based upon experience and performance. In our catchment area, anyone caught begging in the wrong place, at the wrong time, or not from this hostel gets moved on.'

'You personally check all the pitches?'

'Not religiously, but in the course of a day I pass a good few of them, and the beat cops assist me in policing the scheme – subject to a bit of mumping.'

'Mumping?'

'Contributions to their expenses – bribes in other words.'

'But is it worth your while being burdened with checking on beggars?'

'Definitely. Johann Sturtz started this hostel with the objective of rehabilitating its residents as soon as possible. That meant providing them with an income, either by working or begging. Johann, whom I'd known for a few years, and who had helped me out in the past, asked me to take on the responsibility for ensuring that the residents received the best deal possible. So, I broker the jobs and begging operation. Johann pays me, plus I take a commission.'

'You take a slice of the beggar's earnings too?'

'Of course. Without me they would have nowhere to beg. The only exceptions are Gregor and Igor. By virtue of their own friendship with Johann they are a law unto themselves. They beg when and where they want to.'

'And you siphon 25 percent of the takings I suppose.'

'Not exactly. Only 25 percent of an average day's earnings. Anything over the average you keep. But with a good, hassle-free pitch, and by following a few simple rules, the earnings can be higher than a regular job. To keep the pitch you have to pay me six lots of 25 percent in a week. So typically, you'll need to service it six days a week – Monday to Friday; and either Saturday or Sunday, depending on which is the busiest day. You can have days off, so long as I get my weekly cut and the absence doesn't jeopardize my ownership of the pitch. Do you want to know more?'

'I'm still not keen, but if it's the only way to earn money then you'd better educate me.'

Luther sat upright. I felt a lecture coming on.

'Okay. You'll feel self-conscious about begging at the start. After your first day you won't be able to face a second, but the hungrier you get the easier it becomes. Within a week there will be no guilt, shame or humiliation, it will become part of your accepted daily routine.

'You have to be selective about the people you beg from. When a Joe – that's Joe Public – sees a beggar, they react in different ways: embarrassment, anger, guilt and sympathy are the most common feelings.

'The embarrassed ones are often from the upper classes. You can usually spot them by what they wear – overdressed in flashy gear and jewellery – though you rarely encounter them in this part of London. They can't understand why someone has to beg. In an affluent country they think begging can't be necessary; people that beg must have been cast out for good reasons or have a criminal background, otherwise the State would shower them with a range of social security benefits. In many cases they would be right. They can't possibly appreciate some beggars are truly down on their luck, like you, and others are mentally and physically incapable, so that there are no alternatives available to them. They'll avoid beggars; cross the road; start a conversation with a partner; hurry their step. Don't talk to them, rattle your tin or goad them in any way; they'll take exception to your contact, find a copper and attempt to get you moved on or arrested. If you were moved on, you'd have to vacate the pitch until it's quiet again; that could mean the loss of prime begging time. Getting arrested is rare because the law can't be bothered with the hassle of looking after you. But if you do, it's not such a big deal unless the fuzz wants you for something else; you will at least have a roof over your head for the night and possibly a more decent meal than you could have bought with your lost begging income. You shouldn't have any police problems on my pitches though; I know most of the local bobbies and they are rewarded for leaving you alone. By the way, at railway stations always make sure you site yourself outside, since I've no influence, yet, over the British Transport police, and they can be heavy at times.'

The man was human after all – there was something he didn't have influence over.

'Rarely you might strike lucky with the toffs. I've known a toff to show off to his mates by tossing a £50 note to one of our beggars. On another occasion, one smart alec wrote a cheque for a £1000 thinking the beggar wouldn't be able to cash it. Well, the clever bastard was right, only because in shock the beggar gave a false name for the payee. If that ever happens to you, give the name Luther Browncast and then I can cash it for us.

'Avoid the potentially angry ones. Groups of young men, particularly around pub closing time, are the worst. When they've had a skinful their bravado gets reinforced and they'll relieve it on any unfortunates in their path; beggars are easy prey. If you see any group approaching: skinheads, blacks, football supporters, get away from them as discreetly as possible.

'The best punters are the middle class, and ironically, the working class. The middle classes contribute from a feeling of guilt. They will appreciate the difficulties of homeless people because they will compare lifestyles and it eases their conscience to donate a small part of their surplus-to-requirements income. If you work a pitch for a long period, you may find you get regular contributions from the same person. Be particularly friendly to these types. Tell them your name, try to find out their surname and then address them in the future as Mister or Miss so-and-so. With luck, they might adopt you as their very own good cause. The closer you bond with them the more generous they will become.

'The working classes are the salt of the earth and will sympathize with beggars. Many will have experienced being poor or homeless, and while they may not individually give you a lot of money, the quantity of donations will add up. Respect these people. Maintain a sad eye contact with them; talk politely and rattle or point to your money tin. Look disappointed, but don't get angry, if they ignore your pleas.'

This basic street activity was becoming more complicated by the minute. 'Now you make begging sound like a drama course. Perhaps you ought to lecture at a local college – a BA in begging techniques perhaps?' I suggested.

'You may joke, but begging is a profession in its own right. And if anything is worth doing, its worth doing well. If you are successful, can tolerate the boredom of it and have no great ambition, begging can keep you in a reasonable life style. I often tell the true story of a beggar who passed through here around ten years ago. His name was "Rags to Riches" Howard Winston. Ring any bells?'

'No. I've never heard of him.'

'If you were a city dude you would know who I'm talking about. I taught him the techniques of begging, and he had a pitch near the Bank of England. He had a big advantage in that he was a true ruffler from the Falklands conflict, and had bad scars on his face from burns, so he attracted a lot of public sympathy. At his peak he was making almost £100 a day, but he had to because he had an insatiable gambling habit. He'd bet on anything: dogs, horses, football, the weather, elections; but he was unbelievably bad at it. You could toss a coin in front of him 10 times and he'd be wrong every time. He was a bright guy though, and during his begging hours he used to read old copies of the *Financial Times*, arguing the black on salmon colours were more restful on his poor eyesight. Anyway, he became pally with one of his regular punters – a stockbroker – who convinced him that if he wanted to gamble, he should dabble in shares, which in theory would retain some value. History has recorded that over the period of a year, through his broker friend, he transformed £10,000 into £100,000; started a financial consultancy with his go-between; and now heads up Winston Investments, which is one of the most respected investment companies in the City of London. There was an article about Howard in the *Sunday Telegraph* magazine last year and I – anonymously – was mentioned as one of the key people that influenced his life.'

Luther sat back and pushed out his chest in a proud gesture.

Flattery was called for here. 'Don't you think you are wasted in street life? Seems to me your talents could be better deployed in … a PR company for example?'

'I don't think so. I'm too old to change my ways now, besides I actually like what I do. It's down-to-earth, interesting, varied, exciting and has an element of risk to it.'

'How about begging with a woman? Does that improve your chances of donations?' I asked.

'No. It's best to beg on your own. Individuals appear more pitiful, needy and alone. Punters tend to be more reserved when confronted by a group, unless of course you can conjure up a young baby too. Anyway, if a blowze is a relative stranger, you will always need to scrutinize her motives; she may be merely using you for gold digging. And, if she's too good looking, your credibility as a beggar may go down; plus she may attract the wrong kind of interest – punters may assume she's a whore. No, beg alone; the only advantage of a partner is as a lookout in areas where the police are known to give beggars a hard time.

'Anyway, now that Rick's taking over the meat market job his pitch at Stepney Green underground station is available. It's a good one but there's no point in starting today – Sunday is the quiet day. Go there tomorrow morning.'

'Well ... um ... thanks for the offer, but I have other matters to attend to first. I want to follow up the slim leads I have for discovering who I am. But I could start in a couple of days.'

'Not good enough. It's a prime site and I'll miss out on some quality income.' Luther thought for moment. 'I'll tell you what. How about if I keep the position open for, say, two days. For every day you miss you'll have to play catch up on the commission. So, if you start on the third day you will have to pay me 75 percent of the expected. If you don't start at all you will owe me an average day's takings for that pitch, which is currently about £40. Fair deal?'

'£40 seems a lot to earn there. It didn't appear to be particularly busy. How about Whitechapel Station? There was a throng of people around the market.'

'Sorry, that's a no-go area. It's too popular. The traders are afraid beggars will scare off their custom and unfortunately their influence with the police is greater than mine. But I'll let you have Stepney for ... £30, as you are a rookie.'

So Luther's rates were negotiable. I needed to think this through. Would there be enough time in the day to beg and do the other things that were necessary?

'How many hours would I have to beg to achieve the average day's takings?'

'I base it on eight core hours to meet the target. Your best times are when there are most people on the streets: early morning, six-thirty 'til nine-thirty; lunchtimes, twelve 'til two; and going-home times, four 'til seven.'

On reflection, the only time-consuming activity was to scan through the recent newspapers; I could probably do that tomorrow.

If I were truly from the Essex area, then trudging around the local menswear shops to find the possible source of my Burton jacket would be a waste of time. Still, it was an activity I could busy myself with between the begging peak periods.

As for the appendectomy operation, well, I could phone around the hospitals in the area to discover which of them might have performed such surgery in the last few weeks; but what then? Locating the attending hospital staff and then describing myself to them wouldn't be a straightforward task, and anyway, they were unlikely to divulge confidential patient information to an unknown person on the telephone. Despite the difficulties, I knew I would have to try, and registered the exercise as another intra-begging activity.

Lastly, there was the link with Ronnie Kent. Here I had no starting point for my investigation until I had broached the subject with Luther, and there was no guarantee he could or would be helpful. If not, my only other avenue would be to try to wrest information out of Inspector Bradley.

'Are you still with me or are you having another flashback?' Luther said waving a hand in front of my face.

'Sorry? Er ... unfortunately no. I was chewing over your offer. Yes, I will take the pitch, but not until Tuesday. I've decided to go to Ipswich and Chelmsford tomorrow to research archives of the local newspapers. Is there anything else I need to know before my six-thirty start on Tuesday? What if I oversleep? Will you give me an alarm call?'

Luther smiled at my attempt of a joke. 'I don't think that will be necessary. You'll be one of many getting up early to start the day's begging. You haven't been disturbed today because most of your begging compatriots choose Sunday to have a lie-in.' He then stared at me for a moment. 'Your dress sense is about right. Old, unfashionable, but clean; it's a turn-off for the punters if you look too tatty. How those scruffbags Gregor and Igor ever get money beats me. You'll also need a tin or hat for your donations with a few quid in coins as a starter float, and a convincing pleading board.'

'A pleading board? Do you mean like Rick's "Sick Sister"?'

'Yeh. Rick really did have a sick sister in hospital, but that was a few years ago. Choose words you are comfortable with, something near the truth. But I suppose you're going to say you don't have any bad past experiences to draw upon. Therefore, a good choice would be to pretend you are a student saving to go to college. As you're an intelligent bloke, make sure you keep your mind occupied while you are begging. So, get yourself a good second-hand book to read. A small one, so that it's easy to carry, ideally educational, with a prominent title on the cover. Some punters will be impressed with your efforts to keep your mind active through mendicity.'

'Where ...'

'Check with Albert or Jazz; they have a cache of bits and pieces and should be able to find the things you need.'

'There is a favour I need to ask you.' I said. Luther creased his forehead and shook his head slightly like granting any kind of favour would be a serious imposition. 'I've checked the cost of the return train fare to Ipswich and it's a little more than I currently have in ready cash. I was wondering whether you could advance me a couple of pounds until Tuesday?'

The shakes of his head grew. 'A golden rule of the beggardom is to never trust anyone. I preach that all the time, so I won't be duped by an unproven stranger such as you.'

The rejection hit me hard, and then I realized that this was the fabric of survival whether rich or poor. With no credibility established, my decisions would have to be dependent upon my own resources; everything would be a compromise. In my lowest position in society, I would not be concerned with exciting choices such as: Should my next holiday be in Spain or Italy? It was to be petty judgments like: Should I buy food for an aching stomach or a new pair of socks to keep my feet dry? My current dilemma had a solution: only go to Chelmsford tomorrow and keep the balance of my money for food until I had begged the balance for the greater expense to Ipswich. Luther must have recognized the thought processes going on in my head.

He grinned and said: 'Be not made a beggar by banqueting upon borrowing, when thou hast nothing in thy purse: for thou shalt lie in wait for thine own life, and be talked on.'

Luther continued to amaze me. Was there no end to this man's talents? Now he appeared to be projecting biblical knowledge.

'*Ecclesiasticus*, if you were wondering,' he added, answering my puzzled look.

'How about if I did commission-free begging today? A kind of trial run so I am better prepared when I start on Tuesday?' I offered.

He scratched his chin in thought. 'Okay, but it will be at your own risk. I won't have time today to register you with the local fuzz. If you are approached, mention my name. If that doesn't work, move on without arguing. And only stay long enough to get your couple of quid. Alright?'

'Alright.'

'What will you do for the rest of the day?'

'I thought I would explore the area and later call in at the hospital to …' find Charlotte and Kathy I was about to say, but chose a less controversial response, '… visit the guys that were in my ward.'

I don't think Luther believed me, but before he had the opportunity to interrogate me, three of the residents piled into the kitchen: Adrian chatting to someone I hadn't seen before and Jason, who viewed my audience with Luther uncertainly.

'Ah, there you are,' Luther said to Jason. 'Let's go.'

'Can't I get a cup of coffee first,' Jason complained.

'No time. Our meeting's at seven o'clock, and …' Luther looked at his watch, '… that's ten minutes away.'

Jason opened his mouth to complain again, but Luther was already heading through the door and Jason dutifully followed him.

Adrian was pre-occupied with making cups of tea and stroking his friend's backside, so I thought it was time I left too. Strangely, I felt eager to try out my begging techniques, though my motivation was to earn the small amount of extra money I needed for my journey to Ipswich, rather than the activity itself.

Chapter 19

SECOND SUNDAY – 7:00 a.m.

Dorm D was stirring and various bodies were stretching. I recognized Gringo, clad in just underpants, exercising by swinging his arms vigorously in circles and heard the Liverpudlian accent of mop-top Danny attempting to dissuade him from disturbing the early hours of the Christian Sabbath. Gringo broke his rhythm to wave an acknowledgement of my presence then continued his gyrations. In the kitchen I had detected the chill outside so I reached for my warm Burton jacket, which I thought I had left at the end of my bunk with my original shoes – neither were there. Unconvincingly, I examined my bag but already knew from its weight and my earlier repacking, I wouldn't find them there. I tried to remember if I had seen them before I took a shower, but no images came. I searched in vain around the immediate area, including the lower bunk, which was now unoccupied.

'Has anyone been messing with my things,' I called out angrily.

Only Gringo took notice and came bounding over still in exercise mode. 'What's up friend?' he said.

'I've lost a jacket and a pair of shoes. Did you see the new young guy leave?' I pointed to the lower bunk accusingly, 'Wearing a bandanna?'

'Yeh, about a quarter of an hour ago. In a hurry he was and wearing a grey jacket.'

I grabbed my bag and rushed towards the hostel exit. Albert was at reception.

'Has a guy in a bandanna just gone out?' I asked breathlessly and conscious of a nagging ache in my left thigh.

'Don't know,' Albert said, 'I only took over a few minutes ago.'

I continued to the front door and almost fell down the steps as my thigh sought revenge on my sudden burst of energy. I looked up and down the street but there was no sign of my suspect and my leg injury dismissed the idea of a random pursuit.

'Problem?' Albert asked when I re-entered the hostel.

'Who was assigned to bunk D11 last night?'

Albert reached for his clipboard and then stopped. 'That's old Gannet's bed. Nobody's been given that. In fact the police asked we left the bed untouched until they gave us the okay.'

'Well somebody's screwed up and it's led to my jacket and shoes being nicked.'

We debated the issue for a while and Albert filled in a report sheet, which seemed pointless since it had no purpose other than to be filed in an overfull "incident" folder. Several times Albert pointed to the hostel rules notice, which made abundantly clear the staff were not responsible for the security of the residents' possessions – even those deposited in the "safe" – and suggested that perhaps now I would take heed of his original warning. The best he could offer was to follow up the matter with the retired Corporal Mandrake – the old gent who had been on duty overnight. I was frustrated by Albert's unenthusiastic attitude towards my loss, but most of all I regretted the sacrifice of my jacket – a clue to my past which seemed ever more remote.

Pursuit of other clues now had to take priority, so I quizzed Albert about the supply of the begging impedimenta Luther had recommended. Next to the padlocked cupboard, which doubled as a safe, was another cupboard about twice as wide. Albert explained he had a friend who worked at a local Oxfam shop and periodically she would clear out items the shop couldn't sell. Apparently, the public often used the shop as a dumping ground for all kinds of rubbish, mindful that someone, somewhere would pay for the debris of their existence. Anything unsaleable, but serviceable, ended up at the hostel in what was known as the offal cupboard. Mostly the shelves contained clean – albeit poor quality – clothing, but demand for it was high particularly among the residents who chose to discard their filthy clothes instead of washing them. Albert soon found a blue beret, which he thought would serve as a repository for my charitable donations. However, he declined to select a suitable educational book, so instead invited me into his private domain – a great privilege – to conduct my own search. Cheap, dog-eared paperbacks were plentiful but I homed in on a tome – an old copy of *Gray's Anatomy* – that failed the lightweight test, but fitted perfectly in terms of intellectual matter and bold title. The book gave me an idea for my pleading board, which was sourced from the lid of a corrugated cardboard box of toilet rolls Albert had not yet unpacked. I used a thick-tipped black felt pen and neatly wrote on the lid "Medical Student – Honest & Needy". I was pleased with my appeal message; it projected a down-on-his-luck pupil who was striving to qualify in an honourable profession.

With my book and board tucked under my arm and my beret concealed in a pocket (there was no way I would *wear* it), I set off to start my new career. I soon felt the chill of the morning, so I stopped to put on the light coat donated by Miss Springtime. I was content with the new boots; they were comfortable, but heavy, and I consoled myself their weight would gently exercise the throbbing that had returned to my thigh.

The quiet side streets became busier as I neared the Mile End Road, and for the purpose of my task, I was gratified so many people had business or pleasure pursuits this early on a Sunday morning. What I hadn't contemplated was that the station shop would be open. As I nervously surveyed the foyer, there was a resumption of the stomach quavering brought about by yesterday's petty theft, except this time, the churning was fuelled by the celery hearts for breakfast. A mental sickness graduated to a physical one, and I dived into a nearby alleyway that led to a cul-de-sac of flats and lock-up garages. There was just time to note this was named Frimley Street, before I spewed my breakfast – and no doubt, remnants of the guilty apple – against a graffiti daubed wall.

Recovery was slow and beads of cold perspiration appeared on my forehead. I mopped my brow and puke stained mouth with the only handy material – my begging beret. I propped myself against the wall and looked towards the main street. Interested passers-by were regarding me contemptibly like a dog that had fouled the pavement. I feared they could read my thoughts and I wanted to assure them my crime was strictly a one-off. Doubts came as to whether I would continue with my planned parasitic vigil, but I was desperate to sit down and viewed I may as well do this in the guise of a beggar. The taste and smell of vomit in my nose and mouth contributed to my continued nausea, and I resolved that my first task would be to buy something to help combat the sensations.

Shakily I went back to the station entrance and from a distance checked who was serving at the shop; today it was a young girl. There was no sign of the elderly woman who might have perhaps confirmed my shoplifting of yesterday, so I decided to take the risk and approached the counter. The girl gave a smile, welcoming rather than of recognition, so I made my request for the smallest packets of the cheapest brands, of freshen-up tissues and throat and nasal passage cauterizing mints, on offer. I reached awkwardly inside my trouser waistband to the money belt which, by virtue of the earlier sweat-producing panic attack, had stuck to my skin. I withdrew my only £10 note and paid the exorbitant sum – in my terms – of £1.20, and by request received in return small denominations of coins for my starter float.

It was a relief to sit down cross-legged outside the station. I tucked my duffle bag in the small of my back, wiped my face with a tissue, sucked a peppermint and I immediately felt better, albeit hungry and weary. I leant the pleading board against my feet and then sorted through my shop change. I put a £5 float of coins in the beret, which I positioned in front of the board. I temporarily placed the large book in my lap and flopped backwards against the wall with my eyes closed to promote recuperation – from what? Had recollection of yesterday's theft affected my stomach so dramatically, or had I suffered a sudden bout of food poisoning? Maybe a combination of both? Whatever, I was very tired and I must have been asleep within seconds.

Chapter 20

SECOND SUNDAY – 8:30 a.m.

'Medical student, my arse. Is that the best Luffa could fink of?' I thought the condemning voice said.

Arse was the trigger word. My arse felt cold and numb, yet I could still detect a foot prodding it. With effort, I opened my eyes. I must have been in a deep sleep because it took a while to remember where I was and then to focus my eyes on the provocateur. The best description of him was skinhead, an overweight youth – no more than 18 years old – with closely cropped hair, jeans, anorak and heavy boots. I looked around in case he was one of a gang, but he was on his own so I grabbed his leg and gouged with my thumb at the sensitive part below the inner ankle.

''Ere that bleedin' 'urts,' he screamed and with the motion of me jumping up he tumbled backwards onto the pavement. I glanced down and saw my begging hat was missing. I slammed my foot down onto his stomach and said, 'Where's the beret?'

He muttered incoherently through coughs and splutters. I lifted my foot and he rose slowly and unsteadily, clutching his stomach.

Eventually he spoke. 'There wuz no need to do that. I wuz only 'aving a larf.' He reached into a side-pocket of his anorak and took out the beret. 'I wuz gonna give it back … 'onest. I just wanted to teach you a lesson that Luffa probably never taught ya.'

I snatched the scrunched-up beret back and unfolded it to check the contents. My total was now £7.20 by the addition of two one-pound coins and a twenty pence piece. I smiled at making a profit already and for a moment forgot about the skinhead.

'Ya do work fer Luffa, don't cha?'

'Who's asking?'

'People call me Sniffy. I used to 'ave this pitch.' Then as if to demonstrate how he acquired his nickname he wiped his nose on the left cuff of his anorak.

Suddenly I was interested in this lout. Luther had mentioned a Sniffy working for Ronnie Kent.

'Why did you nick the beret?'

'Ya shouldn't doze off when yer begging. Luffa shoulda told ya that. Puntas think yer drunk and nasty bastards swipe yer cash.'

'So you're the world's expert on begging are you?'

'Yeh I reckon. Reglar I used to take home fifty nicker a day from this place,' he said cockily.

'Then why did you give it up?'

'Cos it wuz borin'. Now I've got an exciting job and the money's better too.' He began to massage his stomach again. 'Sharp guy like you's wasted begging.'

'Do you have something I might be interested in?'

'Might 'ave. Gimme a fiver and I'll menshun ya name to the boss.'

'Forgo the fiver and I promise not to break your arm,' I said and took a step towards him.

'Yeh, yeh, okay,' he replied, laughing nervously and taking a step backwards.

'What sort of jobs might be available?'

'Can't say. Boss'll tell ya that.' He paused to snort and then wipe his nose again. 'Who's interested?'

'Robin Forest.'

'You at the Jub'lee?'

'Yes, or I'll be here regularly from Tuesday onwards.'

Sniffy thrust his hands deep into his jeans pocket. 'Okay. See ya, I'll be in touch.' He strode down the street swaggering from side to side, trying to act the hard man, which he clearly wasn't.

He had been an easy opponent, but I was nonetheless surprised at how I had acted. I had considered myself to be mild-mannered – someone who would prefer negotiation and diplomacy to conflict. Resorting to a physical attack on somebody seemed out of character and reckless, and I wondered if this attitude was symptomatic of the lifestyle to which I had been unwillingly initiated. Or perhaps having my limited possessions violated for a third time – my food, my clothes and now my money – in two days had led me to react in an aggressive way. The nausea I still suffered from my vomiting and the return of hunger pangs, had also presumably contributed to my actions. Whatever the reasons, I felt uneasy about my future. Yesterday I had stolen; today I had been violent; and *after all, tomorrow is another day*; but I drew little comfort from those famous closing words other than I had read *Gone With The Wind* to conclusion sometime in my past.

I wish I could have seen who had placed the £2.20 in my beret. Perhaps it would have given insight into who might be a typical benefactor to my begging effort. I followed Luther's advice religiously: choosing likely punters, pleading politely, pointing to my beret, making sure the title of the huge book I was studying could be seen, but the number and generosity of the passers-by was significantly below my expectations. Few acknowledged me or were interested in my plight. The best moment was the attention of an old man who turned out to be a retired surgeon, his interest attracted by my reading material. However, by his enquiries, it was soon obvious to the man I knew little about human anatomy, and the only gain from the encounter was knowledge of the time, which suggested I had been asleep for about an hour earlier. Maybe I ought to sleep again to increase my chances of donations; I wouldn't have to feign it since I was still tired, but after meeting Sniffy, the insecurity of my alms suggested that would be the wrong course of action.

For an hour, I became absorbed in my studies and began to appreciate the natural beauty and grace of the body's interconnected systems and structures. I wasn't familiar with the text; I clearly wasn't a medical student or graduate, yet the lucid topographical descriptions and illustrations were easily assimilated, and I wondered if I was on the brink of beginning a career as a doctor or surgeon.

My concentration was eventually disturbed by a sudden increase in the number of people on the street and exiting from the station. Their target was a building almost opposite which, with the added information of the many skull-capped men heading there, I now recognized as a synagogue, and obviously a popular one too. The Jewish race has a reputation for being miserly and, after half an hour of ambulatory traffic, I was unsure whether the statement was accurate. Numerous individuals had contributed to my starveling appeals, yet on average each had only given a few copper coins. I was encouraged nonetheless that the monetary weight in my beret had swelled, though when the people flow had subsided I gathered the low denomination coins and put them in my coat pocket, lest future donors assumed such tender was the norm.

Obtaining money was the main reason for being here, and I had to keep reminding myself of that fact in order to counter the fatigue of sitting in the same place and my growing hunger. Many times I paced up and down to renew the circulation in my legs. I also took from my bag the small towel Miss Springtime had given me and sat on it as insulation against the cold pavement. I opened the packet of chocolate digestive biscuits and ate a couple, but I found the sweetness in isolation too much and decided fruit would be more beneficial. I returned to the station shop and the young girl there welcomed me like a long lost friend. The selection of fruit was grim; the apples no longer looked inviting and instead I settled on a couple of oranges, which were negotiated at a clearance price of 20p each. From my pocket I counted out the amount in one and two-penny pieces and realizing I was flush with change added a third orange for a mere 10p extra.

As I hungrily ate the oranges, another snapshot of my past surfaced. I was with my brother and his wife and we were playing a computer adventure game. One of those games where the protagonist has an inventory of items and the game player must decide how to use them to further his progress, wealth or escape. For a moment I was that hero, armed with: *Gray's Anatomy*, a limited amount of money, a blue beret, a pleading board, chocolate biscuits, notebook and pen, peppermints and tissues, and miscellaneous clothes; and for amusement I speculated how each of these items might further my own ambitions. But the exercise was wasted, as I kept returning to the sibling revelation. A brother. Now a brother with a wife. I hung on to that thought and tried to envisage the room beyond the confines of the computer screen, hoping for additional enlightenment, but there was no peripheral vision.

Fingers sticky with orange juice, I used another freshen-up tissue to clean them. Putting my book to one side, I turned to creating knowledge instead of trying to absorb it, and brought out my notebook to record the latest happenings in my life.

By late morning a steady stream of people were on the move. By their dress or motion, I tried to gauge their intentions and categorized them first as walkers or travellers. Casually dressed walkers were out for a pre-lunch constitutional, on their way to the pub or about to visit friends; those formally dressed were undoubtedly churchgoers. I classified the travellers into two types: arrivees at the station – nearly all casual – were long distance friends; departees – the majority, formal – were on a day trip to visit one of the many sights or entertainments in central London. In my mind the simple model of human behaviour I had constructed was perfect, because in my solitude there was no one to dispute my observations; besides it passed the time.

One lonely walker I saw was an exception – a policeman on the other side of the road. He stopped and looked in my direction, but fortunately was too lazy, on another mission or recognized I was harmless, to approach or move me on.

Shortly after, I also experienced my first instance of verbal abuse. A heavily built guy, with muscles bulging out of his T-shirt, was waddling by with a female companion. They were arguing. Suddenly he turned his attention to me and, with a statement like: "What're you looking at beggar man?", began to stride towards me with clenched fists and uttering a range of foul expletives. I stood up, not to confront him, but to be in a position to leg it if he got much closer. Thankfully, his woman came to my rescue; chasing after him, hanging onto his arm and promising him she would do as he asked. How I emerged as a character in their disagreement I didn't discover, but I reflected on Luther's warning that often beggars become the victims of acts of bravado.

The return of the Jews indicated the gathering at the synagogue had finished and I put on my saddest, most pathetic face to appeal to their questionable generosity, and it worked to a degree. Again small donations were aplenty, but by the time the flow had ceased, I resolved I had done enough begging for one day. My bum was sore; I had brought my diary up to date; absorbed all I could of human anatomy and, most important of all, I believed I had met my income target. A count revealed my morning earnings had reached – in begging terms – a staggering £8.76. Now I had sufficient for the following day's train fare and some left over for food. With a weekday target supposedly of £30, I thought I had done well. Begging was an easy way to earn a limited amount of money, enough for food with the remainder being saved for the next major expense – clothes; beyond that would be a problem. Surplus money for train fares would require extreme thrift or a steady income from a job. At least for the time being I didn't have to fund my accommodation and, thank goodness, I didn't have – to my knowledge – any dependency on tobacco, alcohol or drugs.

However, there were doubts already in my head whether I had the constitution for begging on a regular basis. Although I had kept occupied during my session, I found the constant vigilance disruptive, rather like fishing (a hobby of mine?). I had to be ever watchful for passers-by, aiming to avoid confrontations with police or troublemakers, but sizing up punters demanded the most concentration. I had soon determined that being an active beggar had brought the greatest rewards. Subtle communication of my wretchedness to likely donors by facial expressions, body language and servile words required theatrical effort, which was easy to conduct but, through repetition, tiring to execute.

Then a fear struck me. Here I was churning through my mind the results of my begging debut, seemingly already committed to this way of life. Temporarily gone from my thoughts was the resolve I once had to quickly return to my past. Was the seamless introduction to begging affecting my desire to unearth my history? Had I cast aside my hopes already?

Having solved my immediate money problem, I turned to my second priority – food. It was ages since I had had any hot food and the thought of soup became dominant in my mind. I packed up my begging gear and returned to the station shop to ask the girl to convert my small change to a £5 note and some silver, which I discreetly stored in my money belt. I established it had just passed midday and worried I might be too late for the handouts at the WI soup kitchen. I knew roughly how to get there, having passed the lane during my tour of Bethnal Green the previous evening so, with the fastest walking speed that my thigh would allow, I set out with mouth-watering excitement.

In Little Lane, I spied an obvious building and I was gratified there were no queues outside, but on closer inspection of the entrance door, it appeared shut, though there was the distinct smell of cooking in the air. The ancient single-storey detached building was squeezed between rows of terraced houses. The two large windows either side of the door had been boarded over and a number of posters stuck to them. The posters were advertising a number of future events for local organizations, but the WI wasn't one of them and I began to think I was in the wrong place. Then the door opened and a red-haired Beatle look-alike stepped out.

'Hi ya, come for some scoff?' he said and lit the cigarette he was holding.

'Yes. I thought I might be in the wrong place. You're Danny aren't you?'

'Yeh. You've left it a bit late, but I think there's still some soup left. Better get in there quick before my lads finish it off. I have to go to sort out the gig for tonight. See ya there maybe,' Danny said and before I had the opportunity to quiz him on his statement, he turned right and hurried down the road.

Inside, across the width of the building, there was a narrow corridor terminating in ladies and gents toilets. Facing me was a double door, which led into a wooden-floored hall. The room was dingy, despite the tall – above eye-level – windows that ran down each side, since the adjacent houses obscured the incoming light. Tables and chairs had been placed around the edge of the room; some were being used, but most of the people were standing around chatting at the centre. Many were drinking from a variety of cups, mugs and bowls, and dunking hunks of bread.

The hall must have occasionally hosted amateur drama productions, because at the far end there was a curtained proscenium. On the stage there was a hive of activity. I made my way across the room and noticed familiar faces from the Jubilee. The remainder of the pop group, Rick, Jason and Gringo were talking loudly and had attracted a small audience, including Adrian who was looking bored and Georgie who was looking spellbound. Brian and Roger were seated at a nearby table; Roger apparently talking to himself while Brian looked protectively towards Georgie.

I joined the short queue before the stage and soon I was facing two witches stirring two cauldrons. On reflection, tainting them as witches was unkind; one did sport a black cloak and the other had a beaked nose, and the huge pots with gurgling contents did remind me of cauldrons, but otherwise the attending ladies (or rather institute women) were receptive, eager to please and had a sincerity about their tasks. However, they must have cast magic somewhere. Each pot must have held three gallons, and each was balanced precariously and miraculously on a tiny portable gas burner. It must have taken hours for the miniature flames to heat up, let alone boil, the contents of the pots. My disbelief must have shown because both the women had spooky knowing expressions.

'Haven't seen you before, young man. You are homeless, are you?' the cloaked woman asked.

'Well, no, not exactly. I'm at the Jubilee,' I replied and she laughed.

'That's alright then. We get local residents popping in now and again to cadge a free meal. So what'll it be? Vegetable or Chicken?'

The contents of the pots looked similar to me, like murky grey water and not many bits floating in them. The embarrassment of the chicken soup saga with Charlotte still lingered, so having determined after a second look that the vegetable soup had a mildly inviting green tinge to it and there was less remaining – suggesting it was the most popular – it became my preferred choice.

'Help yourself to bread, but all the sausage rolls have gone I'm afraid,' beaky said.

The remaining bread was a brown sliced loaf and curled at the edges. Nevertheless, I took four slices when I saw the volume of soup ladled into a king size Coca-Cola cardboard cup. The soup was too hot to drink immediately, so I made a cone out of the bread and, cradling the cup between the cone and my hands to dissipate the heat, I went to eavesdrop on the main attraction.

Rick, Jason and Gringo were relating anecdotes of the group's early days with all three talking excitedly, and surely exaggeratedly, about their eye-opening experiences. We were exposed to remarkable stories of fan devotion: knickers being thrown on stage, devious schemes of groupies to get into their dressing room, and sex in exchange for autographs.

During one of these tales, I heard the history of the group's name. They had formed two years ago and were originally called Les Beats. That was when Les led the group, and named it as a tribute to: himself, his love of the Beatles and his affinity to the French language. The trouble with Les was he couldn't sing or play the guitar well enough, so he was ousted and replaced by Rick. Gringo (whose forenames are Graham Indigo) then took over the leadership and renamed the group as Gringo's All Starrs – his tribute to the Beatles drummer. However, Gringo's ego trip only went as far as playing rather than organizing. The band was now musically complete, but bookings dwindled, and it required another coup and name change before they became regionally recognized. Danny, the quietest and most studious member was voted as the new leader. He re-christened the foursome with the catchy name Millennia and their popularity and bookings swelled. Danny had cultivated the London contact and uprooted the group from their Liverpool beginnings, and he was now trying to extract them from their disastrous debut in the capital city.

'Is the new boy coming to the gig tonight?' Gringo suddenly asked looking at me.

'Yeh, go on, it'll be a hoot. Bring your girlfriend,' Georgie added, taking her eyes off Jason for the first time since I'd joined the crowd.

'Sorry ...' I said, frowning, '... I think I missed out on a piece of information somewhere.'

'Charlotte, your fancy bit,' Georgie attempted to clarify.

Embarrassed and ignoring her assumption I quickly replied, 'What gig?'

Gringo went on to explain how Danny had befriended the landlord at the Howling Wolf pub in Limehouse, who was also the leader of an amateur band – called unsurprisingly the Howling Wolves – that played there four nights a week. The band had no ambitions other than to play and occasionally practice, since the members all had professional and well-paid jobs. For convenience, they left their kit permanently set up at the pub. Tonight the Wolves wouldn't be performing since two of their members were away on business, so Millennia were to take their place. Since they were an unknown quantity the landlord wouldn't pay them an appearance fee, but had offered – because he knew their circumstances – to keep them fed and watered (but not with alcohol) for the whole of the evening.

'It will give us the opportunity to practice, publicize the band and most importantly, sample the pub's food, whose reputation attracts people from miles around,' Gringo continued. 'We want as much support as possible and in return we'll order loads of food and share it with our friends. So, are you coming?'

Everyone was looking at me. The suggestion needed little consideration. What else did I have to do? 'Yes, okay,' I said.

'Bring Charlotte too ... if you want to of course,' Gringo said, more diplomatically than Georgie had managed.

I did want to, but I chose not to comment. Now that the story had been told, conversation fell into a lull. Some people departed; the band to practice its repertoire with Georgie in pursuit of Jason, and comically, Brian in pursuit of Georgie. Some remained to finish their soup and others went back for seconds.

I started to drink my vegetable soup now that it had cooled. It had a passable taste and I did find one or two peas that justified its name. After a few sips my criticism of its flavour was forgotten and I savoured the warm liquid and stale bread as it began to line my empty stomach.

'What have you been doing this morning,' Adrian suddenly asked.

'I had my first stab at begging ...' I said proudly, '... and I made £8.76.'

'Drinks on you tonight then. It's a hostel rule that you share your first begging earnings with your friends,' Adrian said with a straight face.

My chin dropped and I searched for an excuse. 'Well ... er ... it wasn't an official begging – just a trial run.'

Adrian laughed. 'Don't panic. I was only winding you up. There's no such rule ... until Luther invents one.'

An opportunity to quiz someone indirectly about Luther.

'Are you a friend of Luther?'

'You must be joking. Luther doesn't have friends, only various shades of enemies. I presume he's already recruited you into one of his money making schemes?'

'Well yes; a begging pitch and a job soon I hope.'

'And a wealth redistribution scheme too?'

'No, it sounded a bit dodgy.'

'A bit dodgy! Actually it's downright illegal,' Adrian said, but realizing other people were in earshot he continued in a whisper. 'I don't approve in principle of what he's doing, but according to his recruits he's an honourable thief. He only targets private businesses and individuals that are known to be comfortable and, in his opinion, can afford a small loss. He will always endeavour to make as little mess or damage as possible, and he'll only nick goods he deems "surplus to modest needs". His favourite targets are other rogues, particularly anybody making money out of drugs; he really hates those people. After a robbery he phones the police anonymously to report the event, so that the victims can make arrangements to re-secure their premises, in case less considerate burglars arrive for scavenging.'

'What do his recruits actually do?'

'Luther does the thieving, his partners act as drivers, lookouts and removal men.'

'And what kind of things does he steal?'

'Mainly, easily resaleable, transportable household goods: TVs, videos, radios, hi-fis, computers, jewellery, antiques, paintings and money. Of course I don't actually know any of this; I've just formed a picture from various pieces of information I've heard. Luther would never admit to any of it.'

'And he's never been caught?'

'Not that I've heard. I believe a couple of his accomplices have been questioned, but they've never been detained. It's widely viewed Luther either has some kind of Guardian Angel looking over him, or he has a deal or immunity arrangements with the police; the latter presumably.'

'What do the accomplices get in return?'

Adrian started to laugh, then stopped abruptly. 'I guess you don't know what Luther's nickname is? The Fourth Man.'

I shook my head and then I thought I saw the pun. 'Is fourth as in one quarter?' I tendered.

'Very good. Luther takes or gives commission always at 25 percent. It's rumoured he keeps detailed accounts of everything he steals and whenever he sells an item, he passes a quarter of the proceeds to his accomplice at the time. I heard that once he received £4000 for a painting that he stole; he passed the £1000 commission onto his accomplice – a redundant builder – and the next day the builder left the streets and started his own business. So, assisting Luther can bring its rewards.'

Now I knew what Luther was up to, I was unsure whether to admire or despise him. He was certainly a resourceful individual and his stance against drugs probably explained why he was so dismissive about Charlotte. Yet theft was as much a crime as drug dealing, and crime was to be avoided as far as I was concerned.

I was still hungry and wondered if there was any soup left. 'I'm going to re-join the queue,' I said to Adrian.

'I need to be off to Victoria Park now,' he replied. A group of radio-controlled model aeroplane enthusiasts meet there on Sunday afternoons and let me fly their planes. Do you want to come along?'

A glazed look of excitement was in Adrian's eyes. 'No thanks. There's something else I want to do. By the way, do you know the arrangements for tonight?'

'Meet at the hostel at six, or the pub at seven. Don't eat too much soup, otherwise you won't have room for the free food later.'

As it turned out that wasn't a problem: the soup had run out, so I had to content myself with two more slices of curly bread.

Chapter 21

SECOND SUNDAY – 1:00 p.m.

It took fifteen minutes to walk to the Royal London hospital and follow the signs to the Helen Raphael ward. I found the ward sister – a rotund middle-aged woman – and I enquired after the Rensbergs. Being a stranger, I was subjected to a thorough grilling regarding my name, address and why I was there. Without discovering if indeed I was in the right place, I was, in polite and diplomatic terms, told to go away. I attempted to argue my case, but an intimidating hands-on-hips stance from the sister suggested if I were to continue, then security might be called to remove me from the premises. I considered the reasons for such a reaction. If the Rensbergs weren't on the ward, I would have been told immediately I must be in the wrong place – so they must be there. Perhaps hospital policy dictated that critical patients were screened from visitors unless they were immediate family, or on an approved list; I couldn't claim authorization on either count. Most likely, I thought the refusal meant that due to the nature of Kathy's admission, she might be vulnerable to further attacks from her assailant, and hence the police had insisted on no visitors. All this was assuming Luther's accusation was wrong and Charlotte had told me the truth.

I had dedicated my afternoon to seeing Charlotte again, so I resolved I might as well hang around with the hope of seeing her. If she was on the ward, then she must emerge sometime to visit the loo, get something to eat or stretch her legs. The Helen Raphael ward was situated on the first floor down a passageway from the main corridor. A short distance along the corridor – for no obvious reason – there was a row of empty chairs, so I sat down and picked up a discarded copy of yesterday's *Daily Mail*. This was a lighter read in terms of weight and content than my textbook on anatomy, so for the next half hour I updated myself with national news and gossip while remaining vigilant of activity to and from Kathy's ward.

In the sketchy business pages, my attention was attracted to a short article about the projected takeover of a major insurance company. In that short moment, my surveillance had lapsed and, before I had read the first paragraph, I sensed a body nearby. I looked up.

'Waiting for anybody in particular?' Charlotte said nonchalantly.

'Charlotte, where have you been?' I asked and immediately realized it was a stupid question.

'Where do you think I've been? Here, at the hospital, of course.'

'But you didn't return to the hostel last night.'

'You sound like my father the first time I stayed out all night. You're not my keeper you know.'

Her scolding reply came as a shock. 'I … I was just … just worried about you,' I faltered.

She stared at me and I noticed the weariness in her complexion, which was exacerbated by the crumpled jeans and cheeky T-shirt she still wore from yesterday. 'I'm sorry. I've had a tough couple of days.'

'Want to tell me about it?' I said and indicated the seat next to me.

She slumped into the chair and leaned back resting her head on the wall with her eyes closed. I think she dozed for a couple of minutes because she woke with a start then looked around dreamily. She rubbed her eyes vigorously making them redder than they already were.

'I think you need rest. Is there anything I can do?'

'No,' she said stubbornly, but fatigue was taking over and her eyelids were losing their resistance to gravity. 'I just want to lie down for a few minutes – no longer.'

This time her words were slurred like a drunk. Instinctively I sniffed the air trying to detect alcohol on her breath, but I knew it was the tiredness talking. She stretched out on the chairs next to me and laid the back of her head on my left thigh. Her arms were loosely crossed over her stomach.

'Just a few min …,' she struggled to say before the light breathing suggested she had fallen asleep again.

I folded and placed my newspaper on the floor as quietly as possible so that I didn't disturb her. Eager for silence, I became acutely aware of the quiescent sounds that pervade a hospital corridor. The heedful footsteps of nurses and doctors, the subdued voices of visitors and the cautiously wheeled gurneys now conspired in a cacophony of noise I was desperate to screen from my sleeping beauty. Yet, my concern was in vain; even a screaming child, in dispute with its parents over some triviality, failed to wake her. With the depth of her slumber, I contemplated stroking her disordered hair, which had taken on a golden sheen in the dimly lit corridor. But her restful oblivion needed no additional comfort and an attempt to satisfy my own libertine desires didn't seem appropriate during her vulnerability. Instead, I just played voyeur using my visual rather than tactile sense to examine her.

A couple of times she stirred and I had to raise my legs gently so that her head didn't slip beyond my knee. She would regret her supine position when she woke; her back and neck would surely ache – a small sacrifice for the benefit sleep would bring. We stayed that way for perhaps half an hour. Eventually I shut my own eyes and dwelt wastefully upon what may have brought Charlotte to her present state, for surely I would know soon enough. While Charlotte was unaware of her aches, my weakened left thigh began to complain. It started with a dull pain; developed to a pins-and-needles tingling, which then subsided leaving only numbness. I thought that was its final state until the muscle spasms started and my leg twitched involuntarily. I reached down to my duffle bag intending to position it as a pillow substitute for my leg, but the awkward movement aggravated the muscle and with a jerk, I clutched at my leg in response, then at Charlotte to keep her still. She moved in sympathy causing my steadying hand, aimed at her shoulder, to rest on her left breast instead.

She recovered slowly, albeit quick enough to detect my unintentional grope, and then swung her legs to floor and stood up unsteadily.

'What the fuck do you think are doing?' she shouted.

I glanced at my offending hand expecting it to provide an excuse. 'It was an accident ... I ...'

'You bloody pervert, I thought you were ...' She stopped in mid-sentence then continued with marginally less venom. 'How long have I been asleep?'

'About half an hour,' I guessed.

'Oh Christ,' she said and ran towards the Helen Raphael ward.

Leaving my belongings behind I limped after her and watched as she disappeared through a side door before the main ward. Her haste had roused the ward sister who looked surprised and then blocked my pursuit path.

'Where do you think you're going?' she asked.

'I need to see Charlotte. There's been a misunderstanding.'

'By her actions she obviously doesn't want to see you.'

'But ... I ...'

'You had better go or I'll have to call security.'

Behind the sister, I saw Charlotte re-emerge from the room she had entered. 'It's alright Elsie; I had a minor panic. It's not Robin's fault.'

Sister Elsie looked doubtfully towards Charlotte. 'Are you sure? Shall I call Inspector Bradley?'

'NO,' Charlotte shouted and then quickly in a reassuring voice, 'No, really, it's not a problem. Let Robin pass.' She beckoned to me.

I made no movement until Elsie had reluctantly stepped aside. Then I felt her eyes follow me. 'Call me if there's any trouble,' were her parting remarks.

Charlotte placed her finger vertically over her lips as a gesture to be quiet as we entered the room.

It was a large whitewashed room. Opposite the door was a window overlooking a courtyard. To the left, there was an occupied bed surrounded by electronic monitoring equipment, which was emitting gentle background hums and occasional beeps; and there was a rhythmic ventilation sound from a mechanical respirator. On the right, there was a washbasin, cupboards, two straight-backed chairs and a camp bed. Tiptoeing, Charlotte led me to the bed and we sat down.

'What's happening?' I whispered.

'You don't have to whisper. Just don't talk loudly or shout.'

'Okay.'

'Now before I tell you anything, do you swear you didn't touch me up out there?'

I told her about the muscle spasms and she studied me closely trying to detect whether I was telling the truth. I assumed she accepted my story because she immediately changed the subject. 'Kathy woke up last night.'

I looked across the room somehow expecting Kathy to sit up and say "Hi".

'That's marvellous. No wonder you stayed here all night,' I said.

'It was such a strange experience. Every day for months I've sat beside her and talked to her about anything and nothing. I've read books and newspapers to her too. At first, there was a purpose; the doctors said there was a high probability she could hear what I was saying, and it would comfort and encourage her. But after a month with no response, I began to feel stupid and self-conscious about talking to myself; it became a habit and sometimes I thought I was going insane.

'Then last night I was reading *The Hobbit* – her favourite book – for the umpteenth time, when I detected a movement somewhere. I looked around thinking an insect had come through the window, but saw nothing so I carried on reading. Then there was a slight change in the regular sound coming from the respirator and as I glanced at it on the other side of the bed, I noticed Kathy's eyelids were flickering. This had happened before, and the doctor had explained that even in a comatose state, Kathy would still dream and experience rapid eye movements. Yet the flickering appeared to be voluntary like she was struggling to open her eyes and this was confirmed by the audible change in her breathing. I pulled the emergency cord to summon help and seconds later Elsie came in. Her scrutiny confirmed there had been a significant change in Kathy's state and she rushed away to call a doctor. I started to cry as I watched her and prayed she was at last coming back to consciousness. Then, beneath the plastic mask assisting Kathy's breathing, I noticed her lips were moving. I wasn't sure of the consequences of removing the mask but I did so anyway, desperate not to miss Kathy's first words after such a long time. I pulled the mask gently away from her face, ready to replace it immediately if she showed signs of distress, and moved as close to her as I could. I called her name and in a dry-throated, whispered reply she said, "Thank you ... being with me." Her eyes opened briefly and stared towards the ceiling, but I swear she creased her mouth briefly in an attempt to smile. Then she clearly said, "Get better ... soon ... very tired," paused and finally added "Careful ... Chad, Kent ... bad men," before drifting, I hoped, back to sleep rather than a coma. I re-secured the mask, and moments later Elsie returned with a doctor. I related what had happened, and then the doctor spent the next fifteen minutes checking equipment, telemetry, readings and vital signs. His prognosis was encouraging. In simple terms, he believed Kathy had emerged from the coma and her body was now regenerating itself in preparation for returning to a conscious state. Uncertain was how the trauma may have affected her permanently; physical indicators were positive, only time would tell whether the mental ones would be too.'

Charlotte paused and leaned back on the camp bed, which creaked in sympathy. It seemed a relief to her she had been able to share her revelations with someone outside the hospital; but having unloaded, she was fighting to stay awake and I guessed she hadn't slept at all the night before. I was sure there was more to her story and felt I would have to prompt her for the rest.

'Has she said anything else?'

'No. She's opened her eyes a few more times and she's begun to move her head and limbs, but she's said nothing more.'

Charlotte's voice exhibited more than just tiredness; she was troubled too. I thought I knew what it was.

'Who's Chad?'

She took a deep breath. 'I can't be certain, but Bradley's boss is a Detective Superintendent Chadwick Dixon. Bradley and Dixon came here together soon after Kathy was admitted. I distinctly remember Bradley calling his boss Chad, and Chad is an unusual name.'

'Why would Kathy say "Bad men"?'

'I'm not absolutely sure, though a couple of pieces of information tie in. During my conversations with the policewoman I mentioned yesterday – Simone – she hinted strongly the police were eager for Kathy's help because they suspected, though Simone didn't reveal why, that a senior police officer was involved in the drug operation. Kathy's knowledge of who it was may have contributed to her overdose.'

'This man Dixon's involved?'

'It's an obvious conclusion from Kathy's words. But worse, from my point of view, is that Bradley has been over keen for news about Kathy's welfare. Sure, he has a case to solve and, apparently, any information Kathy has is the best lead that the police have. Bradley has asked that anything Kathy says should be relayed to him – and only him – as soon as possible. To me that smacks of collusion between Bradley and Dixon.'

It seemed an emotional rather than logical judgement to me. 'Don't you think you're jumping to the wrong conclusion? It's a reasonable request; after all, if what Kathy knows leaked out, she could be in danger; you might be in danger too. Another possibility is Bradley suspects Dixon and wants to gather information himself so that he can nail him; maybe that's why he's been giving you money?'

'I don't know. I've thought about it a lot since Kathy mentioned Chad. The more I analyze my conversations with Bradley, the more I'm convinced he is involved in this business. I'm scared to leave Kathy alone in case Bradley turns up and … well … does something to Kathy.'

We debated the issue for a while longer, but all we agreed upon was there was no direct evidence to implicate Bradley and we would err on the side of caution with regard to leaving Kathy unattended. I offered to Kathy-sit to give Charlotte a break, but despite the friendship that had grown between us, I don't think she fully trusted me, partly because of the warm way I had spoken about Bradley assisting my own rehabilitation. My suggestion that it would give her the opportunity to get fresh clothes from the hostel was attractive, but she politely refused and said she would discreetly ask one of the nurses to stand in for her later. We felt further speculation would be wasteful, and decided to change the subject to what I had been doing since we met yesterday.

Charlotte moved the two chairs to be next to Kathy's bed so that Kathy could subconsciously eavesdrop on a less controversial conversation. I told her about tailing Luther and Jason, Gannet's death, my recruitment by Luther, the theft of my clothes, my begging initiation, my visit to the soup kitchen and lastly the news of Millennia's coming performance. To me, it was the trivia of Robin Forest's second day; to Charlotte it could have been the narration of a busy day in the life of a celebrity, such was her curiosity in the minutiae of my experiences. Her enthusiasm was no doubt influenced by the mundanity of her last 24 hours, yet I was excited she was genuinely interested in what had happened in my life. Indeed, she was volubly critical of my association with Luther and saddened I had had to succumb to begging to meet the financial needs of my identity research. She made no comment about the invite to the Howling Wolf pub because of her commitments to Kathy, but given the freedom I was sure she would have come. I had to promise to give her a detailed description of the event the next time I saw her.

'When will I see you again?' she asked.

'Is that a cue to go?' I suggested.

'Oh no. You can stay here as long as you like, though I think Elsie will throw you out at nine o'clock, if not earlier, since that's when visiting hours finish. Anyway, you'll have to leave before then to see Millennia and get some decent food.'

'I'd be happy to stay with you instead,' I offered, hoping she would agree.

'No. You go. You'll not often receive invites to pop concerts. Best to take advantage of any social situations that might enhance your life style. Perhaps you could come back tomorrow?'

Now I had a dilemma. As much as I desired Charlotte's company, I was desperate to follow up the smallest lead to my past. I could postpone my trip to Ipswich and Chelmsford until another day, but this would mess up the arrangements with Luther, and I didn't want to get on the wrong side of him. I wasn't sure how long my research would take tomorrow but I would be back by the evening. I explained this to Charlotte and she appeared disappointed, though accepted how important the task was to me.

Prompted by my identity quest, for the next couple of hours Charlotte sought ways of triggering my memories. Initially she tried a serious approach by acting the role of Doctor Westcott in an attempt to spark recollections via association and controversy. Her unqualified methods were similar to the Doctor's, but she treated the exercise empathetically instead of clinically. Some questions did bring faint images to mind, but I was unsure whether these were ghosts of the past or my imagination running wild. I concluded that proactivation of my brain gave misleading results and the most reliable insights would continue to arrive unexpectedly, as indeed they did a little later.

Charlotte was relating the happy days she spent at her student flat in Islington.

'... Julie was a brilliant artist. She funded her way through college by selling portrait sketches of people in the street.'

One of those precious moments had arrived. 'Julie was my girlfriend,' I said suddenly.

'She couldn't have been ...' Charlotte paused. '... Ah, not my Julie – *a Julie.*'

I sat there picturing long black-haired Julie sitting opposite me in a café or restaurant. I was angry, she was sad. I tried to steer towards the periphery of my vision without losing the main image so that I might recognize the surroundings, but the scene faded.

'Was your girlfriend? Do you mean is?' she continued in a jealous tone.

And then another flashback appeared. No pictures this time, merely a recent fact that came to mind 'And Donna did a sketch of me.'

'Another girlfriend?'

'Julie is an ex; I think. I don't know about Donna, I can't picture her, but I think she is young – perhaps a schoolgirl. I have the distinct feeling these are recent memories, maybe from shortly before my accident.'

I wondered what had seeded these memories. Charlotte had spoken two key words – Julie and sketch – which my brain had looked up in its storage banks. Yet, there must have been other occasions when I had been exposed to key words or images. Why now? The only difference I could detect was that I felt relaxed – thanks to Charlotte's company; the most relaxed I had been since waking up in hospital.

'Look, don't take this wrongly ...,' I began and then proceeded to explain my theory to Charlotte.

'It's to do with my voice,' she said. 'Several people have mentioned I have a soothing voice. I was always in demand for baby-sitting jobs because within minutes of reading a child a bedtime story, they would be fast asleep. Friends used to joke that I ought to become a hypnotist when I grew up.'

We both laughed. Then I had an idea.

'If you don't mind, could you carry on talking about ... well ... anything you can think of; perhaps you could read to Kathy. I'll just sit here and if I drift off maybe you could pretend you've hypnotized me and pose me some searching questions? Who I am? Where I live? Where I work? It must be worth a try.'

She laughed again – derisorily this time – but she nonetheless agreed with my mad scheme. She picked up *The Hobbit* from the bedside cabinet and began to read. Bilbo was fighting spiders – one of my favourite bits – which of course was a revelation in itself. Maybe this would work.

I did submit to sleep eventually, though it was, I felt, a combination of Charlotte's soporific voice and the concentrated immersion into the alternative world of hobbits, dwarves and elves. On route to unconsciousness, I absorbed thousands of words, though on reflection the events of Middle Earth were unlikely to contain any that would launch me into my past.

'Hey, it's six o'clock.' Charlotte was shaking me.

I had a dull ache in my neck from my head being slumped to one side and my opening eyes felt gritty. 'Did it work?' I asked excitedly.

'Yes. You're a reincarnated John Lennon, fabulously wealthy, live in a castle in Scotland and have three wives,' she said mockingly.

From drowsiness and frustration, I wasn't amused. 'Don't mess about Charlotte, be serious.'

'Of course it didn't work. I'm no enchantress. You stayed awake for about half an hour. I left you for another 15 minutes then I started asking you questions. And do you know what you said?'

I shook my head.

'Nothing. Absolutely nothing. All I got were a few snorts and grunts. I tried a few more times over the next two hours, but you remained fast asleep. The noise of two doctors, three nurses and the tea lady didn't stir you either.'

'I'm sorry; I didn't mean to be abrupt. I really thought we might have success.'

'Don't try to force the situation. You have the best results when you act naturally. Just keep talking to people; you'll get there in the end. You need to be patient.'

I raised the subject again of staying with Charlotte, but she was insistent about expanding my social life. As I rose to leave, Elsie arrived carrying a coat and bag. It was the end of her shift and Charlotte had arranged for her to watch over Kathy for half an hour while she went back to the hostel for fresh clothes. The hostel was on route to the Howling Wolf pub, so I had the added bonus of Charlotte's company for a while longer.

I'd forgotten about my belongings left in the corridor outside the ward, and was relieved to find my few possessions were still intact, albeit minus *Gray's Anatomy* – even hospitals weren't immune from petty larceny. My hope was that a deserving person like an underprivileged medical student had stolen it.

Charlotte led the walk to the hostel with a haste that brought anger from my hip again. My attention was focused on keeping up with Charlotte and mentally combating my pain, so I had little time for conversation. Not that it mattered, because Charlotte was teasingly speculating what pub food delicacies I might be savouring later. At the hostel, she disappeared to her dormitory and I booked in my bag at reception to avoid transporting it to the pub. Then the persistent Keith appeared.

'Where is everyone?' he asked, a little panicky I thought.

'Sorry, I don't know Keith, I've just arrived ...' I lied and knew what was coming so I continued, '... and I'm ... um ... off to the Doctor's now.' The lie was poorly executed and we both knew it. For the second time I experienced Keith's disappointed look and briefly considered being truthful and inviting him to the pub. But there had to be a good reason why everyone at the hostel avoided Keith's company. I didn't want to spoil the party at the Howling Wolf, so I accepted the moment of embarrassment and privately promised to make amends another time. I had thought about waiting for Charlotte to emerge, but was now eager to leave in case she gave the game away, so I made my way to Limehouse.

Chapter 22

SECOND SUNDAY – 6:45 p.m.

The Howling Wolf pub was less than a mile away. I hurried as best as my thigh would allow, to ensure I staked an early claim to any free food available. According to the clock on the building opposite, I arrived at a quarter to seven. The pub stood out, being an old structure surrounded by modern office blocks. Its façade was clean and brightly painted, and by the number of coloured posters in the windows advertising live music, quizzes, karaoke and hot food all day, was surely a popular retreat. I hadn't passed another pub or café on route, so perhaps it thrived during the week on business customers. At weekends the pub's apparent lack of inherent parking space was probably compensated by a deal with the neighbouring company, whose car park was almost full though no lights shone from its offices.

There was a single doorway to the pub, which led inside to a huge room. A long L-shaped bar faced me, attended by half a dozen staff members, who were moving to-and-fro dealing with a line of customers two deep. To the left and right were raised seating areas with some partitioned into cubicles and diners already occupied many of the tables. I surveyed the area looking for a friendly face or signs of impending musical activity. Then I heard the whines of a guitar coming from the far right and followed the sound to a separate room, a large hall similar in size to the WI meeting place, but devoid of any furniture except for that to augment Millennia's – or rather Howling Wolves's – equipment at the far end. The assembled audience was a strange sight. There were two distinct groups of people. Near the band tuning their instruments, was the group from the Jubilee. I recognized several of them since they were conspicuous by their clothes, and were quietly hanging around chatting, but without food or drink – scavengers in waiting I thought. In contrast, the crowd nearer to me were dressed for a night out; loud, enjoying themselves, and almost without exception, had drinks in their hands.

I joined the sombre party and mingled with some new faces. News obviously travelled fast at the hostel, since my amnesia was well known and I was steered into reciting my short life story yet again, albeit from boredom, I made it the shortest version to date. Meanwhile the noises from Millennia gradually took structure and I avoided another rendering of my past to more new Jubilee arrivals, when Danny proudly introduced the band. He announced they would perform some of their own compositions first and with a frantic drum solo from Gringo they began to play. In the confines of the hall, the music was very loud, so I moved away from the band and observed from the side. Musically I think they sounded accomplished, but it was difficult to be sure since the songs they performed were unfamiliar. Danny was the lead singer with Rick often providing accompanying or backing vocals. The Jubileers looked disappointed, eagerly watching the door for a delivery of food or drink – but none arrived. Gradually they became more animated and eventually a few began to dance. A young man took the lead and Adrian's eyes followed him enviously around the floor.

Adrian was being teased by his colleagues to join his partner, and with a seductive beckoning from him, Adrian's resistance broke down. He was uncomfortable with dancing as shown by his awkward and unrhythmic movements, but soon began to enjoy himself as his friend circled him with a provocative display.

The other patrons were disinterested in the entertainment and continued their raucous behaviour, albeit louder to compensate for the music.

Millennia had been playing for about twenty minutes when two barmaids appeared in the doorway carrying laden trays, and they made their way to a table adjacent to the band. There they deposited four jugs of beer and a dozen half-pint glasses. The band didn't notice the arrival, but the effect on my colleagues was immediate. With the exception of Adrian and partner, the strays gathered round the table – looking, but not daring to touch. I went to join them. At the end of the next song Free interrupted Danny and there was an unheard exchange and glances towards the table. Free came bouncing over with instructions. We were to consume the beer as soon as possible and then notify the bar staff the band wanted refills. The ungrateful ones complained there was only beer, but drank regardless. Instructions were obeyed and even with a small wait to share glasses, the task was complete in less than five minutes. Free and Georgie were despatched to the bar for seconds, and returned as the band was winding up for its interlude. The barmaids followed bearing two enormous platters of sandwiches and then went back to wheel in a trolley, which held numerous stainless steel dishes containing hot hors d'oeuvres. Our eyes were on stalks and in deference to our hosts we held back our attack on the banquet, waiting for Millennia to satisfy themselves first. They did so, quickly and moderately, protecting their nervous stomachs from overindulgence and their heads from alcoholic haze, but asked us to put aside a feast for when they had finished the gig.

Millennia started part two with a rendition of "A Hard Day's Night" and almost immediately everyone was dancing, swelled by the sudden influx of people from the bar. A generation later, the Beatles' music could still work its participative magic. The throbbing and familiar music, and good food, influenced me too. Spurred on by Georgie – with chaperone Brian watching her every move – I joined the heaving throng and discovered I could dance, after a fashion.

As one of the slower numbers began and Free made a beeline towards me, I made an excuse to visit the gents and, when I returned, I spotted Luther watching the band.

'Pretty good, aren't they?' I said.

Luther continued his vigilance then said, apparently to himself, 'I wonder if they have a manager?'

'Wanting to diversify your activities?' I joked.

Luther looked round. 'I have contacts in the entertainment business.'

That was no surprise. I'd have bet my begging earnings against the contrary.

'I was thinking of taking them on myself, but my management fee would only be 24 percent,' I offered as seriously as I could manage.

Luther regarded me with a frown lasting several seconds. 'That's a joke, right?'

I kept my serious visage and shook my head slightly.

'I'm beginning to like you, Robin Forest. You're sharp and witty and, when you get more organized, I reckon we could work well together. How did the begging go today?'

I presumed the Fourth Man had just complimented me and though the thought of working with him disgusted me, I hoped that perhaps I now had his confidence. It was time to put this to the test. 'How do I contact Ronnie Kent?'

Luther looked around to check we couldn't be overheard – somewhat unlikely as Millennia were powering through "I Saw Her Standing There".

'Now there you go again. I build you up and you knock yourself down. What business do you have with Ronnie Kent?'

I told him about Inspector Bradley's suspicion that Kent was involved with my mugging. 'I need to find out if the attack on me was random or premeditated. If the latter, presumably he knows who I am.'

'And if you confront him he might finish the job this time,' Luther said sarcastically.

'I wouldn't confront him directly. I was hoping there might be a backdoor into his organization and that with your many contacts, you could help.'

'Define help.'

Assistance from Luther would be difficult. He would probably be wondering how he could make 25 percent from the transaction, but 25 percent of what? A quarter of my old life? I needed to appeal to his benevolent nature – if he had one. Perhaps flattery would reveal it.

'You are obviously an influential person in the area and have great respect from the residents at the Jubilee …' I lied, but I knew he couldn't contradict me. '… possibly ex-residents too.' I had to pause for the loud cheering of Millennia to die down. 'For example, I bumped into Sniffy today, who was full of praise for your guidance of the homeless.' I lied again, but Luther was beaming. 'You must have the trust of someone who is close to Kent. Someone who might be able to tell you what he and his henchman were doing last Sunday night.'

Luther was still dwelling on my suggestion when Free came over to join us.

'Hello Boss,' she said. 'I didn't expect to see you at a gig like this.'

Luther grimaced. 'Push off Free, I'm busy,' he said angrily.

'There's no need to be like that, otherwise I'll withhold your … rations,' she quipped, glancing at me.

For the first time, I'd just seen Luther embarrassed. Was it the cheeky way she was addressing him or was there innuendo in her words? From knowledge, rations could refer to cakes, though the saucy way she said it hinted at a sexual meaning.

'Anyway, I came to drag *Robin* onto the dance floor,' she continued. Now she put emphasis on my name, seemingly to make Luther jealous.

'He's busy too. So push off if you want to keep your job.'

That struck home and she looked towards me for support. I just shrugged; I wouldn't antagonize Luther now that I had made progress on seeking his assistance. She turned away and launched herself towards a group of unattached young men who were standing near the band.

'Never trust women, they are all whores,' he said in a weak attempt to reaffirm his status.

He looked vulnerable and I wanted to keep him high. 'Well, that put her in her place. She'll think twice next time,' I said.

The praise had the desired effect; Luther emitted one of his growling laughs and then returned to the subject in hand. 'I do have a few spies in his camp. Such information won't come cheap, nor would you be able to afford it.'

I guessed that was coming, but I had gambled there was an acceptable alternative. 'I don't intend paying for it. Would it benefit you if Ronnie were put away?'

'Not especially. Our paths don't cross that often. I'm a small fish to him.'

Not the answer I wanted. 'But I thought you were anti-drugs and Ronnie has apparently cornered the market in the East End. Get rid of him and get rid of the drugs problem.'

Luther shook his head. 'Until somebody else picks up the pieces. I am sure there are plenty of understudies waiting to take over.'

I had one more card to play – a convincing trump card, I hoped. It was a far-fetched theory only, seeded by Kathy's mumblings and Charlotte's deductions. What if Inspector Bradley was a corrupt disciple of Dixon? What if I had stumbled across damning information, which had led to my mugging or failed attempt at my murder? Was that why Bradley had apparently been so friendly towards me, so he could slip me poisoned asparagus sandwiches? It would have been a risk on his part, but who knew he had given me the sandwiches anyway? His word against mine, but he was a public servant and I was a nobody. I had no proof for what I was about to say, but I hoped it would finally influence Luther to help me.

'What if I said Kent was indirectly responsible for Gannet's death?'

'Bollocks. What evidence do you have and what was the motive?'

'Nothing that would stand up in court – yet. But when the autopsy on Gannet has been completed, I'll wager he was poisoned by the asparagus sandwiches or fruitcake given to me by Bradley.'

'No, that can't ...' Luther began, but I was in full flow and didn't want to be interrupted.

'Furthermore, I have reason to believe his organization was responsible for putting Charlotte's sister into a drug-induced coma. And before you say that's crap, I've had the full story from Charlotte and I've seen Kathy myself; she's in a bad way. If you are too afraid to strike back at the drugs barons yourself, give me a lead and I'll do it myself for Charlotte and Kathy's sake.'

These were strong words and I had no idea how Luther would react; but I was becoming fed-up with my artificial subservient attitude towards him. Spurred on by what I had discovered earlier at the hospital and knowing Luther was potentially the most useful ally I had, I was willing to risk the relationship and push him to the limit.

The music suddenly grew louder. Motivated by the reaction of the swelling audience Millennia must have turned the amplifiers up because its improvisation of "Get Back" made conversation impossible.

'Let's go to the bar,' Luther said and we threaded our way through the dancers to the sparsely populated bar. On the way he keep looking around until he spied Free, who was in a dancing frenzy with a gorilla-proportioned young man. She poked out her tongue at Luther but he pretended not to notice. In the bar Luther bought me a beer and we sat down in one of the booths in a quieter area.

'If I were to help you, and I'm not saying I will at the moment, what exactly do you want me to try to find out?'

I seemed to have victoriously argued my case, but concealed it behind a swig of beer.

'Four things. One: Why was someone abducted, mugged or whatever last Sunday night? Two: Who was that person? Three: Specifically, how Kathy Rensberg was involved in the drugs operation? Four: Generally, the name and address of anyone involved in three.'

'I might be able to acquire some insight on the first two points. I'll do that because I think you're a smart kid who deserves a break. Plus, if your speculation about Gannet is true, then maybe justice for him may come from it. But the drug related ones will be tricky and dangerous, and I'll not risk my neck unnecessarily for a young girl who, however it happened, got sucked into that evil world. And if I do discover any information, you never heard it from me. You'll have to run with it yourself.'

I agreed and, to celebrate my progress, I offered to buy Luther a beer. I checked at the bar for the cost of a pint, did a quick mental calculation, and concluded I could afford two pints and still have enough for my train fare the next day. I felt smug with my success and strangely human with my first social purchases.

When I returned to the table Luther was deep in thought and hopeful that he was planning the acquisition of the information I sought, I savoured my beer in silence. I desperately wanted to know what was going through Luther's mind. I studied him, while he studied his pint of beer. When I first met him he came across as the all-powerful godfather of a homeless community in a part of East London. Nothing appeared to faze him. He projected supreme confidence and ultimate knowledge, and I – like my peers around me – regarded him in awe. Since that meeting I felt I had changed considerably: I was stronger, more confident, had adjusted to the world in which I found myself, and had taken on responsibilities for seeking justice for myself and Charlotte. And now I saw Luther in a different light. In reality he was a pathetic creature, just less pathetic than the people over whom he wielded power. He was scared to penetrate the local drugs scene and I wondered if this was real terror or whether a past exposure inhibited him. Perhaps he was the wise one and my fearless, insensitive, attitude was born of my naivety of the situation. Had he recognized that my respect for him had waned and I was now using him, instead of him using me? Maybe he was thinking my stance was undermining his authority and he was planning my downfall? I needed to demonstrate he was still in command of his empire.

'By the way, the briefing you gave me about begging worked perfectly today. I followed your guidance and earned over £8. I am most grateful for your advice,' I said sycophantically. 'When I start properly on Tuesday, £30 a day will be piss easy and your 25 percent investment in me will be guaranteed.'

My words snapped him out of his supposed scheming and he took a long draught of beer.

'Despite the Ronnie Kent theory, you're going to read local newspapers tomorrow?'

'Oh yes. The Kent connection is speculative at best. I still reckon the newspapers offer …' I stopped suddenly. At the bar I spotted a bandanna-adorned youth. He was wearing my Burton jacket, clearly recognizable from the scuffed and torn sleeve.

'Excuse me a moment,' I said to Luther.

The youth was lifting a pint of beer from the counter as I reached him. I grabbed his arm and pulled him towards me. The full glass toppled from his hand and crashed onto the counter spilling its contents in several directions – mostly onto my stolen jacket.

'What the …' he started to say as I took hold of the lapels of the jacket and pulled him down to my eye-level. In my haste to confront him I hadn't realized how tall and broad he was compared to me.

It was now my turn to be interrupted. 'That's my jacket you thieving bas…' was all I could say before I noticed his loose right hand had sought and found the jagged remains of the glass from the bar top. So intent was I on retaining my hold on him that I reacted slowly to the weapon, which was aimed at my head. Fortunately, it was a reaction that made me flinch slightly to the right, probably avoiding a gouged eye, but surrendering a fleshy forehead to a glancing blow.

At the time, the wetness on my brow from the beer dregs registered more than the impact of the glass and instinctively I released by grip, using my left hand to wipe away fluid, and swinging my right arm to land a punch to his stomach. He doubled-up and dropped the glass, but the punch had little effect and he immediately uncoiled. As he rose I hooked my left hand inside his knotted bandanna and held long enough to bring my right knee up for a second assault on his abdomen. He fell to his knees and his free hands, grasping for support, settled on my legs. He pushed forward unbalancing me so that I fell backwards on to the floor. I wasn't hurt, but his reactions were keen and he dived on top of me, his hands grabbing me by the throat. Pressure was applied quickly and, as I fought for air, I saw two spectators attempting to pull him away. It was enough to distract him and I mustered strength to land a finger-numbing punch to the side of his face, which stunned him sufficiently for me to wriggle free. We both stood and he broke free of his captors aiming a right hook to my face. I parried the strike with my left arm and, forgetting my bruised hand, imitated his own action, but connected squarely on his nose. He fell backwards, blood spurting from his nose, but the crowd that had gathered around us prevented him from crashing to the ground. His hands went to his face and he eyed me vengefully, but he had had enough. He staggered for the exit looking over his shoulder. I wasn't satisfied – he still had my jacket – but now Luther was at my side hanging on to my left arm and someone else held my right. My arrestors easily checked the half-hearted movement I made towards my disappearing victim. Suddenly I lost interest in my jacket; it no longer provided a clue to my past nor, in its beer and bloodstained state, did I regard it as fashionable.

The bar was now buzzing with people, the onset of an affray even more attractive than the stimulus of Millennia. The swell of opinion was against me as I had started the fight, and drawn blood from the defendant. There was little regard for his far superior build, and no one thought to question me whether my offensive was justified.

'You're barred and if you don't leave quietly I'll call the police,' said the man to my right.

I turned to face him and winced as I felt a pain above my left eye. I had seen him behind the bar earlier and I guessed he was the landlord.

'But that guy stole …' I began, but Luther squeezed my arm and interjected.

'Come on let's go outside,' he said.

The vision in my left eye became a red blur and I rubbed it with my hand leaving it smeared with blood.

We headed for the door and the crowd parted as if I were Moses; mumbling things they didn't want me to hear lest I gave them bloody noses too. We passed racking containing cutlery and condiments for diners and I picked up a handful of serviettes.

In the street I looked around in case my victim was waiting to pounce with an army of supporters. All was quiet except for the muffled booming coming from Millennia. I spat into the serviettes and then used them to mop the blood from my brow.

Luther inspected it. 'It's only a small cut, you'll live.' Then, reaffirming his status over me, he went into lecture mode.

'You'll have to curb that temper of yours if we work together. Rash onslaughts like that will get you into deep trouble. I don't abide violence of any form, but I must say you handled yourself admirably well. You're a reincarnated boxer, are you?'

I was already thinking about my hot-tempered reaction. Sure, I'd been wronged by the brawny youth, but like Sniffy earlier in the day, my backlash had been excessive and uncharacteristic. Perhaps the beer I had drunk had addled my brain.

'I don't know,' I said weakly, deep in thought.

'I suggest you go home and get a good night's rest. You might need to prepare yourself for shocks tomorrow – if you discover who you are. You could be Lennox Lewis's brother with a skin graft.'

He uttered one of his laughing growls, but I didn't react to his joke. 'What are you going to do?' I was interested because after half an evening at the pub in a social environment, I wanted company; even Luther was better than nothing.

'Well, now you are off the scene I can have a free run at signing up our Liverpool friends.'

Then again, perhaps Luther wasn't the association I sought; I wanted intelligent conversation, not a series of witticisms. Yet, he was probably serious about recruiting Millennia; they were already under his influence and would no doubt be suckered into a disadvantageous commitment. It would be a shame; they had talent and deserved better representation. I made a mental note that the next time I saw any of the group, I would advise them to avoid Luther's tacky schemes.

'Okay,' I acknowledged, 'but don't forget you have a few things to progress for me first.'

The look on his face suggested he didn't need reminding and with a departing mercenary statement, 'I'll update you on Tuesday night … after I've collected my commission,' he grinned and disappeared back into the pub.

I checked the clock opposite – half past nine. Depressed, I began to shuffle my way back towards the hostel, in no hurry for shelter or sleep. I was annoyed with myself that the day had ended so badly. As a curative diversion, I thought of Charlotte and wondered whether I should tell her about my deal with Luther – probably not. She didn't trust Luther and – here was wishful thinking – she might be worried about my safety in such a scheme.

Chapter 23

SECOND SUNDAY – 10:00 p.m.

When I arrived back at the Jubilee, Albert was on duty and mystified by the lack of resident traffic that evening. Word hadn't reached him about the Millennia performance, but he was truly impressed that some of his flock – his term, not mine – were possibly on their way to a better future. I retrieved my bag and, as I neared the unisex common room, I noticed the door was ajar. I could hear the television blasting out dramatic music interspersed with an occasional crash or hand to face thud; it reminded me of my earlier fight. I paused for a moment while I considered whether I was in the right frame of mind to suffer(?) a session with Keith. Why not I concluded? I regretted the way I had treated him so far; the negative statements of my colleagues had influenced me; it was time I made my own assessment of his proffered friendship.

I peered around the door. Keith was the only person there, staring resignedly and disinterestedly at the screen in the corner. He glanced my way, yet his previous enthusiasm to communicate with me appeared to have waned.

'It's *Goldfinger*. I've seen it before,' he simply said and looked back at the television.

This time I wasn't in a hurry to leave. 'Okay if I join you?' I asked.

Keith look surprised – shocked even. 'I can turn the telly off if you like … if you want … to chat,' he said.

'Okay,' I replied, 'I've seen it too – several times.'

Keith clicked the remote control. 'How was the doctor's visit? Sedated you with a bash on the head, did he?'

I didn't want to lie, and fortunately I didn't have to when he added nervously, 'Sorry, none of my business.'

There was an awkward silence. Despite his reputation he seemed reluctant to talk and I was unsure whether to break it with questions about him or statements about myself. I chose a combination of both to see how the conversation developed. 'I had my first stint of begging today. It wasn't the most pleasant of experiences, but I guess I'll get used to it until a job comes along. Do you have a job Keith?'

My introduction appeared to relax him. 'Sort of. It's a black market one while I get some money together. I'm a freelance carpenter at a new office block being built in Hackney. With a criminal record it's nigh on impossible to get a proper job until you can dress smartly and have a private roof over your head ...'

Thus he started, and for the next hour he related a good deal of his life story ...

He was 24 years old, left school at 16 and then studied Art and Graphic Design at college. After two years he joined as a trainee in a small firm in North London, which specialized in designing bespoke kitchens. He dabbled in various disciplines, and developed expertise in the use of computers for designing new products, and carpentry skills for building prototypes. During this placement, he courted Angela who was recruited as a secretary, but who was soon promoted to office manager. At the age of twenty, he married Angela and they occupied – rent-free – the large flat above the premises of their employers, Craftwise Kitchens Limited. Craftwise had acquired a national reputation and Keith was often away overnight on business trips. The Managing Director, Gerald Hopkins, had encouraged Keith to commute most of his salary as a loan account to the business to fund its growth and shortage in cash flow. In return, the loan would eventually be converted to a share holding in the company. So while the Kellertons (Keith's surname) had to manage with Angela's income only, their future prospects were good. However, in anticipation of the good times ahead, Angela acquired expensive tastes, and any surplus money after household essentials she freely disbursed on luxuries for herself and the home.

One evening, two years into the marriage, Keith set out to travel to Birmingham for an overnight stay at a hotel, since early the following morning he had a consultation with a potential client. He had just joined the M1 when there was a call on his mobile phone from the client, who had to postpone the appointment. Rather than make a pointless journey, he u-turned at the next exit and headed home. When he arrived home unexpectedly, he discovered his wife in bed with Gerald Hopkins and – to use Keith's words – he beat the shit out of him. Ever the optimist, Keith had naively thought that would be the end of the matter, but his problems had only just begun. He spent the night at a local hotel, and when he returned home early the next morning, he discovered the front door had been bolted from the inside. Angela refused to let him in. Keith attempted to smash the door down with a jack borrowed from his car, but minutes later the police and a battered Gerald arrived on the doorstep, and Keith was hauled away for questioning. Potentially he could have been charged with assault and criminal damage, but Gerald didn't press charges because he had an alternative revenge plan.

First Keith was fired on the grounds of embezzling company funds; it wasn't true, but amazingly, petty cash records and expenses documentation proved that systematically Keith had been misappropriating funds for a number of months. The reason he had been doing this – according to Angela's statement at the industrial tribunal that Keith instigated on the grounds of unlawful dismissal – was he had an insatiable gambling habit, for which his weekly cash wage was insufficient. Company records proved Keith had been paid in cash and Angela demonstrated that Keith had never put money into their joint account. Gerald refuted Keith's claim about investment of his wages in the company and Keith had no documentary evidence to the contrary. Due to Gerald's benevolence these facts were never presented to the police so no criminal proceedings were forthcoming.

While this was happening, Keith lodged temporarily at a nearby YMCA and took part-time work at a building company, earning enough money to feed, clothe and provide accommodation for himself.

At the divorce proceedings – which had been initiated by Angela the day after discovery of her unfaithfulness – the circumstances of Keith's (false) job dismissal were re-used to paint Keith as an unworthy husband. Angela admitted her adultery, but with her contrived stories of Keith's gambling, embezzlement and negligence, and her Oscar winning performance of a saddened and wronged woman, the Courts had ultimate sympathy for her. The bisection of their joint assets in the final settlement was easy; the few they possessed had been purchased by Angela or were in use by her at the flat, so that's where they stayed. The most deliberated point was Angela's claim for payment to her of the equivalent of Keith's earnings during his gambling period. Keith, representing himself, was disheartened by the whole subject, walked out of the hearing and thereby, in absentia, submitted to the wishes of the Court. It was a rash mistake; he was ordered to pay £15,000 to Angela in instalments over the next years.

For a time he continued with his life and couldn't – and wouldn't if he could – afford the payments. Letters from Angela's solicitor arrived and were ignored. Then summonses appeared and were ignored. He began to move from place to place, and job to job, to avoid the persecution, but jobs were becoming harder to acquire as Gerald, who was a respected businessman with influence, spread the word that Keith was bad news as an employee. Two years ago, the police eventually caught up with him and he was imprisoned for 18 months. He offered no information on his custody and his history was completed with the last six months being spent at the Jubilee, hiding from the authorities and trying to save money to re-launch his life at some future, unspecified, date.

I've reported the story here as opposed to recording the dialogue that took place. Keith was distressed to tell his tale, though no doubt he had done so many times. His discourse was emotional and brought alternating periods of silence and sobbing. It began as a short story with many gaps, which he filled-in non-linearly as he progressed. Thereby the narrative was disjointed and some might consider, potentially untruthful. Yet, by the time I had pieced together the fragments and cross-referenced the events, I concluded the story was a heart-rending chronology of fact, albeit with a reservation it was only his version of the misfortunes that had befallen him.

Keith's naivety and weakness had been his downfall, but nonetheless it was unsettling that he had been the victim of rough justice. I offered sympathy and support, which he rapidly dismissed despite the tragedy of his past. I formed the impression that frequently he had to remind himself of his previous troubles, in order to reaffirm the positive outlook he had of his future. The Jubilee guests had been the recipients of this character building exercise and while I silently criticized them for their lack of compassion, I now understood how distressing it was to sit through Keith's personal soap opera.

I let the final period of silence drift on until I thought Keith and I had both recovered our composure.

'For all I know my past might be equally disturbing,' I said, hoping this would divert any further conversation away from the gloom that had descended upon us.

'Sorry. It helps now and again to brain dump my story. My theory is the more I tell it, the quicker I'll purge it from my memory. It hasn't worked yet though.' His face displayed one final look of sadness then he brightened. 'Anyway, enough about me, what you should be doing is telling me what you've been up to since we were last together, but frankly I'm too tired now to give you my full attention. So, if you'll excuse me I'm off to bed. Save it for another night.' With that he left me alone in the common room.

I wanted to call after him to ask what he had meant by his last statement, but already forming in my mind was a feeling of having been duped. I had just dedicated an hour of new life listening to Keith's sorry tale, and with his departure, I had been left with a small doubt about his integrity. Was the fiction of knowing me a continuation of the story he had just told? I solved the puzzle with one of two possible solutions. Either he was mistaking me with another Robin Forest he had known – after all, this Robin Forest had only been born a few days ago – or this was his gambit to secure an open-ended conversation that would give him an excuse to seek my attention another time.

With the hostel strangely quiet, I simply bathed the cut above my eye and decided to go to bed, too tired and disturbed by Keith's story to seek further companionship. I collapsed on my bed without undressing, noting that Gannet's old bunk had been stripped clean of bedding. I was vaguely aware of the excited noises of early morning arrivals, but otherwise slept soundly until morning.

Chapter 24

SECOND MONDAY – 6:00 a.m.

Luther had been right about not needing an alarm call to get up in the morning. At around six o'clock (I guessed) the hostel was alive with activity as the guests prepared themselves for their begging or slaving jobs. I had planned my day around catching the 8:21 train from Stratford mainline station. Liverpool Street and Stepney Green stations were closer, but the advantage was outweighed by the additional cost, so I had chosen to walk the first thirty or so minutes of my journey. I could have afforded to lie on my bunk until seven-thirty to avoid rush-hour in the kitchen. I felt awake, but I didn't want to take the risk of falling back to sleep, so I sat up and observed the exodus for a few minutes, occasionally acknowledging familiar faces. I saw Rick wearily getting ready for his new job and hopped down from the bunk to talk to him.

'Late night?' I asked.

'And morning, we didn't get back until three o'clock. It was fucking brilliant. I heard you missed some of the gig – a bit of a do with bandanna-man?' Rick replied while searching for an elusive shoe.

'A minor skirmish, except it got me ejected from the pub. Shame, because I was impressed with your performance. And thanks for the food – the best meal I've had in this lifetime.'

'No problem. Can't comment myself, we were too excited to eat much and with all that exercise, now I'm starving.' I recalled Rick had been the liveliest during the show; his borrowed guitar must be recovering now from travel sickness and dizzy spells. 'Luther suggested we employ you as a bouncer for the next gig to keep the wild fans at bay.' He laughed then cheered; he had found his shoe.

'Will there be a next gig?'

'You bet, Luther's working on it today. He has contacts in the entertainment industry, you know.'

'I know.'

'So with any luck this new smelly job of mine will be short-lived.' By now he was fully dressed and with a final 'Must dash, I'll be late,' he was on his way to Smithfields. As naïve as Rick was, I had to give him credit for his enthusiasm for work. If I had been up half the night doing what I enjoyed, I'm sure I would have found it difficult to motivate myself for portering in a meat market. His haste left me no time to lecture him about the misguidance of Luther. Then selfishly I thought that if Rick did give up his job perhaps I could take it over? Would I find this more rewarding mentally and financially than begging? Neither was attractive; anyway why was I dwelling on a homeless future when I had something positive to do today?

I paid a visit to the washroom, this time not bothering to shower or change my clothes – a wash and a teeth brushing sufficed. I looked at myself in the mirror. I didn't look too untidy. Already there was little evidence of the cut on my forehead and the stubble on my chin was itching but gave me a rugged rather than a scruffy appearance. My clothes, despite being slept in, showed no signs of fatigue. I sniffed the air around me and particularly under my armpits. I detected faint pub smells – beer and tobacco smoke – but was satisfied that only someone with a highly sensitive nose placed within a few centimetres of me would detect offensive smells; I would catch up on bodily and clothing hygiene tonight. I headed for the kitchen.

The early morning rush was over; the guests had either set off for employment or were sleeping it off after last night. Amongst the battlefield of dirty crockery I retrieved a clean mug, made coffee, grabbed a couple of slices of bread and then set out on my hike to Stratford.

The sky was overcast with patchy light grey clouds against an emerging blue background. With luck a crisp, clear autumn day was on its way. I enjoyed the walk and strode with little pain from my thigh, though I was relieved when the modern station was in sight so that I could sit down for a while. On route I had chosen to study the developing hustle and bustle of a working day. Examination of cars occupied me for most of my journey. I must have had an interest in motoring since I could easily recognize various marques and models. From an earlier insight I knew I could drive so I tried to picture myself in each vehicle searching for enlightenment of which type I owned. None came, except a strong feeling it might be blue and the colour hadn't been my choice.

When I arrived at the station, I bought my return ticket and a plastic cup of coffee, and thereby reduced my cash liquidity to an all time low of a little over £4. On the platform I searched the litterbins for discarded newspapers and had to settle for yesterday's *Sunday Telegraph* colour supplement. So with half an hour to wait, I read, drank and chewed dry bread.

The train was almost empty when it arrived and on the hour-long trip, I combined thoughts of recent events with an examination of the increasingly rural scenery. It was a lonely journey, made worse by the increasingly negative thoughts that I was on a fool's errand. I considered alternative strategies to resurrect my hidden past, but bashing my head with a heavy object to subtlely and benignly rearrange my grey matter seemed to be the only, albeit extreme, method available to me.

By half past two I was heading back southwest on a train to Chelmsford. At the *East Anglian Mail* offices, I had scoured the issues for the last three weeks, found nothing that prompted memories and then revisited the copies in detail, convinced there had to be something significant I had missed on my first pass. I had been correct in my original forecast of the newspaper's coverage; predominantly it was Suffolk based, mixing National headlines with detailed stories about news in its home county, with barely a mention of events in neighbouring Essex and Norfolk. In the reading room, I had chatted to one of the female staff members who had been intrigued by my dilemma. She had suggested the Internet might prove useful, so I sat next to her while she conducted an enquiry from her terminal. Without a name she had limited search topics, but the most promising was a site called the *National Missing Persons Helpline* which contained profiles and photographs of displaced people, unfortunately none of me. I made a note of the site's address with the intention of revisiting it at a future date.

The results of my research were not unexpected, yet I still felt disappointed at the outcome. Such was my frustration, I wondered if there was any sense in visiting the *Essex Weekly* offices. All I wanted was a copy of this week's edition of their local paper, going back any further would probably be a waste of time. I disembarked at Chelmsford and made my way to the exit and just beyond the ticket barrier there was a newsagents. I added to my financial misery and purchased what I wanted, and I also took a copy of the free *Yellow Advertiser*, which was mainly advertisements, but also had a couple of pages devoted to local news. I returned to the platform and, with twenty minutes to wait for the next train, began to flick through the pages of the local press.

The front-page stories concerned the scandalous activities of a doctor at a local hospital, and a sewage problem at a shopping complex. Mainstream articles continued on the next few pages; thereafter the font size decreased for the coverage of minor parochial events and then increased again for the sports headlines. I doubted the lead stories concerned me, but I read them nonetheless. Pages two and three were more promising: an armed robbery at a post office with a water pistol, two muggings, a woman whose husband had mysteriously gone missing, a drug addict found dead in his flat and speculation about job redundancies at a major regional employer that might be taken over.

On the train I studied the secondary stories more closely.

The first story read like a farce. The robber had threatened to shoot unless the money was handed over, but the postmistress – who had been hard of hearing – had to ask the gunman several times to repeat his demands. In frustration and confusion, he fired and squirted the old woman, who became agitated at the wetness of her dress and lobbed a heavy parcel at her attacker. The comic scene had been observed by a customer outside the shop, who thrust the door open as the hapless thief was about to flee, knocking him unconscious.

The modus operandi of the muggings bore no resemblance to my own. Four in total had been perpetrated by youths in different parts of the county and an accompanying editorial was campaigning for imprisonment of the derelict parents.

The missing husband story could have applied to me. There was no photograph of the husband, but the physical description of him fitted me well, except he was forty-two years old and the wife was forty. Visually I thought I was about twenty-five and I didn't feel older or indeed married; my earlier recollection of a girlfriend named Julie seemed to correlate that. Besides, the wife suspected he had fled to Spain with her sister and the husband's name was Alan; and my name certainly wasn't Alan.

The drug addict was Joseph Carmichael. Not previously known to the police, but he had apparently died from a massive drug overdose. The police had commented that it was the second drug offence within a few days at the same building, so were keeping an open verdict in case the events were linked. Only a tenuous link with me there via Ronnie Kent and Kathy's own fate; but no doubt drug addicts were dying all the time, so any connection was remote at best.

The last of these stories rang a bell, albeit a muffled one. I remembered being attracted to the financial pages of the newspapers I read while I was in hospital. Also, there was the similar article in the *Daily Mail* I had started to read at the hospital while I was waiting to see Charlotte. Both the stories were about an insurance company that had suddenly become prey to a competitor. I searched through the piece in the *Essex Weekly* trying to identify keywords that may have sparked the memory. Was it, Harlow – the town where the company was based? Insurance – the industry in which I worked? Ferndown – the name of the local company? Milton Cern – the predator? Takeover – something I had been involved in? I closed my eyes and bounced these words around my head. Then I read the article over and over until I knew it word for word, but nothing came. As I arrived at Stratford station, I eventually convinced myself that the whole notion had no substance at all.

I still intended to visit Charlotte. I was looking forward to seeing her, but because of my early return, I decided to pursue other priorities first – I was hungry and smelly.

I had only eaten bread since the Millennia feast and thoughts of the hot delicacies, initiated by a rumbling and deprived stomach, had been a background influence all day. It was too late for the WI handouts so I had decided to repeat my raid of the lucky-dip cupboard. Adrian was in the kitchen playing patience at one of the tables. I said hello and then began searching in case there were any new cans.

'Anything you would recommend from the *haute cuisine*?' I jested.

'There were a few leftovers from last night. I brought them back in a doggy bag and put them in the fridge ...' Adrian replied and my stomach rumbled in expectation. '... but I think Gregor and Igor helped themselves earlier.'

My search in the fridge was in vain. There was a screwed-up brown paper bag discarded on the worktop, which Adrian confirmed had been the canine receptacle.

'Oh, and Free brought in cakes and bread at lunchtime ...' (more expectation) '... but they've been eaten,' he added nonchalantly.

'Are you trying to wind me up?' I said irritably.

Adrian looked up sheepishly from his orderly arrangement of playing cards on the table. 'No. Are you hungry? Jazz brought in a couple of jars of homemade jam. They're in the top cupboard.'

The frustration of the day and my hunger boiled over. 'And what the fuck am I supposed to do with that? Eat it with a spoon?'

My outburst made Adrian start and he nudged the table destroying the precise layout of his cards. 'What exactly do you do, Adrian?'

'I'm not sure I know what you mean,' he said softly, trying to reconstruct his game and avoiding my stare.

'You have an easy life around here. Good clothes, never hungry, ample leisure time. Are you sleeping with the owner or something?' I made the last remark to emphasize his apparent trouble-free life and then realized it could be misconstrued since he was gay.

'Who told you that?'

'Don't panic, I was only using a figure of speech.' I turned away to relieve the tension of the exchange and began to re-examine the contents of the lucky-dip cupboard. Undecided, I randomly selected a can and opened it. Surprise, surprise – chicken soup. Just as well I wasn't a vegetarian; but then again, perhaps I was. I found a small glass bowl and emptied the contents of the can into it, liberating the lumpy mass of meaty bits that had congealed at the bottom. I studied the control panel of the microwave oven and had a couple of trial runs. I settled on a three-minute irradiation at full power, which produced a deafening and suspicious hum from the device. Out of the corner of my eye I noticed Adrian occasionally glancing nervously my way.

Avoiding contact, I examined the cupboards and refrigerator looking for something to eat with the soup and settled on the broken remnants of a packet of cream crackers. The irritating hum finally expired with a pathetic ting and I retrieved the lukewarm bowl of soup, too hungry to suffer another ear-bashing to increase its temperature. I took my meal and joined Adrian at the table.

I crunched up the crackers, added them to the soup, and stirred to give it body.

'I used to be a headmaster at a secondary school,' Adrian said as I sampled my soggy mass.

The dejected tone of his voice suggested a tragic story was underway. Calmed by the intake of food, I used encouraging words. 'What happened Adrian?' I said.

'I had an affair with one of the senior pupils. He was eighteen and we were discreet – nothing ever went on at the school. He used to come back to my house a few evenings a week.'

As he spoke, Adrian's quietly assured persona faded. He looked tearful without tears. 'Is that the guy you were with at the pub last night?'

'Yes.' There was a pause while Adrian composed himself. 'He had few friends and he was persecuted by his peers because of his sexuality. One evening he was spotted entering my home and then rumours started to circulate. The rumours developed into misinformation about our conduct and they eventually reached the other teaching staff via the bigoted deputy head. A staff meeting was called and I was confronted with the stories. I admitted the affair and thought I had convinced the audience the perversions in the stories were wholly untrue. What I did in my private life had no effect on my leadership of the school and was none of their business anyway. I thought that was the end of the matter.'

I'd finished my soup. 'Cup of coffee?' I offered as Adrian reached a convenient break.

'Okay, white with two sugars. Does my story disturb you?'

'About you being … gay?'

He nodded.

I rose to make the drinks. 'I don't think so. I have no prejudices to draw on, though I must say I find it hard to … appreciate, a man being attracted to another man. But I don't disapprove.' My answer appeared to satisfy him and he visibly relaxed. I returned with the coffees and an aged, but edible, apple I had mysteriously discovered in the cutlery drawer. I polished the tarnished skin of the fruit as Adrian continued his tale.

'A week later, following a secret meeting of the school governors and the deputy head, I was given a letter terminating my position on the grounds of gross misconduct with a pupil …'

Adrian carried on talking, but I had been transported to another place and another time. I was in my flat opening a letter. *I* had been fired for gross misconduct too, but the background to the dismissal was unreachable. The letter had been posted, but why hadn't I been given it personally? Had I been away on business? On holiday? Of course, I'd been in hospital having an appendectomy operation. The jigsaw of remembrances was beginning to fit together. There was something else though; other items of mail were significant and there were problems with the flat too. Why was my mind teasing me like this? Tantalizing me with snippets of information, which first excited, but then ultimately disappointed me? As before, I dwelt on the images despite knowing that forced concentration would burrow no further into my past. I would have to wait patiently for the next revelation.

'... which is how I came to be here,' Adrian had apparently concluded his story and when I didn't react, added, 'That boring, was it? You've looked rather vacant for the last few minutes.'

I made my apologies to Adrian and explained the flashbacks I had been having without going into details. I was keen to hear his denouement, being genuinely interested and eager for any key words to trigger more historical insights. I encouraged him to an encore of the part I'd missed.

With Adrian's dismissal, he automatically gave up the right to his house since it came with the headmaster's job. The month's grace he had to vacate the premises lasted only a week because of the persecution he had suffered from staff and pupils alike: poison pen letters, protests outside his home and threats to his well-being in aid of ridding the area of a "hideous pervert". Not being financially secure – he didn't exactly explain why, but the innuendoes suggested he was supporting relatives – and without immediate friends to assist him, he was forced to move away from his South London base. His possessions, including an ancient but running Vauxhall Chevette, had been stored in a lock-up garage a few streets away. A fellow teacher had recommended the Jubilee and he had been in residence for the past two months, gradually eroding his meagre savings, but too proud to seek menial work or go begging.

However, the story might still have a happy conclusion. He had sought legal advice on the grounds of unfair dismissal and was soon to attend an industrial tribunal. His solicitor believed his chances of success were high, but reinstatement of his position was not an option since there was little point in trying to overturn the local prejudices that had already been formed. Instead, they would seek substantial damages as compensation for loss of office and a guarantee of headship somewhere else in the country. Of the latter, there should be no doubt. Adrian's previous track record had been exemplary and he was a senior member of a number of National education committees. Meanwhile, Adrian was making the most of his leisure time by pursuing his various cultural and aviation pastimes, and had started to write a fictional adaptation of his experiences. Playing patience had come to be a stimulative prelude to an intense period of authoring activity.

I regretted my earlier anger at Adrian now that I had heard his story. He was a harmless individual who had apparently done nothing wrong, yet had suffered bigotry from his colleagues. I personally could not relate to the subject of homosexuality, but nonetheless he had my sympathy for the way he had been treated.

I was jealous he had an horizon to focus upon, while I had to make do with disjointed fragments of information, which were taking a frustrating amount of time to yield anything substantial. Now I was feeling down, and wanted to get on with the rest of my evening.

'It probably doesn't mean at lot, but if there is anything I can do to help you Adrian, please let me know,' I said, standing up to leave.

'Thanks for the offer, but within a couple of weeks I hope to be out of here, ready to renew my career in another part of the country. I quite fancy the Lake District,' he said.

'Windermere ... is beautiful at this time of year,' I said hesitantly.

'You know the area?'

Strangely I did and recently too. The view from my room had overlooked the lake and I remembered sitting on a bench seat by the shoreline reading a book. 'Apparently so,' I offered uncertainly. 'I've a few chores to do now, but perhaps we could talk again tomorrow evening. The more I talk, the more ... I remember.'

Dutifully I washed up the few kitchen items I had used and returned to my bunk with my head combating on-going hunger pains with diversionary thoughts of the Lake District. I sorted through my duffle bag intending to wash my marginally soiled clothes and then thought better of it. The quantity didn't justify a machine wash nor could I be bothered with hand washing – after all I had no garden party engagements on the horizon. I did choose to shower, thankfully this time with water more than a few degrees above room temperature. I lingered in the shower with my body relishing the warmth and my mind analyzing a possible connection between losing my job, having a flat and being in Windermere. Living and/or working in Windermere didn't strike true. The Lake District wasn't exactly a centre of commerce and I thought I had convinced myself I was based domestically or occupationally in London or Essex. Sub-consciously I touched the scar below my abdomen. Had I had an appendectomy operation in Windermere? Highly improbable, more likely I had been on holiday, or in hiding – but from what or whom? The room overlooking the lake must have been from a hotel. Christ, if only I had transport or sufficient money I could travel there and make enquiries. Surely, with the rate that facts were coming back to me – I had to assume they were facts, not delusions – such plans wouldn't be necessary.

I spent an hour updating my diary and then set out for the hospital to visit Charlotte. I arrived at an awkward time though. Kathy's steady improvement had brought a flurry of doctors' visits and Charlotte was listening to the prognoses. I waited for an hour and eventually Charlotte appeared for a few minutes, deeply apologetic and excited by the positive news of Kathy's recovery. I could tell she was eager to return to her sister's side, so I gave a one-minute summary of my day, and departed, consoled by our joint promises to meet at length the following evening.

I strolled the streets for a while, thinking first of Charlotte and then mentally preparing myself for the official start of my begging career in the morning. Both subjects were still on my mind when I returned to my bunk bed at the Jubilee. My aching thigh and overtired brain conspired again to force sleep as soon as I laid my head on my duffle bag.

Chapter 25

SECOND TUESDAY – 6:30 a.m.

The following morning I was positioned at Stepney Green station by six-thirty. I had slept later than I wanted too, but left soon after rising to avoid the breakfast scramble in the Jubilee kitchen. Instead, I stopped by at reception to choose a new book for my coming vigil, and then headed directly for my destination, oddly with the haste and enthusiasm of a student starting his first job. At the station kiosk, I bought a banana, a can of orange juice and a packet of cheese biscuits for my breakfast and consumed them with a greed that befitted the starveling I felt I had become. I placed my total wealth – reduced to a little over £2 by my breakfast purchases – in my beret as a float and, settled into seated posture, began to read. The book was a novel, whose blurb proclaimed (don't they all?), that I was about to read the best page-turning thriller of all time. So impacting was the book that to this day I cannot recall the author, the title or the plot.

The early morning rush came as predicted by Luther, yet I observed most people were either in too much of a rush to get to work to toss me a few coins, or were well practiced in ignoring the pleadings of a beggar. I had barely doubled my wealth when I inspected my beret at nine o'clock. Thereafter, although the commuter comings and goings subsided, my new audience – comprising mostly of mothers with children in tow – were more aware of my adversity, and the quality of donations surpassed the quantity of the first few hours. The elderly retired surgeon of Sunday reappeared, and this time he complimented me on discarding the charade of attempting to read *Gray's Anatomy*, but still admonished me on the words of my pleading board. We talked and I told him a little of my background including the tale of my book being stolen at the hospital, which for some reason he found immensely amusing. When he left, he dropped a £5 note in my beret and I wondered if I had just enrolled my first regular contributor.

The occasional verbal abuse came my way plus enquiries from a couple of donors who needed reassurance that if they gave me money, it would not be spent on drugs or booze.

At midday, I was torn between forsaking the lunchtime peak for a walk to the WI soup kitchen to secure my own lunch. The decision was made for me when the young girl from the station shop emerged arm in arm with a young man. She looked my way then stopped and whispered to her escort; he nodded and she came over to me.

'Would you like some soup?' she asked.

'Well ... yes, you must have read my mind,' I replied.

She looked pleased and went back into the station.

Her friend looked at me doubtfully then, by way of explanation, said proudly. 'I'm taking Sue to the Burger King so she doesn't need her packed lunch.'

Sue returned carrying a flask. 'It's only low calorie, but it tastes okay. I'll collect it on my way back, or if you go, drop it in at the kiosk.'

I took the flask and grovelled my thanks.

She was right; the soup tasted good, as long as you liked chicken.

Lunchtime at Stepney Green never really happened – not as far as punters were concerned anyway. Stepney Green is a poor cousin to Mile End and Whitechapel in terms of businesses, and particularly shops and eateries, so workers don't roam the streets during their lunch break. Passers-by were rare for the next three hours and comprised of mostly pensioners – not exactly prime candidates to help a needy medical student. I began to doubt that my daily target of £30, less the £7.50 in commission to Luther, would be remotely achievable. Just after three o'clock, the routine was broken.

I noticed the perfume first. I had been absorbed in reading my novel, when I detected a scent waft by. Its strength was sufficient to overcome the ambient smell of traffic fumes so I looked up to ascertain its source. Walking away from me was a woman with long blonde hair and wearing a light grey coat. As I studied her shape and gait – attempting to gauge her age – she looked back and smiled. I glanced around to find the object of her admiration, but the pavement was devoid of people. When my eyes sought her again, I watched her disappear into the cul-de-sac where I had regurgitated my breakfast on Sunday morning. I thought no more of the event until ten minutes later when the clack of a pair of red high-heeled shoes stopped abruptly in front of me.

'I wonder, could you help me?' said a soft, sexy voice. The familiar perfume had already announced the return of my earlier passer-by. I raised my head from the book and, with my mouth agape, studied the woman before me. She was perhaps a few years older than me, with hair too blonde to be natural. Her narrow, sharp featured and lightly made-up face was unusual, yet attractive, and atop – from what I could see from the lay of her clothes – a predominantly slim, albeit invitingly rounded body. Through the unbuttoned coat, she wore a white blouse, and red skirt so short that, from my eye level, the pleasure point at the top of her smooth unadorned legs could have only been a hair's breadth from view.

Odd I thought that she wasn't carrying a handbag and there was a ring on each finger of her right hand. She had to repeat her request as I continued my scrutiny.

'I don't know,' I replied honestly.

'Do you know anything about electricity?' she asked.

'If it's disconnected it causes your fridge to defrost and leave a smelly puddle on the floor.' Why I made such an apparently stupid remark at the time was beyond me, but I knew it had come from a hidden personal experience and I would need to analyze it later.

She appeared unperturbed by such an odd statement. 'I knew you would be able to help. It happened once before you see, possibly a fuse? My neighbour fixed it then, but he's out at the moment.'

I had to stand up because I couldn't take my eyes off her legs, so I studied her pretty face instead. 'Why did you choose me?'

'I need electricity now because there's an important TV programme I need to watch in the next half an hour and … well … when I passed you earlier you looked like an intelligent and helpful person.'

I was suspicious of her reason so I tried to dissuade her. 'I'd be happy to help, but I'm only a poor beggar and you shouldn't take risks with strangers; besides this is my job.' If she was a prostitute, she needed reminding that I was potentially unclean and couldn't – and indeed wouldn't – pay my way.

She may have recognized my uncertainty and read the accusation because, rather forcefully, she countered it. 'Whatever, you're thinking you have the wrong idea. What will you earn in the 15 minutes it might take to help me out? A £1, £5, £10? I'll pay you if you're worried about money ...' Her loud statement didn't embarrass me, but we had a disapproving look and shaking head from the middle-aged woman who emerged from the station, '… and I'll give you something to eat. You look like you haven't eaten properly in a while.'

That clinched it. The prospect of food, real food instead of soup, was the tempter I needed. At my ultimate cost, I gathered my begging bits and pieces and followed her.

The cul-de-sac was deceptive, as was the exterior of the block of flats in which she lived. Both had the generally unkempt appearance I associated with housing in East London. As we entered her first-floor flat, I spoke for the first time on the short walk. 'Smart place,' I offered and dropped my duffle bag to the floor. The door led into a small entrance hall and immediately beyond was an astonishingly bright room. The far wall was almost exclusively a picture window and inquisitively I walked towards it without seeking permission. It must have been twenty feet wide and six feet tall, a single pane of glass except for two smaller fanlights above the transom. I examined it architecturally and was puzzled how the frame and double-glazed panel had enough support to stop them collapsing. The full length was shielded by vertical blinds, which were only opened at a slight angle yet permitted daylight to invade the room. The window looked towards the entrance to the cul-de-sac and I puzzled again why I hadn't noticed the panoramic outlook as we approached the building.

'An ex-boyfriend was a builder,' she explained. 'It's not glass, but some kind of super-strong plastic.'

The brightness continued with the interior. The walls and ceiling were a brilliant white, broken only by the occasional landscape print. A white, short pile carpet covered the floor except for an alcove on the right reserved as a dining area which contained a white table and chairs set on a wood-blocked surface. The wall furniture and bookshelves were white too with respite on the eyes by their darker contents. The large settee and armchairs broke the mould being cream, or maybe an off-white colour. The décor demanded comment, but for my status and reason for being there, I said nothing. After the poor surroundings in which I had become accustomed, I wanted to complete my Samaritan task and move on.

The woman had removed her coat and tossed it over an armchair. My initial guess about her shape was confirmed, curvy in all the right places. The blouse was diaphanous, a white low-cut brassiere holding back ample breasts. Nervously averting my stare, I walked towards the entrance hall. 'Is your electricity meter over here somewhere?'

'The white cupboard to the right of the front door; that's where the electricity bits are housed.'

I found the cupboard and crouched down to open the door to reveal the meter, a fuse box and a shelf containing fuse wire, batteries and a torch. The large rocker switch on the box was in the OFF position. For a moment, I felt dizzy and I assumed it was my awkward stance; then, my eyes blurred and I clearly saw a different cupboard and a different meter, and they were in *my flat*. I stumbled, banged my head on the door, and was immediately transported back to the present day.

There were six fuse blocks and I took out each one in turn. The wires between the screw fittings were intact so I just flipped the switch to ON. I watched the silver disc on the meter begin to rotate and heard music coming from the lounge area. I thought it strange the supply had tripped out without a fuse blowing. I stood up and stepped back to call out a question, thinking she was still in the lounge. 'Did anything happen ...' I started, but she must have crept up behind me and I bumped into her. I swung round and inadvertently brushed against her again and she clutched my arm to steady herself. She took the opportunity to move closer and tried to hold my attention with her eyes.

Above the momentary silence between us, I could hear her accentuated breathing and was conscious of stirrings in my own body. I moved back slightly and she placed her free hand gently between my legs and began a slow stroking action. 'Is something wrong?' she said softly.

I knew she was referring to her advance, but with great will power, an image of Charlotte and assumed innocence, I leant down to shut the cupboard door. 'No. It wasn't a fuse; the mains switch had tripped off. Did you use any electrical apparatus just before it happened?'

The disappointed crease in her naturally red mouth indicated she knew I was refusing to play her game. 'Oh … I … tried to turn the television on, I think,' she said.

I thought the hesitation signalled a lie, but I gave her the benefit of the doubt. 'Could you try it again before I go?'

We walked into the lounge and she retrieved a remote control from a glass and chrome coffee table in front of the settee. She aimed the electronic device at the television, which was resting on a white chest. It came on and stayed on.

'Problem solved,' I said. 'I'll be on my way then.'

'Thank you. I'm very grateful, but don't rush, I'll make you a hot drink first. Tea or Coffee?'

The thought of a hot beverage was tempting – it would be my first of the day. What harm was there? My actions had made it clear I was immune to her flirting. 'Black coffee, no sugar please.'

'Take a seat, I'll be back in a minute,' she said and went to the kitchen adjacent to the dining area.

I cast my eyes around the room, searching for detail this time that would give personal insight to my host. I spied a single framed photo, which showed her sitting in a rowing boat with her arms around a young boy and girl. On the coffee table, there was a copy of *Hello* magazine. The bookshelves displayed several layers of paperback novels and larger hardback books mostly on fashion, pop music and cookery. From that limited intelligence, and heavily influenced by her appearance, my best guess was that she was a model.

She returned with two steaming mugs of black coffee and placed them on coasters on the glass tabletop. As she leant forward, I noticed she had unfastened the top two buttons on her blouse to reveal the cleavage of her breasts. She sat down at one end of the settee and patted the place next to her. 'Sit down, Stella doesn't bite,' she said introducing herself.

Perhaps not, but Stella's suck might kill I mused. I chose an armchair opposite her and picked up my coffee eager to finish it and leave. She slid forward on her seat to expose her upper thighs and a dark space in between that was either black panties or no panties.

'How did a smart and handsome man like you end up on the streets?' she flattered.

I took a few sips of coffee, now with the objective of merely consuming it than relishing it. 'It's a long story ...', I lied and hoping to stall the conversation added, '... and not very interesting.'

'I'm interested,' she countered immediately.

I took another sip, too carelessly and burnt my mouth, but concealed the injury. I cupped the mug in my hands attempting to dissipate the heat from the black liquid so I could drink it quickly. I resolved in any similar future situation to take my coffee white.

'Forgive me. I did promise you food. What can I get for you? A sandwich, piece of cake, a biscuit?'

I politely declined and I wished I had a watch so that I could glance at it and say "Goodness, is that the time?"

With a final mouth scalding gulp I finished the coffee and said, 'I ought to be on my way. Could I use your loo before I leave?' The latter delayed my departure, but I was desperate to take my first pee since I left the hostel that morning. The discomfort had been exacerbated by the erection in my trousers I had been trying to hide since she touched me there.

'Yes, of course. I'll show you where it is.'

We rose and headed towards the front door. The bathroom was the last door on the right.

Stella persisted in her offer. 'There really is no rush. I could prepare you a proper meal within half an hour.'

I declined again and went to relieve myself, making sure I had bolted the door after me. The bathroom was unremarkable in its decor in comparison to the lounge; pink was the predominant colour adorning an averagely equipped bathroom. While peeing, I looked around for signs of male intrusion: shaving tackle, male deodorants, underpants – but there was nothing on display. While doing so it occurred to me that maybe Stella was trying to keep me there for the arrival of a jealous boyfriend. A plausible explanation, though she was taking a risk with a stranger. I could be a complete nutcase for all she knew. Maybe I was being set up for a perverse reason and there was a heavyweight lover hiding in another room, waiting to pounce if I attempted to satisfy the desire any male would have succumbed to in the presence of such an attractive woman. I quickly finished; I needed to get out of here.

She was waiting outside the bathroom when I emerged. I reached for the front door lock. 'Goodbye. Thanks for the drink.'

'Oh, just a moment I promised I would pay you for helping me.'

'There's no need. Treat it as my free good deed for the day,' I quipped.

'No. I insist. I'll get my purse from the bedroom,' she said, and before I had the chance to argue, she disappeared through the door adjacent to the bathroom and left the door ajar.

I should have exited then, but my inherent mercenary nature held me back. A contribution for services rendered – no matter how contrived – would assist my daily earnings target.

A minute passed – an age in such suspicious circumstances – then she called frustratedly from the bedroom. 'Damn ... could you help me with one other little thing?'

Okay, I thought, but then I'm out of here and I stepped into the artificial light of the bedroom. I could see the far end of the room to the right; the heavy curtains were closed and the room was brightly lit by a number of ceiling mounted spotlights, their beams concentrated upon the double bed on the opposite wall. There was a dressing table to the left of the bed and a wardrobe facing it against the nearest wall. I couldn't see Stella initially, but as I crossed the threshold I heard a movement to my left and the door was pushed shut behind me. I turned and there she was – naked; a small pile of clothes at her feet, though my eyes dwelt that low for no more than a moment. Before me was the most perfect female body I had ever set eyes upon. She stood, legs slightly apart; her right arm loose at her side, the left draped diagonally below her breasts with her fingers resting gently on her right forearm. Her pose was blatantly uninhibited and sexually inviting. For once I knew that my memory had stretched into the hidden depths of my past to make its comparison. I'd had girlfriends; I'd seen them naked and made love to them. I could picture faces, and I had explored and enjoyed the bodies that went with them, but I was certain none had affected me the way I felt then. My heart was racing; my mouth was dry and my stomach fluttered, and I could sense – if not physically detect – my body shaking. Part of me was definitely moving, as my growing penis struggled to find an escape route from the confines of my clothing. These bodily and mental experiences had manifested themselves in the few seconds it took me to absorb the situation and for Stella to observe my reaction before she spoke.

'Don't look so shocked. We both hoped this would happen. I'm just not as shy as you,' she whispered and with a single stride had put her arms around my neck and was pressing her body against mine. I started to voice a faltering refusal, but the embrace unbalanced me. The press thus became a push and I felt myself being steered backwards towards the bed. To combat the advance I braced my feet, brought my previously limp arms in to action to steady myself, and clutched at her smooth buttocks. The action was a triple whammy though: it heightened the excitement I was desperately trying to suppress; it gave the wrong signals to Stella; and had the effect of toppling me submissively onto the bed. As Stella bent over me, for the briefest moment, I was tempted to raise my hands and cup her breasts, but a spotlight shining in my eyes made the manoeuvre impractical. What was the purpose of having spotlights focused on a bed? It reminded me of a film set where such intense and expansive light aided the recording of shadow-less detail; I rolled to one side and jumped up.

'I really must going …' I said, '… there's something very wrong about this.' The lust I had felt moments earlier instantly abated.

Stella looked at me with astonishment and then her face turned to anger. 'You bastard, you can't go now.'

But I was already on my way and had reached the bedroom door. I paused and looked back at her.

She switched back to her temptress voice. 'Please come back. Relax … it'll be alright,' she said, rubbing her hands seductively over her body.

I ignored the display; the spell had been broken; whatever she said or did now would have no effect.

I was opening the latch to the front door when I heard her final plea behind me.

'Robin … don't go.'

I stopped dead. Had I heard right? She had used my name. I swung round. 'What did you say?' I shouted.

She knew she had made a mistake and attempted a cover-up. 'Don't go?'

'You said Robin … don't go. How do you know my name?' I moved towards her threateningly.

'I didn't … I don't,' she said, stepping backwards into the lounge and strangely trying to cover her body with her hands.

I followed up and grabbed her by the shoulders now immune to the creamy bare flesh beneath my fingers. I shook her and asked the question again. She jerked her right knee up towards my groin, but I had anticipated her action and pushed her away. She fell backwards and came to rest against a white armchair.

I raised my hand to strike her.

'You'll regret it if you try to hurt me,' she yelled.

'Who put you up to this?' I yelled in return.

Without replying she charged towards me aiming her nailed-tipped hands at my face. Had she not felt vulnerable by her nakedness, I think I would have had a hard time parrying her attack. She moved quickly and I considered myself lucky to receive only a scratch on my right cheek before I managed to seize her wrists and rotate behind her to pin her arms behind her back. Her strength contradicted her beauty, but fitted well with the shower of obscenities she uttered as she continued her struggle. Eventually, I achieved a stalemate situation by wedging her against the armchair and inflicting a painful upward movement whenever she wriggled.

'So will you answer my questions?'

'Fuck off you faggot.'

I realized then that physical or mental persuasion would not work on Stella. I wouldn't try to beat the information out of her. I had the sense to realize that in such a contest I might only be a marginal winner, and she would be more scared of the person she was covering for than me. Besides, violence wasn't in my nature and what crime had she committed against me?

With a final arm twist, I released her and backed away quickly in case she struck out. She turned around rubbing her arm and yelled profanely again. I picked up my duffle bag and opened the front door. I looked back and tried to put together a humorous and threatening parting remark, but nothing fitted the situation, so I just pulled the door to.

When I had descended the stairs to the ground floor I stopped. Throughout the encounter my heart had been pounding, first with desire, and then with anger and exertion. I thought that if I smoked this would be an ideal time to light up, calm down and reflect. I did all of that except sucking a mint took the place of a cigarette.

I crossed the road to sit on a low wall next to some lock-up garages. There I could watch the entrance to the flats and try to make sense of what had just happened.

Until Stella had used my name I had been on the verge of accepting she had to be the sort of woman who occasionally wanted sex with a random off the street. Did such women exist? It was a dangerous way of satisfying a sexual desire. The bogus electricity fault was a plausible and convincing means of enticing someone, and I had fallen for it. So how did she know my name? It could be innocent knowledge. During my begging sessions, I had on occasions given my name to punters that had asked. I certainly hadn't spoken to Stella before today, but it was possible she might have overheard one of my conversations. If I had been set-up then it could have been by anyone that knew Stepney Green station was my pitch, the most likely conspirators being anyone at the Jubilee. But for what purpose? Maybe someone thought I deserved a good seeing-to by a beautiful woman? Or somebody was playing a sick joke? Whatever, I had resolved the event was significant, concerned my present or past life, and needed to be examined further. That's why I had elected to spend a while watching the entrance to Stella's apartment block.

The intention was to observe arrivals and departures hoping I might see someone I knew, or to follow Stella if she emerged. Over the next hour, movements were aplenty, but none that I judged significant. For a while I read my paperback but never progressing beyond a paragraph before my thoughts drifted to a re-examination of recent events. I was close to giving up when a police car entered the cul-de-sac, cruised for a moment, and then drew up in front of me. A uniformed officer climbed out and approached me.

'Everything alright, sir?' he asked.

Now there was a leading question for which I had to consider my answer. I presumed this wasn't a welfare enquiry so something or someone must have triggered the visitation. The something was me, sitting on a wall for an hour. The someone could only be Stella. I stalled a detailed reply.

'Yes, thank you,' I said humbly in case the policeman thought I was trying to be facetious.

'I'm following up a report from a local resident concerning a person sitting on a wall acting suspiciously.' he explained.

I smiled and I couldn't resist highlighting a grammatical blunder. I hoped the officer had a good sense of humour. 'I suppose I'm that person, but I can assure you officer that since I've been here the wall hasn't once acted suspiciously.'

He didn't laugh or smile, and inclined his head slightly towards me. 'Just piss off will you, then everyone will be happy.'

So without saying another word, I did. Inviting questions about what I was really doing wouldn't work, since I couldn't think of a plausible alternative to the truth.

Chapter 26

SECOND TUESDAY – 5:00 p.m.

Unenthusiastically, I plodded back to Stepney Green station and when I arrived it was as busy as I'd seen it. A prime time to be begging, but three women with prams were chatting excitedly by my usual begging position, and the remaining wall space was blocked by various individuals smoking or reading newspapers. I was relieved to be presented with a reason for not working and despite having only £12 in my money belt (I'd counted it while on surveillance), I continued walking along Mile End Road until I came to the caravan eaterie I had patronized when I first came out of hospital. Only three days ago, but an age considering all the events that had taken place. I bought a cup of coffee and a discounted curly bread sandwich filled with fish paste, which I ate with hungry anticipation, albeit minor satisfaction. I felt tired and, recalling how little I had eaten since Saturday, wondered if this was the cause. I had just resolved to raid the hostel kitchen later, when a new food benefactor – Keith Kellerton – walked briskly in front of me.

'Hey Keith, finished work for the day?'

He stopped abruptly and looked nervously around. 'Oh Robin,' he said with relief. 'You scared the shit out of me. I thought for a moment you were one of the court officials.'

I stood up and went to join him. 'Going back to the Jubilee?'

He smiled smugly. 'No way. I'm off to Pizzaland to blow myself out on pasta. Want to join me?'

A mouth-watering offer, but the thought of watching Keith gorging himself would have been more than I could bear. 'No thanks. Such places are beyond my budget at the moment.'

'My treat,' he replied. 'I've had a windfall today and you can help me celebrate.'

He started striding again and looked back when I hadn't joined him.

'Come on, I'm serious.'

He shared his good news in the five minutes it took to get to Pizzaland in Whitechapel. The site manager at the office block where he had been working in Hackney – who had been most impressed with Keith's work – had approached him last week and offered him a moonlighting job at his newly refurbished house overlooking Victoria Park. There had been numerous carpentry jobs to complete at the house, the major one being the installation of a new kitchen suite, so for the last few working days Keith had been employed there instead of Hackney. His boss covered for him at the office by clocking Keith in and out so that he was paid his normal wage, and he had promised Keith a cash bonus for the domestic work. Today he had finished at the house and been given £200 for his efforts. Suddenly I wished *I* was a carpenter.

'You shouldn't do this,' I said as Keith thrust a menu at me. 'You need money for your future.'

'I'll be upset if you order a meal over a hundred quid. Ten quid's worth should be enough to stretch that skinny stomach of yours. Besides, it's for old times sake. We never did reminisce about the school days.'

I studied the menu eager to defer the disappointment he would receive when he became aware of his mistake.

'Try the cannelloni. It's good value for the amount of stodge you get. And we'll add a salad with a double helping of garlic bread and coffee.'

I was apparently no connoisseur of Italian food. The dishes appeared much the same to me, differentiated only by the flavour of the sauces, so after a short debate I accepted Keith's recommendation.

'So. What have you been doing for the last …', he thought for a moment doing a sum in his head, 'it must be … fourteen years?'

His precision was eerie and then it occurred to me that he probably didn't know the circumstances of my unknown past. I hadn't told him and the way that other guests at the Jubilee avoided Keith, it was unlikely anyone else had told him either. A waitress took our order before I had to answer.

'I really don't know,' I started and then proceeded to give him a two-minute précis of my life to date. 'So,' I continued, 'it's impossible that you know me because this Robin Forest has only been in existence for the last four days.'

I thought that would be the end of the matter, but Keith studied my face thoughtfully for a moment. 'No, it's definitely you. I was basing my recognition on your appearance not your name. I'm useless at remembering names, but I never forget a face.'

'Are you sure? Absolutely sure? But you can't remember my name!'

'I recognize your voice too, but your name … it could be Robin Forest, Archibald Twinkletoes – I've no idea. The school will have records.'

'What school did we go to?' I asked excitedly.

'Abbeydale Primary in Leyton. You were in the year above me.'

I was champing at the bit to ask more questions, but the waitress arrived with our meals. She took a frustrating amount of time making room for and placing the dishes, and then used an extraordinary amount of dialogue to check everything was to our satisfaction. Keith attacked his pasta immediately but I was too hyped up to start.

'How do you remember me so well, particularly as were in different years?'

Keith's mouth was bulging with food and I had to listen between chews and swallows.

'On Wednesday afternoons ... the whole school used the playing fields and sports facilities ... of the high school next door. You and I were good runners ... sprinters actually ... and it always bugged you that I could run as fast as you ... even though I was a year younger.'

He paused for another mouthful and noticed I hadn't touched my meal. 'You can listen and eat at the same time. It's not difficult,' he said sarcastically.

I picked up my fork and tucked in. The pasta was good.

'I fondly remember the sports day at the end of your penultimate year there – a steaming hot day in June. We had both easily won our years' 100 metre races and the climax of the day was the inter-house 4 by 100 metres relay race. You were in the Red house and I was in the Blue. At the third changeover, the Red house team was five metres ahead and then it was you against me for the final leg. I passed you in the final straight and beat you by a metre. You were mighty upset about that. You sulked for days and refused to speak to me.'

'You remember that about me, but you don't recall my name?'

'We weren't friends, just rivals. Soon after, you went to your secondary school and I've not thought about you since then.'

The exchange drifted into silence while we both eagerly finished our meal. My head was working overtime with these new, potential revelations. Keith's story had a ring of truth about it. Unlike his troubled story told at the Jubilee, this was delivered unerringly and without hesitation. He could still be mistaking me for someone else, yet three points held my attention. The boy Keith described was a keen runner and I had speculated earlier that if I were interested in sport, the strength of my legs might suggest such a discipline. And, the school was in Leyton – a part of East London less than ten miles away. Age fitted too; Keith was 24, so that made me 25 – about right.

We both sat back contentedly in our chairs. I studied Keith's face and there was the briefest recognition from those past days. His smug look of satisfaction convinced me he was telling the truth.

'What else do you remember about … me?' I asked uncertainly. 'Where I lived? Who my friends were? Anything about my family?'

'Not really. We had little contact other than in sports … there was that scandal about you, your brother and another boy.'

'A scandal? My brother?'

'Yeh, you must remember *that*. It caused a big stir in the school. The other boy left eventually. He was a real roughneck anyway. I think he was expelled.'

'I told you, Keith, my mind's a total blank beyond four days ago. But, my brother … a twin brother?'

'No, I think he was in the year above you. You didn't particularly look alike – he wore spectacles and he was bigger than you … well fatter actually. He wasn't the sporty type. Bit of a joker, always telling funny stories.'

'And the scandal?'

'Something to do with a pupil's father going to prison. It was apparently your fault … well, you and your brother's fault.'

Keith looked around trying to catch the waitress's attention. 'Got room for pudding? The chocolate sponge here is a real treat.'

I was frustrated with Keith. Here I was on the verge of discovering who I am and all he could think about was chocolate sponge.

'Why was it my … our fault?'

The waitress had arrived. 'Two chocolate sponges with cream and …' Keith looked at me for confirmation.

'No dessert for me. I'd like more coffee though.' I was being polite, besides food was no longer a priority. I didn't want any more distractions.

'So, that's two more coffees and … two chocolate sponges with cream.'

I opened my mouth to contradict the order, but Keith held up his hand. 'I'll eat his too,' he said to the waitress and she uttered a nervous giggle as she added the items to the bill before disappearing.

'Keith, I don't think you appreciate what's happening here. You may have just changed my life forever with this information about school. I don't wish to be rude, but could you please relieve the suspense for me?'

Despite my abruptness he wasn't fazed. 'Sure, what was the question again?'

'Why was it our fault the boy's father went to prison?'

'Oh yes. There was a bank robbery. You and your brother had bunked off from school one lunchtime to buy sweets. You passed the bank as the robber was making off in the getaway car. Apparently, you saw him remove his stocking mask as he entered the car, and recognized the boy's father. Your evidence contributed to him being caught and locked up. And, before you ask, I can't remember any names. Obviously the story was in the newspapers. I think it was on TV too.'

'When did this take place?'

'Now let me see,' Keith deliberated for a moment. 'I must have been about nine years old, so it'll be approximately ... 15 years ago.'

Disappointingly the waitress returned with our supplementary order so I lost Keith's attention for five minutes and resigned myself to sipping coffee and analyzing information.

An obvious place to visit was the old school – Abbeydale. There would surely be records of past pupils and, although I wouldn't be able to supply a name (but perhaps I could use Keith's?), it shouldn't be too difficult to find a record of two brothers separated by a year; or maybe a long-standing teacher might recall the robbery incident? And of course, newspaper reports would mention the event and give the name of the thief, though not necessarily the witnesses. So, unless Keith's memory had an onomastic revival in the next few hours, I would be heading to Leyton in the morning.

'Wow, now I'm stuffed,' Keith said coaxing the remains of his second bowl of dessert onto his spoon and delivering it to his mouth.

'What about your own friends at Abbeydale? Are you still in contact with any of them?' This was my last attempt at salvaging additional information from Keith.

'I can't help you there either. There was Alex somebody or other. He was my best friend and we went to the same secondary school in Walthamstow, but he emigrated to Australia and I lost touch with him.'

That seemed to be the end of our conversation. Keith's eyelids appeared to be sagging; perhaps work, money, food and conversation had taken its toll on him. I felt obliged to reward him with further communication and certainly had a tale to tell regarding my encounter with Stella, but I had much to think about without being sidetracked with a restatement of my bizarre afternoon. Keith summoned the waitress for a final time to settle the bill. An amount more than Robin Forest's wealth, but I hoped would have been a paltry sum to the adult version of a nameless sprinting schoolboy from Abbeydale primary.

The wall clock in Pizzaland showed six-fifteen. I had promised to visit Charlotte tonight, but I was also scheduled to see Luther for an update on what he had found out about Ronnie Kent; and I wanted to see Adrian too. It would have been convenient to call upon Charlotte now, since the Royal London hospital was almost opposite Pizzaland, but I knew that once I was with her, I wouldn't want to leave, and the meetings with Luther and Adrian were more important. So I resisted temptation and joined Keith in a brisk walk back to the Jubilee.

When we arrived, Keith headed straight for the common room admitting that a snooze in front of the television would be an ideal end to his day. I went in search of Adrian and Luther. I found Adrian alone in dormitory C. The room was only slightly smaller than dorm D, but had four double bunks, leaving room for eight tall slim metal lockers – all with doors and locks – plus a couple of easy chairs and a small table. In the corner there was a single washbasin, perhaps left over from the original library. If my dorm was one star accommodation, this rated at least three. Adrian was intensely occupied in one of the easy chairs and writing on the back of a used sheet of paper. A pile of loosely stacked sheets was resting in front of him on the table. He didn't look up as I entered the dorm.

'Excuse me for disturbing you, can we chat?' I asked.

He finished writing a sentence before he raised his head. 'Ah, I was just writing about you and your dilemma. Well, the fictional representation of you. I've called you Robert Forrester – the anonymous man.'

'Well, I have an update for you. This anonymous man may be on the verge of discovering his identity.'

'That's marvellous. Sit down and tell me more.'

I sat opposite and told him about Keith and I apparently being at the same school. '… so tomorrow I'm considering a visit to Abbeydale. Do you think they will have details of pupils from 14 years ago, and will they freely give the information I'm seeking?'

'Yes, to the first question. At my own school, I think we had paperwork going back to when it was established, although most was boxed and filed away in the cellar. If I were to receive such a request, I think I would cooperate. After all, the information you want isn't particularly confidential – merely a verification of the names of two brothers who were pupils. I might think twice about giving out the last known address though. But you could have a problem if you went tomorrow. Most of the schools in the area are on half-term holiday, so there may not be any appropriate staff in attendance. Probably best if you ring first.'

Damn. I hadn't counted on that. There I was, a day away from a real identity and now beaten by the education timetable. It explained why I had seen so many children during my begging stint that morning.

'Might a regional office have the same information? One that might be open?'

'Possibly. Would you like me do so some checking for you? I know the procedures to go through and, despite my legal situation, I still carry weight in some educational circles. Anyway, no disrespect, but a nameless individual making enquiries might arouse suspicion. What was Keith's surname again?'

'It's Kellerton. That's very kind of you. I don't suppose you could do it in the morning. And no disrespect to you, the sooner I get out of this place the better.'

'Of course. I'm not exactly overburdened with current duties. Besides it makes an interesting storyline for my book, which I ought to be getting back to.'

I took the hint. 'Yes, I'll leave you in peace now. One more question: have you seen Luther this evening? He's been doing research for me too.'

'He was here earlier with the Liverpool lads. Apparently he's secured them an audition for tonight. A pub in Wapping; can't remember the name of it though.'

I sighed disappointment. 'Okay. If you see him before I do could you tell him I'll be at my pitch tomorrow if he has any news?'

Adrian was already hunched over his papers and I took the grunt to mean yes. 'Thanks. I'll touch base with you tomorrow evening.'

I went to the kitchen intent on a cup of coffee, and quietly collecting my thoughts on the day's remarkable events. The kitchen had been empty earlier; now it was occupied by many residents I hadn't seen before. I was about to leave when there was a shout from my right.

'Hey whats-yer-name, don't leave on our account,' said a familiar female voice.

The odd couples of Brian and Georgie, Roger and Free were seated at the table nearest the door. Free had called out.

'Hi,' I said.

'Have you heard the news about Millennia?' Georgie asked.

'The audition?'

'Yeh,' she replied. 'Good ain't it. What you been up to recently? Haven't seen you since you were thrown out of the gig. Been in a secret love nest with the junkie?'

I was eager to get to the hospital, but the slur against Charlotte made me angry. I reacted with a disclosure to divert attention away from her.

'If you must know I spent the afternoon fighting off the attentions of a beautiful woman who picked me up on the street, and then I had dinner with my school friend Keith.'

My statement brought a chorus of laughter and disbelief that vexed me even more, but Free butted in with diplomacy. 'Don't go Robin. Ignore Georgie; she's an ignorant, insensitive bitch. I know the truth about Charlotte. She called in this afternoon to do some washing and told me about Kathy and ... she was very complimentary about you; had a message for you in fact.'

That stopped my exit and Free's friends looked towards her inquisitively. She presumably hadn't told them about Charlotte.

'What was the message?'

'She's been invited to stay with an old college friend tonight and Elsie's keeping an eye on Kathy, who's conscious and stable. She hopes to see you tomorrow night.'

'Oh,' I simply said. I had been looking forward to spending a few hours with Charlotte. I wanted to share my good news with her and now that would have to wait until tomorrow. Free recognized my disappointment.

'We're off to the pub soon, why don't you join us?' she asked.

I was initially undecided. Realistically was there anything I could do productively for the rest of the evening? Luther had presumably been too pre-occupied with his pop group managerial ambitions to investigate any connection I had with Ronnie Kent. I was dependent upon Adrian to progress my schoolboy history, and Charlotte had found alternative company. The only things that came to mind were laundry, which could survive another day's delay, and updating my log – ditto. The question was whether I really wanted to spend an evening with my present company. Why was I being so choosy? I had avoided Keith for a while and a social meeting with him had been ultimately rewarding. So I accepted and within a few minutes we were on our way to their favourite pub on the Commercial Road.

I learned little about them in the next hour since my earlier rash statement had brought me to the centre of their attention. To my advantage it meant I avoided buying drinks (a financial concern when I accepted the invitation) for the whole evening.

On the story of Stella, Brian and Roger – once they had accepted the event hadn't been a figment of my imagination – wanted intimate details and, later, a description of where Stella lived. The latter acted as a wind-up for the benefit of Georgie and Free, though I feared there was an undisclosed extra-curricular motive. The women immediately judged Stella to be a prostitute, who sought periodic perversions with low-grade people. This did nothing for my ego, yet was nonetheless a plausible conclusion.

In comparison, the story of my past link with Keith held less interest for my audience, other than for them to seek future favours from me should I discover I was a man of wealth or substance.

Much to my surprise, Free and Roger were married. They had been living with Roger's mother in Bow when her sudden elopement with the next door neighbour and a mountain of outstanding debts led to Free and Roger's eviction from a council flat. Roger worked on the production line of a small electronics company in Shoreditch, and of course Free had a part-time bakery job courtesy of Luther. Free's flirtations with Luther were open and sanctioned by Roger as a means of obtaining privileges. Not for the first time I'm sure, Free had to repeat her assurance that the only commission Luther got from her was the occasional supply of bread and cakes. I briefly stirred suspicion in the arrangement when I said I thought Luther took 25 percent of all occupational introductions but, to me, the overzealous denials from Free added to her potential guilt instead of defending it.

Brian and Georgie were unconnected, though even the most unobservant creature would have noticed Brian was permanently trying to change that situation. Georgie had no ambition in life other than to enjoy herself, yet she seemed strangely comfortable with the social boredom of her colleagues. She originated from a troubled family in Sheffield and was hitchhiking her way around Britain, reaching London three months ago. Her next port of call had intended to be Brighton, but the attraction of London – in fun and money terms – had stalled her nomadic way of life. She had no inhibitions and when I discovered how she survived, it was no surprise. Her biggest attribute was her breasts, she proudly announced. Displaying them and the rest of her body to magazine photographers when she was short of money, allowed her to lead a comfortable life and, out of choice, a homeless one. She spent most days in central and west London window shopping and watching people, or "hanging out" as she called it. To satisfy the requirements of the Jubilee, she was supposedly working as a poorly paid shop assistant, trying to raise enough money to rent private accommodation. Money was not a problem to her though since, bar a round of drinks purchased by Roger, she freely and unprompted kept us supplied with alcohol for the rest of the evening.

Brian declared himself a painter; not, as I had immediately assumed, of the decorating kind, but as an artist. A successful man in the past, his downward spiral had begun during an empty period of commissioned work which, combined with failed relationships and a bout of alcoholism, had seen him work the streets as a pavement artist. But meeting Roger had been a stroke of luck for which he had been endlessly grateful. The boss of Roger's company had a passion for art and a prevailing narcissism that suggested to Roger an introduction with Brian might be beneficial. As a result, Brian received a commission to produce a portrait of the boss for the lobby of the building, with the fee being offset by provision of a place in which to work, together with a supply of artist materials. So, each day Brian and Roger went to the same place to work: Roger to affix electronic components to circuit boards, and Brian to paint in the disused toilets in the company car park which had been reclaimed as an artist's studio. The portrait was almost finished and thereafter, for a percentage of proceeds from future work, Brian could continue to use the premises. As far as Brian was concerned, his next project was to be a canvas of a nude Georgie, though despite her propensity to nakedness, it was clear she saw through the hidden agenda of the suggestion.

By pub closing time I felt comfortable with my homeless companions, which was to a large extent promoted by the amount of beer I had consumed. Thanks to Georgie's generosity, we staggered back to the Jubilee and had to curb our loudness and steady our gaits as we passed reception, in case Jazz imposed the house rule about prohibiting entry to drunken guests.

As I climbed onto my bunk, for the first time I felt some comfort with my present life. Today I had: tolerated my second stint of begging; fought off an unexplained attempt at male rape; eaten to satisfaction at Pizzaland; discovered a significant part of my history; and unexpectedly enjoyed an evening with newfound friends. Tomorrow looked positive too: I might make progress in uncovering my past from Adrian and possibly Luther, and I would be seeing Charlotte. In theory, only the begging boredom would hinder my day, but I didn't know that Wednesday would totally reverse the optimism growing in my mind.

Chapter 27

SECOND WEDNESDAY – 5:00 a.m.

The miserable weather gave warning of how the day might turn out. The downpour of rain was so loud on the windows of the dorm, that when I joined the sleep-disturbed early starters in the kitchen, I discovered the monsoonal alarm call had fooled us into rising at five o'clock. An hour earlier than I needed, but it gave me the time to drink a couple of hot black coffees to clear my head and quench the residual effects of my alcoholic dehydration.

I called at the office on my way out to check if there were any umbrellas or raincoats to borrow. The light coat I had was no match for the weather outside and I rued not pursuing my waterproof and hooded, albeit blood-stained, jacket three nights ago. Jazz checked the offal cupboard and found nothing appropriate, but I chose a thin brown sweater and put it on underneath my jacket to act as an additional barrier to the downpour I was about to endure. She enquired after Charlotte and I relayed the latest information I had.

On the walk to Stepney Green underground station, I kept close to buildings seeking shelter wherever possible from doorways and awnings to minimize my drenching, but when I arrived at my pitch, I was soaked through. The rain had saturated my coat – even permeated my sweater in places – and the top of my legs and backside were cold and damp with water that had dripped from the bottom of my coat. The chill also served to remind my left thigh it hadn't fully recovered from its injury. My usual spot outside the station offered no respite from the rain so I risked eviction by perching just inside the station entrance. The position gave protection from the weather, but impacted on my takings by hiding me from the natural flow of commuters, which I accepted was a fair trade of returns.

I wondered what the day would bring. With luck, this might be my last stint of begging. By tonight I might have a real name and then it would be a simple matter to return to my former life – wouldn't it? My name would surely be on a missing persons list by now. If it wasn't, I suppose I would have to search through phone books or electoral registers. What if my name was John Smith? How on earth would I discover who was the real me? A photographic match would do it and assuming I had a passport, that would be the best starting point. My mind said I was familiar with the process of applying for a passport: two photographs had to be supplied and the passport office kept one, and I knew there was a passport office in London. If I was right about the guesses at my background, at the age of 25 I must have been abroad at some time. Concluding my course of action cheered me, though if my name were unusual like Archibald Twinkletoes, my task would be a lot easier. If Adrian couldn't use his influence to obtain the information I needed, then come next Monday, I would be on the doorstep of Abbeydale primary school. And there was still the possibility Luther might uncover a lead. I was almost tempted there and then to give up my begging exercise and dash back to the Jubilee to pester Adrian; yet, whatever the day brought, I would need money, so with my best pleading expression I settled to the task of encouraging the rich to give to the poor.

During the next three hours, I discovered that bad weather must be the bane of the begging community. Punters were moody and desperate to get out of the rain, thoughts of charity cast from their mind. Even those that sought shelter in the station foyer kept their distance from my bedraggled torso squatting in the corner. Despite not getting wetter, my drying-out process proceeded at a snail's pace, and I received little psychological warmth from the infrequent and small denomination donations deposited in my beret. At best, I was a £1 richer and with commission due to the Fourth Man, I calculated that if the situation didn't improve before the end of the day, there was a chance I was on the verge of negative liquidity, and I smiled at the thought of proclaiming my bankruptcy to Luther. I was still smiling when the man himself appeared at the station entrance. He looked hassled and wet.

'Luther, over here,' I called.

He strode towards me. 'Collect your things and follow me,' he growled.

'What's up? Have you …'

'NOW,' he shouted. Inquisitive eyes stared from the station shop.

I folded my coin-laden beret and tucked it into my damp coat pocket. Then I folded my pleading board and placed it with my paperback into my duffle bag.

'Come on,' Luther yelled impatiently. He turned right out of the station and set off briskly down the road. I hobbled in his wake held back by beggar's squatting cramp and twingeing thigh. I caught up with him when he stopped under the canopy of a betting shop. Little rivulets of rain were glistening on the bald part of his head, reflecting the neon lights in the shop window, but his face was dark with anger.

'I'm not usually conciliatory to lying scum like you, but you have one hour to go underground before I put the cops on to you. And if I ever see you in the area again, I'll take great pleasure in personally arresting you. Now fuck off.'

I ran my hand over my face to remove drops of rain. 'Christ Luther, what have you found out?'

'Everything about your sordid past and present. It's no wonder you wanted to fake losing your memory. I'd do the same if my history was as notorious as yours.'

'What history? What have I done? Where did you get this information?'

'I have to spell it out to you, do I?'

'Yes. I've really no recollection beyond a week ago.'

'You're a sick fucker who's spun me a load of lies. You are wanted for drug offences, are a suspect in the murder of a drug dealer ...'

'Impossible. There must be a mistake. Who told you that?'

'There's no mistake. DI Bradley says there's been a fingerprint match. And there's more. They want to talk to you about Gannet's death and apparently you raped a woman yesterday.'

'That's all a load of crap manufactured by Bradley. When did you see him?'

'He and a couple of his stooges were at the Jubilee when I called in looking for you earlier. They were questioning everyone as to your whereabouts and grilled me for fifteen minutes. They knew I knew, but the rule of the homeless is you don't split on your mates, even the sick ones. But the bastards will wear somebody down; it wouldn't surprise me if they were on their way to the station already. They didn't follow me though. They know I'm too slippery for them, but I'm not hanging around to be seen with you. You're on your own and I hope they catch up with you.'

Luther looked up and down the street, thought for a moment, then disappeared right at almost a jogging pace. I slunk back into the doorway of the shop rapidly trying to assimilate what I had just heard. The accusations had to be rubbish and my first thought was to confront them and let the justice system take its course. But presumably the fabricated evidence against me was sufficiently sound to detain me in custody, and without friends or family to come to my aid, I would have no means of clearing my name. With the leads I had, surely even as a fugitive, I could gather information in my defence. First priority was to get away from the immediate area. I guessed any search for me would be confined to places I was known to frequent – a big list of three: the Jubilee; Stepney Green station and the Royal London Hospital, all along or south of the Mile End Road, so I decided to head north for my safe haven.

I self-consciously donned my beret as a weak disguise, turned west along Mile End road and then took the first turning right. I hurried, concentrating more on vigilance than on a plan for my freedom. In my travels so far, I couldn't recall ever seeing a policeman or police car, yet now I was trying to avoid them, they – or rather their counterparts – appeared to be everywhere. My stomach churned every time I saw a uniform, spied a distinctly marked car or van, or heard a siren; though the majority were other non-regulatory officials or emergency vehicles. On the positive side, it had stopped raining and, after zigzagging through streets for fifteen minutes, I turned through a gate into Haggerston Park. The weather must have deterred the nature lovers, so I had a choice of any of the green painted seats. I chose one facing away from the road and partially hidden behind an evergreen bush, brushed the water away with my hand and sat down to think.

So, the cunning temptress had reported me for raping her. Was this how she sought retribution on her unwilling partners? Or had it been a set-up that had failed? If so, orchestrated by whom and for what reason? She had obviously notified the police with my name and description, but it had taken until today for them to look for me. Maybe they had tentatively earmarked me as a suspect regarding Gannet's death and the rape had eventually spurred the police into action. Were these two events connected in some way? Had I been correct about the possibility of Bradley wanting me out of the way? But why?

However, these events were trivial and defendable in comparison to the drug offences Luther had mentioned. He knew I had nothing to do with Gannet and he must have reasoned I was no rapist; the mysterious drug angle had turned him against me. From where did Bradley conjure that information and a matching set of fingerprints? Was it possible to fake a set of prints? At the hospital, Bradley had said there was no match against existing records, but what if some had recently become available? I shivered as I remembered the déjà vu feeling when Bradley took my prints. Suppose they had been taken in my not-so-distant past? It might account for the remembrance and that they had only recently been filed on the police computers. The possible explanation was revealing and shocking. Maybe the doctors' diagnoses had been right after all – my suppressed memory was a result of shutting out something awful before my mugging. Something connected with drugs and a murder. I shook my head and said 'No, No' to an empty park. That couldn't be true. I didn't feel any guilt, but perhaps a hardened criminal never felt guilt for any of his wrongdoings. Maybe it was only a matter of time before my recidivistic tendencies took hold. Despair descended upon me, as did another downpour of rain from the swirling black clouds overhead so I moved to shelter under the veranda of a worker's shed to complete my deliberations.

I knew as a fugitive the police would eventually track me down. No doubt by tomorrow my description would be with every copper and homeless refuge in the area. I could attempt to flee by public transport, but that would need money. Maybe I could hitchhike? But going away wasn't the answer; the few clues to my past were local, so for the time being I would have to carefully balance my concealment with exposure to information sources. Following up the school connection via Adrian was my immediate priority, but contacting him was now fraught with danger. I couldn't go to the Jubilee or anywhere nearby. The Jubilee was possibly being watched or someone was bound to split on me if I were seen. Even if I could contact Adrian, say by telephone, he may have been primed to seek a meeting with me as a trap. Ideally, I needed a go-between and who better than Charlotte? She would be a perfect ally and with her own concerns about Bradley's integrity, if she had heard the news about me, she wouldn't have been taken in by his drugs story. I set off to look for a telephone box.

Two blocks away at a busy intersection I found one, located the number for the Royal London hospital and selecting a few silver coins from my money belt, made the call. Within a minute, I was speaking to a nurse on the Helen Raphael ward who went to find Charlotte.

'Hello?' Uncertainty.

'Charlotte? It's Robin.'

'… Yes?' Hesitation.

'I need your help. Can I meet you somewhere in about half an hour? Away from the hospital.'

More hesitation. 'Oh … hello Sandra. Yes, I did leave my gloves behind.'

What was she talking about? 'Are you okay? It's me … Robin.'

'No. Don't bother; I have another pair.'

Either she had flipped or she was trying to signal to me. 'You do recognize that it's Robin … Robin Forest talking to you?'

'Of course.'

'Is it difficult to speak to me now? Do you have someone with you?'

'Yes, that's right. I'm sure it's nothing to worry about. Why don't you ring me later when you return from the doctors.'

Clever girl. I understood what she was trying to do. 'Is Bradley there with you?'

'No, but that's close to the truth.'

'Is there … another policeman … asking questions about me?'

'Yes.'

'And he said I'm wanted for drug offences?'

'Yes, isn't that awful?' She said in a sympathetic rather than a critical way.

'I'm sure there's a mistake, but I think the story must come from my past. Has he mentioned the real name of who they are looking for?'

'No, I'm afraid not.'

'If you can discover that piece of information, it would help enormously.'

'Yes, I understand.'

'So, could you meet me in half an hour?'

'I shouldn't think so. You'll need four times as much as that.'

Without a watch, I didn't know the time, but I guessed about ten-thirty. 'You don't have to respond to this, but I don't want to meet you in the hospital in case it's being watched. Then again, I don't suppose you want to leave the hospital for too long. I noticed when I last visited you there was a side entrance in Mount Street. How about if I meet you there at ... twelve-thirty? If you think you're being followed or there are any problems, stand outside with your arms folded.'

'Perfect. If there's anything else I can do for you Sandra, you will ask won't you?'

'Well done Charlotte. That's all for now.'

'Okay. I'll hear from you later. Bye.'

I was relieved from our coded conversation that Charlotte appeared to be on my side. All I had to do now was to keep scarce for the next two hours. I wondered how seriously the police were taking my disappearance. Were there droves of constables combing the East End right now? They would have a detailed description of me from Bradley's visit while I was in hospital. I wasn't equipped to effect a change in my appearance though, and the stupid beret I was wearing (a personal opinion from my past presumably) and the stubble on my chin – now almost a beard – would do little to conceal me. I looked outside from the dry confines of the telephone box. There were umbrellaed people on the street, but no police in sight or anyone observing me. I pulled up my coat collar, stepped out and backtracked hurriedly towards the sanctuary of the park. I resisted the temptation from the smells oozing from a café, but then paused outside a public launderette. I peered through the window and noticed the shop was currently unoccupied, although some machines were clearly in operation. I opened the door and the warmth of the air invited me to enter. I made my way to the far end of the shop and chose a seat positioned behind an industrial sized tumble drier and next to a red-hot radiator. On the facing wall was a large clock, which showed ten minutes to eleven.

I took off my damp jacket and hung it over the radiator and then stood with my legs pressed against the white painted metal. Within a few minutes, small puffs of steam began to rise as the heat penetrated my clothes. I was beginning to feel more comfortable when I heard the shop door open and I instantly became a statute, breathing as lightly as I could.

'Forest? You in 'ere?'

I heard the door close and then approaching footsteps.

'Ah, there you are. Can't hide from me mate,' Sniffy said as he came into view.

'What are you doing here?' I said looking over his shoulder in case anyone was with him.

'Just doing me job; keeping an eye on ya.'

'How did you know I was here?'

'Man of my skill could tag a snowman in a blizzard. Wuz easy. So what ya been up to? You upset Luther then phoned yer Mum?'

'Why have you been following me?'

'Boss said I 'ad to follow ya since ya failed the test yesterday. Find out what 'e's up to, 'e said, then offer 'im a deal.'

'What test? What deal? What are you talking about?'

Sniffy sniffed and then laughed so loud I looked towards the door in case anyone passing had heard.

'Ya know yer in a spot of bovver with the cops, don't ya?

I kept silent unsure of where this was leading.

'I 'spose Luther tipped ya off. That's why yer on the run.'

'And what exactly do you know?'

'Ya poor bastard. Fancy not being able to get it up Stella. I'd 'ave no trouble given the chance.'

'How do you know about that?'

Sniffy smiled and attempted to wink conspiratorially, but it came across as a twitch.

'Christ. You were at Stellas? I bloody knew it. It was a set-up, wasn't it?'

'Really couldn't say. Anyway ... it's up to the cops to sort out now.' Sniffy was beaming with the game he was playing with me.

'What's there to sort out?' I tried innocently.

Sniffy chose not to sniff this time, preferring to wipe his nose on the sleeve of his jacket. 'The rape charge of course. Yer sunk when they catch ya.'

'You and I know that's a load of bollocks. Nothing happened.'

'Stella says otherwise; so does the witness.' Sniffy now had a sickly grin. I wanted to physically remove it, but I felt there was a bottom line coming.

'The witness is presumably you?'

The grin grew wider.

'So cut to the chase Sniffy. You said there was a deal.'

'Of course ... Stella and 'er witness could withdraw their stories in exchange for a few favours.'

'What kind of favours?'

'I'm sure the Boss has a few things in mind which would be a lesser evil than doing stir for rape.'

'I need to think about that. How can I contact you?'

'You've got a day – that's all; assuming the fuzz haven't caught ya by then. I'll meet ya here, tomorrow, midday.'

'I need two questions answered though.'

'I'm not sure whether yer in a position to get questions answered. Try me.'

'Why so much interest in recruiting me?'

'My personal recommendation from our first meeting and it's known ya can handle yerself. Word's got round about yer fight at the Howling Wolf.'

'Okay. If I'd had Stella, would I have passed the test? And then what would have happened?'

'That's three questions, but who's counting? Ya would still be on a rape charge, but I would also 'ave photos of ya at it, which might prove useful sometime in the future.'

I wasn't satisfied by his answers, but felt it was as far as I would get in this session. Anyway I wanted Sniffy out of here. He gave me the creeps and I thought perhaps I'd underestimated his abilities – or rather his influence – from our first encounter. 'I'll see you tomorrow then,' I said, hoping I would be left to complete my drying out process. Yet Sniffy just stood there staring at me and I stared back. He cracked first.

'I'm still waiting for answers to my questions.'

I thought back on our conversation and realized I needed to vary the truth a little. 'Luther said the police had called at the Jubilee looking for me in connection with a rape. He was a bit pissed about that and told me to disappear. The phone call was … to a hostel in North London to check they had vacancies. I thought it would be safer away from this area.'

'And yer here to dry out before ya move on there?'

A good reason, so I nodded agreement.

'And yer come back here tomorrow?'

'Absolutely. It sounds like my best option,' I said to encourage his confidence in me.

'Right then I'll leave ya to get warm. Midday, tomorrow,' Sniffy said and swaggered to the door, opened it and turned right along the street. I waited twenty seconds then rushed to the door to watch him disappear into the distance to ensure he wasn't laying in wait to follow me again.

Several aspects of this encounter puzzled me. Stella had deliberately reported her "rape" to the police and it had reached the ears of Bradley. Yet if this was a plan instigated by Ronnie Kent, and Bradley was in his pay, wouldn't Ronnie, and therefore Sniffy, know about the other accusations against me? If they did, what was the point of setting me up with Stella? In their eyes I would already be a criminal who would gladly exchange refuge for a few favours. I had to conclude that whatever the connection between the police and Kent, their information network either wasn't timely or complete.

My recruitment was an enigma too. Was Kent's organization so desperate for servants to his cause that a relatively unknown homeless person was being blackmailed to join? My street cred had only been peripherally examined. Wouldn't my background need study too? I could be an uncorrupted police spy set to infiltrate the Kent camp.

And the biggest puzzle of all – did any of these events relate to my apparent abduction and mugging? It seemed unlikely. Bradley had pointed the finger at Ronnie Kent, which would be a strange thing to do if they were in collusion. It possibly explained why Ronnie (via Sniffy) had not realized that his muggee of ten days ago and the Robin Forest he was trying to recruit, were the same person.

As I steamed to comfort on the radiator, I continued to debate the solutions in my head. Whichever way I analyzed the information there were too many unknown variables to solve this complex equation. Then my concentration was disturbed and the security of my hiding place breached when two customers returned to collect their wash loads. An old woman who kept looking nervously over her shoulder at me, and a man of my age who I was sure was considering engaging me in conversation. The tension of discovery became too intense so I fled back to the glisteningly wet street ensuring I averted my face from the interlopers.

Chapter 28

SECOND WEDNESDAY – 11:30 a.m.

With another hour to kill, I strode meanderingly south towards the hospital, this time vigilant for police and the presence of Sniffy behind. Many times I ducked into shop entrances and alleyways to await the arrival of a tail, but none came. Via Whitechapel Station to check the time, I reached the Mount Street rendezvous approximately ten minutes early. I took shelter from the rain and observed from an entranceway in an office block opposite. Office workers came and went, but fortunately no one seemed interested in me. Even the building concierge came out once, looked around, nodded to me and then went inside again. So my vigil continued untroubled for ten minutes ... then twenty ... thirty. At forty minutes – half an hour beyond our scheduled meeting time – a small panic began to take hold of me. I had placed my reliance on Charlotte turning up and without her as an ally I didn't currently have a plan B. I extended my lateness tolerance minute by minute as I considered my options, or rather option, since I kept coming back to the only thing I could do – telephone Charlotte again. Then she appeared at the top of a small flight of stone steps that led from street level to the side entrance. I resisted the temptation to rush across the road, fearful we were being watched. She kept looking up and down the street apparently unaware I might be directly opposite. Her arms were unfolded, but nonetheless I stayed put for a couple of minutes sneaking looks from my hiding place behind a marble pillar, before venturing across the road. She saw me approaching and beckoned with her hand to follow her inside. It was gloomy as I entered the hospital, and at first, I couldn't see Charlotte and then I heard a hushed call.

'Robin ... Robin ... I'm here.'

I followed the sound left and spied Charlotte in an alcove beneath a grand wooden staircase.

'What have you found out?' I asked eagerly.

'Not a great deal I'm afraid ... in fact what I do have, came from Kathy.'

'She's spoken again?'

'Yes and she's been sitting up and taking light food, but she is still very woozy. I'm so happy for her Robin. The doctor thinks she will make a full recovery,' Charlotte said with a cheerful tone and then immediately became sombre. 'But I'm anxious about her safety. She has key information about the drug ring and I don't know who to trust anymore.'

'What does she know exactly?'

'The night she was planning to break into the secret room at BioRemedy, she observed an unmarked van draw up outside. It stopped adjacent to a door, which was possibly another entrance to the secret room. There was a flurry of urgent activity to load heavy cardboard boxes onto the van. She phoned her police contact number to report what was happening and was told to do nothing but wait for police backup. While she was watching and waiting, the mobile phone of the skinny man overseeing the loading rang. He answered it with the name of "Ronnie Kent" and then said "Chad, why the fuck are you ringing me now of all times?" He then listened for a moment before talking agitatedly, albeit at a subdued level Kathy couldn't hear. Ronnie finished the call, issued instructions to his colleagues and then seconds later three men burst into Kathy's lab. Before she had a chance to react, they had bound and gagged her, and thrown her into the back of the van. That's the last she remembers.'

'You've drawn the same conclusion as me?'

'Assuming Chad is Detective Superintendent Chadwick Dixon, somehow he intercepted Kathy's call and tipped off Ronnie Kent.'

'Christ, that's key evidence. Who have you told?'

'You're the first. I only heard this last night. I was wondering what to do this morning when a policeman turned up to interview me about you.'

'Who knows Kathy is awake and talking?'

'Some of the staff here.'

'Could they have leaked anything to Bradley?'

'I don't think so. As far as I'm aware, only Elsie and I have been asked by Bradley to advise him when Kathy is conscious. I trust Elsie; she's aware of my concerns about Kathy's safety.'

'Could the copper this morning have heard about Kathy?'

'No. I spoke to him in the corridor and he was only concerned with your whereabouts. I gained the impression he didn't know anything about Kathy's circumstances.'

'And when was Bradley last here?'

'He called in yesterday morning. Presumably since then he's been too busy looking for you. After all, according to DC Dryland you are a double murderer, a drug dealer and a rapist. Do you have your alibis lined up or should I turn you in now?' Charlotte looked serious for a moment.

'What exactly did Dryland say?'

'He was vague at first. He said the police needed to locate you urgently to help them with enquiries and it was known you had recently visited me at the hospital. Because of Kathy's revelations, I was suspicious about his motives, so I was vague too. I said that I assumed you were at the Jubilee and if I saw you, I would pass on the message. But he looked troubled and added I should avoid contact with you because you were possibly a dangerous criminal. I said that was impossible. You came across as a kind person who had fallen on bad times because of your amnesia, and I insisted he qualify his accusations. He then said you were wanted in connection with two murders, a rape and drug offences. I pushed for details, but he wouldn't say anymore. What are the details Robin?'

I told her all I knew starting with my recent confrontations with Sniffy and Luther. She was sympathetic about the Gannet accusation since I'd mentioned his death previously, but was shocked (or jealous?) with her perception of my naivety in my encounter with Stella.

'I'm sorry Charlotte. My only excuse is it seems I've already succumbed to the habits of street people. It was the prospect of money or food that attracted me, not her. I had no idea she had a hidden agenda.'

Charlotte still looked doubtful.

'Look, I'll be completely honest with you. If my affections weren't placed somewhere else, then maybe I would have been tempted by her advances, but all I could think of while it was going on was … you.' There, I'd said it. A spur of the moment statement not designed to find favour, but one from the heart. I immediately wondered if she thought it was the former or the latter, but her response yielded nothing.

'And the drug business?'

'I don't know … really. The apparent fingerprint match is pretty damning, but I don't remember a thing before last Tuesday. I'm not a criminal and I've had nothing to do with drugs. My head says so, but I can't prove it to you.'

Charlotte sighed. 'I must be crazy. My sister's been at death's door because of drugs and I'm apparently associating with a major contributor to the drug's underworld. God help me, but my intuition says you are innocent … If I'm wrong then I'll do everything I can to make sure you rot in hell.'

Her last sentence was bitter and seemed final. A moment of silence followed, where I didn't know what to say and feared Charlotte was waiting for me to leave.

Eventually she said: 'How can I help you?'

'First help yourself. You must keep knowledge of Kathy's recovery secret for the time being; at least until you know whose side Bradley is on.'

'And how do I find that out?'

167

'I'm hoping to find out via Sniffy, but I don't know how long that will take. In the meantime speak to Luther at the Jubilee …'

'You're joking. Luther would sell his own mother to make money.'

'Hear me out. I know Luther is a villain and doesn't like you, but he is so anti-drugs and has the ear of the police. He might not know if Bradley or Dixon is involved, but I'm sure he will know a high-ranking copper who isn't corruptible that you could trust. Don't say I recommended you speak to him, it might dissuade him from helping you. Also contact Adrian...'

I went on to explain yesterday's revealing afternoon with Keith and how Adrian had offered to try to discover my identity. 'Adrian may have found out something by now. Be careful though. I think he's a decent guy, but the police may have turned him against me. Also, if the fingerprint story is true the police must have a real name for me. When they visit you again, do your best to get more information.

'You'd better return to Kathy now. Make sure she understands the importance of feigning recovery and forgetting what happened to her, just in case the police try to interview her when you're not at her side. Phone the Jubilee as soon as you can and ask Adrian or Luther to come here. I'll phone you later for an update.'

'Where will you be?'

'Not too far away, but out of sight.'

'Did you mean what you said earlier?'

I frowned puzzlement. 'About what?'

'Your … affections,' she replied awkwardly.

She looked the way I felt, sad and tired. I reached out nervously and put my arms around her. She stood like a statue for a moment then relaxed and nestled her head on my chest. 'Yes,' I said, 'and if I get out of the mess I'm in, I'll prove it to you.'

We stayed that way for a minute, holding each other gently, a comforting embrace that might be experienced between brother and sister. I wanted it to be more and hoped Charlotte felt the same way, but we knew our circumstances prohibited any deeper expression. Then she broke away and with a plea for me to take care, disappeared down the corridor.

When I went outside the rain had stopped and there were patches of blue appearing through the lightening grey clouds. Panglossian reappeared in my head and as I walked quickly west along Whitechapel Road, choosing to conceal myself in the crowds of the busy thoroughfare, I attempted to analyze the reason. The word's connection with my past failed me, but the meaning persisted. A sudden euphoria had consumed me. It shouldn't have been like that. Here I was a fugitive from the law accused of heinous crimes, yet my outlook was full of optimism. I was convinced I was about to discover my true identity and I believed with it an exoneration of indictments against me. No doubt, the less inclement weather helped too, but the overriding influence was surely the few moments I had held Charlotte in my arms?

I headed towards Liverpool Street station. The attraction was that it would be bustling and I would feel less exposed in a crowd of people rather than pacing lonely roads. I made my first ports of call to the sandwich and bakery kiosks asking for cheap or free out-of-date food (a tip I'd picked up from Free), but it must have been too early for cast offs and I came away empty handed. I wasn't starving and could afford a decent meal, but I was mindful of the days ahead. Begging for income wouldn't be a safe option and I would need money for phone calls and who knew what else. I would have loved a cup of coffee, but I visited the public toilets instead and slurped water from the cold tap. I considered touring the waste bins for a newspaper or food rejects, however Liverpool Street was now a modern station devoid of receptacles presumably to forestall the deposit of suspicious packages. Did commuters really take their waste home for disposal?

I paced up and down for a while, and every now and again looked up at the clock on the departures board. I wanted to give Charlotte a couple of hours to make contact with Luther and Adrian before I called again, but time dragged and I became bored with the station. I stepped outside to wander the streets, passing the Stock Exchange and the Bank of England then killed time by people-watching at Bank station. I chose a different route back to Liverpool Street and as I was waiting to cross Apollo Street, I glanced at the building opposite and noticed a familiar name – Winston Investments. Of course, a few days ago Luther had told me about one of his past disciples – Howard Winston – who had made good in the City. As I crossed the road, I distractedly hit on an idea and was almost run down by a despatch rider in a hurry. I entered the modern lobby of an old building bedecked in marble, glass and leather, and enquired at the pivotal circular mahogany reception desk. The mature bespectacled woman smiled her corporate smile, but her voice betrayed her suspicion and contempt.

'Can I help ... you?'

'Would Mr. Winston, Mr. Howard Winston be available?' I asked.

'Is he expecting you?'

'No, but ...'

'Mr. Winston doesn't entertain casual visitors. You'll have to phone for an appointment,' she said dismissively.

I tried a bluff. 'I'm sure Howard would see me if he knew I was here. Perhaps you could relay a message to him?' She reached for a notepad. 'Now. It's very important,' I added loudly and as authoritatively as I could. She looked to her right towards a uniformed security guard who was positioned by the lifts perhaps checking he was close by in case I became abusive.

'I'll phone his secretary. Your name is?'

'My name is Robin Forest, but you need to mention I am a close friend of Luther Browncast.'

She dialed a number. 'Jo, I have … um … a street person … in reception who is asking to see Mr. Winston ... Yes, I know … Robin Forest … He says he is a friend of a Luther Browncast … smells a bit … He's very insistent … Yes, I'll hold.'

She avoided my eyes while she waited for a response. This was the first time I'd been recognized openly as a street person. I caught my reflection in a square pillar that had ceiling high mirrors on all four sides. I did look a sorry state: my hair was untidy and matted from the rain; the stubble on my face gave me a dark – sinister even – unclean appearance; my clothes were crumpled; my stance looked weary like I'd run a marathon, and I detected an odour about me, not BO more like stale rain.

'Yes … Really? … Okay, I'll tell him.' The surprised receptionist finished her call. 'Mr. Winston will see you now. Take the lift to the third floor. His secretary will meet you.'

As I stepped out of the lift a younger woman, unprejudiced by my appearance, greeted me warmly and I followed her down a deep-pile carpeted corridor. We entered a glass-panelled secretarial area where she knocked on a stout door above which there was a red light shining. When the light went green, she opened the door and ushered me in. From the prevailing décor I expected a plush office. It was brightly lit, but contained simple furnishings and a plain wooden desk, behind which sat a tall, rakish man of about fifty and wearing glass-bottomed spectacles. He rose and came to shake my hand. At first sight, he appeared deeply tanned, but as he approached, I saw the dark wrinkled patches of skin that covered his face – the Falklands burns Luther had mentioned.

'Good afternoon, young man, please sit down,' he said and pointed to a high-backed chair in front of the desk. 'How is that contemporary Fagin these days? I haven't seen him for a few years. Still up to his old tricks?'

We sat down. 'He's fine, sir. Saving homeless souls such as myself.'

'Call me Howard by the way. Luther sent you to see me?'

'Not exactly, but he said you were now a key man in the financial world. I'm here on the off chance you might be able to help me.'

'You have some money to invest? Sorry … poor joke, carry on.'

I told Howard about how I became homeless, keeping the story as simple as possible and omitting the build-up to my current predicament. I dwelt on my suspected links with the world of finance and in particular, the affinity I might have with the Ferndown or Milton Cern insurance companies. Despite the bizarre tale, Howard was attentive and nodded in a few places. When I'd finished he sat back in his chair and placed his hands together as though he was praying.

'I'll tell you one thing for nothing – you certainly don't belong on the streets. That's obvious from your delivery. Degree education I would guess and from London. However, it's not immediately obvious to me as to how I can assist you.'

'I was wondering if you had any contacts at Ferndown or Milton Cern who might be in a position to tell you whether any of their employees had ... well ... gone missing or maybe had a nervous breakdown in recent weeks. I know it's a long shot, but I don't exactly have many avenues to pursue about my identity.' I did have a few of course, but I didn't want them to jeopardize the co-operation I was seeking from Howard.

'Coincidentally I do know the Financial Directors at both companies. Between you and me, I have been speaking to them recently about the speculations in the press; seeking clues that might aid the investment strategy of my portfolio managers. I take 25 percent of their commission earnings for every piece of profitable information I give them,' he said smugly, and I wondered whether the scheme was his invention or Luther's. 'Anyway, why haven't you contacted them yourself?'

'I didn't think there was much point. What would you do? A strange person rings you up and says his current name is Robin Forest. He doesn't know his real name, but he may have worked at your company some time ago and then disappeared without trace. Who is he? It sounds ridiculous.'

'Isn't that what you are asking me to do?'

'The difference is, you are a respectable person. If you pose a question, someone will listen and respond. I'd be treated as a crank and have the phone put down on me.'

'But each company employs thousands of staff.'

'Yes, but how many suddenly go missing? Not many I'd bet.'

'What would you bet?'

'Sorry? I don't follow you.'

'I used to be a betting man and it was almost my downfall. I don't gamble anymore because investing in stocks and shares is a science. Gather intelligence about your market, analyze trends, spread the risk and I'll guarantee a rate of return way above the market average. It's rigorous and sometimes mundane, but you can't beat the excitement of a wager with unknown odds. I'll never stake money on such an event again, but if I'm to help you, I want some reward. You presumably can't pay me in cash so how about staking yourself?'

I didn't like the sound of that. It smacked of one of Luther's perverted schemes, but I was intrigued by the offer. 'Meaning?' I asked.

'I am renowned for my judge of character. I am always involved in the recruitment process of my senior staff by interviewing them personally. Without exception every person I have employed has been loyal, reliable and a credit to my company. Despite your present state, I recognize a similar quality in you. If I succeed in discovering who you are I insist you pay me back by joining Winston Investments. If I don't, I still want you to join Winston Investments, but it would be your call.'

'What would you pay me?'

'Enough. Commensurate with my perception of your abilities.'

'I might be worth more?'

'That's the magic of the bet. I might be winning a whiz kid or a dodo. You might earn a packet or a pittance. You decide.'

I couldn't believe my ears. A vagrant had turned up on the doorstep of the head of a prestigious City company and within minutes, they were playing employment power games. This was bizarre. The man was crazy or he knew more about me than he was letting on. At the moment I couldn't hazard a guess at where the truth lay, but what did I have to lose?

'Go for it,' I said.

He picked up the phone and asked his secretary to contact the Finance Director at Milton Cern. When connected, he explained the situation and sought an introduction to the Personnel Director, who then promised to phone him back within the hour. He did the same with Ferndown and was put straight through to Paul Richardson, its Human Resources Director. From the conversation, I detected he was boasting about the sophistication of his personnel system, and that if Howard held for a few minutes, he would give him an answer.

'Pop outside and ask my secretary to fetch refreshments while I'm waiting, would you?'

I did as he asked, and as I was returning, there was a buzzing in my head. My immediate thought was that it was coming from one of the neon tubes on the ceiling, but then I felt a slight tingling on my scalp, followed by a dizziness that forced me to grab the back of my chair to steady myself.

'Are you okay?' Howard asked.

There was a vision in my head: a brightly lit office, like this one. I was nervous. There was a man interviewing me. This flashback was different to the others though. I was convinced the earlier ones had come from the recent past. This emanated from another part of my brain, more distant, years ago. 'Paul Richardson … I know him,' I stuttered.

Howard looked apprehensive and motioned me to sit down. As I did so, the mental picture changed to one I had seen before – a black-haired girl in a café.

'Ask him if his secretary is called … Julie. Yes, Julie,' I said excitedly.

Howard nodded and then there was a response from the phone. 'Yes Paul, I'm here … I see … You're certain? … No, that's okay … I'm much obliged to you. One final question: Could you tell me name of your secretary? … It's all to do with the same enquiry … Thanks again … Goodbye.'

I couldn't contain my anticipation. 'Well, who am I?'

Howard's face betrayed both our disappointments. 'Ferndown have no record of any missing employees. A number, as you would expect, are on scheduled holidays. Four employees are on long-term sickness – three women and one man close to retirement. Paul's secretary is called Debbie Roberts.'

There had to be a mistake. I was as certain as I could be that I had found the link I was looking for. I didn't know what to say and was saved from an inadequate response as Howard's secretary arrived with coffee and biscuits. When she had gone Howard said, 'Don't despair. We've yet to hear from Milton Cern.'

'I'm not hopeful. Ferndown, Paul Richardson and Julie …' There was another flash, '… Julie Rawlinson – that was her full name – all meant something to me. How far did they go back in their records?'

'Paul mentioned he'd searched back over the last 12 months, which if you've been anonymous for about two weeks is presumably long enough?'

'I suppose so. But maybe I didn't go missing. Perhaps I'm on their records as being on holiday. I might have been fired or I resigned.'

'It's a possibility, but how many people would match that criteria? Besides, your Julie connection failed too. I'm sorry Robin, I think you must be on a false trail.'

The phone rang. I drank my coffee and pocketed the biscuits for later. I eavesdropped the conversation with Milton Cern, but it was another blank – no missing persons, no delinquent employees. Dejected, I stood up to leave. 'Thanks, Howard, I'm sorry to have wasted your time. I've a few more ideas to follow up, so I'd better be off.'

'What if you are right about Ferndown? I could try one other avenue. Sit down for a moment.' Howard picked up his phone and asked someone to come to his office. 'One of my IT guys is popping up. I'll get him to take your photograph with a digital camera. I'll e-mail the image to Paul Richardson and ask him to check it against his records. It's worth a try. How can I contact you?'

I thanked Howard again and said it would be easier if I contacted him instead. He reiterated his offer of a job and I promised I would consider it when I resolved my identity problem. I washed first in a cloakroom and tidied my hair with a borrowed comb. Then I was taken down a floor to a room full of computer equipment where the IT guy acted the role of portrait photographer and took half a dozen head and shoulders shots of me. I stopped at reception on my way out.

'Howard said it would be okay if I used the phone before I left,' I said to the dragoness. A lie, but I knew she wouldn't query the request and I received great satisfaction from her discomfort. She nodded reluctantly to a spare phone on the counter.

'Where have you been? I've been worried.' Charlotte said with urgency when she came to the phone.

'I've been following a new lead about who I am. A dead-end sadly, but an interesting experience nonetheless. I'll tell you another time. Any news from your end?'

'Quite a lot ... Peter.'

My first thought was Charlotte was playing a male version of the Sandra game she had played earlier. 'You have someone with you again?'

'No, no. It's your name. Peter Shadwell,' she said excitedly.

'Adr ... Adria ... Adrian's ... he's ...found out?' I stammered.

'Yes, yes ... You sound disappointed.'

'I'm ... I'm shocked I suppose. You're sure?'

'Adrian was. The facts fitted. You started at Abbeydale Primary school 20 years ago. Your brother Andrew joined the year before you, Keith Kellerton the year after ... Hello ... Are you still there?'

'But I ... I don't feel like a Peter Shadwell. I thought the name would open a floodgate of memories, but ... there's nothing.'

'Don't force it. Relax, go for a walk. The memories will come, you have to be patient.'

'It's so frustrating though. This should be a big breakthrough not an anticlimax.'

'Do you want to hear the rest of my news?'

'Yes, of course.'

'Luther was here a couple of hours ago. I had to work hard to get him to come because he still didn't believe my situation. Now he's met Kathy and heard her story, he's full of co-operation, particularly if it means exposing police involvement in the drugs scene. His motive, I believe, is more for his kudos than bringing about justice, but who am I to argue so long as he succeeds. He guessed that you suggested I contact him, which puzzled him considering your own involvement in drugs. He said if I were to speak to you and you needed a roof over your head, to contact your artist friend. Make sense?'

I thought for a moment. 'I think so. What's Luther going to do now?'

'He's gone to see a trustworthy police friend of his, a Bill Haynes?'

'That's probably a good move. Bill's the local copper on Luther's payroll.'

I enquired after Kathy's health and was pleased to hear she was improving by the minute, although we laughed about the sudden relapse she had had a couple of hours ago, when Inspector Bradley had looked in. I wanted to be sociable with Charlotte as she was in good spirits, but I needed to think, and miss fuddy-duddy at reception was becoming overly absorbed in my conversation.

'I have to go now. It's not private here,' I said giving my observer the evil eye.

'Could you call me later, Robin ... I mean Peter?'

'I'll try to, but stick to Robin for now. Robin's a good guy, we don't know about Peter yet.

Chapter 29

SECOND WEDNESDAY – 4:45 p.m.

Peter Shadwell. Peter Shadwell. Peter Shadwell. I replayed the name repeatedly as I left Winston Investments. I should have been ecstatic. Ever since I woke up in hospital discovering my name had been the number one objective, yet now I felt uneasy. Indications were that Peter Shadwell was not as innocent as I had assumed he might be. I should now be ploughing through phone books, contacting the passport office, searching the Internet, but I dismissed the actions, I was now afraid of what I would find out. For once I had no direction, no drive and no enthusiasm for much at all. Hunger didn't help and I remembered the biscuits I had pocketed. I nibbled at them as I aimlessly strolled the streets. Avoiding Peter Shadwell, I reflected on my conversation with Charlotte. She too had reached a new phase of her life. With Kathy on the mend and hope that the perpetrators of her suffering might be brought to justice, Charlotte would be free to continue her studies. I envied the simplicity of her future.

I found myself in Shoreditch. By accident or fate I couldn't decide, yet this was the area where my artist friend – Brian – worked. I presumed he was the friend Luther had meant, and his place of work, rather than the Jubilee, was where I was supposed to contact him. It was getting dark and the streets were quieter. I'd forgotten I was a fugitive and my police vigilance had waned. I stopped and look around, fearful I was being followed or observed. Pedestrian and vehicle traffic were oblivious of me, and the resumption of rain reminded me I needed shelter for the night. How Brian might solve that problem was beyond me and I didn't know the name or address of the company where he painted, nor did I know if he kept regular office hours.

I was at the north end of Commercial Street, which was a promising name for industry, so I headed south inspecting each adjoining road for outward signs of my vision of an electronics business: modern, purpose-built two-storey structure with brightly illuminated signs. Minutes later I was attracted to a turning off the main street by virtue of the number of trucks and vans parked. It looked a likely place and sure enough, I passed a carpet warehouse, a second-hand car showroom, a DIY store and other wholesale premises before they merged disappointingly into rows of terraced houses. I was about to turn back when I noticed a Ford Transit emerge from a narrow street between a gap in the houses. Emblazoned on its side in variegated colours were the words Rainbow Electronics. I turned into the street, but it soon terminated in a cul-de-sac headed by a rectangular, red-bricked, three-storey building, which at first sight appeared to be an old school. A sign outside listed three companies one of which was Rainbow. There were the expected railings defining the perimeter and the "playground" in front was now a car park, which was busy with an exodus of people presumably about to depart for home. I stood at the main gate and observed the eager employees emerging and then on the left side of the car park I saw a single-level brick building with a corrugated iron roof. There was an entranceway at either end guarded by full height L-shaped walls. It must have been a recollection from my school days that helped me recognize the block – despite the changes – as once being an outside toilet for pupils. A skylight had been set in the roof at one end and there were two windows symmetrically placed on the facing wall. I strode over to the nearest window; the room behind was lit, but obscured by closed vertical blinds. The door adjacent to the window was ajar so I pushed it gently and called out.

'Hello? Brian?' I called speculatively.

'Come in Robin,' echoed a voice from inside.

I steered through the narrow porch and entered a room the size of a modest lounge, but the décor of, I suppose unsurprisingly, refurbished toilets without the plumbing. The interior walls were whitewashed bare brick and the floor was grey concrete scattered with a few mats made from carpet offcuts. There was a door at the far end, which presumably led to the second half of the building. The fittings were Spartan: a wooden bench strewn mostly with artist's materials, a small hand basin, a camp bed, a couple of upright chairs. An electric fan heater purring in a corner was keeping the room warm. Brian was obscured behind an easel in the centre of the room.

'You were expecting me?' I said.

A head appeared at the side of the canvas on the easel. 'Luther said you might come. Make a brew would you, I'm gasping. Kettle's on the bench somewhere.'

I dropped my duffle bag on the bed and glanced at Brian's painting. 'That's brilliant Brian. I didn't know your benefactor was a young woman.'

'The boss's daughter. I'm painting this between sittings. It's cheating really, I'm only copying a photo,' he said modestly and, with the blunt end of his brush, tapped a photograph clipped to the corner of the easel.

'Nonetheless, it's a stunning picture,' I said as I prepared the kettle.

'What do you think of my studio then?'

'Basic, functional and … bright.' I was referring to the bank of four white neon strip lights that hung from the roof.

'A painter must have light. The natural light from there,' Brian pointed up to the skylight, 'is perfect during the day, except it leaks when it rains,' then he pointed down to the bucket to his left which was catching a steady drip from above.

I commented how noisy the rain was on the metal roof.

'The sound keeps me company. It's soothing,' he said. 'Be quiet for a minute I have a tricky bit to finish.'

I made the tea and watched in awe as Brian used different brushes and colours to master the shadows on his portrait's hair. I was no expert, but Brian had undoubted talent. Satisfied, he sniffed and took a long drink from his mug of tea.

'There's a funny damp smell in here. Is it you?'

Embarrassed I said, 'Probably. I've been out in the rain a lot today.'

'Stick your butt in front of the fire, otherwise you'll catch a cold. You need to be fit when you're on the run.'

I moved to the warm corner. 'You've heard about my problems then?'

'Bit difficult to avoid with the police raid this morning. You're the talk of the Jubilee.'

'Aren't you afraid of supping tea with a notorious criminal?'

He laughed so hard he spilt tea on the concrete floor. 'If you're a notorious criminal then I'm Leonardo Da Vinci.'

'It's Luther's opinion.'

'Luther can be a prat at times. Look, us homeless folks need to scrutinize their companions closely after the way life has treated us. Everyone at the Jubilee has you down as a good guy. We don't believe a word the police said. You a rapist and a Gannet killer? What a load of bollocks.'

'And the drugs offences? Luther seemed convinced.'

'Luther is so anti-drugs he won't even take aspirin to combat a headache. He has a good reason I suppose.'

'Does he?'

'Don't you know why?'

'No.'

'His wife died of a drugs overdose. Someone mistakenly spiked her drink with a cocktail of drugs at a party. She was dead within two hours. You didn't hear it from me, okay?'

I nodded. It explained a lot.

'Anyway, Luther's on your side now. He was here an hour ago and told me the story about Charlotte's sister. I've never seen him so agitated; he was like a man possessed. Said he was going to do something he should have done a long while ago. Added that you might be turning up and I was to look after you. Then he disappeared in a great rush. So, are you staying here tonight?'

'If it's okay. Will your employer mind?'

'No. I've often stayed here myself. Sometimes I get carried away with my painting and work all night. There's heat, light, running water – only cold I'm afraid – and the box under the bench has food in it. Only things like crisps and chocolate bars, but there's a chippy five minutes down the road. If you turn up shortly before it closes at ten-thirty you can often stake a claim on any free leftovers.'

'Toilet?'

'Ah. I usually use the one in the main building, but that will be locked after about seven o'clock. You can do your number ones round the back; number twos – I'll leave to your imagination.'

We continued chatting for a couple of hours over endless mugs of tea and then coffee when the tea bags ran out. I favoured talking about Brian's past and projected future, but he was genuinely excited in my plans to avoid the police, and the resurrection of Peter Shadwell. I had little that I wanted to share. My best course of action majored on discovering why I had been mugged in the first place. That meant infiltrating Ronnie Kent's organization (unless of course Luther's efforts beat me to it), but I kept that course of action to myself. So, I talked about unlikely investigations such as phoning hospitals about appendectomy patients, visiting my old school, checking with the passport office and so on, all of which would be difficult now Peter Shadwell was on a wanted list. Soon Brian became the topic of conversation and I let him reminisce about his happier pre-alcoholic days. They had been spent in artistic and sexual bliss with his departed girlfriend coincidentally in a house in Shadwell, an East London district a few miles away. This occupied us both until Brian decided to go.

'Well, I'll leave you to it.' Brian said and made a gap in the blinds to look outside. 'The boss's light is still on. I'll tell him that his daughter's portrait will be ready tomorrow night and then I'm off to the Jubilee to see what the lovely Georgie has been up to today. Do you want to come over and use the loo?'

I did and then on the way out Brian explained the security procedures for his studio.

'I suggest you leave before eight in the morning; that's when the early shift starts. The workers know about me, but if a duty-bound employee sees a stranger coming out of the studio, they may raise the alarm. When you go, use these two keys to secure the door and hide them here.' Brian indicated the base of some wooden pallets resting against the sidewall.

Back in the studio, I quickly became restless. The room lacked any distractions for non-artists: no TV or radio, not a book or newspaper in sight. An old wind-up alarm clock kept reminding me how slowly time was passing so I made more coffee, tidied my rucksack, and washed – all to avoid thinking about Peter Shadwell. My head had a kind of fuzziness about it, which I tried to associate with hunger; yet, secretly I was convinced a torrent of memories was waiting to be unleashed and I was fretting I couldn't handle its arrival. I hadn't written in my diary since Monday so I killed almost two hours bringing it factually up to date albeit keeping away from private thoughts and speculations in case they stimulated the flood. I helped myself to a chocolate bar while writing and my stomach growled with contentment and begged for more. I checked the clock – close to chippy closing time; perhaps I could satisfy my stomach with fish and chip leftovers?

I easily found "Your Plaice or Mine" on a nearby street corner and was vexed to see there was still a queue of paying customers being served. I sheltered from the rain in a shop doorway opposite and waited patiently for the patrons to disperse, hoping the proprietor's policy was to overcook in anticipation of custom, rather than cook to order. There was a five-minute gap when no one arrived, and then I saw a white-aproned man go to the front door to flip a hanging sign from "Open" to "Closed". I hurried across the road ready to adopt my hungry and penniless look. Halfway there I saw two shabby bundles magically emerge from the shadows and shuffle at an unlikely speed towards the door. There was a sign of recognition from the man who beamed a welcome and opened the door. When he saw me gaining pace he looked uneasy and the two brown overcoated, bobble-hatted bundles turned to see the reason.

'Hey look Igor, it's the fucking nosy bastard,' said the left bundle.

'Don't worry Nikolai, he's … an anonymous friend,' said the right bundle.

The bundles were Gregor and Igor – or their English-speaking clones. They looked the same, but their accents were East London not Polish. 'Gregor? Igor?'

'Thought you'd left the country after the bother this morning,' one said.

'You want us, or some grub?' asked his brother.

'Well … er …you speak English,' I said.

'What do you expect after living here for 56 years?'

'Come in out of the rain,' Nikolai interrupted in an accent that I assumed an English-speaking Pole might have. 'You've not been fooled by these two dummerers, have you?'

I nodded embarrassingly.

'You wouldn't be the first. Now what'll you have? There's a couple of pieces of cod, haddock, sausages in batter and a dozen helpings of chips.'

I chose cod and chips, and ate while the three Poles jabbered away in their native tongue and Nikolai degreased his frying equipment. I knew they were talking about me. Periodically I caught English words and they looked my way, but they seemed at ease with an alleged murderer in their midst.

When Nikolai had finished his cleaning, he glanced to me. 'Good Polish food?'

'Excellent,' I said, though I was worried about the quantity of fat in my stomach looking at the unctuous layer on my fingers.

'Good, Good. Now you pay.'

'Pay? ... I thought ...' The Slavonic threesome laughed.

'It is Polish custom,' Nikolai said. 'Nothing is free. You pay what you can.'

'We'll pay for him. He's our guest,' said Gregor or Igor – I still couldn't tell who was who. He unbuttoned his overcoat to reveal a dark interior festooned with different sized pockets, some with bulging, unseen objects. He began feeling the lumps and occasionally put his hand into a cavity to extract and examine the contents. His coat was a repository of misplaced treasures. I saw: miscellaneous cutlery; pens and pencils; a torch; foreign bank notes; various keys; sweets; small packets of biscuits and no doubt there was a lot more, but he was satisfied when he brought out a small screwdriver with exchangeable bits stored in the handle. 'Here, this should pay for the three of us,' he said to Nikolai.

'I already have one of those,' he replied ungratefully. 'Give me three pens and we'll call it evens.'

The trade was completed and the homeless trio each took a final bag of chips. Nikolai motioned us towards the door and took a spray can of air freshener from a shelf. As we left the chippy, my last vision of Nikolai was seeing him liberally spraying the area we had occupied in the shop. I suspected the combined smell of frying oil, two tramps and me, would have been too much for anyone.

Without a goodbye, Gregor and Igor disappeared in the opposite direction and I ambled my way back eating greasy cold chips.

At the studio, I sat on the bed feeling uncomfortably full and began yawning. I was mentally tired from the day and was looking forward to sleep – the perfect means of shutting down my brain activity before the Peter Shadwell memories changed my life for better or for worse. I mustered enough energy for another wash and cleaning of teeth, but undressing was beyond me, besides, the studio was now cold and I didn't want to leave the fan heater on all night. I stretched out on the bed fully clothed and pulled the blankets over me. But sleep didn't come straightaway as I had anticipated. A tap was slowly being opened. A tiny drop of water began to form, which grew until just before it dripped, I saw in the clear reflection ... myself in a room holding a bundle of letters. Then another drop took shape, quicker this time … and there I was again in a public phone box. The third drop flashed by; not my image, but a man and a young girl. Now a trickle and mirrored in the dancing water I began to see … a woman; and the flow became stronger and wider … and I recognized … Julie; but she has disappeared as the flickering water becomes a gush … a torrent … a waterfall; and then there were too many images to take in …

Chapter 30

FIRST FRIDAY – 4:00 p.m.

The front door to my flat is difficult to open because of the stack of mail behind it and I give the door a whack with my suitcase to budge it. The pile for two weeks is less than I expect, but it shouldn't have been there in the first place if my sister-in-law had kept her promise to keep a check in my absence.

I sift through the mail. Much of it is advertising crap, which I toss it on the coffee table for scrutiny later. My eyes settle on two personal envelopes. The most eye-catching has a franking of Ferndown Holdings – my employer. Initially I think this is odd; Ferndown had never written to me at home before, except when they offered me a job two years previously. Then, as I tear open the envelope I realize my period of absence has spanned a month-end, so it is probably my payslip. It is, but there is a letter enclosed too.

Dear Mr. Shadwell,

It is with regret I have to inform you that effective immediately your employment with us is terminated in accordance with company disciplinary procedures for evidence of gross misconduct.

During your absence, we carried out a security audit of all company PCs. On the PC allocated to you, we discovered files and messages that were in clear breach of the company policy relating to computer misuse of Internet and e-mail facilities.

In view of the serious nature of this matter, we request that you or any prospective future employers do not contact this office regarding references.

On your return from vacation, please telephone Miss Julie Rawlinson so that immediate arrangements may be made to collect your company car. Personal effects from your desk will be sent to you separately.

Paul Richardson
Director of Human Resources

I stare incredulously at the letter before me. There has to be a mistake – none of the accusations are true. I regard myself as a model employee: hard working, ambitious and loyal. Ferndown are a tough company to work for, so I know they are intolerant of poor performance and are strong on discipline, but I also view them as a fair employer. An instant dismissal without counselling is out of character. I am intrigued by the possible content of the incriminating files and messages; I can't think of any data that could cause such a vehement reaction from my employer. I should perhaps have been concerned by such a letter, but know I haven't done anything wrong and an audience with my boss or personnel will surely resolve the misunderstanding.

I check the payslip in case it holds further clues. I do some swift calculations – I've been paid up to today. The letter is dated last Friday, so being pedantic I assume I should have been paid a month's notice, unless gross misconduct has nullified that. And, the two week's convalescence I'd just completed should have been shown – as agreed with personnel – as one week with sick pay and one week's holiday. But these issues are irrelevant; as far as I am concerned, I still have a job and the error needs to be resolved as soon as possible.

It is four-thirty on a Friday afternoon; the Ferndown switchboard will be open for another half an hour. I resolve to call Julie. She, if anyone, will know what the hell is going on. Julie is secretary to the personnel manager; I know her, and her body, quite well; we have been a casual item for about three months. Casual means we see each other outside work once a week – from Saturday morning to Sunday morning. The rest of Julie's leisure time is devoted to either studying for various exams or tending her frail mother. Parental-sitting relief on Saturdays is provided by a visit from Julie's married sister. Despite the intimacy of our Saturday nights, I have wondered whether the weekly relationship is merely an outlet for her domestic incarceration or whether the affair will evolve into something more meaningful than sex and companionship. I doubt it somehow. We have never expressed any love between us, nor have we ever planned the future beyond the next Saturday. It seems as if we are using each other as a convenient stepping-stone until someone better comes along. But, I like her and she appears honest and trustworthy; plus she has my sympathy about the plight of her ailing mother. Fortunately, my own parents are alive, well and thriving in Canada.

I pick up the phone – the line is silent. I shake the handset, press buttons randomly and trace the cord back to the wall socket. Temporarily satisfied I go to the bedroom to test the second phone, but encounter the same problem. I then remember a British Telecom letter in the post pile still in my hand. I rip it open angrily and an itemized bill tumbles onto the floor. Nothing odd about that, except I recall my last quarterly bill was received and settled before I went away. A letter is left in my hand, headed Cancellation of Service. I gaze in disbelief at this latest bombshell and search for text, which might reveal the reason or the originator of the annulment – but I had already guessed.

The cancellation is dated a week earlier and is another event marked as effective immediately. Of course, this is one of the risks associated with being employed by an enormous multi-national company that views company cars, mobile phones and domestic phones as perks of the job. Lose the job and the perks go with it. Ferndown paid for the installation of my home phone, and continue to pay for business related calls and pro rata rental, but I pay for my private use. It is totally unreasonable to me that my employer should instigate the termination of my home phone without a notice period. Indeed, how am I now supposed to call Julie about my car? Isn't it strange how helpless one can feel without immediate contact with the outside world? I had a company mobile phone of course – I needed it for my job – but strictly speaking, I wasn't allowed to use it privately, so to resist temptation I'd left it in my desk drawer at work. Besides, I knew if I'd carried it to the Lake District, there was a high probability I would have been bothered with questions from work colleagues, which I wanted to avoid.

All is not lost however. I have an acquaintance residing in the flat opposite – he has a phone I could use. Josh Carmichael moved in a couple of months ago. He's a kind of thirty-year-old shaggy red-haired hippie, very animated – can't keep still for a minute. He appears to be a popular person and gets many visitors. He likes his rock music loud at times, but never after ten o'clock at night. He often calls round for a chat and is interested in my background and job, although he's less forthcoming about himself. He likes to borrow things; usual commodities like tea, coffee, sugar and milk, but mostly condoms – lucky bastard.

I step out into the hall and rap on his door. No one comes to answer, but I feel certain he must be in – I'd noticed his van outside when I arrived home. I rap a second time – hard enough to make my knuckles sting. I am sure I hear a movement behind the door and I have that observed feeling from the spy hole in the door. I call out, 'Josh are you there? Can I use your phone to make an urgent call?' There is no answer.

I don't know anyone else well enough in the block to beg use of their phone, despite the urgency. Besides, what I need to say or shout down the phone is not something I want to share with a casual neighbour. My best choice now is to hurry outside to a pay phone.

I go back to my flat and raid the dish on the sideboard in the bedroom, which contains discarded loose change. I grab a few pound coins and some silver, and set out for the short walk to the call box at the slip road leading to a parade of six shops. It is ten minutes to five already and much to my relief the booth is empty and in service. I dial the Ferndown number and Debbie, the bouncy boob blonde receptionist answers.

'*Ferndown Holdings. How may I help you?*'

'*Hello, Debs. How's things?*' I use a familiar form – I know her well and had been out with Julie, Debs and her boyfriend Rhys as a foursome. '*It's Pete, Pete Shadwell, back from convalescence. Can you put me through to Julie?*' I ask.

There is a pause before she replies. I imagine her biting her nails – she does that when she is nervous.

'*Yes, Mister Shadwell. I'll try her extension for you,*' she says emphasizing the Mister to give her reply an unexpected formal tone.

There is another delay and I envisage Debbie debating my call with Julie.

'*Hello, Pete.*' At least Julie is using a civil address, but her voice is a whisper without it's usual confidence.

'*What's going on Julie?*' I ask. '*Can you talk?*' She shares an open plan office with her departmental colleagues including her boss Paul Richardson, the Human Resources Director.

'*It's rather difficult at the moment. Could you return your car to the office tonight and put the keys through the letterbox?*'

'*No I bloody can't,*' I shout. '*Not until I've had an explanation of what this is all about. If you can't help then transfer me to Paul.*'

'*That's not possible; he's left for the day. Don't make things difficult Pete. Everyone here is pretty pissed with you. It's best if you just ... well ... do what's asked of you.*'

'*I'm not doing anything until I've had my say. Look, can I see you later? Perhaps then you can tell me what you know.*'

'*I can't discuss this with you, and anyway I have to look after my mother tonight.*'

'*I'll pick you up tomorrow morning then, as we arranged before I went away.*'

'*No Pete, after what you've done I don't think that's a good idea.*'

'*And what have I done exactly? Everyone knows except me. Christ, Julie, I've been judged in my absence. I would have thought at least you would be interested in my side of whatever story is being put about.*'

'*Alright, but don't come to my home. Meet me in the Wimpy bar in the High Street at ten o'clock. I won't be coming back to your flat afterwards though. I'm sorry it's over between us now.*'

'*Okay, Julie. I'll see you tomorrow,*' I say and put the receiver down.

Although Julie and I are not close, the severing of a relationship is usually a heart rending experience, but I feel nothing – being dumped by a casual girlfriend is not high on my current list of wrongs to rectify.

Next, I phone my brother's house. He won't be in from work yet, but my part-time teacher sister-in-law should be home from school by now. There's no answer. I try Andy at work and his phone is answered, but it is a work colleague, who says he hasn't seen him today. I briefly consider driving over to my brother's, but I could do that later. First, I want to shower after my long journey from Windermere, eat and dwell on my immediate problems.

I stop at the newsagents and general store. I purchase a few essentials to keep me going such as bread, milk and biscuits and start back. About 200 metres from my flat block I notice someone carrying a heavy plastic bag emerge from the shared entrance and head for Josh's Escort van. I immediately assume it is Josh. It is certainly a man of the same build cloaked in a knee length grey raincoat turned up at the collar, which is possible since Josh – a freelance graphics designer – does wear strange clothes. I break into a jog, but as I approach, the man's body language, and the fumbling way he opens the rear door and throws the bag inside, cast doubts that it is Josh. I call out to him, but with his back to me, he hastens his entry to the van. I catch a glimpse of his black (not red?) hair, before he fires the engine and with a squealing of tyres disappears ungracefully down the road. The opaque non-standard tinted windows of the van prevent me from ascertaining who the driver is. It has to be Josh. I begin to puzzle why my return from forced exile seems to be having an adverse effect on everyone I know.

This time, when I return to the flat, I detect a smell that I had noticed before, but had disregarded as a general mustiness from being empty for two weeks. It isn't a dusty odour; it has a sour food tang to it and my nose tracks the source to the kitchen. Then I realize how strangely quiet it is in the flat. Ambient noises usually come from two sources: the central heating system – but since this was late summer I haven't turned the boiler on yet; and the ancient fridge/freezer which sits ominously silent in the corner with a small puddle of coloured water at its base. I curse when I open the door of the old white monolith as more food and tainted water seeks freedom from its rubber-sealed entrapment and cascades around my shoes. The day gets my vote as the second worse in living memory – almost as bad as the horrible scare from a couple weeks before.

I'd had a few stomach cramps and dismissed them as a viral infection, being similar to complaints from some work colleagues. Following a walk into town one lunchtime, I was browsing the shelves in a bookshop when I doubled-up in pain, and was promptly sick over myself and the display of top-ten fiction paperbacks. Frozen in agony, an ambulance was summoned and I was operated on immediately for a ruptured appendix. I was discharged three days later, and with approval of my employers, decided to take a long-overdue break as a period of convalescence. I had gone to the Lake District – a favourite location of mine – and had spent almost a fortnight in relative isolation, with gentle therapeutic walking, sight seeing and catching up on a *backlog of reading material. Refreshed and fit, I had returned to a new nightmare.*

The fridge problem has to be something trivial, albeit damaging, like a blown fuse in the wall plug; the unit is old, but it has always been reliable. I bend down to the cupboard beneath the sink to retrieve a screwdriver and notice the digital display on the electric cooker is blank. Then I check the same on the microwave oven – that is blank too. I flip the light switch – nothing. I go to the entrance hall and peer into the small cupboard that houses the electricity meter. The trip switch is in the ON position, but the spinning disc that registers electricity flow is stationary. A general power cut could be the answer, but surely not lasting long enough to cause my fridge to defrost? Frustratingly I waste ten minutes cleaning up the mess.

I step out into the corridor intent on breaking my silence with a neighbour other than Josh. I've lived in this block for six months and though I have seen people come and go I am not even certain of the identity of the residents in the adjacent flat, which I stand before now. As I ring the doorbell I know there isn't a general power cut, I can hear a TV inside announcing the opening theme tune of the evening news. A mid-teenage girl in a navy blue and white school uniform opens the door.

'It's for you Dad,' she says and disappears.

It is thirty seconds before a mid-thirties man in a dressing gown takes her place.

'Oh, it's you. I thought you'd left the country,' he says curtly.

Before I can convert my puzzled look into words, he continues. 'They haven't caught up with you yet then?'

'I'm sorry I'm not with you,' I say.

'You're definitely not with me son. I haven't seen you. Okay?'

'Look, I've been on holiday for a couple of weeks and my phone and electricity have been cut off. Do you know something about it?'

He draws his gown together, tightens the cord and leans forward to glance left and right down the corridor. Satisfied there are no onlookers he grabs my arm, pulls me through the gap and shuts the door.

'D'ya want a cuppa? It looks like ya could do wiv one.'

My face must reveal such a thought is high on my list of priorities.

'Donna, put the kettle on love,' he shouts to the girl who had answered the door and subsequently taken the opportunity to switch TV channels to watch an episode of The Simpsons.

With a complaining sigh she uproots and goes to the kitchen. My mind-reading host leads me to a threadbare sofa and uses a remote control to click the TV off. I sit down, but he remains standing and leans towards me.

'She's a good girl really,' is his apparent explanation for the sigh, then he adds in a whisper, 'even though her mother's fucked off to live with an ex-workmate.'

And I think I have problems.

'You an American?' he asks.

'No, but I spent the first five years of my life in Canada. I didn't think I still had an accent,' I say.

'Thought so,' he says knowledgeably.

'You implied someone was looking for me?'

'S'right son. In some trouble are you?'

I presumably was, but I said, 'Not that I'm aware of. Who came?'

'It was like bleeding rush hour here yesterday. The landlord was looking for you in the morning; the police during the afternoon; and a long-haired yob was hanging around your door last night before going into the flat opposite. I'd seen him doing the same thing once before ... must have been just after you went away. The landlord and police were a bit twitchy, but none of them said what it was about, except I had to contact them if I saw you. Buggered if I'm gonna do that; landlords and police are bottom of my list of people to co-operate with.'

Now I'm seriously worried, but try to stay cool in front of my neighbour. 'I don't suppose I could use your phone,' I ask, thinking I ought to take every opportunity to reach my brother.

'Sorry,' he says, 'my wages don't run to such fancy devices.'

Donna returns from the kitchen with a couple of chipped white mugs containing a steaming light grey liquid. I eye it suspiciously and take a sip. It tastes vaguely like tea, drowned with milk and is sickly sweet.

'Thanks,' I say to Donna, grateful only that the drink is hot. She sighs again when she realizes the TV had been switched off and slumps noisily into an armchair facing us.

'I'm sorry I haven't introduced myself. My name's Pete Shadwell,' I say and stand up to offer my hand.

He taps me gently on the arm. 'Sit down lad. We're not formal in this home. Call me Reg.' He looks at his watch. 'Christ, it's late. Gotta get me togs on. I'll be back in a mo. Keep still though, Donna's got her pad out.' He adds and disappears into a bedroom.

I sit down again and I look over to the girl who is now holding a large artist's sketchpad in front of her. She keeps peering around the side and I can hear the slight scratching sound of a pencil. 'Are you drawing me?' I ask.

'Might be,' she says nonchalantly from behind the pad.

I take a swig of the syrupy liquid and her head reappears.

'Keep bloody still, will ya,' she swears with the experience of a hard-nosed villain.

My hand freezes, half expecting a gun to emerge.

'Don't be so bleeding rude,' Reg says as he returns to the room dressed in dark blue overalls. *'Pete here's our guest.'*

Reg is clutching a piece of paper. 'I've one of them emergency numbers if you want it?' When I look puzzled he adds, *'For the 'lectricity company, about your lack of volts.'*

'Thanks,' I say, *'but I'm not sure if ringing them will do any good. The master switch for each flat is in a locked cupboard in the entrance hall. I remember it being switched on when I first moved in. My guess is the landlord has arranged for the supply to be cut off. It might explain why he is looking for me.'*

'Not been paying your rent?'

'Well, yes. It's paid by standing order regularly each month, but there's a few strange things happening in my life at the moment. The lack of electricity is another example.'

'I'd like to help ya out, but I've gotta get to work. If you're stuck for the night you can stay here if you like. Sleep on the sofa. My shift ends at four o'clock so I may disturb you when I come in. Donna won't mind and she'll keep you company.'

I look at Donna who has put the drawing pad face down on the floor. She has been following the conversation intently and I catch the remains of a grimace on her face. It doesn't seem smart to be alone overnight with a strange female teenager in a strange flat. I am surprised Reg has entertained such an idea having just met me, but I don't want to appear nervous or ungrateful.

'Thanks for the offer Reg but I have a stack of things to sort out in my flat. If you have a few candles spare though they would be useful.'

'No problem,' he says nodding to Donna. *'I've got to go, but Donna will give you the box of nightlights that are under the sink'.* In an instant, he grabs a duffle coat by the front door and leaves the flat. Donna gets up and goes to the kitchen. She returns clutching a red and white box and passes it to me. I stand up ready to leave.

'You can stay if you want. It'll be alright, I won't rape you and I won't let you rape me. I can finish my drawing then.'

I am taken aback by her streetwise comments. *'I'll ... er ... just finish my tea and ...'*

'Sit down, I'll only be a few minutes.'

It is ten o'clock before I leave. Despite the initial impression, Donna is a bright girl, who is deeply inquisitive about appendectomies, my job, the Lake

District, my girlfriend – especially my girlfriend – or any other subject she cares to raise. I form the impression she is lonely or interested in me. I should have left earlier to drive over to my brother's – it is only fifteen minutes away – but I am worn out from the day and decide to walk down the street and telephone him again. Fortuitously it is the right decision; there is still no answer and then I remember – Friday night is badminton night. Andy and Kylie are both keen players and much of their social life revolves around the badminton club and its members. I assume they have gone back to their playing partner's house for supper. My distress call will have to wait until morning.

As I enter my flat, I intuitively flick the light switch inside the front door and in the prevailing darkness curse I had forgotten to take Donna's candles. I don't want to frighten her by knocking on the door, so resign myself to a search in the hall cupboard for a small promotional pocket torch I recall I had been given when I purchased my computer. I eventually find it, but not before I have grazed my knuckles on a wooden shelf, and stabbed my hand a few times on unseen sharp objects. A pile of dislodged invisible bric-a-brac lies at my feet, which will have to stay there until daylight comes. To make matters worse the search has been a waste of time; the pathetic yellow glow from the torch lasts all of ten seconds before I am plunged into darkness again. I cautiously make my way to the bedroom and sit on the bed for a few minutes letting my eyes adjust to the gloom. Cat-like, I undress and go to the bathroom to brush my teeth and return without further injury. These truly are my dark ages, with sleep the only option once I have planned my agenda for the following day.

Chapter 31

FIRST SATURDAY – 7:00 a.m.

Without the prompt from an electricity-dependent alarm clock, I am awake at seven o'clock unrefreshed, and laze under the duvet contemplating my situation and plan of action. Of course I've already done plenty of thinking; goodness knows what time I had got to sleep, barely a few hours ago based upon how tired I feel and the diversity and extent of the explanations that I recall from my pre-slumber deliberations.

I know I am innocent of all employment charges levied against me, but proving that fact or stating my side of the story, will have to wait until Monday. Today the best I can achieve is to obtain details of the accusations from Julie and restore telephonic access to my fellow humans so I can start making calls that will bring order back into my life.

Breakfast is a disappointing affair. I like toast, and hot milk on my porridge, but powerless I have to be content with the cold and uncooked equivalents.

I walk the two miles into town. I am still groggy from the restless night and view the exercise and fresh air will clear my head. Besides, overnight I had concluded that using the car might be risky, as (currently) an ex-employee of Ferndown Holdings, there is the possibility I am no longer covered by insurance. I don't need a conviction of Driving without Insurance to add to my woes.

The shops aren't open yet so I wander aimlessly around the streets. Then I sit for a while in a small memorial park observing a convoy of dog walkers and attempt, unsuccessfully, to test a theory that there is a strong visual correlation between dogs and their owners. I need to visit a mobile phone shop, and my bank, since I barely have any cash left from my holiday, but I am concerned the transactions might make me late to meet Julie and I am eager for an explanation of the employment termination. Eventually I settle on a bench seat outside the Wimpy, half an hour before Julie is due to arrive.

I have lost my appetite for food and am keen to preserve what little cash I have rather than squander it on an overpriced cup of coffee in the Wimpy. I choose instead to observe the passing of problem-free shoppers. About the time Julie is due, I spot Dave Chalmer chatting intimately with a pretty redhead. Dave is a work colleague at Ferndown. I rise from my seat and call out to him. Two other Daves turn towards me, but the one I seek continues walking – amorously pre-occupied. I catch him up and put my hand on his arm. Startled, he swings round and looks down. His height is more fitting to a basketball player and a good six inches taller than mine, but he is usually a gentle giant so I'm not prepared for the coming exchange. The encounter starts out friendly enough.

'Hello Pete,' he says, 'this is my girlfriend Michelle.'

'Hello,' *I say nodding and smiling at Michelle. She smiles back and offers her hand to be shaken, but Dave intercepts it.*

'This, my darling, is Pete Shadwell – the treasonous pervert I told you about. Look at him closely and ensure you always walk on the opposite side of the road to him in case he stabs you in the back or tries to touch you up.' *He puts his arm around her waist and drags her away, failing to see the dumbfounded look on my face.*

I hesitate long enough in the chase after them to notice Julie stop at the entrance to the Wimpy and look nervously inside. I recognize Julie by her long brown hair, black leather jacket, knee-length red skirt and red shoes – red is her favourite colour. I walk up behind her.

'Am I glad to see you. I was beginning to think nobody in this world would spend the time of day with me.'

She turns around and takes a halting step backwards. Her face is cheerless and apprehensive – not the look of the Julie I know.

Without a greeting, I follow her into the restaurant and she chooses a two-seater table next to the entrance. I take off my jacket in the warm surroundings and hang it over the rear of the seat. Julie keeps hers on and buttoned as though she isn't staying long.

'I can't stay long,' *she confirms.*

'Long enough I hope to tell me what's happened at Ferndown.'

There is a waitress hovering already.

The food smells have stimulated my appetite. Whenever Julie and I have eaten out, I have always paid the bill despite her arguments. Today I'm in no mood for chivalry and Julie appears intimidated enough by my presence to not refuse my next request.

'Could you buy me a burger and a coffee? I'm light on cash from my holiday and I haven't been to the bank yet.' *I lied, but I wasn't feeling in a particularly accommodating mood.*

193

She hesitates. *'Okay,'* and turning to the waitress says, *'and a Veggie burger and coffee for me.'*

The waitress continues to hover, presumably about to ask whether we want fries with our order, but we ignore her so she gets her answer by default.

'Are you fully recovered from your operation?' Julie asks me. It occurs to me that she won't see my appendectomy scar now, but I quickly dismiss the thought; I want to ask the questions.

'Yes. What's in the file Julie?'

She tries to give me a baffled dumb look, but I press on.

'My personnel file. Ferndown wouldn't risk dumping me in absentia without having written evidence.'

She can't deny its existence. It's her role to maintain the personnel records and she knows the disciplinary procedures as well as I do. Ferndown is a staff conscious company. Its philosophy – as explained during the two-week induction programme for new employees – is simple: look after the employees and they will be loyal and motivated to get their work done, and the rewards will come. Step out of line and you'll be on the way to the Job Centre.

Julie draws breath. *'It started on the first Tuesday you were away. A newly recruited contract worker – Sebastian Tate – carried out routine maintenance on your PC.'*

Another contract worker.

Locating its headquarters in Essex had been economically sensible for Ferndown from a site costs point-of-view, but the company was constantly struggling with recruitment, influenced by the lucrative salary scales available in nearby London. Attracting qualified computer systems people, in particular, was always a problem because they were in short supply, so Ferndown often had to resort to recruiting highly paid contract staff.

'On the Wednesday I heard there had been a commotion around your desk and your PC had been taken away to the IT Director's office. The following day I was summoned to a meeting in my boss's office and the IT Director was there too, although he said nothing during the interview. Paul Richardson stated that I didn't have to answer any of his questions, but he was investigating serious allegations against you, and any information I could offer would be treated in strict confidence.'

'Why did he pick on you?'

'He didn't specifically. Apparently anyone known to mix with you at work was interviewed too. I assume one of your colleagues must have known about our out-of-hours meetings. Anyway, I was asked if you had ever mentioned anything about your use of the Internet, e-mail or Milton Cern plc. I replied honestly that you hadn't.'

Julie and I haven't been an item long enough to set rules – except one. We both felt strongly that if a work initiated relationship had to resort to conversation about our respective day-to-day activities, then it was doomed to failure. Besides, the declarations we had to sign when we joined Ferndown were stricter than the Official Secrets Act and talking about our work – even to spouses – was strictly prohibited. Presumably, that was why Milton Cern had been mentioned – they are the biggest competitor to Ferndown in the Insurance business.

'*By last Monday they had completed their interviews and examination of your PC, and then your termination letter on the grounds of gross misconduct was given to me to type.*' *Julie pauses apparently not wanting to go any further, but I just stare at her. My intimidating look is making an impact when the waitress reappears with our order. A minute passes while the food and drink is laid out. Julie starts on her burger and I continue my stare.*

'*Well?*' *I have to prompt.*

'*Well what?*' *she says and a slither of mayonnaised lettuce slides down her chin and drops on her plate. She wipes the residue away with her serviette.*

'*The details Julie.*' *I raise my voice for the first time and she looks around in case anyone had heard.*

'*You know the details,*' *she whispers.*

'*That's my problem, I don't. I've done nothing wrong to my knowledge; so just tell me everything that went in the report.*'

Her expression changes; doubt and confusion appear briefly on her face.

'*There was nothing from the interviews. I think they were trying to discover whether you had an accomplice. On your PC they found copy e-mails to Milton Cern with large attachments disclosing financial details of Ferndown and its customers. There were also return e-mails from someone with an address of* middleman@miltoncern.com *confirming receipt of the data, and that the agreed fee had been transferred to your bank account. That was what caused them to go crazy about you, the rest was insignificant by comparison.*'

I am a statistician at Ferndown – an actuary to use the posh term. I dabble with numbers, probabilities, interpolations and extrapolations of summary data – data that I need to do my job. So I had permission levels to retrieve summary data, but not individual details. I mention these facts to Julie.

'*They were aware of your assigned access levels, but they examined the database logs, which revealed you had given yourself level 1 access, extracted the data, then set the level back again.*'

'*I've no idea how to change access levels and certainly don't know anyone at Milton Cern. This is total madness Julie. If I had done such things I wouldn't be so stupid as to use the company e-mail facilities to conduct such* transactions. Everyone knows that e-mails and Internet access are monitored. A more discreet way would have been to copy the data on to floppy disk and post it.'

'The analysis of your actions considered that, but the volume of data e-mailed would have filled hundreds of disks, which could have been noticed by someone. Besides, the conclusion was that you knew you would be discovered and would not be concerned with being detected. You would have a handsome fee from Milton Cern and probably a job there too. Your dismissal may not be the end of the matter either. The company solicitors are considering whether they have any criminal redress over you too.'

'I've been set up Julie, don't you realize it's not in my nature to do such a thing?'

'I don't know you that well. Anyway, they even suspect you had probably dated me with the view to using me to obtain personnel information. Did you?'

'Don't be stupid. I dated you because ... well, because I thought you were bright and beautiful and nice to be with.'

She ignores the flattery. 'Well your actions have alienated you to the whole company. It's been spread around that you have threatened everyone's job and the next few weeks will be critical to Ferndown's survival. Our Chief Exec has met with his equivalent at Milton Cern, who has claimed he knows nothing about the industrial espionage. The Chief doesn't believe him of course and everyone in Ferndown is on red alert watching for any suspicious events regarding Milton Cern.'

'The espionage thing is a complete fabrication. You said the rest was insignificant. What's the rest?'

She looks at me nervously and drinks her cooled coffee in one session. I take the interlude to drink from my own cup, but the anger I feel deters me from tackling the burger.

She returns her cup to the saucer. 'They also discovered you had been using the company e-mail facilities for personal messages.'

'Oh big deal. I assume they mean a handful of urgent e-mails I had exchanged with my parents in Canada last month. This was while they were attempting to sort out the transfer of funds to me from a Canadian bank. I had permission from my manager for that. I don't suppose anyone thought to check with him?'

She doesn't answer the question, but says quietly. 'And then there was the porn.'

'Porn? On my PC? That's ridiculous.'

'Apparently they looked at something called a cache and found you had visited porn sites. There was also a hidden folder, which had about a thousand hardcore images.'

Julie starts to cry.

'Julie, you have to believe me. None of this has anything to do with me.'

'I do believe you, but as a result there have been ugly rumours circulating about me. They say you needed dirty pictures because I couldn't satisfy you in bed. It's become so unbearable having to deal with the innuendoes and sniggers behind my back, I've started looking for a new job.'

We sit in silence for a while. My mind is frantic about everything she has said. The whole situation is like a bad dream. I search my mind for any clue, which could explain what's happened. I have only one idea.

'I'm sorry about this Julie. What do you know about this Sebastian Tate guy? It seems he was the only one who had access to my PC.'

'Nothing really. He started just before you went away. He fitted in well; fairly quiet; well educated; had good references, a bit scruffy though.'

'Is he the person with thick black hair tied back in a short ponytail. Bit younger than me perhaps?'

'Yes, that was him.'

'Was?'

'He was only on a probationary two-week contract. Ferndown wanted him to stay, but apparently he had accepted a contract elsewhere.'

'Damn. He was hanging around the office on my last day. What was his previous contract?'

'I can't remember.'

'Could you find out for me? And where he lives. He's the only entry point I have at the moment to clear my name.'

'Okay. I'll look it up on Monday and call you.'

'You can't. Remember, my phone's been cut off. I'll have to call you.'

She glances at her watch. 'I ought to be going now.'

I detect a half-truth, but choose not to raise it as an issue. The exchange has troubled her and I think it is best not to push our remaining fragile friendship to the limit. I need an ally to discover what has been happening at Ferndown and Julie is perhaps the only one I have now.

She stands and says 'I'm paying the bill then?'

I nod shamefully and she heads towards the pay desk. I study her on the way. I notice for the first time the sexy walk she has. She doesn't look back as she leaves the restaurant and I experience a brief pang of regret that our relationship is over through no fault of my own.

My coffee and burger have gone cold, but I finish them merely to satisfy my thirst and hunger. I replay the conversation with Julie in case any new trains of thought come. They don't and I resolve not to wait until Julie's call. Instead I will risk turning up at the office on Monday morning and will confront those that have mistakenly decided my fate.

Now I need to sort out a phone ... but there's a loud knocking and someone is calling out a name, 'Robin, Robin ...

Chapter 32

SECOND WEDNESDAY – 11:45 p.m.

'... Robin, Robin, are you there?'

I opened my eyes. It was dark and despite the urgency of the noise, I laid there trying to understand what had happened. Had I passed out in the café? Why was I lying down on a bed fully clothed and covered in blankets? I tried to sit up thinking maybe I was injured, but movement was easy. Then confusing memories intermingled; I remembered where I was, but couldn't work out how Brian and his studio fitted in to my world at Ferndown. And why hadn't I seen Julie at the Jubilee? I got up; the banging on the door was preventing me from concentrating. I headed towards the source of the noise stubbing my toe on a bucket of water in the process. I paused before the door somehow knowing there was a light switch there and pressed it. The sudden bright light hurt my eyes and I reflexively closed them as I opened the lock on the door. A wet shape burst in with a gasp and quickly shut the door again.

'Christ, you take some waking,' said the unseen shape. My eyes were still avoiding the light and my head was busy unravelling the visual conflicts. Hands shook me, 'What's wrong with you?'

'I ... I ...', I recognized the voice and forced my eyes open for confirmation, '... Luther, it's you.'

'Of course it's me. Oh Shit, you're not on drugs, are you?'

'No, NO ... I ... I've just had a bad dream, that's all. I'll be okay in a minute.' But already the presence of Luther had brought me back to the present day.

'You'd better sit down. I have serious news for you,' Luther said.

I staggered to one of the chairs and sat down with a thump. Luther sat on the edge of the bed. I glanced at the alarm clock – it was shortly after midnight. I'd only been asleep for half an hour yet almost a day of my past had filled my head.

'If it's about my real name then I already know. You're talking to Peter Shadwell.'

'You've spoken to Howard? I only spoke to him an hour ago.'

'Howard? No. I've seen him, but he drew a blank in helping me. Keith and Adrian made the discovery. Keith turned out to be a school friend and ... what have you heard from Howard?'

'He dug me out at the Jubilee. Told me about your visit and the result of the photograph he sent to your ex-employers. He thought I or you ought to know urgently'

Suddenly the mystery about Ferndown clicked into place. I had guessed correctly. I hadn't gone missing – I'd been sacked. And presumably, Julie was no longer Paul Richardson's secretary because she must have left for a new job.

Luther continued: 'Once again your activities never cease to amaze me ... murderer, rapist, drug dealer and now ... industrial spy and pornographer.'

His voice was serious, but not threatening, and he was exhibiting his poker face. I went on the defensive. 'Look Luther, I know I keep giving you excuses, but I am innocent of the reasons Ferndown had for firing me. I've been set up.'

'Again? What I don't understand about your latest charade is why you bothered to contact Howard if you already knew about Ferndown.'

'I didn't at the time. Since then Adrian has uncovered my name from school records and within the last half an hour I've had the most vivid dream about what happened at Ferndown. Apparently ...' and I went on to describe what I'd discovered. 'Does that correlate with Howard's information?'

'Certainly the reasons for your dismissal; but did you know as a result of your supposed treachery, Ferndown is in financial difficulties. Its share price has slumped and it will possibly go under or more likely be absorbed by Milton Cern with hundreds of redundancies?'

'I had read in the press about its problems, but surely that can't be anything to do with me?'

'Officially no, unofficially yes. Reading between the lines Howard reckons you are not exactly the most popular person at Ferndown.'

So now I knew what had happened to me. It was nothing to do with Ronnie Kent after all. Somebody with a stake in Ferndown had sought revenge on me – physically. This didn't explain why my electricity had been cut off; maybe that was just an administrative error by my landlord and the reason he wanted to see me. I aired my thoughts with Luther.

'It's a plausible explanation for the story that you know; but how do you account for the drug offences and fingerprint match?'

'I can't Luther, unless you have more details about the accusations.'

'No, but I will later when I see Bill Haynes.'

'Drugs doesn't fit at all into my memories of Ferndown. But there's a discrepancy about the prints.'

'Which is?'

'Bradley took my fingerprints when I was in hospital. Two days later he assured me there was no match on file.'

'Perhaps he made a mistake and … rechecked them when the rape was reported?'

I had a more believable idea. 'Or the first set of prints was filed between the two events?'

'Why do you say that?'

'There was a recent familiarity about the procedure when they were taken in hospital.'

'Which makes you guilty again. Either someone has a vendetta against you, or you are one of the most versatile crooks I've ever come across. Which is it, Robin, Peter or whatever your latest name is?' Luther said.

'After my dream I'm convinced I'm Peter Shadwell, but the jury's still out on my integrity, though I have the feeling they will return their verdict within the next twenty-four hours.' The decision would come from another flurry in my cortex, or from my dealings with Sniffy.

Luther stayed for another half an hour, and I told him about my meeting with Sniffy and the rape set-up. He warned me about the danger of playing games with anyone involved with Ronnie Kent, but it was my life and if I wanted to endanger it, that was my look out, he said. I changed the subject and instead we gossiped about people at the Jubilee to avoid any further speculation about Peter Shadwell's pedigree. There was still a degree of mistrust between us – it showed in the uneasy way we spoke to each other. We agreed to meet at the studio the following night and compare our findings.

When Luther had gone, I realized how little I knew about this trickster: where he really lived; what his ambitions were; whether his intentions were truly honourable. For now, I had to believe he was marginally on my side and thus an asset to my cause, but I feared how I would fair with him as an adversary.

Most of all I feared sleep. I could feel the pressure building in my head again; the throbbing over the eyes; dizziness, shivering and nausea. I went outside and sucked in deep lungfuls of cool air; paced up and down; pressed my thumbs into the sensitive areas on my forehead. Now there was real physical pain and I wanted to scream, but the effort was beyond me. My legs began to buckle and I crashed to my knees adding to the pain as I hit the concrete floor. For a moment I crouched on all fours and then, as I attempted to stand, I was violently sick, my fish and chip supper spewing three feet to stain the studio wall. The shivering and nausea abated immediately and I rued the wisdom of gorging on the greasy dregs of a Polish fish shop. Weakened and with a volcano about to erupt in my head, I staggered back inside. With eyes almost closed, I searched the bench in vain for a small bottle or packet that might contain a painkiller. I knew what was coming; I had to lie down and let the magma flow ...

Chapter 33

FIRST SATURDAY – 12:00 p.m.

I walk into the mobile phone store and a spotty young salesman accosts me. He looks familiar. I am sure he is the same individual that had sold me a home computer two years ago. He obviously hasn't improved his personal hygiene – the zit on the left side of his nose is still there and is again a notable distraction.

He proudly announces he knows absolutely nothing about mobile phones, which he declares is to my advantage since I need to answer a simple questionnaire on a computer. This will guide me, in an unbiased fashion, to the exact model and charging tariff I require. After the tenth question, I become frustrated with the amount of time the exercise is taking and resort to an impulse purchase of a pay-as-you-go brand I have seen advertised on TV recently. Cost and fancy facilities don't matter I just need a working phone NOW. This irritates zitface – perhaps it's a commission thing. I give him my Visa Card and he swipes it casually through an electronic reader. The two-tone beep signals all is not well.

'It's on stop,' he says, as if I don't already know by the smug look on his face. Why did I know this would happen?

'Try it again,' I say.

He does. 'No luck. I'll have to keep it,' he says.

I proffer my bank's Switch debit card as an alternative. He shakes his head knowingly and studies the details. He looks up and then back to the card, like there should be a matching photograph.

Beep-beep. Beep-beep. He tries it a second time without being asked.

'I'll have to keep that too. It's not your day, is it?' he says.

I thought disasters came in threes – I am on about my tenth without a break.

I put my hand into my back pocket and draw out the ready cash I have with me – £40 in notes and a few coins.

'How much is this phone?'

'£65,' he says.

'And the cheapest you have?' I ask.

He stares contemptibly at the two £20 notes in my hand and turns around to examine the display of telephones lined up on the shelves. He scratches his zit and selects a device about twice the size of the one I had chosen. He shows it to me from a distance as though I am about to snatch it from him and run from the shop.

'This is £35, but the minimum credit voucher to prime it is £10.'

'£30 for cash?' I say with my best pleading look.

He shakes his head. 'It's already discounted.'

'Look, give me my Switch card back and I'll pop over the road to the bank and have the card verified, and then use it to draw more cash. It'll only take a few minutes.'

He looks unconvinced by my plea. I try a gamble.

'Think of the commission you'll get. I'll even buy a more expensive phone.'

I try not to sound too desperate and I've no idea whether he is a waged, commissioned or both type of employee. It strikes a chord though.

'I'll have to keep the Visa Card,' he says as a compromise.

'Okay, a deal. See you shortly,' I say picking up my Switch card and dashing out before he changes his mind.

My bank is immediately opposite and I am thankful that by chance I have selected a brand and a branch that is open on Saturday mornings. The General Enquiries desk is closed, but there are two counters open, so I have to join the single queue. As I listen frustratingly to the customer transactions it vexes me that banks have not adopted the method employed by supermarkets: a quick till for short/urgent proceedings and a normal till for the prolonged labours of such things as opening a new account. Ten minutes later, I stand before another young man and explain my Switch Card problem.

The clerk rattles entries on his keyboard and studies a screen only he can see. 'I think the reason Mr. Shadwell,' he explains, 'is that you are currently overdrawn by £103.87 and haven't arranged an overdraft facility with us.'

'That's crazy, I had over £2,000 in the account on my last statement and I was expecting some large deposits.'

'I'll print a statement of the last month's transactions for you,' he says in a manner that does little to hide his disbelief.

He presses a few keys on his keyboard and the buzzing behind him signals printing is in progress. He collects the plain listing paper tabulation and stares at it for a moment. 'There was a large debit transfer a week ago,' he says as he passes the statement under the dividing window.

I study the entries. Large is an understatement – over £20,000 had disappeared in a single transaction on the previous Friday.'

'This is a mistake, I didn't authorize this payment.'

'You must have, sir.' His calm demeanour now has an irritable trace, influenced by the impatient sounds coming from the queue that has formed behind me. 'The code against the transaction indicates it was initiated via your PC banking access.'

'But that's impossible, I haven't been near a PC for two weeks.' I raise my voice. He startles in response at my outburst and then shrugs his shoulders dismissively.

'I need to speak to the manager.'

'I'm sorry, the branch supervisor is not on site at the moment.'

'I don't need the supervisor, I need the manager.'

'This branch doesn't have a local manager. He's based at the regional office in Chelmsford.'

'Can you ring him?'

'It's a woman actually, but she doesn't work on Saturdays.'

'Then who's going to sort this out?'

'I can raise a query for you which could be investigated on Monday.'

'I need this resolved NOW, not on Monday. There's been a VERY BIG mistake here and if these people ...' I turn and indicate the attentive and frustrated group behind me, '... get to know about how you are mismanaging accounts, then you'll lose more customers.'

'Mr. Shadwell, please, there's no need to make a scene. I assure you any mistakes will be rectified first thing on Monday morning.'

'Can you authorize a temporary overdraft for me until then?'

'I'm sorry, that's not within my power.'

I guessed that would be his answer. The shit is getting deeper – about waist level, I estimate.

'Then can you change this £20 note into 20p pieces for me? Or do you need approval for that too?' I offer as my parting gesture.

I decide to walk back to my flat. Arguing further with a guy who is out to preserve his job would be pointless. Besides I have hit on an idea – use my cheque book. I rarely use it these days except to periodically draw out cash for funding a month's worth of day-to-day purchases. The rest of the time, I use my debit or credit card and increasingly direct payments by PC banking. I can pay for my new mobile phone by cheque and use my Switch plastic as a *guarantee card, which is good for £100. That way it won't be swiped through a card reader and rejected.*

I look at the statement again. The £21,619.85 that has disappeared from my account is clearly a mistake. It was a close call though; another £10.34 or two days earlier and the transfer would have bounced. Two large sums have been credited to my account a day before the transfer. One is from a bond that has recently matured; the other is a gift from my parents – part proceeds from the sale of one of their smaller businesses. I have opened a high interest, Internet savings account intending to deposit these funds on return from my convalescence. This is a temporary measure to ensure the best return on my capital while I go through the agonizing process of identifying and buying my own house. I feel I have wasted enough money on rented property and am sufficiently secure in my job and income to join the ranks of homeowners – the money is to serve as a deposit. I am sure the erroneous financial plight can be rectified, but I am not so confident about the job prospects.

Further scrutiny of the statement shows a few additional cheques have been honoured after the big debit that led to the overdrawn situation, but not the standing order to the landlord for rent. That could explain why my electricity has been cut off.

As I near the flat, I immediately notice my car has gone. The car has a sophisticated alarm system and although the area isn't especially up-market it is not renowned for car-crime – or any crime – so the conclusion I jump to has to be the correct one, Ferndown have repossessed the car. The transport department always retained the master keys for a company car and the user is issued with the spare set. Julie must have tipped off someone that I have returned from my sick leave. I wonder whether I have left any of my personal possessions in the car. There may have been an old pair of driving gloves in the boot, but besides those I think I have removed everything of mine when I returned home yesterday. I consider phoning the police, but what was the point? I have been told it is no longer my car so if it has been stolen it is Ferndown's problem – not mine. Anyway I have more important calls to make without spending what little money I have for the benefit of my ex-employer. To make calls I need a phone; to buy a phone I need my chequebook.

In my flat I go immediately to the filing cabinet in the lounge. I don't close the front door, meaning to collect my chequebook and head straight back to town. I open the top drawer and I notice that instead of the hanging files being crammed together they are loose like some are missing. The file labelled Bank isn't there and trying to remember the structure of my filing system, I conclude the Insurance, Savings and Documents files are missing too. I know they were there before I left for Windermere; one of the last things I did was to empty my pockets of various credit card receipts and file them away. I first assume this explains my banking problem, but then recognize an anomaly. Money has disappeared from my account by a computer-initiated

206

transaction not a cheque and I know I have no paper record of my computer password nor have I ever written it down anywhere. A small consolation, but whoever now has my chequebook won't get far with the account being on hold. Yet the theft may explain my credit card being on stop. With its number being on my statements and purchase slips, using it to buy goods on mail order would be easy. My only recent purchase was to pay for my holiday; that came to £400 so the present holder must have blown the balance on my credit limit of £1000. 'Shit,' I say aloud, not at the loss of money – which I assume will be borne by the credit card company – but the arrangements I'll now have to make. Ring the police to report the burglary; ring the credit card company, the bank, the building society and – based upon the documents I know are missing – go through the undoubted laborious processes of obtaining a replacement passport and birth certificate. I slump into my armchair with the frustration of it all and say 'Shit' again. I hear footsteps nearby.

'That's no way to speak with ladies present,' Donna says. 'Something up?'

'Oh, sorry Donna. Yes. I've been burgled.'

'Is that why the police were here again this morning?'

'I don't know. It could be. I'll have to ask them to come back again.'

'There's no need. They said they would come back at two o'clock.'

I checked my watch; that was forty minutes away.

'What's been stolen?'

'Documents, cheque book, things like that. Donna, I need to pop out for a short while. I shouldn't be more than half an hour, but if I'm longer and the police arrive could you ask them to wait?'

'Sure. You want me to stay here?'

'No. You better not in case you disturb the crime scene,' I invent on the spur of the moment. I have enough problems without an under-age girl being found in my flat.

'Have you seen Josh today?' She looks puzzled. 'The guy opposite.' She hasn't. I knock on his door as we leave my flat, but there is still no answer.

Nor is there any answer from Andy's when I call from the public phone a few minutes later. I do reach the credit card company and they confirm my card has been over-used for purchases in London and is now on a black list. I tell them all I know about the loss, but they will want verification from the police. I also reach a few mutual friends of Andy and me, and ask if they have seen him recently. Nobody has, although a work colleague of Kylie's says she hasn't been at the school this week and doesn't know the reason why.

Chapter 34

SECOND THURSDAY – 7:10 a.m.

There was a ringing in my head; it didn't make sense. More mechanical than a telephone, and why should someone be calling me in a public phone box? I reached out towards the noise and grasped – empty space? Gravity signalled that my arm was vertical not horizontal, and it was dark. I opened my eyes and looked in amazement at my raised hand and let if fall to my side. The ringing was becoming fuzzier, slower like a spring unwinding. My head was throbbing and I felt a chill, but the ambient air was stuffy and warm. My skin was cold – cold from evaporating sweat. I sat up and perspiration ran into my eyes. I blinked away the drops and focused upon the source of the noise which I knew now was an alarm clock. Ten past seven; present day; Brian's studio; East London.

There was a rancid taste in my mouth and the acidic smell of puke traces on my shirt, and I recalled the prelude to my overnight images. But they were more than images – these were hard facts unleashed from my cerebral archives. I was no longer just an unconfirmed industrial criminal, but a bankrupt victim too. Lest I forget these and earlier revelations I took out my journal and noted key memories.

Thus far I'd experienced three flashbacks. As best as I could determine they'd been in chronological order.

Part 1 – Friday. I've had an appendectomy and been on holiday in Windermere to convalesce for two weeks. On my way back I call in at the local library and my name is missing from the computer records. My recollections had started there, so was that moment the start of my downfall?

Part 2 – Friday and Saturday. Back at my flat (in Harlow?) I discover my name is Peter Shadwell; I've been fired from my job at Ferndown and my phone and electricity have been cut off. Josh(?) ignores me. I meet Reg and Donna, who say the police and the landlord are looking for me. I meet Julie – now my ex-girlfriend – who says I lost my job because I leaked confidential information to Milton Cern, sent personal e-mails and collected porn. We agree to talk on Monday.

Part 3 – Saturday. My bank account's been raided (how?). My flat's been burgled; my credit card compromised and various documents stolen. Andy and Kylie are missing(?)

Had I forgotten anything significant? I studied the notes looking for a pattern. Did I really perpetrate the events at Ferndown? With no memory before my holiday I had no idea. My recall said the large deposits into my bank account had been bona fide. What if Julie had been right that Milton Cern had rewarded me for my treasonous efforts? How did the police have my fingerprints? Was I already a convicted criminal? And, most mysterious of all, what was the drug connection? I was mugged on the Sunday night so there was a gap in my past from mid-Saturday. Obviously, something of consequence had happened during that time to transport me from Harlow to London. The dreams had provided some background, but had made the unanswered questions even more frustrating.

I glanced at the clock again. I had intended to tidy myself up before leaving, but it was time I wasn't here. I picked up my duffle bag and caught a glimpse of a stranger in the mirror over the washbasin. I stopped to compare the face looking back at me with the one I knew of Peter Shadwell. Three aspects struck me: the gaunt countenance, the sunken eyes and the vomit infested beard, which showed I'd become a true man of the street. I quickly splashed water over my chin in a cursory attempt to improve my appearance, but the outcome was merely a plain black growth instead of one flecked with yellow. Disturbed by what I saw, I returned with reluctant haste to the streets of East London.

Today the weather was kinder. Overcast and damp from the previous night, but not raining. I made my way slowly, evasively and vigilantly to the Bancroft Library and was waiting at the entrance when the doors opened at nine. The library would be a safe haven for a couple of hours while I conducted research into the background of Peter Shadwell.

First, I looked up Ferndown in a business directory and I noted the address and telephone number of its head office in Harlow. That led me to examine the phone books for the Harlow area and I found two Shadwells – one with an initial A, which could be my brother Andy. I checked out the Rawlinsons – no J – but four others that might be Julie's mother, since I only knew her as Mrs. Rawlinson. I also added two S Tates to my list. Then I moved on to other local places of interest: hospitals, libraries, the tax office and council offices. The electoral register for Harlow would have been ideal, but I established at the enquiry desk I would need to contact or visit the main library in Harlow for details of voters.

Next, I wanted to use one of the two Internet-connected PCs, but they were both occupied, so I picked up that day's copy of the *East London Gazette* and took it to a reading table nearby. Disinterestedly I browsed through the headlines and then I turned the page … and there was Peter Shadwell staring at me from the top left corner – a passport sized, black and white, head and shoulders sketch. Unlike a normal police photo-fit picture, the sketch was uncannily accurate and I knew – despite the cleaner image it portrayed – I would be easily recognized. The accompanying headline said "Suspected Murderer seen in Stepney". I looked around to make sure nobody was watching then drew the newspaper closer to read the story.

Peter Shadwell, wanted for possession of drugs and the suspected murder of a drug dealer in the Harlow area two weeks ago, recently stayed at the Jubilee homeless hostel in Stepney. Using the alias, Robin Forest, he arrived at the hostel last Friday, and according to the resident warden, appeared to be a genuine homeless young man who was suffering from amnesia. 'It came as a great shock to his new-found friends that he was possibly a notorious criminal,' said Albert Thompson. Detective Inspector Bradley, who is leading the local investigation, said that Shadwell might also be able to help the police in its enquiries concerning the death of a long-standing resident at the Jubilee on Saturday and the rape of a young woman at her home on Tuesday. 'The man is dangerous and if anyone sees him he should not be approached – instead contact the Bethnal Green police immediately.'

So, my supposed crimes were now public knowledge. The article did plug one gap in my knowledge, my supposed victim had been murdered two weeks ago. If the time of death was accurate, two weeks ago I was in Windermere. My vigilance would have to extend beyond avoiding the police to averting the scrutiny of any crime-conscious, *Gazette*-reading civilian. I had viewed I was safer closeted in the library than being on the streets, and the press exposure had accelerated my need to discover as much as I could about Peter Shadwell.

Making sure I wasn't observed, I tucked the *Gazette* inside my duffle bag in the naive belief that one copy less in circulation would help forestall my apprehension. I then hovered behind the unlikely Internet users hoping my frustrated presence would make a strong hint. There was a female pensioner moving shaky hands on the keyboard and mouse, and absorbed in studying pictures of flowers. The other appeared to be a housewife, who was surrounded by shopping bags and scrolling up and down through a list of recipes. Eventually, she clicked on one depicting lamb cutlets cooked in bread sauce, gave a departing satisfied grunt, and sent the instructions to the printer. I took her place.

My first visit was to the *National Missing Persons Helpline* pages I had originally seen at the *East Anglian Mail* offices – nothing new there. I hoped the service was unknown to anyone looking for me, instead of nobody being concerned with my disappearance. I found the Ferndown corporate pages, which were dedicated to marketing of its services – no mention of people or its current problems. Then I tried a general search using various combinations of my real name. I was looking for anything that might lead to my address: perhaps I had a hobby, which I had felt the need to publish on personal pages; maybe I was an official for a sporting club; possibly my name was on a mailing list somewhere. I wasn't sure what I might do if I found an address; the police were surely watching my home, but it seemed a vital piece of information I ought to acquire. Predictably I found hundreds of links to P, Pete and Peter Shadwell and it would have been fascinating to explore the more bizarre references that contained my namesake. One in particular caught my eye – a presenter on *Radio Essex* – and I was about to click on the link when I registered someone looking over my shoulder. I turned round and there was the flower-loving granny – wide eyed – staring at my screen.

Innocently I enquired, 'Can I help you?'

She shifted her gaze to me and her mouth gaped open, first in surprise and then as her lips began to move, I suddenly knew what was coming. I had already shuffled my chair backwards and grabbed my duffle bag as she stuttered her initial words in a nervous whisper. 'You ... you're ... that murderer.' She moved aside, perhaps fearing I would attack her. As I braced myself to run I cast her a pleading look, hoping she would reconsider the oncoming outburst. But my imminent departure strengthened her resolve. 'Murderer,' she said again, loud enough to attract curious attention in the quiet of the library. Curiosity grew to serious interest as I began my escape run. Serious interest rose to mild panic as granny's confidence grew with my increasing distance from her and the frailty of her body belied the rising volume of her voice. 'Peter Shadwell ... Murderer ... STOP HIM.' Yet I was fortunate; the library held perhaps half a dozen patrons and as no one was in immediate danger the audience merely looked on in surprise. But I ran and kept running for five minutes until my lungs were burning and my injured thigh threatened to topple me to the ground. I knew my haste had drawn scrutiny from pedestrians as I weaved through the streets, but distance from my discovery outweighed caution.

When I slowed to a walk, I was close to my ultimate target. Hot and with a pounding heart, I entered the cul-de-sac that led to Rainbow Electronics and the assumed safety of Brian's studio. The assumption was wildly wrong. As the studio came into view from the entrance to the converted school, the white and yellow livery of a police car parked outside, halted my progress. Presumably too soon to be connected with my granny encounter, I guessed the police investigations were expanding to include visits to the environs of my

Jubilee acquaintances. With no other hiding places left to me, it was probably only a matter of time before I was apprehended.

Despondent, I headed for my rendezvous with Sniffy. I was nervous that an association with Ronnie Kent's organization wouldn't further my claims of innocence, but the gamble was worth it, if only to temporarily provide shelter from the police.

Thursday must have been a favoured washing day since the launderette was busy, but when I noticed from outside that several people were studying newspapers, I kept moving in case they were *Gazette* readers. My increasingly accurate body clock told me I was early anyway and this was confirmed when I passed a jewellers displaying timepieces variously indicating I had about another hour to kill. I took a risk calling in at a newsagent to buy a £5 phone card and then found a kiosk to make calls.

Three people headed my dialing list: Charlotte, Andy and Julie.

I phoned the hospital first and spoke to Elsie since Charlotte had gone to the Jubilee. She was due back soon so I left a message I was okay and I would try to call back later.

I then studied the list of phone numbers I'd prepared at the library; A. E. Shadwell was my next choice. I keyed the numbers nervously. What would I say if someone answered? I had no time to compose my introduction before the connection stopped ringing. There was a mechanical click then silence at the other end.

'Hello ... hello,' I said. Listening closely, I was sure the line wasn't dead – I could hear a regular tick-tock of a clock in the background. 'Hello ... Andrew, are you there? ... Please answer, this is Peter, your brother.'

'Peter Shadwell?' asked a voice.

'Andrew? Thank God I've reached you, something awful has happened to me.'

'This isn't Andrew. But we would like to know where he is. Where are you?'

'Who are you? We? What's going on? Where's Kylie?'

'Peter, calm down. I am a friend of Andy and Kylie. Tell me where you are. We can help you.'

'What ...' I started but my hand was shaking. 'I want to ...'

My head registered a throbbing again. The call had triggered something in my memory, but it was recalling the feeling of pain rather than physically experiencing it. To kill the memory I had to kill the call, so I hung up the phone. There was instant relief. What was happening? A major objective had been to contact my brother and here was a *friend* who might be able to help. For an instant, I had recognized the voice – but only the voice, no name or face. Yet in that brief moment I feared it wasn't a friend. The dealings with

212

Sniffy would have to wait. I needed immediate help and there was only one source on which I could rely.

I made my way quickly and openly to the hospital, not caring I was a public fugitive. By the time I reached Whitechapel Road, the thumping in my head had started again – physically this time – and I was thankful the traffic barred my haste. I clutched at the post of a pedestrian crossing signal for support, waiting for the one opposite to display a green man. The red light appeared to be waxing and waning in brightness, then it occurred to me the pulsing was synchronized with the drumming in my head. I knew I was about to faint, but was conscious enough to know I had to reach Charlotte first. I stepped out into the road, hearing, but not taking heed of the warning voices and car horns around me. My legs had gone to jelly and onlookers must have sympathized at my apparent disability or mocked at my drunken stagger. I climbed the steps to the hospital entrance with the effort of a mountaineer, then through the doors with the fading consciousness of a long distance runner crossing the finishing line. As I ventured into the corridor that would lead me to Charlotte, I was aware of hospital staff gathering around me and then my body dissolved, and I slid slowly into someone's arms saying, "Sam Rapley. Get nurse Rapley."

Chapter 35

FIRST SATURDAY – 2:00 p.m.

I hurry back for the appointment with the police. I feel privileged my burglary is so important, for outside the flat I see two police cars parked and one uniformed policeman standing at the entranceway. As I approach, I nod to the constable.

'Mr. Shadwell?' he asks, stirring from his guardsman stance.

'Yes,' I say.

'Inspector Huggins is waiting for you. I'll accompany you, sir,' he says and falls in line behind me.

As we climb the two flights of stairs to the first floor, I become uneasy about the constable's concern for my welfare on such a short trip.

It looks like a delegation in the corridor outside my flat. I assume it is Huggins talking in whispers to Clive Gifford – the landlord; another plain clothed officer is studying a piece of paper, and a uniformed officer is chatting to Reg and Donna. They all look engrossed in what they are doing, and it takes the attention seeking clearing of the throat behind me to divert their focus. An eerie silence prevails for a moment until Inspector Huggins (I guessed right) takes control of the situation and introduces himself. He is a short, shabby individual that reminds me of the TV detective called Colombo.

'Ah, Mr. Shadwell, I'm pleased to meet you at last. I am Detective Inspector Huggins. Did you have a good holiday? I'm sorry to hear about your break-in. I've examined your front door and can't find any signs of a forced entry.'

While he is speaking, Reg and Donna disappear into their own flat and shut the door behind them. Huggins doesn't offer his hand in greeting, so with embarrassment I steer my rising hand to detour into my jacket pocket to retrieve my door key.

'Don't touch anything when you go in, we'll arrange for the SOCOs to take fingerprints later.'

Clive is hovering behind the policemen. I catch his eye. 'Did you want something Clive? Like restoring my electricity supply?' I say sarcastically.

He looks nervously towards the Inspector, seeking approval for his reply. I spot a slight shake of the head from Huggins then Clive says, 'I ... er ... wanted to check nothing has been damaged.'

'There's no damage,' I assure him, 'just some missing documents and missing electrical current.'

Clive opens his mouth to speak.

'We'll deal with this for now Mr. Gifford. You can settle your domestic differences with Mr. Shadwell later,' Huggins says. His tone is forceful, as though he purposely doesn't want Clive present.

I insert the key carefully into the lock and turn. I gently nudge the door with my knee and usher three of the policemen into my flat. The guardsman stations himself outside as I close the door with my toe.

The three have found their way into the living room and are casting their eyes inquisitively at the furniture and fittings.

Huggins speaks. 'This is Detective Sergeant Gordon Willow and PC Chris Ringwood'. He indicates his colleagues.

'I can't offer you a hot drink for obvious reasons. Can I get you water or fruit juice,' I say, more to break the atmosphere that charges the room than to be a concerned host.

'No thank you,' Huggins replies. 'Could you tell me what's been taken and from where?'

I point to the filing cabinet in the corner of the room. 'I keep important papers in the top drawer. Four files are missing; the ones labelled Bank, Insurance, Savings and Documents.'

'And did these files contain anything of value?'

'Not directly. Other than correspondence, the Bank file contained spare cheque books, statements and credit and debit slips. Insurance had photocopies of policies; Savings – old and new pass books; Documents held principally my passport and birth certificate.' I then go on to relate the experiences I have had with the phone shop and bank that morning.

'You think these events are the result of the burglary?'

'The credit card must be. I'm not sure about the bank. My guess is the bank has made a cock-up. The missing money was obtained by a PC Banking transfer – not by cheque. I keep the computer access codes for that in my head.'

'Won't those details also be on your PC?' Willow asks.

'Possibly in encrypted form, but it doesn't look like my PC has been tampered with. I can't be sure since there's no power for me to turn it on.'

'And nothing else has been disturbed?'

'I don't think so.'

'Would you mind if we had a look around?'

'No, of course not; but there is one question I wanted to ask first, Inspector.'

Huggins widens his eyes as a sign for me to continue.

'How did you know I had been burgled?'

'I didn't. The first I knew of the burglary was from the young lady a few minutes ago.'

'But I believe you came here earlier in the week.'

'Correct, although that was regarding an entirely different matter.'

'Which was?'

'We'll get to that in a moment, sir. One thing at a time.'

Huggins and Willow both don gossamer gloves. Ringwood goes to the window and looks out. Willow steps towards the bedroom; he stops short and turns to observe Huggins, who has made straight for the filing cabinet. Curiously, he bends down, pulls the handle of the bottom drawer slowly with his plastic covered index finger, and peers inside.

'What do you keep in this drawer?' he asks, moving things aside.

'Miscellaneous stuff like photographs, guarantees and domestic appliance instruction manuals,' I reply.

'Ah, ha,' Huggins says triumphantly and Willow strides excitedly to join him.

'Some evidence Inspector?' I question naively.

'Most certainly,' he answers, 'but for a different crime perhaps?'

I am arrested on a charge of Possession of a Class A drug with intention to supply and taken to Harlow police station. The custody sergeant retains my personal property and I am led to an interview room. I refuse legal representation; this has to be a mistake and I believe I can deal with the situation personally. I try unsuccessfully to contact my brother. Huggins and Willow interview me. They are friendly and gentle to begin with, but as time passes, Huggins in particular, gets frustrated at my non-cooperative nature.

'It's no use, Inspector. You can shout and bang the table as much as you like, but I've told you the truth. I don't sell drugs; I don't use drugs; nor have I ever been associated with anyone who does,' I holler. My patience has run dry. For the last two hours I have been the model detainee, politely and calmly answering the constant stream of questions thrown at me from Huggins and Willow. I am now tired, hungry and frustrated from the day. This latest episode in my downfall has ground away at my restraint; now I want to *fight back. I can detect that Huggins is about to use my distress against me, but I continue my tirade before he seizes the opportunity and I lose my flow.*

'Surely you've worked it out Inspector? I've been set up. It's all part of a conspiracy against me. I've lost my job under mysterious circumstances; my bank account has been raided; my phone's been disconnected; my electricity's been cut off; files are missing from my flat, and now you've conveniently discovered a hidden stash of white powder which you suspect is cocaine. I freely allowed you to search my flat because I knew I had nothing to hide, and yet you went directly to the bottom drawer of my filing cabinet. Is that where all drug dealers keep their stock, or is there the slightest possibility you received a tip off about its location? I think your nark should be in this interview room. Not me!'

'The information was received anonymously. We don't always follow up anonymous information except we've had independent reports that a drug dealer was operating from your building.' Huggins says defensively. 'It's just as well we did though. You had enough dope in your filing cabinet to keep an army high for a week.'

'And your snout knew I would contact you about the burglary. How convenient.'

Huggins has been pacing up and down to curb his anger. Now he sits down opposite me and leans forward across the table threatening me with his eyes. 'Or just an unfortunate coincidence on your part perhaps. Let me tell you what I think has been going on'.

'You are a drug dealer Mr. Shadwell who has perhaps over-stretched himself somewhat; become a little greedy perhaps. I reckon you owed your suppliers a lot of money and they'd become a bit impatient. Therefore, they decided to wipe you out financially and expose you to the police in order to teach you a lesson. A crime against a criminal which, in their twisted way of thinking, is possibly the ultimate justice. Had you paid them off earlier maybe none of this would have happened? The large sums of money transferred recently to your bank account – presumably because of your illegal dealings – arrived a little too late to keep the wolves at bay. Your enforced convalescence came at an unfortunate time.'

Huggins sits back satisfied with his deduction.

'Nice theory, Inspector, but I believe flawed in several respects. I can prove the legal source of the money transfers. I can call upon character witnesses who would vouch for my integrity and movements in recent weeks. Furthermore, it is quite implausible that these suppliers could or would infiltrate Ferndown so quickly and dramatically just to get at me. What would be the point? If they'd stolen all my money and had me convicted of drug dealing, I would have lost my job anyway.'

My statement has impact because Huggins and Willow confer privately for a few minutes. Eventually Huggins sits opposite me again and smiles.

'Mr. Shadwell, I have to agree there is a small – very small – doubt in my mind about your guilt. While that is the case, you can have the opportunity to redeem yourself. Give me a full statement of your involvement in your drug dealings, including the names of your accomplices, and I promise I will present your co-operation to the courts in the most favourable light. If you refuse, when I discover the full extent of your crimes, I will ensure you receive the full quota of the sentence you deserve. Do I make myself clear?'

'Perfectly.'

'Do you now want a solicitor to be present to guide you in your statement?'

'No, inspector. I have nothing to add to what I've already told you – several times.'

'Very well, then I will need to detain you overnight ... while we check parts of your statement.'

Inspector Huggins's closing remark is a shock, yet apparently a reasonable and legal response to my alleged offence. I argue my personal situation requires urgent attention, but he is nonplussed with my plight. I reconsider enlisting the assistance of a solicitor, but have no contact of my own and I am advised the duty solicitor cannot be present until the morning. Instead, I rely on being able to contact my brother, but after many attempts and a hot, albeit tasteless meal from the canteen, at ten o'clock I resign myself to my first night's detention at Her Majesty's pleasure.

Chapter 36

FIRST SUNDAY – 2:00 a.m.

There is some satisfaction about my overnight stay in a cell: I have artificial light from the single light bulb dangling from the ceiling and a Saturday newspaper with all of its supplements to divert my attention, but most of the time my mind seeks explanations of my problems. Eventually around two o'clock I sleep, though fitfully.

Breakfast is at eight, more fulfilling than dinner in taste and need. Willow arrives with news, good and bad.

Good: I am to be released on police bail. Reg and Julie have been contacted, and have vouched for my integrity, which is a relief, but surprising, since Reg hardly knows me, and Julie no longer wants to know me. Reg also mentioned the suspicious activity outside my flat, which must have helped.

Bad: The white powder is cocaine. I am still under arrest while further investigation proceeds. My fingerprints are taken. I am told not to leave the country (unlikely without a passport), and to report to the police station on a daily basis.

I am released at ten o'clock. There is of course no transport available to deliver me back home, so I slog for three miles through drizzle and arrive wet and dejected at my front door. I immediately notice a difference. The usual tarnished brass coloured lock has been replaced with a shiny silver version. I know my key will not fit, but nonetheless go through the motions of inserting the key in the slot – which works; and then trying to turn the key – which does not. I kick the door in frustration and utter a loud 'bastard' at the absent landlord. I bang on Josh's door hoping he's now home, but still there is no answer.

The noise attracts the interest of Reg, who calls from down the corridor. 'Hey, Pete, you're back. I thought we'd seen the last of you. You better come in.'

Reg despatches Donna to put the kettle on. 'I saw the cops take you away yesterday. What happened?'

I tell him the story of the last twelve hours in the time it takes to drink two cups of Donna's milky, sweet tea. Unlike Huggins and Willow, Reg immediately concludes I am innocent. 'Bleeding obvious to me,' he says. 'You've been stitched. Who've you rubbed up the wrong way then? Miffed somebody big time I reckon. Cough who it is and I'll find someone who can sort them out.'

'That's the mystery, Reg. I don't know. The nearest I've been to upsetting anyone in recent memory happened a few weeks ago when I shouted at a woman for allowing her dog to pee against a wheel of my car.'

My remark brings a laugh, but the story is true. I racked my brains in the cell last night and that was the worst I could come up with.

'So what are you gonna do now?'

'My brother is the best ally I have. I'm sure he has some contacts that will be able to help me out, except he seems to have disappeared. I was going to visit him this morning, but I can't get into my flat for the spare key to his place. My lock has been changed.'

Donna has been listening attentively and speaks for the first time. 'While you were at work last night dad, that slimy Clive and another guy arrived and made a lot of noise next door. That's what they must have been doing.'

Reg looks thoughtful for a moment and then goes to a cupboard in the hallway. I hear metallic sounds: tools banging together, keys jangling. Reg reappears holding a small leather Dorothy bag. 'Donna, make some more tea, love. I'll be back shortly.'

I look to Donna for an explanation, but she just grins and goes to the kitchen.

'Could I have hot black coffee?' I call after her; the lingering sweetness of the tea needs cauterizing. Before she finishes, Reg is back.

'Okay, Pete, let's go,' Reg says and beckons me.

I follow him outside and he stands by my gaping front door waving his hand in an obsequious gesture. I inspect the door thinking it's been forced open, but the woodwork is clean. Reg puts a finger to his lips indicating silence and ushers me inside. I close the door after me, and pick up an envelope from the floor. I look at Reg suspiciously. Suddenly I have doubts about my neighbour. Did he break into my flat? What does he do overnight?

Reg says: 'I know what you're thinking. I'm not a burglar. I drive a breakdown truck and have acquired a knack of breaking into things – cars and garages usually.'

'Frankly I don't care what you do Reg. I'm just grateful for your help. I hope you don't get into trouble about this.'

'No tell, no Hell – as they say.'

I am not sure who they *are*, but I am too distracted by the envelope to enquire. It's a letter from the landlord's solicitor full of legal stuff, the upshot of which is that I am an undesirable for a) non-payment of rent and b) illegal acts in my flat. Very sneaky I think. How was I supposed to see this with access denied? Henceforth I am homeless. I show the letter to Reg.

'That bastard Clive. Wait 'til I get me hands on 'im.'

'Don't get involved Reg. You'll only make matters worse for me – if that's possible. I'll go through the official channels. However, there is something you can do for me.'

'Name it.'

'Could I store my personal stuff in your flat? It would only be for a day or two until either I resolve this problem with Clive or I shift my stuff temporarily to my brother's. If I don't move it now my guess is that it will be moved for me, possibly to the local tip.' Reg looks doubtful. 'There's not much. With a couple of small exceptions the furniture and fittings are rented with the flat,' I say, which satisfies him.

I change into a fresh set of casual clothes and then for the next hour the three of us work as a team. I identify my property and Reg and Donna transport it in convoy to their flat. I comment about a decaying smell in the corridor, which perhaps is coming from Josh's flat, but Reg dismisses it as the odour of a hot curry.

When we finish, the sum of my possessions is stacked untidily in the corner of my neighbour's living room; unordered in foreign surroundings it is a pathetic sight.

I express my thanks for the nth time and set out for my brother's with a promise to call back later or tomorrow to remove my chattels.

My brother is the one person that can help me right now, but his unanswered phone troubles me. There is probably a benign explanation; maybe he is in the midst of a heavy bout of social engagements; perhaps he and Kylie have gone away for the weekend; more likely the timing of my calls has been unfortunate. As three-month-old newly-weds, I know they are devoting much of their spare time to refurbishing their new home. My guess is they are working outside or touring DIY centres selecting paints, wallpapers and other decorating materials.

In comparison to my urban existence on the northeast side of Harlow, Andy and Kylie live out in the sticks in a hamlet called Nazeing Tye. It is six miles distant, four across town and two down twisty country lanes.

I presume I can catch a bus to take me closer to my destination; the costly alternative of a taxi doesn't seem appropriate. I can't recall the last time I used a bus. Trains – yes, particularly for trips to London, but a bus? There is a bus stop at the end of the road, and I only know that from recollection of driving past a neat queue of people each morning on my way to work. I often had a tinge of guilt in wet weather when the commuters were huddled beneath umbrellas or cowering from the rain. As for the destination and timetable of the (green and cream is it?) single-deckers, I have no knowledge and remain ignorant when I examine the glass-covered frame attached to the bus stop pole. I assume it will provide the information I require – it probably did once – but instead is now skilfully and permanently obscured by a notice advertising the dubious services and phone numbers of the Harlow Mobile Masseurs Club. The sign at the top of the pole implies that bus numbers 10 and 12 stop here, but in isolation, the digits are meaningless. For me it is analogous to being instructed how to start the engine of a car, but not being told about the motion enabling aspects of a clutch, gear lever and throttle. On reflection, I am pleased with such ignorance. I am in no mood for company, even with aloof fellow passengers or a preoccupied bus driver; today I prefer solitude.

To walk the distance in my terms is trivial – I have done it a couple of times before. First: when my company car was receiving minor body repairs after being hit from behind by a distraught wife, who was attempting to follow her husband to a rendezvous with his girlfriend. Second: not long after I joined the local gym, following a lecture from a doctor friend, whose sermon of the evils of stressful sedentary deskbound jobs made them sound like they were a single step from devil worship and an premature coronary. The walk will take me about 90 minutes, maybe less. The weather conditions are ideal for a brisk walk. It has stopped raining and the clouds are now fluffy white unlike the earlier water-sodden light grey. There is a fresh damp smell wafted by the light breeze and the temperature is comfortable.

With all that has happened in the last 36 hours, I assume thoughts on my walk will be consumed with those events and possible explanations, but I have already dwelt on them long enough overnight. I am optimistic, Panglossian even, about the outcome. Tomorrow morning will see me climb rapidly from the present nadir. So instead, in a kind of rambling trance, I study the urban then rural surroundings, and somehow find distracting interest in housing estates, light industrial complexes, road layouts, the countryside and farm buildings. It is only as I near my brother's home that my mind returns to my temporary jobless, moneyless, homeless and drug accused state, and I imagine the fun I will have in relating the crazy story to an undoubtedly disbelieving sibling.

Nazeing Tye is an attractive hamlet of about twenty near identical terraced cottages, in a single street surrounded by open, flat farmland. For such a quiet and picturesque location one would have expected the cottages to be spacious and luxurious, but a century ago they were working tenants' dwellings commissioned by the owner of the long demolished Nazeing Hall farm. The properties had originally been small dwellings, but pairs have been amalgamated into single homes to better accommodate today's average household's demand for utility and leisure rooms. History, and the wishes of the parish council, have ensured that the facades of the cottages and extensive front gardens have remained unchanged. Pressure for the storage of cars has however necessitated the building of garages at the rear, but these have been cleverly disguised to appear as vehicle-sized outbuildings constructed of brick with wood cladding. A solid yellow line in the gutter of the road outside the cottages has been painted as a deterrent to parked cars, but this merely contradicts the other ancient preservation measures. Indeed, because there has been no corresponding enforcement notice erected (because it would spoil the aspect – said the council), few of the car-owning residents comply with the restriction. So, despite the immaculately kept gardens and buildings, Nazeing Tye never reaches the finals of the best-kept hamlet in Essex.

I recall these facts, imparted by my brother, as I stride up the inclined road that plateaus at the cottages. It is not immediately obvious whether Andy and Kylie are at home; their car would be parked around the back. They were thankful that they had obtained a country residence as their first home, so chose to pay heed to the parking ban.

I make my way up the part muddy path to the south-facing front of their cottage. The path leads to the right hand side porchway, which has been nominated as the main entrance. The mirror image porch of the converted symmetrical dwelling is now merely ornamental and contains an array of colourful pots and hanging baskets stocked with bright autumn flowers. There are half a dozen newly laid paving stones near the entrance way and an unlaid pile resting inside the porch, suggesting this may be Andy's current maintenance project. Andy is a disciplined person, who having started a project would see it through to completion before starting another. With favourable weather conditions and lack of outside activity I deduce that Andy probably isn't at home, but I hope Kylie is.

There is no bell and only the metal remnants of where a door-knocker used to rest, so I rap on the solid wooden door with my knuckles and at the same time scuff my hiking boots on the coconut mat to remove traces of mud. There are no new sounds to add to the drone of a distant lawnmower and the occasional bird tweet. I step on to the damp lawn in front of the bay window and peer in. I don't expect my view to reveal any useful information since it is designated as the spare bedroom, but several things bother me. I go back to the front door and let myself in with the spare key. I call out, but all is quiet except for the loud tick-tock of a decorous ancient grandfather clock in the hall. I turn left into the spare room to examine it more closely. The bedding and pillows are rumpled and the covers tossed aside; the drawers in a chest have been left open. I speak regularly to my brother so I am usually aware if he has any guests staying overnight. To my knowledge I have been the only person to stop over thus far and the fastidiousness of Kylie precludes her leaving any room in disarray. But what do I know? I have been incommunicado for two weeks and considering what has happened to my life during that time, it is anyone's guess whom Mr. and Mrs. Andrew Shadwell might have had staying with them; it could even have been a Russian spy using the cottage as a safe house. This last statement is not as frivolous as it sounds, because Andy is employed – as far as I can determine – in a secret Government job. I sit on the disorderly bed and reflect upon his history.

Andy is 26 years old and I am 25, yet we both graduated from the same university in the same year. Andy always had a flare for languages and he graduated from Reading with a first class honours in German; his third year of four being spent teaching English at Bonn University. As a mildly xenophobic brother, I had no interest in the non-English speaking world – despite speaking passable French – and misspent my three undergraduate years struggling to a lower second-class degree in Mathematics. Yet, I secured a job with Ferndown within weeks of graduating. Graduate status, irrespective of grade, was sufficient for my employer to grant me an interview; grill me before panels of staff; subject me to four hours of psychometric tests and then instantly offer me a junior position at a rate of £2,000 per annum above the average I could have expected for my mediocre qualification. It was a while before Andy was offered a job and although he implied he was having great difficulty obtaining satisfactory employment, I was sure this was for my ears only; the truth more likely being he was spoilt for choice and was playing one potential employer off against another. When he did make his choice, I am convinced that I made a big contribution to his recruitment.

I had been working at Ferndown for about three months and I was sitting at my desk analyzing demographic data of recently deceased policyholders, when my phone rang. There was a man in reception who needed to see me urgently. He would not give a name, would not say where he was from, only that it was in connection with my brother and – bypassing in-house security – was on his way up to see me. My immediate thought was that Andy must have had an accident and a messenger had arrived with bad news. I rushed to the lift to greet my envoy and encountered a smartly blue pinstripe-suited man of about fifty. He quickly reassured me Andy was fine, then – without explanation – insisted he was immediately introduced to my boss. His manner was assertive and as a naïve recruit to Ferndown, I felt obliged to comply.

My boss had an enclosed office, which was shut to me after the introduction, but I nervously observed proceedings through the glass-panelled door. The interchange lasted no more than a minute, during which time the man produced an identity card and then invited my boss to use the telephone. He declined, stepped out of the office and then ushered me in giving me the strangest look.

The man was John Ingram; well, that's what his ID indicated, but based upon the ensuing interview I doubted the accuracy. His title was Government

224

Security Officer and I had to sign the Official Secrets Act before he would continue. His job was to investigate the background of applicants, but he chose not to explain for what. Then began a two-hour grilling that would have done justice to a scene from a spy movie. I was asked the most intimate and searching questions about me, my brother, and any known joint associates. If I hesitated or was uncertain about my answers, he would pose the questions again later. Many questions were similar or phrased slightly differently, I assumed to corroborate earlier answers. With a final warning about the confidentiality of our meeting, he left as abruptly as he came. As ordered, I have since never discussed the interview with my boss, brother or any other person. Andy has never mentioned it, nor has he ever been forthcoming about his job, even to his wife.

I quizzed Kylie once about his secretiveness, but she had learnt to live with it. What she had found difficult to accept was how unemotional he could be at times, particularly when it came to tragic events. When asked, he skillfully dismisses his occupation as a boring research function based in London, which strangely demands impromptu and extended visits to Europe. I wonder if that is where he is now, except that doesn't explain Kylie's absence, since she never accompanies him.

I check the other rooms for suspicious activity but they appear normal. There's no sign of a distant departure: unopened mail deliveries or pristine newspapers. In the kitchen there are a couple of used tea plates and mugs, nothing unusual in that, but when I put my hand on the kettle it is still warm – warm enough to have been boiled within the last hour. I must have just missed them. No matter, I'm not going anywhere; I'll make myself a drink and a snack, and await their return.

Sipping my coffee, I look out of the kitchen window into the large rear garden. Privacy is guaranteed by the six-foot high fencing along the borders of the plot. It's mostly laid to lawn with freshly dug – albeit uncultivated – flower beds in strips down each side. There are stepping-stones across the lawn, which lead to a side door in the garage positioned on the left at the far end of the garden. Although there is a facing window in the nearest garage wall, from here I can't see inside. I don't expect Andy's car to be there, but I decide to investigate anyway.

It's peaceful in the garden. The distant lawn mower has completed its task and the birds must be taking an afternoon nap. As I near the garage, I think I witness a movement through the window, but dismiss it as a trick of the light. I open the door and peer in. I have just enough time to recognize who is wielding a jack handle, before my head screams with pain and blackness envelops me.

Chapter 37

SECOND THURSDAY – 2:00 p.m.

I forced my eyes open expecting nausea and pain, but there was neither. I expected to be lying in a pool of blood on the floor of a garage in Nazeing Tye, but I wasn't. I moved my head gently from side to side bracing myself for a burning sensation that didn't come. I did have a floating feeling like waking from the after effects of a general anaesthetic. In particular, my head felt clearer than I believed it had done for some time. No pressure, no tightness, like a heavy cold had suddenly been flushed from my airways.

I was lying in a bed and I comfortably eased myself into a sitting position. I wore just underpants and next to the bed there was a chair with outer clothing which belonged to me. I recognized my surroundings as a private room of a hospital; telltale signs were all around: clinically decorated walls and ceilings, trolleys of equipment, a wash hand basin in the corner – not dissimilar to Kathy's room. Kathy? I closed my eyes to picture the comparative scene and I saw Charlotte at Kathy's bedside reading from a book. Then I realized I had been jolted back to the present from another snapshot of my recent past.

I heard the door open and saw a head peer cautiously through the gap. Seeing me awake a nurse strode in.

'Couldn't keep away from me then? How are you feeling?' she said closing the door and coming to stand by the bed.

I looked up. 'Sam?'

'Don't look so surprised. I do work here and you did ask for me.'

'Did I? When?'

'About an hour ago you staggered into the hospital and collapsed. Are you sure you're okay?'

'I think so – physically anyway. Actually, I feel … well … pretty good. Hungry even.'

'Excuse me saying so, but you look a lot worse than when I kicked you out of the hospital a week ago. You're thinner and scruffier. Have you been living on the streets?'

'No. I've been at the Jubilee except for last night.'

'You could have fooled me. What have you been doing, Robin?'

Use of my old name reminded me of my current situation. 'Who knows I'm here?'

'Only me, and the staff who brought you here. Is there a problem?'

'You've not read the newspaper about me?'

'No. So you *are* someone rich and famous?'

'Not rich, but certainly famous,' I said.

I needed Sam's help so I confided sufficient detail of the events in the last week to illustrate my plight and my innocence. The news was a surprise and shock to Sam, but her faith in me remained intact.

'If you stay in this holding room, you'll have to be formally admitted to the hospital.'

'I've no intention of staying, but first I need to see Charlotte Rensberg. Am I safe in this room for a while?'

'Yes, but only a short while. I've requested a doctor to come to examine you.'

'Can you cancel that? Say I've recovered and discharged myself. Could you then fetch Charlotte instead? I'll only need a few minutes with her then I'll be away.'

When Sam had gone, I washed and dressed. In the mirror above the sink, the reflection confirmed how terrible I looked, but I consoled myself that a shave, shower, fresh clothes and a hot meal would considerably improve my appearance.

There was a knock on the door and I froze. 'Who is it?' I said.

'Charlotte,' said a whispered voice that I recognized.

'Come in,' I called.

Charlotte entered and ran towards me. 'Oh, Peter I've been …'

I motioned her to be quiet and sidestepped to close the door behind her.

'Sorry, I have to be careful. I'm headline news.'

She hesitated, inhibited by my reaction. 'Elsie showed me the *Gazette* this morning.'

I wanted to make immediate amends, but I had to get my priorities straight. 'Sit down, I need your urgent help.'

We sat on the bed and I held her hand, merely as a gesture of urgency, but she smiled and looked submissively into my eyes. I had to stand up to concentrate.

'Since I last saw you I've recalled most of the few days before I was found dumped in Hanbury Street. I think I know who attacked me – not why; but it's nothing to do with Ronnie Kent. Furthermore, I believe the same person set me up on a drugs charge and may have murdered a drug dealer. I think I have enough information that, if followed up by the police, would prove I'm right. That's my problem though. Who can I trust? And I, in fact we – but for difference reasons – won't find out unless we have feedback from Luther. If Bradley is clean ...'

Charlotte interrupted: 'Bradley was here early this morning. He took great pleasure in telling me his network was rapidly closing in on you, so I might as well save him police time and tell me where you are hiding. He certainly doesn't like you anymore.'

'It's because he thinks I've conned him. In his eyes, I've gone from a sad victim to ruthless villain. I think it suggests he's on the right side of the law, but we need to be certain.'

'So what do you want me to do?'

'You need to get in touch with Luther and find out whether we can safely reveal our information to either Haynes or Bradley. I was scheduled to meet Luther at Brian's studio tonight, but I think that's now being watched by the police. Phone the Jubilee and leave a message that Luther should contact you immediately. Meanwhile I'll stay here as long as I can. Sam will cover for me.'

'Okay. I'll do that straightaway. Then I ought to get back with Kathy.'

'How is Kathy now?'

'She sleeps for about twenty hours a day, but when she's awake she's cheerful and lucid. If she continues her progress the doctor thinks she could go home in a week, except of course ... there's no home to go to.'

Charlotte's response was a mixture of joy and sadness, and when she had gone, I paced and tried to think of what else I could do to accelerate events.

I could present myself at the nearest police station and demand the officer in charge listened to my story before contacting Bradley to takeover. The idea was flawed since I was a high profile fugitive who would be instantly recognized. Even if I wasn't, there was the danger the local police corruption might extend beyond Bradley and Dixon. Maybe I could enlist an intermediary who could pass on my knowledge to a senior officer of another police division? Now there's a thought, though I wasn't exactly overrun with friends I could call upon, at least not ones my memory had revealed to me. Yet there were two: Julie and Reg. I had doubts whether Julie would be on my side, but Reg – my new found neighbour – was a good choice; a man who had little respect for the law, but who unfortunately didn't have a telephone. Perhaps Adrian could be persuaded to extricate his car and give me a lift to

Harlow? I filed these thoughts as contingency plans I would have to seriously consider if Luther's co-operation wasn't forthcoming.

On a personal note, I needed to visit the loo and something to eat would have been welcome. I wasn't sure of my exact location in the hospital. The window in the room faced onto a quadrangle at ground level, which yielded no information regarding the nearest toilet, canteen or vending machine. Food I could stall, a pee I couldn't. I opened the door carefully and peeked out. The corridor was quiet; the few doors I could see were closed and only had numbers on them. I decided against exploration, instead, I shut the door and then quickly relieved myself in the sink. As I was scrubbing the sink afterwards with liquid soap and tissues I caught sight of a shadow pass in front of the window. At the same time the door burst open and the shape of DI Bradley filled the doorway.

Chapter 38

SECOND THURSDAY –2:30 p.m.

Despite my recent suspicions of Bradley, I couldn't forget the friendly toothy smile he had when we'd previously met. This was the main reason I was ambivalent about his integrity in the police force. Now I saw him in his authoritative state: a grimace, not a smile; tall and powerful, not seated and concerned. It only briefly crossed my mind there was a chance to escape. I reasoned his arrival in this room must have been planned and even if I was skillful and strong enough to manoeuvre past his imposing frame, there would undoubtedly be other police officers stationed to apprehend me. The figure standing outside the window was confirmation. Yet without my freedom, I stood little chance of clearing my name. The best I could achieve was to play straight and attempt to convey my innocence as convincingly as possible.

I stood still and acted unsurprised. 'Hello Inspector, I was hoping I might see you again.'

My composure only stalled his resolve for a moment. 'I'll have to work on my first impressions theory. I really thought you were a good guy. You can restore some of my misconceived faith in you by coming quietly.'

A huge uniformed constable appeared behind Bradley as if to emphasize that *quietly* was the only option open to me. I thought Bradley was imposing, but the constable had a bulbous and misshapen nose that would have befitted an impotent boxer, and his girth and weight were more akin to a weightlifter. The thin black moustache struck me most of all. It rendered the man with respectability, but more importantly it jogged a memory of my first day at the Jubilee and suddenly I had a plan.

'I'll do as you ask, but could I have a private word with Bill first?' I looked towards the constable. The constable and Bradley looked at each other.

'Do you know this man, Haynes?' Bradley asked. The constable shrugged, but my guess that he was Bill Haynes was confirmed.

'No guv, well not personally,' Haynes said.

They both turned to me for an explanation.

'Before you take me away I have crucial information to impart which could lead to the arrest of major criminals. However, for reasons which I can't go into now, I have to make this privately available to Bill first.' I could see they thought this was a trap. 'I'm serious. If you doubt my probity then by all means handcuff me to the bed first.' I stretched out my arms in submission.

'No harm in it boss. Underwood can see what's going on from the window and Shadwell's a bit smaller than me,' Haynes suggested.

Bradley looked impatient, but the tiniest hint of crime-busting information had him hooked. 'A few minutes, that's all,' he said and swapped places with Haynes, keeping his eyes on me as he closed the door.

'Has Luther been to see you about Bradley?' I asked immediately.

'Yes.'

'Did he explain why he wanted the information?'

'No.'

'Will you tell me what you told him?'

'Why?'

'Because the information I have may be compromised depending upon Bradley's ... allegiance.'

Haynes looked angry. 'I've known Bradley for about five years. We've worked together many times and he's straight as a die. He has commendations and has turned down promotion twice in order to stay in the field. He's like Luther, obsessed with tracking down drug offenders. He might bend the law now and again to his advantage, other than that you couldn't find a better copper.'

'You would say that of course, since you're not exactly clean yourself, are you?'

'What do you mean?'

'I know about your dealings with Luther. Supplements your lowly PC earnings does it?'

Haynes clenched his fists and took a step towards me. I gambled and stood my ground.

'I like my job and it's my choice to stay as I am. Not that it's any concern of yours you fucking lowlife.'

'So your extracurricular income is sanctioned by your bosses, is it?' I had raised my voice deliberately threatening that Bradley or Underwood might hear.

Haynes motioned with his hands to turn my volume down. 'Every penny I receive from Luther I donate anonymously to the police benevolent fund.'

'But you didn't answer the question, you see, and that's my problem. For all I know you're as corrupt as Bradley and wouldn't utter a word against him.'

'Bradley's clean and I don't have a guilty conscience.'

'Then presumably you don't mind if I declare to Bradley what you and Luther have been up to?'

'You wouldn't do that.'

'Oh, but I would, unless you can help me with a little problem I have.'

Haynes tensed as if to argue, then relaxed and said 'Which is?'

'I need you to convince Bradley somehow that he must listen to what I have to say, and act on it. Without your support, I fear he will just lock me up and throw away the key, particularly as I am allegedly heavily involved in the drug scene. Brief him; bring him in here and then I want you to go to the Helen Raphael ward and get Charlotte Rensberg to join us.'

'You'll have to whet my appetite with some information I can give him first.'

'It's a trade I want. I want him to seriously consider facts I have about my innocence and in return I'll give him details that will implicate a senior police officer in the local drugs scene. With luck the information should lead to the arrest of Ronnie Kent.'

Haynes's expression showed I struck a nerve. A broad grin appeared on his face making his droopy moustache lift to horizontal. 'That should do nicely,' he said and left the room.

I looked towards the window and Underwood looked bemused by the activity. Cheekily I gave him a little wave, but he turned away not wishing to consort with an enemy.

I was encouraged the Haynes/Bradley consultation was taking some time. If Bradley had dismissed my proposals out of hand, he would have returned quickly. Haynes had appeared sincere enough about Bradley's integrity, but if Bradley had conned Haynes, and Haynes had conned me, then Kathy's, Charlotte's and my demise were now a forgone conclusion.

Bradley re-entered the room after a few minutes. He went to the window, opened it slightly and whispered to Underwood before directing me to lie on the bed so that he could keep an eye on me. He began strolling up and down the room. 'I don't know what hold you have over Bill, but he's convinced me to listen to you, albeit against my better judgement. I should add though, that if you or the Rensbergs have been withholding key information, I reserve the right to book you all for obstructing police enquiries.'

'You agree to my terms?' I asked.

'You're in no position to barter with me Shadwell. Get on with it,' Bradley replied impatiently.

I described, as best as I could remember, the content of my dreams and flashbacks from the previous day. Bradley was sceptical about my recollections, convinced the details were contrived to fund an alibi. I persisted with my story and offered that Reg and Donna would be able to confirm much of what I related. I emphasized matters relating to my bogus drug bust, and my neighbourly connection with the murdered drug dealer I had originally read about in the Chelmsford local paper. I proposed a conspiracy theory centred on the theft of Josh's van, the lack of response from Josh's flat and the smell I had detected coming from the flat two days later. I seemed to be making impact with Bradley, since he had begun to make notes in a little black notebook. He thought for a while when I had finished.

'You're certain that this Sebastian Tate was the man who stole Carmichael's van and who hit you in the garage?'

'Absolutely. The black ponytail was the giveaway, plus I caught sight of his face as the jack handle hit me.'

'Perhaps you could satisfy me with a reason for his motive?'

'I'm afraid not, Inspector. To the best of my knowledge I'd never met him until he joined Ferndown. Nor can I explain how poor Josh fits into all of this.'

'Which takes us back to where we started from. What you've said doesn't account for drugs being found in your flat or give you a solid alibi for Carmichael's death.'

'Maybe it does,' I countered. 'There are two things you could check. Find out the time of Josh's death. I believe it happened before I returned from the Lake District. Also get the fingerprint records checked out from the scene of the crime and my filing cabinet. I've been in Josh's flat enough times for my prints to be there, but if Tate's prints are there – bingo. Someone planted those drugs too and I'll wager Josh's or Tate's prints are on my filing cabinet.'

'Assuming they were careless enough to leave any behind,' Bradley said. 'Besides, there are other unknowns. What's the relationship between Tate and Carmichael? Why did Tate steal the van? Where's the van now? Who's at your brother's now? Why was Tate using one of Kent's cars when he abducted you?'

'Valid points. Maybe the van was used to transport drugs and could be at my brother's. Your last point must be a coincidence. You had no proof it was the same car as Kent's.'

'Equally valid, except coincidences often give the police the breaks they are looking for. And there's a drug connection.'

'Well, isn't the best course of action to pick up Tate and lean on him for answers to these questions? Will you pass these facts onto the division handling the hunt for Peter Shadwell?'

Before Bradley could answer, the door opened and Haynes came in with Charlotte. She saw Bradley and looked nervously towards me. I started to rise from the bed, but Haynes stiffened and quickly shut the door.

'It's okay, I was only going to give Charlotte a chair,' I explained.

'You stay where you are,' Bradley said and guided Charlotte into a chair on the far side of the room.

'Peter, what's happening? I haven't heard from Luther yet.' Charlotte pleaded.

Bradley looked questioningly towards Charlotte.

'I've been explaining to Inspector Bradley about my drug related past. I hope he's about to agree to help me,' I said.

'To answer your question before Miss Rensberg arrived: yes, I'll pass on the information you've given me, plus I'm holding you as a suspect for the murder of Gerald Fullerton – also known as Gannet – and the rape of Stella Mackenzie.'

'Inspector, are you telling me Gannet really was murdered?'

'He was poisoned.'

Charlotte gasped and put her hand over her mouth.

'That doesn't answer the question. Deliberately? By asparagus sandwiches for example?'

For the first time during the interview Bradley permitted himself a thoughtful smile. 'You're more resourceful than I appreciated,' he said. 'Not only do you have influence on PC Haynes, but it would appear you also have access to the police pathologist. I had the report on Fullerton's autopsy yesterday afternoon, which among other things confirmed the asparagus sandwiches he consumed shortly before he died, had not contributed to his death. There was a note in the report the request to conduct such a test had come from an anonymous source.' Now Bradley laughed. 'Of course, you must have theorized I had doctored the sandwiches to poison you. But what motive would I have? Maybe this explains why I'm aware that somebody's been checking up on me at the station.' He glanced accusingly at Haynes, whose normally ruddy face had suddenly flushed scarlet.

Well done Luther, I thought. He must have been the anonymous source. 'How was Gannet poisoned then?'

'Salmonella. Present in dodgy meat, it is assumed he ate at Smithfields.'

'So why did you accuse me?'

'You were the last person known to be in contact with him and it added weight to the story for the press. The more scandalous the accusations the greater coverage they give. And since we are trading secrets what on earth was going through your head to think *I* had poisoned … Gannet?'

'That will become clear when Charlotte reveals what she knows. I'll tell you more about the rape when she's finished.'

Everyone's attention turned to Charlotte. 'Are you sure it's safe … in present company?' she asked.

'I have it on good authority that the Inspector is trustworthy.' I purposely didn't look at Bill, but I sensed another flush from him, and Bradley's renewed scrutiny.

Charlotte admitted Kathy's recovery and revelations had been concealed from the police because of her fear that Kathy might be exposed to danger. When she reached the part about "Chad" and Ronnie Kent, I watched Bradley closely for signs of a reaction, but he merely uttered a small sigh as he took an abnormal inhalation.

Haynes was more voluble. 'Bloody hell guv. That's major stuff. We could …'

Bradley interrupted. 'Don't jump to conclusions. All that this young woman's sister heard was one reference to the word she thought was Chad. It was probably "Dad".'

'Ronnie Kent's father died two months ago. You know that since you went snooping at the funeral looking for villains,' Haynes countered.

'Alright,' Bradley said reluctantly, 'but Chad could be a nickname that's nothing to do with Chadwick. Do you know what Chad actually means?'

'It's a country in North Africa?' I offered.

'Yes and it's also a kind of fish; the little bits of paper or cardboard punched out of paper tape or cards and, it's the name of the character in those facetious sketches during the 1940's. Chad was portrayed as a bald head peering over a wall, with a caption beginning "Wot no ...?", in protest at wartime shortages. So our "Chad" could just be … a bald man.'

We all stared at Bradley, maybe in awe of his knowledge, but for me it re-aroused my suspicions he might be protecting Dixon.

'I know what you are thinking, but put yourself in my position. I can't investigate my own boss based on one reference to the name of Chad. Can I?'

'Can't you have his phone tapped or have him followed?' Charlotte asked.

Bradley laughed: 'No way.'

'Presumably you won't tell him what Kathy said either?'

'I'll want my own statement from Kathy, but I'll keep it to myself for the time being. And I'll guarantee Bill's discretion.'

'Yes sir,' Bill said formally in confirmation.

'And can you guarantee Kathy's safety? If there was a leak she's conscious and talking, she could be in danger,' I said.

'If I'm convinced by her statement then I'll consider putting someone on guard outside her room. Bill's my first choice so we can keep a closed shop on the information.'

We fell into silence for a moment dwelling on each of our options. I rose from the bed – this time without opposition – and stood by the window looking out. Underwood was close by, sitting on a low wall, smoking. I turned back to the room.

'I have a proposal,' I said and went on to add details of my two encounters with Sniffy I had omitted earlier.

'Not only should what I've told you exonerate me from the rape of Stella, but it gives us, or rather me, a way into Ronnie Kent's organization.'

'To what end?' Bradley asked.

'To obtain information for you of course. This was the trade I had in mind. You pursue the leads I've given about Tate and Carmichael and although I've missed my appointment with Sniffy, it shouldn't take too long to find him again.'

'You're assuming I let you walk away from here. I'm duty bound to arrest you. Besides, there's no certainty Sniffy would recruit you, let alone allow you intimate contact with information sources.'

'On the contrary, since my last meeting with Sniffy my infamous face and criminal career have been in the headlines. My transfer value and credibility must have soared.'

'Not necessarily. Recruiting a public enemy might be a turn off.'

'But it's worth a try, surely?' Bradley was thinking. 'If I don't succeed within a couple of days, I promise to turn myself in.'

'It might work …' Bradley said. '… but there's perhaps a better method of infiltration. We know Kent hires street people for his shady schemes and he often approaches anonymous strays from the Charing Cross and Strand areas at night. The tunnels at Charing Cross underground station are a good bet. We planted an undercover man there about a year ago, but he was found out and ended up as a stiff in a skip.'

'I don't think it's a good idea,' Charlotte said protectively. 'It's far too dangerous.'

I detected a concern for my welfare that warmed me, but without my offer – in the short term at least – I was destined for jail. My life was going nowhere at the moment, and I was willing to take almost any risk to give it some direction.

Bradley ignored her and grinned. 'Okay. We'll … I'll … give it a shot. Mercenary bastard that I am, using you as a pawn sacrifice to capture the king is a good return.'

Charlotte didn't like being bypassed and tried discouragement one more time. 'You're crazy Inspector. How will you cover up Peter's escape?'

'Bill will be discreet and I'll tell Underwood we have a case of mistaken identity. No one else in the force knows I'm here. I'll not be able to give you immunity from the rest of the police looking for you, so you'd better make damn sure you aren't picked up. If you do, then our arrangement never took place. Bill and I will be able to confirm that.'

'So you'll set the wheels in motion to follow up my Sebastian Tate lead?' I asked.

'Yes.'

'Then you'd better brief me on what you know about Kent and his organization.'

'I don't think you need to hear this Miss Rensberg,' Bradley said. 'Would you go back to your sister and tell her I'll be along to interview her shortly.'

Charlotte stood up reluctantly and moved towards me. 'Will you see me before you go?'

Bradley answered for me. 'I don't think that's a good idea. Peter will need to slip out of here as discreetly as possible. Best say your goodbyes now. We'll leave you alone for a couple of minutes.' He nodded to Bill and they both left the room. The Inspector recognized Charlotte's needs more than I did; my mind was still buzzing with the responsibility I had just taken on.

'Are you sure you know what you are doing, Peter?'

'Yes, of course. Above all, the plan buys me time and freedom while Bradley gets the evidence he needs to clear my name. Anyway, it must be fairly unlikely the idea will work as easily as we assume, but don't tell Bradley. If I do succeed in being recruited, I should be able to bale out if the going gets tough, or earlier as soon as the charges against me are dropped.' It was the answer Charlotte wanted, but I was already committed to pursuing the cause against Ronnie Kent as far as I could.

'Do you promise me that's what you'll do?'

Her eyes held mine seeking reassurance and, perhaps something else. I didn't want to lie to her and if I told the truth, I was afraid our parting would end in an indeterminate campaign of dissuasion. As I thought of my response she came closer.

'Charlotte, I …' I started and then my following action meant an immediate answer wasn't necessary.

I ran my fingers through her hair then pulled her gently towards me. I kissed her forehead and then moved my mouth towards hers testing her reaction. She put her arms around my waist and began caressing my back; it was the positive sign I needed to kiss her in a way I had only dreamed of up to now. We embraced and held each other for a minute, but then I sensed tears roll down her cheek. I broke away fearing I had upset her.

'Something I've said or done?'

'No. Something you *haven't* said. The promise. You're determined to get to Ronnie Kent. Why?'

'I think the resolve has been in my mind since I saw Kathy lying in a coma. It sickened me to think there were people in the world who could inflict such tragedy and potentially get away with it. I do promise to be careful though. After what's just happened, I couldn't bear the thought of not being able to kiss you again. Can I remind myself what I have to look forward to?'

I kissed the tears away and then sought her lips again. The kiss was shorter, but more passionate this time. From its effects, I knew my impetuous conviction to accelerate Kent's downfall would need moderation; I was desperate to return to Charlotte, unharmed from my self-imposed assignment.

'When you come back for the next kiss, can I make two requests?' She was smiling.

'Anything.'

'Promise not to be offended?'

'Another promise? Yes.'

'Have a shower and a shave. You smell like a drain and I'll be itching for the next week.'

We laughed and held each other again. It was a light-hearted way to depart.

She walked to the door and stopped to look back. 'You'll have to come back to me Robin Forest ... Peter Shadwell ... whoever you are. I'd like to find out more about the man I've fallen in love with.'

I had no time to dwell on Charlotte's parting words. Bradley and Haynes returned immediately and Bradley launched straight into the background I wanted.

'For the last ten years *Barrimore* Kent – Ronnie Kent's father – had been number one gangster in East London – allegedly. He was believed to be behind numerous blags, some murders, prostitution, porn and worst of all a drug-running business that had grown uncontrollably. Alleged, believed, suspected, whatever word you choose, he was definitely the local Godfather, but we've never been able to prove it and now it's too late.

'Barry was never directly involved in any operation; he had so many levels in his organization chart that it made the civil service appear parochial. Whenever we've caught one of his suspected hirelings, one of our major objectives has been to get him or her to squeal on their immediate commanders and we've had some success. However, the higher we climb in the hierarchy of command, the harder it gets to break down. On an armed bank robbery, a few months ago, we penetrated four levels of command above the crooks at the sharp end and we still believed we were nowhere near the top of the tree.

'Barry owned loads of houses and flats in the East End and asked peppercorn rents in return for co-operation from the tenants; co-operation covers: harbouring criminals, storing stolen goods and selling drugs. We've raided dozens of premises in recent years after tip-offs and surveillance, and with few exceptions, when we go in we find ... nothing. Barry and Co always seemed to be one step ahead of us. The law's not in our favour either. By a quirk of the Misuse of Drugs Act, we can arrest houseowners and tenants who let their property be used to supply cannabis or opium, but not in the breed of drugs that Kent deals in, such as crack and heroin. For prosecution we have to rely on civil action by the local authorities, but their priorities are vested in other social injustices. Nowadays, because of our previous abortive attempts, we've been instructed ...' Bradley stopped suddenly and blew air sharply through his mouth. He frowned and appeared to be studying Haynes, who began to fidget.

'Sir?' Haynes said, thinking he was the object of Bradley's attention.

Bradley ignored him then a few seconds later said to himself, 'Hmm, it stacks up.'

'What does?' I enquired.

'We've been instructed by the Super to be 110 percent sure of our facts before any other raids and to always seek ... *his* prior approval.'

'Super meaning Superintendent Dixon?'

'Exactly. Although in isolation, it proves nothing. I know the Assistant Commissioner has had significant representation from ethic minority groups about harassment, and to protect his political backside he has merely passed down his caution.'

'You've been talking about Barry in the past tense; Bill said earlier that Barry was dead.'

'Yes, I'm coming to that. Even if Barry had wanted to become personally involved with any of his operations, he would have been physically incapable. Ever since he descended on our patch, he's been bed-ridden. He had a wasting disease, which progressively ruined his body, but left his acute brain intact. He masterminded everything from between the sheets, and was tended day and night by his wife and a succession of highly paid and incorruptible loyal nurses. Instructions are issued – we believe – to his *field marshals* via the Internet. He rarely had any visitors of note to his comparatively modest house in Bromley, and nothing revealing has ever been communicated via the telephone – we have it tapped of course – other than obscure references to e-mail accounts and websites. We are sure that somewhere he has a sophisticated computer operation. Now we have a cybercrime unit permanently devoted to monitoring his sites, and attempting to crack codes and messages. If we could locate that operation, we would be able to close down the Kent organization in one swoop.

'A couple of months ago Barry contracted pneumonia and was dead within three days. He was only 55 years old. Now we come to Ronnie.

'Ronnie's about your age and height, skinny, triangular shaped and scarred face, black hair, usually scruffily dressed and foul mouthed. Years ago he got into all kinds of petty troubles: shop-lifting, smoking cannabis and a few con-tricks, but his father soon put a stop to that because – we assume – it was drawing too much attention to the Kent household. As far as we know, Ronnie was kept out of the mainstream business because he was too immature and unreliable. He was spotted harmlessly hanging out in clubs, bars and snooker halls. However, in recent years, as his father became more infirm, we think he was trusted to take over the less lucrative, non-drugs part of the Kent Empire. We've certainly had more arrests in that period and think that has been partly because of Ronnie's less meticulous attitude to crime than his father. Now Barry is dead, we hope Ronnie is in control of the drug trafficking and is less conscientious in that area too. That's the resume in a nutshell. It should be enough for your purposes. Any questions?'

I thought for a moment. 'Barry started his criminal career at a late age; what turned him?'

'That's always been a mystery to us. Most villains start young. The records show that before coming to London he ran a respected carpet fitting company in Birmingham. He had no previous convictions.'

'How do I get in touch with you if I find out anything?'

'It'll look suspicious if you carry a mobile phone and I can't spare the resources to have you tailed. The best I can do is give you my mobile number to memorize.' He recited the number and I echoed it for confirmation. 'You'll be able to reach me any time of day. Phone me whenever you can and tell me where you are; if the Sebastian Tate story doesn't check out I'll need to pick you up. Anything else?'

'Can you advance me some money ... for expenses?'

He reached into his back pocket and took out a wad of notes, reluctantly peeled off two £5 notes and passed them to me. '£10 should be enough. You're a stray remember; you can't be too flush. Keep you're head down, if not for me then for your young lady. Now fuck off to Charing Cross. I haven't seen you.'

Chapter 39

SECOND THURSDAY – 3:30 p.m.

I picked up my bag and made my way to the side entrance of the hospital where I had met Charlotte the previous day. This brought back memories of our first embrace and the more recent intimacy. I hesitated for a moment daydreaming about being with her, but the passing of a police car on the street shook me back to the task I had assigned myself, and I set off with a vigilance that matched the determination of my resolve. From memory, Charing Cross was about five miles away and it was only around three o'clock. I had plenty of time to get there before nightfall, so decided to go via the launderette where I had arranged to meet Sniffy. I doubted he would still be there, but it would accelerate contact if he were.

The launderette was still busy and this time I ventured inside to look around. There was no sign of Sniffy there or anywhere in the nearby streets. I returned to the telephone kiosk I had used earlier and made a call to Ferndown. I hadn't decided what to say, but I asked to speak to Julie Rawlinson and was informed she had left the company at the end of the previous week. Presumably, the difficult situation regarding her involvement with me had forced her to move on. The call confirmed why Howard's enquiry about Paul Richardson's secretary had drawn a blank. To test the reaction I also asked to be put through to Peter Shadwell and received a similar answer without any elaboration. I then tried my list of Rawlinsons; one unobtainable, two not answered and the last not the right person. The Tates were no better; a retired police officer who wanted to chat and a salesman working from home.

I found a quiet pizzeria and ordered a pepperoni pizza and a bottle of water. I sat on a bench in the grounds of a nearby memorial gardens and, in concerned deference to my sensitive stomach, spent the first minute discarding the indigestible pepperoni pieces before rewarding my hunger. After eating, I lingered, afraid that pacing the streets would be unnecessary exposure. I replayed my flashbacks, searching for vital clues I may have missed in previous analyses and when nothing new surfaced, I thought of

Charlotte. Adversity had brought us together, but our futures looked bleak. Even the possibility of bringing the perpetrators of our downfalls to justice brought me no solace. Charlotte, Kathy and I were penniless and homeless, and the status of my brother was currently unknown. I wanted to dwell on the positive side of my relationship with Charlotte, but knew in the present climate this was foolhardy, lest there be a negative outcome. I spent a lonely hour with my thoughts and, deflated and resigned, picked up my belongings and mingled with the throngs of commuters as they left their offices homeward bound.

I headed for the River Thames with my head hung low to minimize visual contact with anyone. When I reached the Embankment, I lightened my outlook, encouraged by river breezes and the less energetic flow of pedestrians. I passed Charing Cross and roamed for a while studying the solid and ornate architecture of the Government buildings around Whitehall. It was in my mind that this was the working territory of my brother, and the Foreign Office and Ministry of Defence complexes stood out as likely candidates for his employment. Where was he now? Was he involved in the same conspiracy as me? I was already tempted to ring Inspector Bradley for news, but so far I had none of my own to trade; it was time to make steps to correct that. I made my way straight to Charing Cross station to reconnoitre the area.

There were no obvious places at this time of day where the homeless hung out overnight, so I bought a copy of the *Financial Times* and found an empty bench seat in the Victoria Embankment gardens adjacent to Embankment station. It was a great relief to sit down. The head-numbing trauma of the morning and the long thigh-aggravating walk had drained me more than I realized. With the pink newspaper on my lap, I was reminded of Howard Winston's resurrection from the streets and wondered whether my fate was equally rosy. I had intended to begin reacquainting myself with the supposedly familiar world of insurance, but a brief exploration of the front page of the FT had my head nodding in submission to the needs of sleep. I fought the suggestion for a few minutes then using my bag as a pillow stretched out to the full length of the bench. I had sufficient presence of mind to hide my face with my beret before drifting into unconsciousness with renewed trepidation of revealing more of my resurfacing past.

Two things woke me: I was cold, colder than I'd been since Sebastian Tate hit me with a jack handle; and a rough tongue was licking my hand.

'Come away Tootsie,' said a female voice nearby.

I shivered and removed my beret to peer through the gloom. An overcoated old woman was tugging a long lead that terminated in a tall white poodle wearing a tartan body warmer. The dog was slobbering the residual taste of my pizza. I swung my legs to the ground. The woman kept her distance no doubt fearing the close proximity of a tramp. Simply removing my spittle-covered hand solved the problem, but the dog in a parting gesture of defiance cocked its leg, weed on my trousers and hurried away to sniff trees with its mistress in pursuit. I stood up, shook my leg and experienced general body stiffness from my bench slumbers. I stretched and shook other body parts to loosen and warm my muscles. I appeared to be the only person in the gardens now, hardly surprising since it was dark from the evening, and the park lighting and shallow glow from the overlooking buildings did little to brighten the spookiness of the place. The sky above was star filled and the wind blowing from the Thames accounted for the chill. There was a muffled roar of noise coming from the passing traffic on the Embankment.

I kept to the shadows of the gardens and made my way towards the exit nearest to Charing Cross station. My discretion was wasted since the gateway was chained and padlocked, and I recalled that many of the parks were closed at dusk for security reasons. This didn't explain why I hadn't been moved on or why an old woman had been walking her dog at this time of night. I would have accepted the latter was a dream but for the reminding dampness of my trouser leg. I solved the entrapment by scaling the lower branches of a tree and climbing over the encircling railings of the gardens, but in my haste, a spike speared a foot long tear in the back of my jacket.

At the station, the central clock showed nine o'clock meaning I had been asleep for around four hours. It had been a deep sleep; no dreams or flashbacks that I could recall. Either my brain had needed recuperation or the flow of information from my past had now come to its natural end.

The mainline and underground stations were still busy; the commuter flow now replaced by diners and theatre goers heading for the Strand or Leicester Square. I surveyed the tunnels and walkways of the underground, and there were beggars and dossers dotted everywhere together with the occasional busker. The beggars and buskers had comparatively healthy donations in their collecting snoods, hats or instrument cases despite the signs warning of hefty fines. Luther's pitch allocation presumably didn't extend to this part of London and I wondered whether someone else was the beggar's overlord or if this prime location was a free for all. Whatever, I had no intention of begging; I needed to avoid the scrutiny of the regular police, transport police or a Luther equivalent. The clusters of sleepers were the most pathetic sight: completely cocooned in their moth-eaten blankets and stretched out on panels of large cardboard boxes often with remains of fast food and their cartons littered around them.

If Bradley was right that homeless people were recruited at Charing Cross, it was a difficult decision for the most strategic place to be, such were the multitude of locations to bed down for the night. A hopeless task; the odds were surely against me being in the right place at the right time.

The tunnels that led away from the underground ticket hall looked the most promising. The ramp leading to the exit on the north side of the Strand was the resting place for perhaps ten homeless souls. Three of them were chatting in a group and one was calling out to passers-by for small change. If someone refused they were politely bade to "have a pleasant evening", but the tone of the voice was ambiguous as to whether the statement was cynical or sincere. I chose not to join them, favouring solitude, and viewing as a singleton, I might be more approachable to any prowling recruiters. Further along there were some shops, closed for the night, though offering doorways and alcoves that provided shelter from the wind chill concentrated by the tunnel. I found one recess that held abandoned packing material and at the risk of usurping someone's overnight accommodation seized it as my own. The smell from the area probably explained its unoccupied status, the pervading odour suggesting this was used as a local urinal. There were currently no damp patches, but the white stone backdrop was stained a yellowish-green colour. I was tempted to transfer the bedding to another cell, but I already smelt of dog's pee and anyway, the position – at the apex of the slight curve in the tunnel – provided a strategic outlook to the left and right. The large cardboard box had once contained packets of cornflakes, and from a two-foot square cube, it had been cleverly made by the previous owner, into two six-foot by two-foot strips. I used one in an L-shape as a backrest and base, and the other as part base and "blanket", and felt proud at my ingenuity. The design certainty shielded me from draughts and I settled reasonably comfortably to study the FT crossword, sip water from my bottle and observe the passers-by.

Despite my earlier sleep and a need to be watchful, I drifted in and out of consciousness. I was woken several times by noisy groups of youths and prayed I didn't become a victim of their collective recklessness. Twice during my wakeful periods, pairs of uniformed policemen paraded along the tunnel like nuns, but fortunately they appeared more concerned with their dialogue than with the detritus of human society.

I guessed it was near midnight that my true resilience to street life was severely tested. The recess and cardboard bed were serving their purposes as a shield from the wind, but the dropping ambient temperature had penetrated the insufficient layers of my flimsy clothing to skin depth, so that I awoke shivering uncontrollably. Coupled with the impassivity of my body I began to question the sense and healthiness of my task. I strode up and down the tunnel to bring circulation back to my numbed and frozen limbs. My homeless compatriots didn't stir and I envied their practiced resistance to the elements and noise. After five minutes or so, I returned to my sleeping quarters hoping I wouldn't have to spend another night in such demeaning conditions.

Chapter 40

THIRD FRIDAY – 1:00 a.m.

I felt the beret whipped from my face.

'Well fuck me, if it ain't the man I'm looking fer.'

In my drowsy state I thought the police had found me and then I recognized my visitor's voice. I had rehearsed many times for such an encounter and quickly reverted to the role of a desperate Robin Forest. I opened my eyes slowly and then twitched as if shocked.

'Sniffy. It's you. Thank God,' I said feigning relief. 'How did you find me?'

'Wuz easy. Ishmael said there wuz a stranger in the camp.'

'Ishmael?'

'The schnorrer three shops down from ya.'

'But how did you know to look here?'

'It's a favourite spot to look for new talent. Most of the new bums in town head for Charing Cross. But why're you 'ere?'

'A guy at the hostel in Camden last night said this area was a good place for begging. I've spent most of the afternoon working pitches around Covent Garden. Didn't get much money though because the police and other beggars kept moving me on; but lots of food handouts.'

'So why didn't ya meet me at the launderette. Didn't ya like the deal?'

'No. No. I did go there, but I was too late. Some flush blokes I met last night took me on a bender. I was still sleeping it off at midday.'

'Bloody dangerous working CG with your form, amazing ya didn't get picked up.'

'So you and Stella haven't withdrawn your statements?'

'Yer kidding me right? Are ya really as dumb as ya look ... *Peter Shadwell?*'

I had decided the best course of action was to play ignorant of my past, so I gave Sniffy my best confused look.

'Sorry. You're mixing me up with someone else. My name's Robin Forest.'

'It's alright, I'm not the fuzz, ya don't have to play games with me.'

'Well, that's the name I'm using; I don't know my real name. I didn't tell you earlier that I had an accident and lost my memory.'

'And ya ain't seen the local paper?'

'No. What? Was there something about me? Someone looking for me?' I said with fake excitement.

He reached into his inside pocket and took out his wallet. From it he produced the newspaper cutting from the *Gazette* and handed it to me. 'Oh yeh, someone's looking for ya alright.'

I pretended to study it and displayed rising panic. 'There must be a mistake. None of those things are anything to do with me.'

'The rape is and I heard about Gannet. Perhaps yer conveniently forgot about the drugs stuff?'

'You set me up on the rape and Gannet ... I'd only just met him ... why should I want to hurt him? And the drugs things ... I can't believe I had anything to do with that. But why are you carrying that press cutting?'

'I tole me boss about ya before the newspaper report. But when he'd read the story he said he *definitely* wanted to see ya.'

'What does he want with me?'

'As I said once before, if ya can 'elp 'im out on a few projects then ... well ... we'll get the rape charge dropped, although that's the least of yer problems at the moment. I'm sure he'll have some ideas about yer other difficulties.'

'What's your boss's name?'

'Why'd ya wanna know that?'

'If he's going to keep the fuzz away from me, then I ought to know his moniker.' I surprised myself with my language. The exposure to Sniffy seemed to be bringing out the East End roots in me.

'I don't suppose it'll hurt to tell ya. Ya'll probably meet him tomorrow – his name is Jake.'

'Jake?' I queried with a disappointed tone.

'Yeh. Ya got some problem with the name of Jake?'

'Um ... well no ... I guess not.'

'Good. So pick up yer gear and we'll be orf.'

We set off down the tunnel and a beggar stirred from his cardboard bed. 'Hey, got any jobs for me Sniffy,' he called out.

'Not tonight Carlos,' Sniffy shouted back, 'maybe tomorrow.'

'You're popular. What sort of things do these guys do for you?'

'This and that. Dunno exactly. I just recruit and then the boss assigns the jobs. He's good at matching the right person to the right job. The weaker or less reliable guys get involved in the simple scams and the fitter, student types, like you, get the juicy stuff.'

We entered a bustling part of the Strand. 'What sort of ... stuff?'

'Yer too full of questions for my likin'. So shut it, there's too many ears about.'

'At least tell me where we are going.'

'Ya'll find out soon enough.'

Meeting someone called Jake didn't hold a lot of promise, but I reflected upon Bradley's statement about the hierarchy in Kent's organization. I was stupid to think there would be a direct route from Sniffy to Ronnie. If I was being recruited at the bottom rung of the ladder, even with my public pedigree, it could take ages to reach the top, if ever. I'd stick to my task until I had the all clear from Bradley and then he would have to take over.

When we reached the end of the Strand, we took to the back streets so I tried to reinstate my questioning, albeit at a subtler level.

'So you're just a hustler for the management, are you?'

'Na. I'm a recruitment executive,' he said proudly. 'I get reglar wages an' everything. I ain't been in this job long, but my boss says I'm one of the best execs he's ever 'ad. Reckons I'll be promoted soon and I'll get a company motor.'

It sounded like complete misguided bullshit and I had great difficulty holding back laughter. To cultivate his confidence in me though I continued my charade.

'Bloody hell. Wish I could fall on my feet like you. So, you'll have blokes working for you and a car?'

'Yeh, sort of. I'll become assignment manager and I'll get a moped when I've passed me test. Won't be long before I've got a car though.'

I supposed a youth like Sniffy had never been in a proper job. If I'd mentioned working conditions, health and safety at work, notice periods, payslips, tax, national insurance and other esoteric matters of an employer/employee contract, his limited brain would have undoubtedly gone into overload.

I lost the initiative from that point. He began to pose me questions about how I had lost my memory and what I had recalled from my past. I chose to ignore my earlier theory that I was the victim of a Kent mugging, just in case there was still a connection somehow. Instead I spun a tale of suddenly finding myself wandering in Stepney without documents or an identity. I speculated I'd perhaps had a nervous breakdown that, from his revelation in the newspaper, may have been brought on by murdering someone.

'Aren't you scared you may be escorting a killer through the streets of London?'

'Nah. I'm sure ya had good reason to take someone out. You ain't no nutter and I can look after meself alright.' Like you did when we first met I thought.

We walked south of St. Paul's Cathedral then north beyond Liverpool Street station until we reached a turning off Worship Street. It was a narrow, run-down street, and we passed an Indian takeaway, an electrical retailer, a newsagent and a couple of boarded-up shops before we reached a stretch of familiar looking terraced houses. At the third house – number 17 – Sniffy slowed down, looked around and then took two strides up the path to the front door, beckoning me to follow. Before joining him, I hesitated when I thought I recognized a vehicle parked on the other side of the street. The house was in darkness. He took out a large bunch of keys from his anorak and examined them, finally selecting a silver key to open the door.

'Try not to make too much noise, ya might wake the residents,' Sniffy said flicking a switch.

A dim bulb lit the hallway, which looked like it hadn't been decorated for years. The walls were decked in faded floral wallpaper and there was a musty smell combining age and tobacco smoke. There was a facing staircase with threadbare green carpet.

'Isn't this your house?' I asked innocently, but guessing the reply.

'Nah. It's one of the safe houses we use. George and Jessie live here rent-free on the understanding they accommodate the occasional guest. Ya'll be safe here until Jake decides what to do with ya.'

Sniffy led the way to the kitchen at the far end of the hall. The kitchen was fully equipped and clean, but the appliances, except for a new microwave oven, were from a generation earlier.

'Want some grub before ya get yer head down?'

'You just help yourself?'

'Sure. Wanna sandwich?'

'Just black coffee for me thanks.'

'Sit in the back room, I'll bring it through.'

The back room was adjacent to the kitchen and furnished as a lodger's one room flat. The furniture comprised of a bunk bed, a second-hand chest of drawers, a wardrobe and two-seater settee. Piled about ten high in one corner were identical light brown boxes that, by their markings, contained video recorders. Familiar floral wallpaper covered the walls, but otherwise they were devoid of ornamentation. There was a curtained window, which by shielding the light, I could see faced a mostly concrete yard skirted by high walls. It was a cold and depressing room, but for the transients passing through I supposed it was shelter, and provided semi-private modest comfort. I inspected the stack of boxes and their immobility indicated they were full rather than empty.

Sniffy came in greedily eating a sandwich and was oblivious to the cascade of crumbs falling to the linoleum floor. I took the proffered coffee and chose not to complain it was white. I started to ask about my surroundings and hosts, who were presumably asleep upstairs, but Sniffy's suspicions were aroused.

'Questions, questions,' he said. 'Just be thankful yer off the streets. Jake will tell ya what ya need to know later.'

So I left it at that. I used the small WC off the kitchen to wash and clean my teeth and when I returned Sniffy was fast asleep on the bunk bed. By default I curled up on the settee marginally warmer than in my earlier cardboard bed. Without the knowledge to occupy my mind about the following day, I thought of Luther and video recorders, but soon fell asleep too.

Chapter 41

THIRD FRIDAY – 8:30 a.m.

Despite the cold, I slept soundly. Again no dreams or flashbacks, and still with a freedom of mind, which suggested the earlier flood of memories had abated for the time being. Sniffy using a mobile telephone woke me.

'Yeh, Yeh … No problem … I'm orf to do me scouting after breakfast.' Sniffy was saying and sniffing between replies. He noticed I was awake then added for my benefit, 'He won't be going anywhere if he knows what's best for him … pick him up at ten … okay, I'll tell 'im.'

'I'm moving on already?' I asked, unfurling my cramped body from the settee.

'Yup. The boss'll be 'ere in his Ford Cortina at ten. It's a white one. Ask George to check the streets are clear before ya get in.'

'And then what happens?'

'Can't say. That's up to Jake.'

'But you are obviously a key man in the organization, what do you think might happen?' I flattered for a response.

'Bearing in mind yer profile, I'd keep ya hidden for a while and then involve ya in something juicy to pay me back for me kindness.'

'Like what?' I could tell from his reaction he was about to tell me to mind my own business, but there was a knock at the door and the head of a grey-haired woman peered in.

'Hello, Jess. Come in. Got some brekkie for us?'

I knew the answer already; greasy smells of bacon had wafted into the room with her.

'Yes, dear,' she said making her short round body fully visible in the doorway. 'For two, is it?' she continued when she saw me.

'Yes, luv. No fried bread for me, gives me indigestion,' Sniffy said. I wasn't given a choice.

'Two minutes in the living room,' Jess said closing the door as she left.

The living room was at the front; cosy in comparison to the lodger's quarters, with soft furnishings, carpet and a television which Sniffy switched on to a raucous breakfast programme. Jess served breakfast on metal trays and the meal must have been on a par with the best a trucker's transport café could offer: double fried egg, rashers of crispy bacon, fried bread, a mountain of liberally buttered toast and heavy mugs of sweet tea. In my previous life, I didn't think I would have indulged myself with such a fatty fare, but the inviting smells overruled any concern for a healthy intake, so I ate hungrily.

Sniffy was more reserved with his eating and when the TV presenter announced nine o'clock Sniffy pushed aside his unfinished breakfast. 'I've important things to do so I'll leave ya to it. Might not see ya again. Good luck, ya'll need it,' he said, wiped his nose on his sleeve as a parting gesture and left the room.

I heard a whispered exchange with Jess then a slam of the front door. I switched the TV off to finish my tea and toast in silence. A few minutes later, Jess arrived to clear away the dishes and offer more tea. I politely requested black coffee and she obligingly returned with a steaming cup shortly afterwards.

'Thanks for the breakfast, Jess,' I said. Then tried to add casually, 'Whose blue van is that outside?'

'It belongs to ... actually I dunno who it belongs to, but my George uses it for ... errands,' Jess said nervously.

'What kind of errands?'

'I ... er ... can't say ...' she started, then lowering her voice to a whisper added, '... it's clan ... cladestine, yes cladestine,' apparently having trouble with an unfamiliar word.

'Does George lend it to other people? Luther Browncast, for example?' I whispered too.

'You know Luther?'

'Yes. He's a close friend of mine.'

'Oh, that's alright then. Yeh, Luther borrows it sometimes when he has some cheap goods to collect. George sells them on for him.'

'Like video recorders?'

'Yeh, that sort of thing.'

I wondered if Luther knew he was trading with a member of Kent's organization. If he did, it was a worrying link considering the confidences I had shared with him, and his apparent criticism of all things Kent.

'Where's George now? I'd like to meet him.'

'Poor soul, he's still in bed. Had a bit too much booze last night. He's sleeping it off. He'll be up soon. You relax here until it's time to go.' She sniffed. 'Unless – if you don't mind me saying so – you want to take a bath?'

I was feeling persecuted about my smell, particularly as I could no longer detect it, but a bath was a luxury that would have to wait. I put my hand in the inside pocket of my jacket and then slapped the side pockets. 'Not just now, Jess. I could do with a fag, but I'm right out of them. I'm going to pop to the newsagents down the road to buy some.'

'Oh, I don't think that's a good idea. You're not supposed to go out until you're picked up. Have one of George's to tide you over,' Jess said and retrieved a packet from the top of the television.

'Not my brand, they make me cough. I'll only be two ticks. I'll be back before you can blink.'

'If George finds out he'll murder me.'

Without meeting George I had no way of knowing whether I ought to take this literally in present company; nor had I managed to discern Jess's allegiance to her husband. I stood up. 'Why not give him breakfast in bed. I'll be back before he finishes.'

'Alright dear. It's his birthday tomorrow. I'll say it's a pre-birthday treat. Hurry now.' She attempted a furtive wink. 'Leave the door ajar so you don't have to knock to get back in.'

Outside I turned right. There were no customers in the newsagents so I popped in and bought a random packet of twenty cigarettes as evidence of my errand then scanned the streets looking for a phone booth. I found one two blocks away and thankfully it was unoccupied. I dialled Bradley's mobile number. A gruff voice answered.

'Yes. Make it quick I'm busy.'

'Peter Shadwell. Want to trade news?'

'Where are you?' Bradley sounded impatient.

'I'll get to that. I need to be quick before I'm missed. Have you found out anything?' The line was quiet for a moment and I heard a background conversation.

'Tell me where you are and I'll give you a progress report when you've been picked up.'

'I will if it's news in my favour,' I said.

'It can wait. It's more important we bring you in … NOW … your life may be in danger.'

Bradley's tone was perplexing. The danger statement came across as an afterthought – I wasn't convinced. 'But I can't wait, Inspector. Goodbye.' I paused long enough to test my bluff and then Bradley continued.

'Okay, Okay. Some of it's good for you, some not. There's no trace of Sebastian Tate. The address and phone number from the personnel department records at Ferndown don't exist. His references were from bogus companies.

If it's any consolation, Ferndown now think he was a plant from a competitor and they may have been hasty in your dismissal.

'The estimated time of death of Joseph Carmichael was three o'clock, plus or minus a couple of hours. That spans the time you said you arrived back at your flat. Carmichael's fingerprints were on police records from previous drug offences, but only your prints were on your filing cabinet.

'Josh's van was found about a mile from your flat and contained traces of white powder. The forensic team has taken the van away for examination.

'And the most important bit, your brother has gone missing and your sister-in-law is in hiding. Some government heavies were staking out his place. The shit's hit the fan and I can't help you anymore. They or we need to pick you up now for questioning. So, where the hell are you?'

Bloody hell, that's more than news – it's major headlines, I thought. I was quiet for a moment taking this in.

'Shadwell?'

'Yes, I'm here Inspector. Does this conflicting news mean I'm not yet immune from prosecution of Carmichael's death?' I said. The answer was obvious but I was interested in Bradley's reaction.

'Not yet, but I'm sure we can sort out that little problem.' Bradley said with a conciliatory tone.

As far I was concerned it wasn't a little problem. I feared that once I was in custody, the pressure to find the real killer would be scaled down. The longer I delayed my surrender, the greater the chances that Sebastian Tate might be found and my innocence proven.

'Sorry Inspector, you'll have to make do without me for the time being. I'm making good progress at this end which could sort out your *little problem*.' I said mimicking Bradley's statement.

'I've been overruled on that matter. I had to declare the arrangement I made with you. My neck's on the block unless you come in.'

Bradley sounded desperate now. I had a conscience I was betraying the trust he had invested in me, but I needed to buy time. I wasn't yet in any danger with my infiltration, and I could bail out whenever I wanted. The news about my brother troubled me, but what could I do? I had nothing to offer and since Andy's employers were involved, surely they would make progress without my presence.

'Keep looking for Tate. I'll be in touch,' I said finally, and put the phone down.

Bradley's urgency was worrying, yet he had taken the time to tell me what he had found out. Then it occurred to me that perhaps he had organized a trace on the phone number. I hurried away and went straight back to George and Jess's house.

'You were a long while,' George said suspiciously when I returned. George was not an advert for healthy living: a couch potato with a beer belly that was protruding from an egg-stained vest and hanging over creased beige trousers. His sunken eyes, ruddy face and tousled thin hair confirmed his distress from the previous night.

'I was browsing through a car magazine while I was waiting to be served. Couldn't put it down. I quite fancy one of the new Alfa Romeos. You a motor enthusiast George?' I conjured the response from nowhere, banking on the fact that George had no interest in cars. I struck lucky.

'If I had enough bleeding money I might be.'

'My problem too. Just window shopping.'

George wasn't sidetracked. 'Check with me in future if you want to go out. That silly mare of mine doesn't know what she's doing or saying most of the time. And ... don't say anything to Luther about our mutual ... friends. He might get a bit miffed and I make a tidy sum from his ... er ... what's he call them?'

'Wealth redistribution schemes?' I offered.

'Yes, that's it. Clever with words is Luther.'

'Don't worry. I'll keep your secret.'

'Thanks. Well, your lift should be here soon. I'm off to tidy myself up.'

Chapter 42

THIRD FRIDAY – 10:00 a.m.

At exactly ten o'clock a battered – more rust-coloured than white – Cortina drew up slowly and stopped just past the house. A tidied George – with egg-less vest – spotted it too and went immediately outside. He sidled up to the passenger door and opened it, after looking up and down the road rather obviously. He exchanged words with the driver then nodded towards the house – my signal to leave.

I picked up my duffle bag and unhurried I went to the car mentally noting the registration number on the way. George slammed the door after me. The driver was a tall skinny guy, about thirty with a shaven head. He waited until I had fastened the seat belt and then guided the car away slowly and smoothly.

'Hi, you must be Jake,' I said to break the silence.

'We don't use names,' he said angrily, adding 'I'll kick that moron Sniffy when I see him,' thereby immediately breaking the rule.

I chose not to say anymore preferring to concentrate on where we were going. Less than three minutes later we crossed Old Street into Pitfield Street and pulled up outside a betting shop.

'Out. Don't try a runner otherwise I'm after you. Check in at the bookies. You're expected.' said my short-term chauffeur.

The thought hadn't entered my head. I obeyed.

It was too early for punters. The door to the shop was locked, although the metal shutter that protected it had been hoisted to head level. I tapped gently on the solid door and waited. I noticed my driver was talking into a mobile and then I heard the other half of the conversation behind the door. '... Okay, opening it now,' said the voice as bolts were drawn and locks freed.

The door opened and I was urged in by the smaller of two contrasting Japanese men. The first, about my height – tall for an oriental – was casually dressed and strangely pince-nezed. His companion was more the norm in stature, but grossly abnormal in girth, a sumo wrestler in a suit came to mind.

The wrestler escorted me silently to a back room beyond the betting booths while the other made busy re-securing the front door before joining us.

'Preez to sit down,' said the tall man and pointed to a stool in front of him.

I did as he asked and the big man stood behind me. The atmosphere appeared friendly, but I was troubled by their intimidating positions. I flinched as the bespectacled Japanese quickly put his hand into his bulging trouser pocket and withdrew a black object which I feared might be a gun; it was a mobile phone. He punched two numbers, waited a few seconds, and then began jabbering in Japanese. I had the impression he was describing me to someone since his small eyes were wandering over my seated body.

While he was speaking, I heard movement above me then footsteps descending the stairs. A middle-aged white man dressed in brown trousers and pink shirt stopped in the doorway and waited. The manager of the bookmakers? When the call had finished he asked, 'Everything okay, Chiko?'

Chiko dismissed the question with a nod and the white man returned upstairs. 'You go in ten minutes. Must blindfold you,' he said to me, followed by something oriental to the silent wrestler, who grunted an acknowledgement. I spun round on the stool to see the sumo unwind a black band from his enormous waist. He waved a finger in a circle indicating I should spin back again and then tied the band tightly around my head.

Chiko came forward to check that my eyes were completely covered. 'You take off and Taro hurt you. Okay?'

'Okay.' It wasn't okay, but I was in no position to argue. This whole situation was becoming bizarre. I figured that – for reasons currently beyond me – I was being passed up through the Kent hierarchy of command, and presumably the security arrangements now in place meant I was about to be delivered to a sensitive area of the organization. I smiled at the thought of Sniffy's jealously if he had known I was being promoted so rapidly in the company. What perks awaited me I wondered: private health insurance; a pension; *four-wheeled* transport?

'What funny?' Chiko demanded.

'Oh, nothing, Where am I going?' I asked superfluously.

'You not speak now. Taro hurt you.'

I wagered Taro was used to hurting people and probably enjoyed the experience, so I stayed silent. In reality, I had no reason to smile; it hit me that the blindfolding exercise might not be for my discretion, but a prelude to a ghastly demise. I dismissed the thought and focused instead on the one-sided conversation between my two captors – Chiko talking, Taro grunting – attempting to identify any English names or places I could file away in my spying portfolio.

Ten minutes or more in darkness, with an unintelligible monologue for company is a tortuous existence, which was broken only by a short pause for the lighting of a cigarette. It came as a relief when I heard the sound of a car horn signalling it was time to move on to the next stage of this charade.

I didn't leave the same way I had arrived. We must have exited by a side door to the alleyway I had noticed earlier at the side of the shop. Deprived of my sight I consciously attempted to sharpen my other senses. A car door was opened just beyond the exit. I was bundled into the rear of the car, followed by a huge body, presumably Taro, as I felt the plush seat sag next to me. The cold of the previous night had been inherited by the day and the temperature inside the car was low too, so I reasoned it hadn't travelled far to get here. The seats were leather and the fresh smell suggested the car was relatively new. I had plenty of legroom and the resonant sounds led me to believe I was inside a large saloon car. The passenger door opened and someone sat in front of me – I guessed it was Chiko since nobody spoke. The doors were closed with a gentle click and when the engine fired up instantly and purred quietly, I was convinced I was sitting inside a quality built car. I failed miserably however on the next perceptive task. I endeavoured to kept track of the motion of the vehicle: left at the main road, ten seconds turn right, slow down for something, weave right and left, twenty seconds stop and turn left, and then the uncertainty began. Left and right turns came quickly – more than seemed necessary for a direct route to our ultimate destination; perhaps the zigzagging was deliberate to confuse where we were heading. Five minutes into the journey we stopped at a quiet place and the well-spoken driver turned towards the rear and spoke for the first time.

'Handcuff the prisoner,' he said. I heard a metallic rattle and Chiko barked an instruction to Taro. He leaned across, grabbed my left wrist, and clamped it into a metal loop. The other end was looped through – I supposed – a grab handle above the rear door, leaving me hanging awkwardly above my seat. Taro tugged at this fastening, painfully and unnecessarily twisting my arm in the process, at last inflicting the injury which he hadn't had reason to deliver earlier. Taro and Chiko then got out of the car, and the driver and I continued our directionless drive for another ten minutes. Having a contorted body suspended in the back of a car wasn't exactly a common and discreet occurrence, so I rationalized the windows of the car were perhaps tinted to keep prying eyes out.

When we eventually stopped, I detected an electronic beep and then the noise of a shuttered door being raised. The car moved forward for a moment followed by the same door being lowered. Finally, a parking manoeuvre and then the engine was switched off. The driver got out and I was left alone for a few minutes before two bodies arrived to man handle me out of the handcuffs. They led me across a stone floor, which from the echo was at the base of a large warehouse. There was a strong smell of new carpets. We climbed an open metal staircase and halted at the top. I heard six different electronic tones like a pass number being keyed into an access unit and then the mechanical click of a door opening.

We entered a chilled, maybe air-conditioned room, and there was a background hum of electrical equipment. I was led through another door then spun around and pushed backwards onto a creaking wooden chair; only then was the black band removed from my head. I squinted my eyes against the bright neon strip lights in the ceiling and examined my surroundings. I was in a large windowless office, thirty feet square. Across the room was a grand mahogany-coloured desk, which might have been a valuable antique, but for the well-worn appearance it had. Behind it was a more modern executive brown leather chair. On the desk there was a telephone, a single pile of papers and a three-tiered filing tray with labels of "in", "out" – and amusingly – "shake it all about". There was a bank of four-drawer filing cabinets lining the wall opposite the door. My chair backed on to an empty plain table, against which leaned sumo wrestler version two. He was taller, narrower and occidental in comparison to Taro, but still with strength that oozed from his body.

The door was ajar and through it, I could see three men chatting. The tallest had his back to me and appeared to be issuing instructions to the other two, flapping his gangling arms for emphasis. As he did so, his long black hair waved in unison with his movements. For a moment the hair reminded me of Sebastian Tate then he turned round and marched into the room. Based on Bradley's description, I knew I was about to meet Ronnie Kent.

Chapter 43

THIRD FRIDAY – 11:00 a.m.

Ronnie Kent was a lean untidy wretch, dressed in faded jeans and crumpled T-shirt, but the giveaway was the deep scar on his left cheek, which ran from eye to mouth. He appeared to me like a scruffy mature student. How he commanded respect as head of a major criminal organization was visually beyond me.

Kent stopped in front of me with his hands on his hips. 'Do you know who I am?'

I wasn't sure how I was supposed to react. Should I show recognition I was in his renowned presence or deny all knowledge I knew who he was. I was unsure how much of my unknown past and present circumstances had reached his ears from Sniffy so I knew I ought to err on the latter. Yet at that moment, the person standing in front of me reviled me, and this led to a response I was to regret.

'You look like a drugged dropout from a rock band,' I offered.

Kent's first reaction was a twitch in the scar and then he raised his right hand as though he was about to hit me. I stiffened, preparing myself for the blow. The brute still behind me forecast the action by grabbing my arms behind the chair to protect a backlash against his boss and to give Kent a stationary target. But Ronnie fooled us both; perhaps he was afraid of hurting his hand or realized his lightweight frame couldn't deliver the force he wanted to inflict? Instead, he aimed a kick with his amply booted, right foot. The target was my left shin and the sickening crack I heard registered with me before the pain. With the agony I felt, I was convinced he had broken my leg. Despite being held, I involuntarily lurched forwards and I noticed with relief the horizontal strut between the two legs of my chair had snapped in two because of a ricocheted impact from Ronnie's boot. The solace was brief.

'I've been wanting to do that for a long time, you bastard,' Kent said as he leaned towards me, and dragged my head backwards by grabbing my hair. It seemed an odd thing to say, but before I could dwell on the thought, the foulness of his breath wafted over me as he moved his face closer to mine.

'Another fucking smart remark like that and you'll be found floating in the Thames. Do you understand?'

I couldn't speak because of the pain or even nod my head in acknowledgement, but the submissive look in my eyes answered his question.

'So, I'll ask you again. Do you know who I am? And have we met before; you look familiar?'

This time he let go of my hair. 'I presume you are the boss of this organization. We may have met in the past – if I knew my past.'

'We've met alright. Hang on to the cunt and check him over,' Kent said to my restrainer, who placed one of his massive arms across my windpipe and pulled me upwards while he used his other hand to grope my pockets and body cavities. Kent smiled at my increased displeasure. Satisfied I wasn't harbouring anything of interest he turned his attention to my duffle bag lying on the floor. He bent down to pick it up, tugged at the drawstring and tipped the contents onto the table. He used a finger to prod my belongings like they were diseased and then paused at my notebook.

'What's this?' he said flicking through the pages.

Oh shit, I thought. I'd forgotten about my diary. I struggled to recall what I'd written in it. I knew I hadn't recorded any details about my major flashbacks, but I was unsure if I'd mentioned anything about Kent in my notes. I tried to gurgle an answer, but the pressure across my throat inhibited me. Kent nodded to the big man to slacken his grip.

'Just random notes I've made in the last few days, hoping it might help me to remember my past or who I am,' I eventually said with painful gasps between words.

Thankfully, my answer held more interest than the notebook and he tossed it on top of my bundle of clothes.

'I know who you are. The police know who you are, and some of your criminal past has been documented. I can't understand why you can't accept it.'

'I suppose I'll have to ... accept it. So can you help me out?'

'Why should I? I've no place for a murderer in my company, particularly one that's had his picture spread around the newspapers. You'd be a fucking liability.'

'So why am I here?'

'I may not be able to regularly employ you, but you could still be useful to me. A one-off assignment in return for a completely new identity.'

'I might be interested.'

Kent laughed. 'You don't have a fucking choice mate. If you refuse, I either feed you to Brutus here or you get dumped unconscious outside the nearest cop shop, and then you'll spend the rest of your life in the nick with someone's cock up your arse. What'll it be?'

'What do you mean, a new identity?'

'Are you stupid? What do you think it means? New name, new appearance, official documentation, references plus a bundle of cash. It's then up to you. You can go abroad if you want; Ireland or Spain's a good choice.'

'And it's foolproof?'

'Course it's fucking foolproof. Done it loads a times before. Even my old man did it. Do the job and you could be a free man two days later.'

'Depends what I have to do.'

'Now look you little shit, I've told you already, you don't have a choice. If you don't do this job, we'll skip the police, I'll fucking skin you myself.'

Kent was beginning to sound desperate – the reaction I wanted, to draw out his bravado and confidences. Already he had revealed that his father, and therefore he, had a manufactured name. Was that why Bradley hadn't been able to trace Barry Kent further back than ten years? If I pushed my obstruction anymore, I had no doubt Barry's son would have great pleasure in getting rid of me. Now I had to pretend to play along with his demands; possibly the only way I would get out of this place alive.

'Okay. What's the job?'

'That's better. I knew you were a sensible guy. Let him go Brutus. If he makes a false move, eat him.'

'Sure boss,' Brutus growled for the first time. Brutus by name and brutish by nature, how fitting I thought.

'Right. I believe you know Kathy Rensberg.'

I sat there silently not knowing how to respond. Kent nodded to Brutus who snatched both of my ears, folded them over and then squashed them into the side of my head. I screamed thinking my head was about to cave in from the pressure.

'Fucking hell Shadwell, don't you have the message yet. You play ball or get hurt. I'll make it easy for you. You've been seen with her sister, and you've visited them both at the hospital.'

'Y ... Yes,' I forced myself to say. Brutus immediately let go. I reached for my ears to check they were intact and not bleeding. 'Yes,' I said again. 'She's in a coma. She might die.'

'Correction. She will die ... and her sister. That's the little job you're going to do for me.'

'I can't ...' I began and instinctively put my hands over my ears, but that left my midriff undefended, and in a blur, a clenched fist descended from behind me and slammed into my stomach. I doubled up, clutching the source of the pain and choking for air. I was hauled back into an upright position by sharp nails gouging my ears. Spots of blood appeared on my jacket.

Kent was enjoying this game. I was losing my way; I had to join in.

'Okay. Okay. Get this brute off me and I'll co-operate,' I pleaded. Without instruction, Brutus released me. I massaged my ears and recoiled at the sight of blood on my hands.

'Why do they have to die? What have they ever done to you?'

'Never you mind. That bitch Kathy should have died a while ago. You'll be completing some unfinished business for me, and you'll be doing her a favour.'

'Why kill Charlotte too?'

'A witness, and you'll have to kill her first to get to Kathy. So, how do you want to do it? Gun, knife, syringe? All three?'

'Hmm ...' I started, faking deliberation. '... Knife and syringe are too risky if Charlotte struggles. I need an element of surprise. A gun would be quick. For Kathy, I'll just unplug her life support system and smother her with a pillow to make sure. The gun would have to be a small revolver – silenced.'

'Now you're talking my language. You've obviously used a gun before?'

'Of course. Bit of a marksman too,' I lied. I had never seen a real gun in the flesh, let alone handled one.

'Thought you'd lost your memory?'

'Some things you never forget. I know I'm good, but can't tell who taught me, where I've used one or what I've used a gun for.' Total bullshit, but credibly delivered to an easily impressed thug.

'Well, well. Shame you've got to disappear, you might have been useful.'

'What's the plan? It will be risky. There could be police guarding them,' I said, opening my eyes wide to portray enthusiasm for the task.

Trying to be too casual I'd offered a fact and Kent jumped on it straight away. Narrowing his eyes he asked, 'Why should there be police guarding them?'

They would only be protected if they were in immediate danger from Kathy revealing information about the circumstances of her coma. 'I mean, maybe the police are waiting for me to turn up?' I said to cover up my slip.

'I doubt that. They don't have the resources to station cops at the places you might go. Anyway, they'll believe you'll have left the area by now.'

'I hope you're right, but I've still got to get past the nurses.'

'Not a problem – this is how you'll do it. You'll be taken back to George and Jess's and will stay there until it gets dark. Jess will disguise you as best she can. Someone will arrive to deliver the hardware and brief you in detail about the operation. A car will pick you up and take you to the hospital. The driver will wait in Stepney Way at the rear of the hospital. You'll be accompanied by one of our team into the hospital and if necessary, he will create a diversion while you deal with the girls. When you're done, dash to the car and you'll be driven back to G and J's. Our guy at the hospital will hang around discreetly until he knows the hit has been successful. He'll relay the result to me, and then you'll be given your exit package and taken to any mainline station of your choice. After that, you're on your own. Okay?'

'I can't see any flaws.'

'There are no flaws, dickhead. One final point. Your actions will be monitored at every stage and if you try to opt out, they'll be two dead brothers as well as two dead sisters.'

'I don't understand. I thought you said two dead brothers,' I said as calmly and innocently as I could, but I knew then the link I had speculated on earlier had finally been made.

'So. Your memory doesn't include your brother? Take it from me you have a brother and he's worried about you, even if you're not worried about him. If you fuck up the show, you both go down.'

I had to show some recognition of this fact. I was acting the amnesiac role as best as I could, but I didn't think I could handle the endangerment of a brother without a telltale sign of emotion. 'I … I've dreamt I have a brother, but thought that's all it was … a dream. I don't believe you. You're bluffing. Where is he then? Let me speak to him.' I tensed my legs to stand up, but remembered my battered ears and changed my mind.

'I'll do better than that. You can see him now if you want to.'

'How will I know he's my brother?' I challenged.

'You'll know,' Kent said. 'Gag him. I'll be straight back.' He left the room and Brutus picked up the discarded blindfold and secured the band tightly round my mouth. For good measure, he punched me in the ear to check how much my scream penetrated the gag. Not satisfied, he tugged the band one more notch and hit me again. This could have gone on forever, but Kent returned.

'Follow me,' he said.

Brutus fell in line immediately behind my limping body. Just before we stepped into a corridor, I slowed and glanced left at what I had first thought was a picture on the wall. It was a pornographic calendar for the current year and still positioned at the photograph for June. The background was comprised of tall rolls of carpet. In the foreground, there was a naked blonde girl prone on a large pale blue rug fornicating with the handle of a carpet sweeper. The girl I recognized as my temptress Stella, but I was more interested in the initials BQC emblazoned on the headband she was wearing.

'No time for fun,' Brutus said and pushed me forward.

I followed Ronnie down the corridor passing closed doors. As the corridor turned right, facing us was a large room visible through large windows, which extended from ceiling to waist height. The scene was reminiscent of one I was probably familiar with from Ferndown's computer centre. On the far side, I could see racks of electrical equipment with obligatory flashing coloured lamps. Fat communication cables emanated from the units and clung to the wall before disappearing into the roof space. To the left there were dozens of freestanding grey boxes, which I assumed contained the main processors. Beyond the glass panes there was a long table, partitioned for individual workstations, and many were in use by casually dressed operators. Some of the monitors displayed pornographic images, which I assumed were being maintained rather than being viewed. There was little doubt in my mind I was looking at the hub of the Kent's computer operations that were being so eagerly investigated by the cybercrime unit Bradley had mentioned. I had dawdled again and received another shove from behind.

We came to a door that led to a gloomy staircase. We descended two long flights of concrete steps and went through another door. I expected to emerge into a cellar, but the area was like a plush waiting room: thick pile carpets, leather suites, rich furniture, grand ornaments, and a blended smell of freshly percolated coffee and a familiar perfume. Stella was sitting on a settee and was wearing her micro red skirt like a wide belt. She was chatting to a smartly dressed middle-aged man who was caressing her leg. They briefly glanced our way, but were more interested in each other than the unusual sight of a gagged person being frog-marched across the room. Then Stella did a double take and jumped up, 'Bloody hell, if it isn't the queer beggar that nearly broke my arm.' She charged towards me like she had at her flat, intent on her revenge.

Brutus stepped in front of her and held her back with a well-aimed grasp of her throat.

'Lay off Stella, get back to your business,' Ronnie shouted.

Her companion stood up and took a diffident step forward, but Brutus cast him a threatening look and pressed harder on her throat. Stella gurgled then Brutus pushed her away. She caught her breath and gasped, 'Fucking ape shit.'

Drama over, our threesome left the room by a door opposite and entered a narrow passageway. At the end, we passed through a heavy door then down a wooden staircase into a converted cellar.

'It's only me Seb,' Ronnie called out.

The walls were bare stone and the floor was covered with mottled grey linoleum. To the right were rows of shelving units containing various sizes of brown and white cardboard boxes. Lighting came from strip lights precariously attached to a false plywood ceiling. At the bottom of the stairs, we turned immediately left through a bricked archway, into an area equipped as temporary living quarters. Facing us was a metal framework bed with a mattress, and a man sprawled out on it with hands and legs secured to each end by handcuffs. Muffled sounds came from his mouth silenced by packing tape. There was a brief surge of memories in my head and I knew without doubt it was Andy lying there. I recognized features, shape and clothes: the brown tousled hair, spectacles and slightly Roman nose. A leaner body than I remembered. The jacket of one of his smart business suits was in a bundle on the floor next to his black leather shoes, and he wore tailored, but crumpled shirt and trousers. He was still wearing one of his favourite blue silk ties.

I looked to the left, and standing next to the bed was Sebastian Tate.

The tale had come full circle. It had started with Sebastian Tate and now he had resurfaced at the climax. There were so many questions I wanted to ask and the smirk on Tate's face showed he was revelling in my dumb frustration and the security of my brother. I lunged forward tugging at my gag, uncertain whether my objective was to strike Tate or console my brother, but I knew both would be fruitless as Brutus forced my arms up my back.

'Have you briefed the shitbag?' Ronnie said to Sebastian.

'Yes. He knows what he has to say and the punishment he'll receive if he doesn't.'

'Remove the tape.'

Tate reached down and pulled the tape from Andy's mouth with a vicious tug. I cringed at the ripping sound.

Andy yelled then looked sad-eyed towards me. 'Pete ... you have to do what they ask, otherwise they'll kill us. They're not bluffing ... believe me. Then they promise to let us go ... tell John Ingram ... and don't ...'

But that was as much as Andy could say before Sebastian grabbed his hair and re-secured the tape.

Ronnie shouted, 'Who the fuck is John Ingram?' Sebastian shrugged. 'Well?' Ronnie growled at me and then kicked my shin for a second time. I mumbled a scream through my gag and shook my head before Brutus relieved the pressure on the black band so I could answer. But Andy's message meant nothing to me. Fortunately, I knew the name of John Ingram; he was the security man that had interviewed me at Ferndown. This was the only other name I knew from Andy's covert employment. Was that a coded request to notify his employers what had happened? Another kick reminded me to reply.

I scowled at Kent. 'I haven't the faintest idea. I've lost my memory, remember?'

'I won't let you down Andy, we'll be ...' I managed to add before the gag was replaced.

Ronnie steered Sebastian to the far end of the cellar and they spoke quietly for a few moments. Ronnie then finished audibly with 'I'll let you know when you can let him go.'

I discerned the closing words were purely for my benefit as an attempt to convey sincerity about the terms of Andy's release. Yet, even without Andy's coded message, I knew our fate. It was obvious to me Ronnie did not intend to keep his side of the bargain. Once I had done his dirty work of killing Kathy and Charlotte, I was certain Andy and I would mysteriously disappear. The most naïve observer of the situation would acknowledge that our freedom would be dangerous to the Kent organization, whether we knew the location of the operations centre or not. The unknown quantity was whether Ronnie would wait until I had completed my task before he disposed of Andy, or would he keep that in reserve in case my attempt at murder failed.

We headed back the way we had come. Stella was in an advanced state of undress, but was too pre-occupied with the seduction of her visitor to acknowledge our passing. I collected my duffle bag and belongings on the way to the exit of the inner sanctum, and the black band was transferred from my mouth to my eyes. Ronnie muttered something inaudible – but not a friendly goodbye – and I was on my way back to George and Jess's. A simpler journey this time, no passengers, no car swaps, but still more left and right turns than my brain could memorize. Just before we stopped, I heard my unseen driver make a phone call announcing my imminent arrival. The car door opened and someone leaned in to unharness me from the grab handle and remove my blindfold – it was George. He pulled me out of the car and steered me urgently towards his house. I glanced round in time to see a silver Mercedes accelerate away, albeit too quickly for me to note its registration number.

Chapter 44

THIRD FRIDAY – 12:55 p.m.

Inside the house George ushered me into the front room. 'No funny business this time,' he said sternly.

'I don't know what you mean.'

'No wandering off anywhere. I'll get a rollicking for letting you out to the shops. You stay put until you're picked up later. It's for your own benefit. Understand?'

I understood, but I had been relying on being able to call Bradley to pass on the information I had for him. I wondered if George knew what I was involved in. It was time to find out. 'Yes, no problem. You know who I am?'

'You're Shadwell, the drug murderer, I read it in the paper.' He pointed to a copy of the *Gazette* lying on a sideboard. 'I don't approve of killing, but I've just been instructed to keep an eye on you.'

'Then the other eye won't mind if I use your phone. I ought to ring my old lady, tell her I'm okay.'

He thought for a moment, but didn't acknowledge my joke. 'Nah, you can't talk to no one. Sit down and be quiet.'

I sat down in an armchair and George left the room. The clock on the mantelpiece showed almost one o'clock; it would be getting dark at about seven o'clock. I had six hours to come up with a plan. There weren't many options if I couldn't get to a phone. If I escaped from the house, George would relay the information to Ronnie Kent and Andy would undoubtedly be killed. If I followed the scheme, several things could go wrong. Perhaps there would be police around the hospital guarding Kathy and Charlotte, and if someone other than Bill Haynes recognized me, I was sure to be arrested. My best chance was to make discreet contact with Bill, seek his co-operation and fake the deaths of Kathy and Charlotte. And then what? Make my way to the getaway car and be driven to my certain death, followed by Andy's. It wasn't much of a choice. Yet, if I could physically disable George and Jess, I could phone Bradley and give him a few hours head start to locate Andy, but I had no idea how I would achieve that.

I took my diary from my bag and opened it at a blank page. Should the opportunity arise, I wanted a piece of paper to pass on with the facts I had gathered so far about the Kent organization. I started to make notes. I listed details of the current house; my trip to a carpet warehouse (?); BQC; Ronnie, Sebastian and Andy; the silver Mercedes and anything else I could think of that might be relevant. I was almost finished when George returned.

'Jess is making some sandwiches,' he said. 'Hey, whatcha doin'?'

'Updating my diary,' I lied. 'When I start my new life, I'll sell my memoirs to a newspaper. They pay good money for stories like mine. More profitable than robbing a bank this is.' I cockily stabbed the notes with my finger.

'Better not mention me,' George warned.

''Course not. Everyone and everywhere are strictly anonymous. I don't owe the police any favours; besides, I don't want the big boss coming after me. Have you met him?'

'A few times. Jess ... knows the boy's ma quite well. She used to buy her old man's fags from the shop I ran until he started getting his own supply from lorries – if you know what I mean?' The statement prompted George to reach for his cigarettes, 'Want one of these?' he offered.

'No thanks, not my brand,' I said, corroborating my comment to Jess earlier.

'What's your poison then?' he said lighting up.

'Er ... these,' I said retrieving the random purchase from my pocket. A nod from George invited me to join him. Reluctantly I unwrapped the packet and took out a cigarette. From uncertain memories I gleaned smoking would be a new experience for me, and hoped my action and reaction wouldn't advertise my ignorance. He lit my cigarette from his lighter and I tried to draw confidently without inhaling. The taste was foul, but I hid any signs of displeasure. I resolved to keep talking to avoid frequenting my new habit. 'What's happening for the rest of the day?'

'You stay here until you are picked up tonight. Jess will be weaving her magic with make-up later and your accomplice will soon be joining us.'

'Accomplice?'

'Don't know the details, but apparently somebody will be helping you with whatever you are doing tonight.'

I had assumed my accomplice would arrive in the pick-up car. If I were to incapacitate George and Jess, I would have to do it soon. On the other hand, I could try a softer option.

'George, I need your help; I desperately need to make a phone call. The job I'm doing tonight is something very big. When it goes wrong, at least four people will die and you could end up as a liability to the boss, or wanted as an accessory by the police. If I can make that call, the lives will be saved and I'll guarantee that you'll come out of this in the best possible light.'

'And if it doesn't go wrong?'

'It will, believe me. The job is badly conceived and is doomed to fail.'

'Perhaps it will fail if you do make the call. I can't take that risk, I'm on a fat bonus for doing what I've been told.'

'What sort of bonus?'

'£500.'

'I'll give you £1000 to make the call. Who would know? Are your phone calls monitored?'

'No, but the calls are itemized on the phone bill and that goes straight to the boss.'

'It's only a call to a private mobile phone. Look, by the time it appears on a bill you won't have a boss to worry about.' I used George's pause to stub the remains of my unsmoked cigarette into an ashtray.

'What's going to happen to the boss?'

Perhaps I'd gone too far, now he was anxious. 'Nothing. What I mean is I can set you up as your own boss. Nobody to answer to but yourself.'

'Who are you exactly?'

'Just a man who's innocently stumbled into some trouble. I haven't killed anyone and now I'm desperate to save my own life, the life of my brother and the lives of two innocent girls.'

'One phone call?'

'Yes.'

'And the grand? I want cash.'

'You'll have to trust me. I don't have that kind of money with me.'

George still looked doubtful. 'When will I get the cash?'

'If we can sort this out now, tomorrow. I'll deliver it personally or Luther will bring it to you.'

George nodded towards the phone. 'Press those buttons so that the number's not sent. I'll be listening. If you say anything dodgy I'll cut you off.'

George watched closely as I picked up the receiver and dialled Bradley, inserting 141 before the number so the caller wasn't identified. George sat by the phone poised to cut the call. Frustratingly it rang a dozen times before it was answered.

'Hello.'

A voice I didn't recognize. I hesitated. 'Bradley?'

'Not available. Who is that?'

There was a tone to the voice that bothered me: stern, authoritative. I chose to be cryptic. 'Urgent info. Get Bradley.'

'I'll pass it on if you tell me who's calling.'

I had to lie convincingly. From somewhere came: 'Rawlinson. National Crime Squad.'

George's hand hovered over the disconnection button. I put my hand over the mouthpiece, 'Trust me George … Please.'

The silence from the other end suggested my credentials were being examined. I took the initiative and bellowed: 'I said this was urgent. Who the fuck am I speaking to?'

'Okay, Rawlinson, let's have it. This is Bradley's superior, Superintendent Dixon.'

Dixon? Why was Dixon answering Bradley's phone? Whatever the explanation, I didn't want to speak to Dixon. I pushed George's hand down and the line went dead.

'What's going on? You a copper?'

'No, but something's gone wrong and I need to make another call.' I had to call the hospital and speak to Charlotte.

George began to protest. 'Now look, this is getting too risky. I'll …'.

There was a loud knock on the front door. We kept silent for a moment waiting for Jess to answer. When she didn't appear, George left the room to see who had arrived. I took the opportunity to tear the page of notes from my diary and place it in my trouser pocket. I heard the front door close. George returned and then Jess timidly entered the room. 'Luigi is here to see our guest,' she said and stood aside to reveal the arrival in the doorway.

To me Luigi was the archetypal Latin gangster: medium length, slick black hair; tanned complexion; narrow face with sharp features; superfluous sunglasses; and dressed all in black: polo neck sweater, shiny shoes, leather jacket and cord trousers. His average height and girth were swamped by his swarthy appearance. As a companion in crime he would stick out like … pepperoni on a pizza, seemed an appropriate analogy.

'You leave,' Luigi said to George, who looked towards me for confirmation.

All I could do was shrug, it was George's home, but the tone of Luigi's order was not one to be countermanded. George ushered his wife from the room and followed her.

Jess looked back. 'I'll bring you some sandwiches and drinks,' she said graciously.

'Nothing. We will be busy,' Luigi said dismissively. I was hungry after the nervous energies of the morning but didn't argue. He waited for the door to close, and then removed his sunglasses.

'So my friend, we discuss business. I tell what we do. Okay?'

His plan took over an hour to explain. It wasn't the detail that consumed the time, more his stunted English and strong Italian accent that necessitated frequent repetition. He had already been to the hospital to reconnoitre entrances, exits and the location of Kathy's room. I casually enquired about signs of police protection around Kathy's ward, but apparently, there was none. This was a disturbing fact that would hinder my own plan. Either Kathy had not convinced Bradley about her observations at BioRemedy, or the police presence was ultimately discreet. I doubted the latter since Luigi portrayed the thoroughness of a seasoned professional.

There was no subtlety in what was to happen: enter the hospital by a side door; go straight to the ward; use my friendship with Charlotte to gain access; kill Charlotte and Kathy; leave by a rear entrance. I detected many flaws, but chose not to highlight them. I played my part in showing enthusiasm for the plan, but the cold reality of the exercise hit me when he lifted his sweater and undid the retaining straps of a gun with holster. He explained the gun was a Beretta 92 semi-automatic pistol with a silencer – a "Very nice piece" in his language. It was magazine loaded and held eleven rounds. He drifted into technical details about its design, most of which I ignored since I did not intend to use the evil-looking weapon, though I did listen carefully about the safety features. With the silencer attached, it was a foot long and weighed heavy in my hand at about three pounds. Luigi donned a pair of thin leather gloves and before securing the holster and gun to my body, he meticulously wiped them with an impregnated tissue which smelt of alcohol. Tucked under my armpit the gun felt cold and unnatural. He insisted I shoot both girls in the head, more than once if necessary. Luigi thought my plan to simply switch off Kathy's life-support system was too prone to failure. "Head mean Dead" was the phrase he used.

He then took off a shoe and rolled up his trouser leg. Tucked inside an elastic bandage around his calf, was a soft leather sheath containing a four-inch bladed dagger honed to hair-splitting sharpness. The knife was to be used as a contingency should there be any doubts about the fatality from the gun. With the clinical precision of a surgeon brandishing a scalpel, he began his description of the appropriate entry points for the blade tip in the chest and neck to inflict certain death. As a distraction from the sickness churning in my stomach, I lit and really smoked a cigarette, but then with the nausea from its side effects, I had to absence myself to the bathroom to throw up my breakfast. Jess and George were in the kitchen. Jess wanted to fuss about my health and George wanted to continue our earlier conversation, but I deferred on both lest Luigi became suspicious.

271

'You feela okay?' Luigi asked when I returned.

'Cigarette on empty stomach,' I explained.

'No problemo, I fix knife then we eat.'

Luigi used another tissue to clean the weapon before he transferred it to my own leg. I had to stroll up and down to test security and bodily comfort. Both tests were passed, though comfort of my mind was lacking. Finally, he passed me the leather gloves and stressed that I wear them whenever I handled the gun or knife. Satisfied, Luigi opened the door and called out: 'Bring food now.'

It was Jess's big moment to rush in with an enormous dish of sandwiches. Luigi despatched her to fetch a beer for himself and a black coffee for me.

'You need clear head for …' Luigi said and completed the sentence by aiming two fingers on his hand at my head like a gun and making a popping sound with his mouth.

We started on the sandwiches and when Jess arrived with the drinks, she hovered until Luigi acknowledged her presence. 'When do you want me for the beauty treatment?' she asked.

'My disguise,' I said for Luigi's puzzled benefit.

'Now … is … good,' Luigi replied with a staccato delivery, his mouth full of food.

Jess studied me for a moment, 'Hmm … I need to do your hair first. Let's go to the kitchen.'

I followed her hoping to use the opportunity to speak to George privately, but Luigi joined us wanting more beer, and stayed to watch the show.

Jess offered to wash my hair, but I chose to do it myself in case she detected the gun inside my jacket. It was awkward leaning over the sink and avoiding my battered ears, but a joy to get rid of the grease and grime that had accumulated over the last few days. I then sat in a chair and Jess expertly cut my hair short and finished the styling with a trimming razor. She left my embryonic beard, arguing that in comparison to my picture in the *Gazette*, it was already an integral part of my disguise. I caught a glimpse of my face in a mirror on the wall and the transformation was already impressive, but there was more to come. Another visit to the sink, this time Jess took control and rinsed my hair with blonde dye, rubbing hard with her fingers. Three times I yelped like an injured animal when the burning liquid touched the raw parts of my ears. I had to sit again wearing a plastic shower cap while she used a pastry brush to ingrain the dye into the growth on my chin. George and Luigi, now supping beer together, found the proceedings increasingly funny as time and alcohol passed. When Jess had finished, George fetched a box containing various styles and colours of spectacles, all fitted with clear lenses. I selected six pairs which fitted comfortably and then Jess chose the pair which best suited my face and hair colour. Satisfied, she removed the shower cap and then used a hair dryer and brush to complete her masterpiece. I studied myself in the mirror while Jess tidied and swept up my brown locks from the floor. Now the transformation was remarkable.

Luigi and I adjourned to the living room, excluding George and Jess on the grounds we had further business to discuss – it wasn't true. With approximately two hours before we left, Luigi proposed I relaxed and took a nap perhaps. According to his doctrine of killing, it was important to be rested and have a clear mind for the task ahead. I didn't want to sleep, but I needed a quiet time to reflect upon my increasingly hopeless circumstances. I closed my eyes and left Luigi to finish the sandwiches.

After my painstaking conversion from a brown-haired beggar to a blonde hit man, I began to wonder about the futility of the exercise. Kent was desperate to have Charlotte and Kathy removed from endangering the exposure of himself or Dixon in their drug operations, and he had placed his faith in me to carry out the assassinations. Why me? In Luigi, he appeared to have an experienced man to do the job. I supposed the difference was that I was expendable. But Kent was running the risk that if I cocked up and were caught, or I simply surrendered to the police, I could potentially incriminate a number of people: Kent, Tate, Luigi, George, Jess and other people I had met in the last two days. The police would soon discover I had no motive to kill the girls – quite the opposite – and then they would surely follow up the information I had obtained. Maybe Luigi had a bigger role to play than a lookout at the hospital? Perhaps I was the means to gain a guaranteed entry to Kathy's room, and the elaborate disguise was the way of ensuring access. If I didn't complete the job then Luigi would take over. Success or not, I was convinced the hidden agenda of the plan meant I would not survive the operation. Luigi would kill me at the hospital or if I escaped, no doubt the getaway car would be last place on earth I was seen alive.

There was a more recent consideration too – Dixon's involvement. Ronnie's misguided trust in me was born from his belief I had no recollection of my past. Conveniently I was already a murderer, easily blackmailed into another to gain freedom for a new life. Was he so easily duped into believing I was still an amnesiac? If he knew to the contrary, say via Dixon, would it make any difference? Bradley was aware of my real situation and Dixon was answering Bradley's mobile phone. Furthermore, according to Luigi, there were no police protecting Kathy and Charlotte. Did this mean Dixon had somehow intervened? In my earlier call to Bradley, he had said to me: ' … your life may be in danger … I've been overruled … I had to declare the arrangement I made with you …'

I kept my eyes closed, but didn't sleep. I analysed and re-analysed every piece of information I had gathered since my recruitment, and waited in vain for divine guidance.

Chapter 45

THIRD FRIDAY – 6:40 p.m.

At twenty minutes to seven, the telephone rang. Luigi jumped up and went to fetch George to answer it, but the call was for Luigi. He listened intently for a couple of minutes, responding occasionally with a "Si" and once with a "Sheet" – the Italian version of "Shit" by the troubled look on his face.

At the end of the call, he said: 'Problemo. We go now.'

'What problemo?' I said, sarcastically imitating his accent.

'Strange men in car at end of street watching house.'

Perhaps my get-out clause had arrived. 'Police?' I asked with anxious enthusiasm.

'Maybe. We go back way.'

I picked up my duffle bag.

'No, no. Leave here,' Luigi said and started towards the kitchen.

In that short moment I had to decide if this was the opportunity I had been seeking. There were three options: follow Luigi; draw the gun on him; or run out of the front door – I chose the latter. I took one step in that direction before Luigi yelled.

'What you doing, English?'

As he spoke, I heard Jess gasp and I guessed the reason. Without turning around, I said weakly in mitigation, 'I thought I'd take a look outside.'

'I kill you first,' Luigi said, brandishing a gun at me.

Luigi grabbed my arm and pushed me towards the rear door in the kitchen. In the backyard, we ran towards the rear wall. At the base there was an old coal bunker. Luigi intimated with his gun that I climb up and haul myself over the wall. There was a six foot drop on the other side and I tumbled into a cushioning pile of rotting flowers and wreaths – the discards from the graves of the church grounds in which I'd just landed. I looked around; there was no one in sight. Luigi quickly followed, his gun restored to its hiding place. He led the way, zigzagging through gravestones, until we were hidden from the road at the back of the church. He issued instructions for our next moves and restated his threat to shoot me if I strayed. I set off first, walking casually along the church path until I came to the road. There I went right and followed Luigi's directions, conscious he would be behind me at a distance. Finally, I turned into an alleyway, which emerged at the end of a cul-de-sac surrounded by six-storey blocks of flats. Unheard, Luigi immediately appeared next to me. Nearby, there were young boys kicking a football.

A few minutes later, a red BMW entered the cul-de-sac and motored slowly towards us. A horn beeped to disperse the footballers and in unison they made obscene gestures to the driver. The BMW stopped and we climbed into the back seats. The driver and passenger were scruffy student types; reminiscent of a breed of rough sleepers I had seen at Charing Cross. We moved away and the passenger punched a number on his mobile phone and said 'Safe pick-up confirmed.' Nothing else was said until our short, but circuitous journey had deposited us at the side entrance to the hospital in Mount Street. Luigi confirmed the escape arrangements and we climbed the steps to the hospital.

Luigi's reconnaissance must have been comprehensive because he strode out with familiarity along the corridors, checking periodically I was in tow at a discreet distance. As we passed the corridor that led to the designated escape exit, he pointed and gave a thumbs-up, and then we climbed a staircase to the first floor. Luigi appeared casual and at ease, not concerned with the civilians and medical staff en route. I was shaking with fear inspecting each person, hopeful one of them might be a police officer in disguise. The holstered gun and strapped knife felt like enormous growths on my body that I was sure someone would notice. I had a desperate plan in the back of my mind, but an increase in my courage and confidence, and an opportunity, were required for its execution.

I followed Luigi along the main corridor. As we neared Kathy's ward my eyes went to the row of chairs where I had sat when I first visited Charlotte last Sunday. Sitting on his own was a casually dressed man whose width required more than one seat. His face had been hidden behind a newspaper, but he lowered it as his attention turned towards Luigi – it was PC Bill Haynes. The uniform wasn't necessary, I recognized him by nose and moustache. As arranged, Luigi turned right into the passageway opposite the one leading to the Helen Raphael ward, his intention being to pretend he was using a wall phone a short way down. As Luigi changed direction, Bill looked towards me and our eyes briefly met. Uncomfortable and without recognition, he returned to his newspaper, but I could feel he was still watching me. I reached into my trouser pocket for my sheet of notes and carelessly let it flutter to the ground. With the same hand, I ran my fingers through my blonde hair, hoping the action might trigger scrutiny in Bill's mind. I listened for a reaction behind me, but detected none above the noise of my footsteps. As I turned towards Kathy's ward I glanced quickly right and saw Luigi acknowledge me from the wall phone. Ahead of me in the distance, I could see activity in the main ward. Most of the chairs outside the entrance were occupied by reserve visitors, waiting for their turn to visit the patients. Without knocking, I opened the second door on the left and closed it swiftly behind me.

Kathy was sitting up in bed and Charlotte was at her side, reading from a book. In a well-practiced manoeuvre to conceal Kathy's consciousness, I noticed her immediately go limp and close her eyes. Charlotte jumped up and shouted, 'Who the hell are you?'

I briefly removed my spectacles to aid recognition. 'Charlotte, it's me Pete … keep your voice down.'

'Pete?' She started laughing. 'What have you done to your hair?'

'Listen to me, this is serious. Ronnie Kent is blackmailing me to kill you and Kathy. If I don't, my brother Andy will die.'

Kathy opened her eyes. Charlotte started to walk towards me. 'How are …'

I spat my words out: 'Stay where you are and just listen for Chrissake. One of his gang is outside waiting to verify you are both dead. If you're not, he'll kill you himself. He'll be here any moment. I'll have to take him out – kill *him* if necessary – and then immediately call the police. It's the only option I have. Get Kathy up. Both of you lie down on the floor hidden behind the bed and keep absolutely quiet.' Charlotte was rooted to the spot with her mouth open. 'Do it, NOW!' I shouted.

I could see a problem. Kathy was wired up to various items of equipment and there was an IV drip in her arm. But I had underestimated Kathy's degree of recovery. She threw the bedcovers off and began frantically tugging at the electrical and fluid connectors on her body – obviously monitoring rather than life-sustaining lines. I prayed her actions didn't trigger any nurse-summoning alarms. Charlotte leapt to Kathy's assistance. I positioned myself behind the door and I reached into the armpit of my jacket to withdraw the long-snouted pistol; I didn't bother with the leather gloves. I flicked the safety lever, but kept my finger away from the trigger. I balanced the gun in my hand, viewing it solely as a blunt instrument and attempting to overcome the disbelief that I could be in such a situation. Kathy was now hidden on the floor and Charlotte looked my way as she reordered the bedclothes. The panic and concern was evident as she stared motionless at the gun. I signalled her to get down. All I could hear now was the disconnected rhythms of the machines and the thumping of my heart. The seconds dragged like hours and I wondered whether I would have to entice Luigi into the room. How long would it take him to realize something might have gone wrong and he needed to finish the job? Perhaps there were people outside the room delaying his follow-up?

I heard the door squeak open. From my position I could see the reflection of the doorway in the mirror above the sink. As the gap widened I saw blackness, then a black shape and finally the clear outline of my black-clothed minder. Too late I realized my voyeur privilege was two-way – I could see Luigi's reflection as he could see mine. In an instant a gun appeared in his hand and the door was thrust open. I guessed his objective was to knock me off balance, and with little time to move I braced myself for the impact. But the mounting of the door was in my favour; with thirty degrees of angle remaining the hinges reached their extent of travel and the door bounced back towards Luigi. It was enough distraction to allow me to emerge from my hiding place with my gun held high and bring it down with the maximum force on Luigi's head.

The plan worked – after a fashion. The blow struck home, but with the limited surface area and weight of the gun barrel and silencer, my nervous aim and Luigi's movement, the glancing blow to a resilient Latin head had little disabling effect. Shock had a role to play though on his trigger sensitive finger. The muffled spit of a discharged bullet, the thud into an unintentional target and a female scream echoed around the room within microseconds of each other. I looked towards the scream and saw Charlotte's and Kathy's heads briefly peer over the edge of the bed. My action was misjudged and allowed Luigi an opportunity to react similarly by smashing his own gun against the side of my face. My already battered ear cushioned the force of the attack, but old and new wounds wept blood, and dazed, I collapsed to the floor.

Content that I was temporarily immobilized, Luigi moved quickly towards the girls' hiding place. Another scream would surely bring assistance from outside, but I could hear the girls talking urgently, then Charlotte whimpered 'Oh Kathy, No, No' as Luigi took aim. With great effort, I managed to rotate myself into a sitting position, and still holding my gun, fumbled blindly with the safety catch until I heard the satisfying click. At the same time, I called out to Luigi. Both sounds had the desired effect of diverting his murderous intent towards me, and for a moment he was spoilt for choice. Our eyes met and radiated hate to each other, and it was the signal for two more bullets to be expelled. I felt a sharp blow and my whole body spasmed before a black veil was drawn over my consciousness.

Chapter 46

THIRD FRIDAY – 11:00 p.m.

By now, I should have been familiar with the process of waking up in a hospital bed: a post-appendectomy, which I still didn't remember, and a post-mugging and fainting, which I vaguely did; yet, as I briefly opened my eyes on that Friday night, the predominantly blurred and white surroundings registered something celestial rather than clinical. I was convinced that I was about to meet my Maker and minutes later one of His messengers spoke to me. The female voice was appropriately angelic and soothing. She told me I was in a safe place; my problems had passed; I would be alright; above all, I was loved and missed. I felt my hand squeezed gently.

Chapter 47

THIRD SATURDAY – 9:30 a.m.

For some time I was aware of the sounds around me. A dawn chorus first, which was progressively swamped by the drone of distant traffic. I heard far-off doors opening and closing, and one nearby which I assumed was the entranceway to wherever I was confined. Voices were present too. Periodically, there were whispered conversations between a female I recognized and two males that I didn't. My body told me it was unwise to qualify sound with sight or movement. But I remembered my right hand being squeezed, so I waited for the next whispers then fluttered my fingers to gain attention.

'Mr. Shadwell, are you comfortable?' asked a male voice.

'I'm not sure. Is it safe to move or open my eyes?' My mouth was very dry, but I could speak.

'Try not to move, but open your eyes ... slowly.'

I attempted to raise my eyelids and I could feel resistance like they were stuck together. Suddenly the viscidity that held them fast gave way and they sprung open. I felt a pain on the left side of my head as I stirred. There was a white-coated shape leaning over me and shining a pencil beam of light into my eyes, forcing me to make gritty blinks.

'Would you bathe his eyes nurse? I think they've been weeping following the general anaesthetic.'

There was preparatory noise then the nurse said: 'Keep still with your eyes closed.' The nurse was Sam Rapley. She gently dabbed the sticky area with a liquid that smelt like seawater. 'Try again.'

This time my vision was clear and I saw a young doctor and Sam standing either side of the bed. 'Are you my Guardian Angel?' I said to Sam.

She smiled. 'With the scrapes you've been in, I think I must be your Seraphim rather than a lowly Angel.'

I discerned her remark as a religious pun, though the subtlety escaped me. 'What's happened to me now?'

The doctor leaned over again and continued his light beam experiments. I obviously reacted positively. 'Excellent,' he said. 'I'm Doctor Henderson by the way. I've removed a bullet from your lower chest and attended to your head injury. Your nurse is Sam Rapley. I believe you've met. She asked specifically to look after you.'

His words immediately triggered the memories of my last waking moments. I tried to push myself upright from my prone position and managed to gasp, 'Charlotte? Kathy? Andy?' before I slumped back with severe complaints from my head and chest.

'Easy now,' Sam said. 'Charlotte and Kathy are fine. Charlotte was by your bed for part of the night. I don't know anything about an Andy.'

'My brother ... Andy.' I said gritting my teeth against the pains.

'There are policemen outside waiting to interview you. They will probably be able to answer your question,' Sam said.

'Not yet, nurse. I don't think Mr. Shadwell's ready to receive visitors. Check the dressings on his chest and head, and let him rest a few more hours.'

'But the police insisted they see him as soon as he was conscious.'

'This is *my* territory, not the police's. You tend our patient. I'll deal with them.'

Doctor Henderson left me alone with Sam.

She peeled away the gauze on my head and drew breath. 'Nasty. Six stitches. It'll scar, but it won't show. It's above your hair line.'

'Tell me what you *do* know, Sam.'

She didn't answer until she had finished with my head and had drawn back the bed covers to examine my chest. 'Left side, just above the abdomen, clean bullet wound, cracked two ribs that got in the way, no internal damage. Three inches higher and you would be dead,' she said indifferently.

'Not my body, Sam. Char ...' I stopped as she touched a sensitive part of my wound. 'The Rensbergs.' Again, she ignored me until she had finished her administrations. 'I said, they are fine. Kathy suffered no adverse effects from the ordeal. Charlotte is frantic with worry and is on the waiting list to see you.'

'Waiting list?'

'It appears you have acquired a number of friends during your homeless days. Let me see ... in addition to the police and Charlotte, you've had visits from ...' she pulled a scrap of paper from her uniform pocket, '... Luther, Adrian, Keith, Brian, and a couple of smelly tramps called Gregor and Igor ... oh, and a phone call from Howard Winston. But they are all out of bounds until you've had more rest – Doctor's orders. So, take these couple of pills and I'll leave you alone for a few hours.'

I took them and a full glass of water to slake my thirst. 'One more question before you go?'

Sam hesitated by the door.

'Luigi … the Italian … the man who tried to kill me?'

'The police will tell you.'

'Sam?' I persisted.

'He's dead, Peter.'

I had been asleep for three hours when Doctor Henderson returned and announced I could receive my first visitors. 'Come in Superintendent. I can permit you a maximum of thirty minutes.'

Two men entered, one of them I'd seen before. The stranger, the shorter and older man smartly dressed in a blue pinstripe suit spoke: 'Good afternoon, Mr. Shadwell. I'm sorry to trouble you so soon after your … incident. My name is Detective Superintendent Dixon. This is my colleague Detective Sergeant Underwood.' Dixon drew up a chair by the bed and Underwood remained standing.

'What's happened to my brother? Where's Bradley?'

Dixon displayed an irritating smirk. At a glance his face was a pasty grey, which matched his hair, but not his bushy black eyebrows. 'Your brother is safe. He is currently helping us with our enquiries. He will be brought to see you when he's finished, and I've finished with you. In the meantime, tell me how you killed Ricardo Santori.'

'Who is Ricardo Santori?'

Dixon sighed with frustration: 'The man who allegedly attacked you and the Rensbergs.'

'Tell me about Bradley first.'

'Mr. Shadwell, I'm here to ask *you* questions, not the other way round. I have a murder to investigate.' Dixon's manner was patronizing and suspicious.

'You are accusing me of killing someone. Shouldn't I have legal representation?'

'There you go again, asking questions. You are already under arrest for other crimes Mr. Shadwell. Not yet, for this particular matter. I am merely seeking your version of events.'

'You already have a version from Charlotte and Kathy?' Another question; Dixon sighed again and said nothing. 'I think I'd rather make my statement to DI Bradley.'

'I'm afraid that's not possible. Bradley has been suspended from duty.'

'Suspended. Why?'

Dixon dismissed my question. 'That is irrelevant to my enquiries.'

'I believe it's very relevant to any information I can give you.'

'Very well. I am aware of your deal with Bradley and of the incriminating statement Miss Kathy Rensberg has made about me. But you have been conned Mr. Shadwell. Bradley has been under suspicion for several months regarding his *co-operation* with the Kent organization. I believe he felt endangered by your knowledge and contrived to have you and the Rensbergs killed. It's because of his actions you are lying in this bed.'

'That's rubbish. The evidence says otherwise.'

'Oh, so you have evidence to the contrary, do you? I wonder whether it competes with the box file of evidence I have in my office?'

In the seconds I dwelt on this statement, I recalled the details of my meetings with Bradley and everything I had heard about him. Ignoring the suspicions I once had about the asparagus sandwiches, I was now convinced about his innocence regarding Kent. No way had I been conned. Dixon had to be lying.

'Well?' he said impatiently.

'Kathy Rensberg heard Ronnie Kent talking to you.'

Dixon laughed. 'The infamous Chad story?'

I decided not to comment.

'On the night in question the records show that Underwood here took the call from Kathy and relayed the information, as instructed, to *Bradley*. When Kathy's drugged body was found, we put two and two together. This was our first lead to justifiably start investigating Bradley. The story you heard confirms that. Has it never occurred to you that *Chad* could easily be confused with *Brad*?'

'No, but there are other ....'

Dixon leaned towards me to interrupt. A scowl had appeared on his face. 'Now look you little shit, you are wasting your time. Bradley's going down and there is nothing you can say that will change the situation.' He sat back in the chair, realizing his outburst was irregular. He continued calmly: 'I have an alternative theory to pursue about your involvement in this. Maybe Bradley's deal with you went further. Perhaps he arranged for you to be recruited in order to kill the Rensbergs and offered you sanctuary as a reward. A new life somewhere? How convenient that Bradley suggested you go to Charing Cross station and miraculously you were picked up on your first night there.'

Sadly, everything Dixon had said made sense. Admittedly, I had been exposed to only a small part of the case against Bradley. I wasn't happy about how gullible I might have been. For now I had no option but to defer to

Dixon's greater knowledge, at least for his benefit. Did it matter I had been mistaken? Kathy, Charlotte and Andy were safe. I was alive and presumably, the Kent Empire was in rapid decline. Resignedly I said: 'Okay, Inspector, I'll tell you what happened.'

I started from the time Sniffy found me at Charing Cross station and finished with the shooting. Dixon took no notes and asked no questions during my story, just an occasional nod or shake of his head at a few key events. It was a lot of information to commit to memory. Either he had a brain like a sponge or most of the detail was already familiar to him. When I'd finished he smiled, though whether it was with satisfaction or relief, was impossible to tell.

'How do you know you met Ronnie Kent?' Dixon suddenly asked.

'I don't follow.'

'It's a simple question Mr. Shadwell. Did the man you say was Ronnie Kent formally announce himself? Give you his business card? Did someone say "Hello Ronnie Kent. How are you?" Did you recognize him?'

'I recognized him.'

'Ah. You had met him previously?'

'No. Bradley described him to me.'

'Hardly reliable information considering his particular situation.'

It sounded like an argument by the defence counsel at a trial. Was Dixon building to discredit me as a witness?

He moved quickly on. 'There is a discrepancy about your shoot-out with Santori. You say you fired a single shot. Are you sure?'

'Yes. We shot at each other at the same time. I was hit and then, I assume, I passed out.'

'Now there's the puzzle I'm trying to unravel. Santori had *two* wounds. One was a flesh wound to his upper right arm; the second was a fatal one into his brain.'

It was a great relief to see Sam arrive at that critical and timely point. I was fading rapidly from the physical and mental energy required to deal with the interview. Despite protests from Dixon, she exercised her rights for patient welfare and summarily dismissed my visitors from the room. Dixon had insisted he was to be advised at the earliest opportunity when I could be seen again, but Sam had countered with a "Don't call us, we'll call you" kind of reply. Dixon had the final say when he employed his rights for prisoner protection and demanded that I should be refused visits other than from medical personnel until his return.

'Did he give you a hard time?' Sam asked.

'That man is evil, Sam. Keep him away from me.'

'I can't forever, but I can invent a relapse or two to stall him.'

'Thanks. Is there any chance I could see Charlotte? There's some urgent things I need to discuss with her.'

'I fear not. There's a policeman stationed outside the room with specific instructions to bar anyone from seeing you.'

'I can't be seen except by medical personnel. Could you cloak her in a white coat and hang a stethoscope around her neck?'

'That might be difficult. She and Kathy are under guard too.'

'But you said Charlotte was here last night.'

'She was accompanied by a policewoman. It was while they were moving Kathy to another room. Her original room has been sealed off for forensic examination.'

'Is there anyone else waiting to see me?'

'I don't think so. The Superintendent shooed them away.'

'Then I need to get a message to Bill Haynes – the big policeman who came with Bradley yesterday ...'

Sam was eager to co-operate in any action against Dixon. She had her own suspicions about his character based purely upon an assessment of his behaviour to the hospital staff. "Arrogant pig" were the words she used, which I thought was tame in comparison to my own thoughts. I asked her to try to locate Luther. He would know how to reach Bill, and Bill might be the best person who could shed light on what was going on.

Sam agreed to help, but first she had to check my dressings and general welfare. She offered lunch and I amazed myself by choosing chicken soup, a cheese sandwich and coffee, more from Sam's insistence to eat than any desire to satisfy hunger. While she fetched lunch, Doctor Henderson visited and forced me to parade up and down the room to test my mobility. Vertically I was surprisingly pain free, albeit unsteady on my feet. The doctor escorted me to the toilet under the additional watchful eye of a uniformed officer and there I discovered that a sitting position was more troublesome, as the creasing of my side stitches caused me to flinch and catch my breath. Comfortable once more in bed, I ate, drank and drifted to sleep.

Less than an hour had passed when Sam woke me saying there was a Doctor Browncast to see me. And there was Luther standing beside the bed, bedecked in a white coat and stethoscope hanging around his neck. Sam smiled and winked, then left us alone.

'I knew you would be trouble when I first met you. Now you really are a murderer and a blonde one too; but congratulations are in order, you downed one of the drug bastards.'

'I'm not proud of what I did, Luther. In fact, I feel quite sick when I think about it. What else could I have done?'

'Aimed for a limb instead of the head? Don't fret about it. The story's not over yet. I've spoken to Bill.'

'You have? Why isn't he here?'

'Not possible, he's been suspended as well as Bradley. He'd never get past all the coppers in this place. They all know Bill Haynes; besides it's difficult to disguise his bulk even in a Doctor's overalls.'

'I don't understand. When was he suspended? He was outside Kathy's ward when I arrived last night to … assassinate her.'

'It's a good job he was, otherwise the situation would be worse than it is now. He and Bradley were suspended, supposedly because of the deal you made with them about letting you go. Bill is adamant that only Sergeant Underwood could have leaked the arrangement, but the true reason they were suspended was the incriminating information about Dixon. Bill reckons Underwood is in league with Dixon.'

'Are you sure Bill's not covering for Dixon? Dixon interviewed me earlier and he says he has a volume of evidence which proves Bradley is in cahoots with Ronnie Kent.'

'I trust Bill and he trusts Bradley. That's good enough for me.'

'So why was Bill at the hospital?'

Luther sat down and began to fidget with his stethoscope.

'Bradley was held in custody pending an investigation, but Bill was told to just go home. When Bill heard from a colleague that Dixon had called off the protection for Kathy and Charlotte, he was suspicious and worried for their safety. He visited them at the hospital, told them what had happened, and posing as a civilian, elected to keep a private look out. Your disguise certainly fooled him and it only clicked who you were after he was minutes into deciphering the note you had dropped.

'He was the first to arrive on the bloody scene in Kathy's room. He quickly found medical staff to attend to you, but the Eyetie was beyond help. Then he had a dilemma, whom should he call at the police? He wasn't supposed to be there and he didn't want to call Dixon. Instead, he relayed the details to a trusted colleague on the duty desk at Bethnal Green CID. One team was despatched to the scene of the crime and another started to analyse your cryptic information. Luckily, one of the DC's recognized BQC as Best Quality Carpets – he had bought a carpet from there on the previous weekend. Feeling smug about his discovery, he phoned Dixon with the news, but it was another fifteen minutes before he was called back and given the go ahead to mount a raid on the premises. By the time the team arrived there, the operations centre at the warehouse was deserted except for your brother who was chained to a bed in the cellar. For such a comprehensive disappearing trick it's reckoned the operation must have had well rehearsed evacuation procedures. The fifteen or so minute delay would have been critical to their getaway.'

How convenient I thought. 'Dixon must have used the time to tip off Ronnie Kent.'

'Possibly, but who can prove it? At the time he was apparently in a car in Stratford being driven by *Underwood.*'

My mind was working overtime looking for flaws. 'The call log for his mobile phone … it could be checked to see what number he rang around that time.'

'Bill thought of that too, but Dixon's not stupid. He probably has a separate untraceable mobile just for such eventualities.'

'So Kent and Dixon have got away with it?'

'Not necessarily. Bill thinks there must still be evidence left at BQC and there's the information that you, your brother and Kathy can provide. Assuming of course it's not swept under the carpet by Dixon.'

'Then we have to convince another senior officer to listen to what we have to say. Can't Bill help out with that?'

'Maybe. Except everyone is shit scared of Dixon, and Bill's suspension discredits him.'

I returned to thinking mode. My brother was employed by the Government. Possibly a long shot, but surely he had some contacts that could go above Dixon's head. I offered the solution to Luther. 'I wonder if my brother can help.'

'Just how does your brother fit into this? A few days ago you didn't know who you were, and now your brother is found imprisoned at Ronnie Kent's HQ.'

'I don't know and I won't be able to answer until I can speak to him, but …' I paused because I recalled a fact about yesterday which potentially didn't stack up. 'When were Bradley and Haynes suspended?'

'Friday morning, I think.'

'Then it's possible that it wasn't because of Underwood. I didn't think Underwood was within listening distance when I did the deal with Bradley. I spoke to Bradley on Friday morning and at the time he was still on duty, which he wouldn't have been if Underwood had acted on the information he might have acquired early on Thursday afternoon.' I told Luther what Bradley had said about my brother going missing and the government involvement. 'I expect MI5, MI6 or another intelligence agency leaned on Bradley to reveal why he had staff snooping about at my brother's home. Dixon would have been party to the process and probably used the incident as his opportunity to remove Bradley from the investigation, and set him up as the scapegoat for collusion with Kent.'

'So how do you think your brother could help?'

'If his employer – presumably the Home Office – was angry about its employee being kidnapped, they might want to be involved in apprehending the perpetrators. I'll try out the idea on Andy when he gets here. Meanwhile, could you keep in touch with Bill to monitor the police situation?'

Luther agreed and with a reminder there was still a list of well-wishers from the Jubilee waiting to see me, he elected to leave in case Dixon's return blew his cover.

'One more thing Luther. Your friends in Grace Street – George and Jessie.'

'What about them?' Luther sounded surprised at my knowledge.

I told him about their involvement with Kent then added controversially: 'I didn't know you were working for Ronnie all along!' His departing embarrassment at this unwelcome news removed the remaining small doubt I had about whose side Luther was really on.

Dixon did return about half an hour later. I overheard Sam's valiant attempts at sending him away, but as Dixon became loudly vociferous, her resolve faltered and he entered the room, this time accompanied by a young uniformed policewoman to act as scribe for a ruthless interview. Ruthless, because as the interview progressed, I became increasingly frustrated with the repetition of the questions, aimed, it seemed, as an attempt to compromise my consistent answers. Moreover, I reasoned, Dixon was attempting to convince me he had no prior knowledge of my brief foray in the Kent organization. His persistence grew as my tolerance faded. The policewoman kept looking nervously at Dixon, perhaps disturbed by his aggression, which conflicted, with her textbook training on interviewing techniques. Strangely, the killing of Santori was hardly mentioned. There was no threat of accusation or arrest, and it occurred to me that maybe this was by design. Subjecting me to the formal processes of arrest would require official statements and possibly a trial, and that would publicly reveal information Dixon might want to suppress. The interrogation ended when, on the verge of losing my nerve, my body chose to protect itself from the verbal onslaught, and I began to drift into an exhausted sleep.

Sam woke me at six o'clock and was apologetic about the intrusion of Dixon. I didn't complain; she had already put herself at risk enough for my benefit. A crowd had strolled down from the Jubilee and had formed a ptochocracy to gang up on the lone policeman keeping watch outside my room. Led by the physical presence and charisma of Jazz, the pressured constable had conceded they could come in, albeit one at a time, after a body search and with my prior approval.

Adrian entered first to say hello and goodbye. I thanked him for unearthing my real name, but he dismissed the discovery in favour of the important news he had received that morning. His solicitor had negotiated a substantial out-of-court settlement for his unfair dismissal and Adrian was heading north the next day to be headmaster at a school in Darlington. He didn't say whether his younger friend was joining him and I was too embarrassed to ask. He did say he still intended to finish his novel, and wanted to keep in touch to further document my experiences, as potential material for his fictional work. I was happy to agree and gave him my brother's address for communication. I was still technically homeless and unsure whether the forwarding address might be one of Her Majesty's prisons.

Keith was next and wildly excited. 'It's all come back to me. I was talking to Adrian and when he said he had found out your name is Pete Shadwell everything clicked. Your brother is Andrew; my best friend was Alex Mountjoy and the bank robber's son was Alan Tremlett.' I offered my thanks for the information, but sadly it had come too late. If he had remembered last Tuesday, I probably wouldn't be in the situation I was now, but I didn't trouble him with such detail. Keith told me that due to the non-availability of a policewoman for a body search, Jazz, Free and Georgie had left to mount a separate campaign to visit Charlotte and Kathy. I was jealous about such contact, and courtesy of a biro and scrap of paper from Keith, I penned a hastily written note for him to transport to Charlotte.

Roger didn't have a lot to say. He had brought me biscuits and unwrapped grapes; the latter he had stolen from a stall on the way to the hospital. He did make me laugh though. I almost split my stitches when he related how Gregor and Igor had reacted to the idea of a body search before they could see me. He reckoned he saw their faces go white beneath the grime that covered them. It would have been a classic moment to see the policeman's expression had he ventured into the glory holes concealed beneath the Polish brother's coats. They left a soiled mini packet of biscuits for me and had then nervously scurried away with a parting "Fucking nosy bastard" aimed at the constable.

Brian appeared last and was the most inquisitive about my fate and injuries. Few details of the shooting had yet reached the public domain and I declined to add any information fearing Brian was the kind of person who might blab to the information hungry reporters he said were conducting a vigil at the hospital. I steered the conversation towards his current painting and he beamed with satisfaction. The painting of his boss's daughter had been completed and delivered. His boss had showered praise on him and promised to introduce him to a number of influential colleagues for other commissions. Unexpectedly Brian had also been paid a heap of cash for his efforts and he had purchased an expensive bottle of wine for me as a get-well gift.

I was truly touched by the visit of my Jubilee friends. I had only known them for two weeks and already I was enamoured by the camaraderie amongst the homeless community. If the current course of events continued, it was likely my brief encounter with such disadvantaged people would soon be at an end.

As I ate my evening meal, I recalled the apprehension I had felt when I left this hospital for the first time to join the homeless. Now I was having similar feelings as I prepared myself to return to my previous life. The proverb "better the devil you know" kept popping into my mind. The devil I currently knew was life on the streets. Could I adapt to the unknown devil of Peter Shadwell, whose knowledge of his past was less than Robin Forest's? The debate occupied my mind for some time, and when sleep took control, the issue was into extra time with a penalty shoot out on the horizon.

Chapter 48

THIRD SUNDAY – 7:00 a.m.

I was awake at seven o'clock, out of bed five minutes later, and washed and dressed within twenty.

Washing was a big relief. Parts of me had undoubtedly been cleaned to attend to my injuries, but the rest had been left in its unwashed, though not visibly, grimy state. I didn't wash my hair, since bending forward over the sink for more than a few seconds painfully compressed the stitches in my side; instead, I examined my hair with interest. My head had been partly shaved above my left ear to accommodate the stitches. In the region around it, presumably aided by sterilisation, my blonde tinge had reverted to brown; it gave me a freakish look.

And dressed was an overstatement; I had simply donned a hospital dressing gown hanging on the door.

I paced up and down the room for exercise, and even ventured as far as stretching and limited bending without too many bodily complaints. I could hear the hospital beginning to stir outside the room and went to the door to peek outside. My police guard was sitting in a chair opposite the door. He looked extremely uncomfortable: his head bent back, mouth wide open and arms hung loosely at his side. An open paperback was balanced precariously on his lap and he was broadcasting heavy breathing sounds. For an instant, I considered escaping to visiting Charlotte, but I realized I didn't know my own location in the hospital, let alone Charlotte's, and a dressing-gowned patient wandering the corridors would soon be noticed.

An Asian nurse spotted me and came rushing over to enquire if I was okay. I confirmed I was and indicated to her to keep her voice down pointing to my snoring guard, but approaching footsteps and a call of 'Christ, am I glad to see you' from my left was loud enough to disturb the quietude I was seeking. The sleeping policeman spluttered once and stood up with a jolt, tipping his book to the floor. We all looked towards the intruder. It was Andy.

Conscious of his dereliction to duty, the constable leapt between Andy and me, and stood his ground. He twitched slightly as Andy reached into an inside pocket to produce a small folder about the size of a credit card. Andy flicked it open and waved it in front of the officer, who studied it carefully before saluting and standing aside.

Andy spoke to me, but I was staring with a shock brought about by the encounter. Of course, I had seen him two days earlier at the warehouse, yet that was a detached and constrained meeting, and now I had the chance to really communicate with him. It was a strange feeling; I *recognized* the person in front of me and experienced a feeling of love and warmth one has for a sibling, but I didn't *know* him, except for the events that had returned as flashbacks. Even those had shown there were gaps in my past knowledge. What employment status did he have to make a constable react in such a submissive manner?

'I said, you're looking good ... but a little distant?'

'I ... I'm sorry ... Andy,' I said awkwardly. 'It's weird talking to you like this.'

The audience was gawping. 'Let's get some privacy,' Andy said.

I led Andy into my room and shut the door. 'Is it safe to hug you?' he asked.

'Er ... yes ... avoid my left side.'

He stood on my right, put his left arm across my shoulders, squeezed and held tight. 'After our encounter on Friday ... I thought ... I'd never see you again.' His voice was choked with emotion. The sorrowful life I'd led since my mugging, and the trauma of the last few days, suddenly caught up with me, and I sobbed, and Andy sobbed with me. It was minutes before we composed ourselves. We both had so much to say and ask, but the bonding we had been through inhibited us from speech, and we drew comfort from just being together. I lay on the bed and Andy sat in the chair alongside. We stayed that way in an easy silence until my breakfast arrived a few minutes later.

Andy declined my attempt to get a breakfast for him, settling for a cup of black coffee. He was keen to begin our exchange of information and I was too, so I ate the distractions quickly. Yet, having eaten and with my mind eager for explanations, a physical tiredness from the nervous energy I had consumed began to take over. I fought sleep, but succumbed to its demands for over an hour. When I awoke Andy and Charlotte were standing by the window, chatting quietly. I watched them for a moment, content that I was rejoined – as far as I knew – with the two people who meant most to me.

'I see Andy has been using his influence again.' I said, referring to Charlotte's presence.

Charlotte started and looked towards me. Her stance was weary, but otherwise she was radiant. Up to now I had only seen her in T-Shirt and jeans. Today she wore a plain pink blouse and dark grey slacks, and her golden hair neatly encircled her joyous face. She came to my side.

'I've been so worried about you,' she said, looking puzzled as she ran her fingers gently through my hair.

'An assassin looks much better as a blonde, don't you agree?'

'That's not funny,' she scolded.

I regretted my flippant remark and asked: 'How's Kathy?'

'Physically fine, but she's finding it difficult to come to terms with ... the shooting. Like me, she wants to get out of this hospital. It has too many unhappy memories.'

I felt the same way and was looking forward to discussing the future with Andy. Perhaps he could help Charlotte and Kathy too. I took Charlotte's hand and pulled her towards me. She leaned carefully over and kissed me lightly on the lips. I was disappointed with the ephemeral greeting, but she looked back nervously at Andy, embarrassed to be intruding on a family reunion.

'And I thought the last few weeks had been bad for you, when all along you've been falling in love with this gorgeous new friend,' Andy said with a touch of irony.

Charlotte visibly blushed and my cheeks felt warm.

'We are just good friends brought together with a common end,' I countered.

This time Charlotte appeared disappointed and Andy leapt to allay her worries.

'For Charlotte's benefit let me say that although you may not know me very well, I have 25 years of experience of you, and I've never seen you look at a member of the opposite sex like *that* before.'

We laughed together, each I felt for different reasons, though with a shared goal to move on to more important matters. Andy sat astride a chair and Charlotte rested on the edge of the bed holding my hand.

'Where do we start?' I asked.

'Well,' Andy said, 'I've heard a lot about your viewpoint from Charlotte, perhaps I ought to begin with everything I've been involved in. It's a long story. Are you sure you're up to it?'

'I've been in limbo for two weeks wondering what the hell has been going on. If I pass out or go to sleep, wake me and carry on. I think it's time I knew the truth.'

Chapter 49

THIRD SUNDAY – 9:15 a.m.

Andy adjusted his spectacles and positioned himself comfortably on his chair. 'The logical, rather than chronological, starting point is when I woke up in the cellar at BQC on Tuesday morning – with Sebastian Tate standing over me. I demanded to know why I was being held against my will and instantly he was strangely forthcoming. It soon became apparent the man was a complete egomaniac and wanted to bask in the pleasure of boasting how he had achieved your downfall. But before he got to that, he insisted on giving me some background. The conspiracy apparently started when Barry Kent was on his deathbed. He called for his two sons, Ronnie Kent and Sebastian Tate to be by his side, so that he could tell them a story.'

Andy had lost me already. 'You mean son and ... step-son maybe?' I suggested.

'No. They are true brothers; Kent and Tate are adopted names; their original surname is Tremlett. For Barry, Ronnie and Sebastian substitute Victor, Alan and Trevor.' Andy looked at me expecting a reaction. I just shrugged.

'The change took place about ten years ago, soon after Barry – I'll use current names otherwise we'll get confused – had spent five years in prison.'

I mumbled to myself. 'So that's why the police had no earlier record of Barry, they should have been looking for Victor Tremlett.'

Andy had paused, waiting for my attention, 'Barry had been in prison for a bank robbery ...' and I finished, '... in Leyton.'

'You do remember.' Andy exclaimed.

I briefly explained what Keith had told me in Pizzaland and his recall of the name Alan Tremlett yesterday. Some of the story threads were coming together and I was eager to get to the climax. 'But what story did Barry relate to his sons? They presumably knew about the robbery.'

'Yes, but not the full story, because Barry didn't know it at the time. I need to give you some of *our* background too ...'

Andy went on to relate the events of that period of our school days.

Ronnie was ten years old at the time and in the same class as me; Sebastian was only eight. In comparison to the lanky Ronnie of today, he was big then, inches taller than Andy or me, and maybe a stone or two heavier. He was already notorious for bullying and misbehaviour – probably a budding chip off Barry's block – and by contrast, Sebastian was a well-mannered kid with a studious nature.

Andy and I had witnessed the bank robbery, and I had recognized Barry from the times when he had to collect Ronnie from school following one of his disrupting pranks. We didn't go to the police straightaway because we were scared our lunchtime absence from school would land us in trouble. But we had been seen outside the bank by one of our mother's friends and when mother confronted us, we owned up and were promptly marched to the police station to make a statement. As it turned out, our statements weren't essential for a conviction because stupidly Barry had used his own car for the getaway, and another witness had recorded the registration number. Furthermore, when the police visited Barry's house they found the stolen money. That damning evidence was too much to refute, so Barry and his accomplice had no option but to plead guilty. However, before Barry was sent down, rumours began to circulate at school that two pupils had recognized Barry, and this had led to his arrest. Andy and I kept silent about our grassing and our involvement never became public knowledge.

Ronnie became even more unbearable after that and began a school-wide campaign of bullying to discover who had informed on his father. To avoid adding to his notoriety inside school, Ronnie used to confront pupils before or after the school day. When it was the turn of Andy and me to be questioned, he followed us from school and waited until we had reached a small park. He drew up alongside and started asking us what we had been doing on the lunchtime of the robbery. Andy apparently used to have a stammer at school and when he stuttered an excuse, Ronnie read his hesitation as an admission of guilt. Ronnie threw Andy to the ground and started cursing, and kicking him in the face. Before Andy could react, he had pushed two broken teeth through his lip and there was blood everywhere. I attempted to come to his rescue by swinging my satchel into Ronnie's body, but to Ronnie these blows were merely irritating than harmful. On about the fourth blow Ronnie turned to deflect the satchel with his arm. As he did so, one of the straps on the satchel came undone and the edge of a metal ruler from inside wedged itself in the satchel flap. The parry by Ronnie had the undesirable effect of steering the ruler towards his face to slash open his cheek. It was a deep wound and his bloodletting soon surpassed Andy's, amid murderous screams that attracted attention from around the park. An ambulance was summoned to take Ronnie to hospital. Father took Andy to the dentist for emergency treatment and I was left to answer questions from the police. There had been ample witnesses nearby to confirm the unprovoked attack by Ronnie, yet the police chose to write off the event as merely schoolboys' exuberance.

When Andy and I returned to school a few days later, we discovered Ronnie had been expelled. His attack on Andy had been the final straw as far as the headmaster was concerned because, unbeknown to us, many parents had already complained about Ronnie's strong-arm tactics. Sebastian was removed from the school too and until recently that was the last time Andy had seen them.

I had sat spellbound by Andy's story. I searched my mind for recollection of the incident, but nothing came. The past encounter with Ronnie potentially explained a lot, yet still left many questions unanswered.

'So little brother, twice you've rescued me now. And you don't remember the first time?' Andy asked.

'No, nothing,' I said. Andy frowned at my reply; I wasn't sure whether it was from worry, disappointment or disbelief. I was eager for the modern day encounter with the Kents, but the mention of our parents in the story had raised a more pressing question. 'Mum and Dad? I can picture them … in Canada … but I don't know …'

'They're fine. I've telephoned them and apologized about us being incommunicado for a few weeks. I said we've had a few minor problems to sort out so that they didn't worry, and we'll be in touch again soon.'

'So, back to the present day and Sebastian's story,' Andy said and my eyes lit up in anticipation as he continued to relate the information he had obtained from Sebastian.

Barry had maintained that the disease, which had rendered him immobile, was contracted while he was being treated for a minor respiratory infection in the prison hospital. He didn't levy blame with the prison authorities, rather the individuals who had supposedly secured his capture in the first place. While he was busy mugging and drugging in East London, his thoughts never turned to seeking retribution, because he had no way of knowing who the culprits might have been. However, when he knew he was going to die, he instructed his cultivated sources in police records to root through the old files to discover who had originally blown the whistle on him. As a result, he came into possession of the statements Andy and I had made after the bank robbery. He kept this information to himself until his deathbed, where his dying wish was that suitable suffering was metered out to Messrs Peter and Andrew Shadwell.

I had a question about why Sebastian had apparently been out of the limelight all this time, and why he adopted a separate surname. Andy had gleaned that information too.

Ronnie had been the brawn and Sebastian the brain. When the Tremletts moved away from Leyton they went to live in Birmingham. Without the influence of his father, Ronnie moderated his brutality, but was intellectually still a no-hoper. Sebastian however, did well at school and excelled in the sciences. Thanks to illicit proceeds, the Tremletts had been comfortable financially and Sebastian was installed in a fee-paying boarding school. The arrangement suited him because he was now old enough to realize he could make a name for himself, without having to resort to the criminal ways of the rest of his family.

When Barry was released from prison after five years, he took on the name of Kent and moved the family – minus Sebastian – back to his old hunting ground. Sebastian, keen to divorce himself completely from his roots, took the name of Tate and eventually went to Southampton University to study Computer Science. There Sebastian was the brightest undergraduate until he discovered drugs, and finding himself short of cash to feed his habit, in desperation he contacted his father to bale him out. Barry did, but not without coming to an arrangement to further his own criminal ambitions. In exchange for helping Sebastian kick the habit, he had to leave university and work for Barry, who had an increasing need for a trusted person to oversee the computer dependent side of his activities. Barry had been using computers for all kinds of things: money laundering; investment scams; porn sites; and most of all as a secure means of controlling operations at arms length from his bedside. He couldn't involve Ronnie, whose peanut brain even had difficulty with controlling the TV from a remote control. So, Sebastian *had* been heavily involved in the Kent organization for a few years, albeit as the chief backroom boy indulging his technical brain at its operational headquarters.

I asked Andy how the Kents had found out where we lived.

Sebastian had been given that task. He went through the usual sources of telephone directories, electoral registers, the Internet and apparently found more A and P Shadwells than he could cope with. It was pure chance that he and I had a mutual acquaintance – Joseph Carmichael – known to the Kents as Josh the Tosh. Josh was an addict recruited from the streets and acquired his nickname from his trait of searching drains and sewers for lost valuables he could resell to fund his habit. He was a bright guy, and became a pusher of some standing in the organization. When Barry decided to expand his drug dealings into Essex, Harlow was a prime site and Josh the ideal person to handle distribution. Then, during a chance conversation between Sebastian and Josh about neighbours, the name of Peter Shadwell had cropped up, and bingo, Sebastian had found me.

Josh had been assigned the task of discovering everything he could about me, which explained why he had been so interested in my background and job. With such knowledge, it would have been easy for Sebastian to kill me or arrange to have me killed – his ultimate aim – but Barry had wanted us to suffer first and Sebastian hit on a private idea. Before delivering me to Ronnie, he wanted to indulge his own form of perverted pleasure. He had found out from Josh I was to take two weeks leave in the Lake District to convalesce after my appendix operation. In addition, while he was conducting research about my job at Ferndown he discovered they were advertising for systems specialists. Such a job fitted his expertise perfectly; all he had to do was to fabricate glowing references, attend an interview and he was employed immediately on a two-week contract.

His first week at Ferndown coincided with my last week, and during that time, he impressed his new employers with his enthusiasm and willingness to work long hours; but the overtime was spent on remotely keeping tabs on the Kent computer operations and hacking through Ferndown's computer security. The latter gave him all he needed to apparently engineer my electronic downfall. Andy didn't know all the details of what Sebastian did, since these were "trade secrets" that Sebastian had been unwilling to disclose.

I took over for a while and explained what I had recalled about the incriminating evidence he had planted on my machine. 'He did a thorough job. He stole customer records and sent them to Milton Cern; invented private e-mails and filled my PC with pornographic pictures. It was no wonder Ferndown dismissed me *in absentia*. Who was Sebastian in collusion with at Milton Cern?'

'Nobody,' Andy said. 'He falsified the e-mails so that it looked as though there had been two-way communication. Then he leaked a story to the financial press to compromise Ferndown.'

'And then he set out to ruin me domestically and financially too,' I said.

'Yes. On the first Sunday you were away, he broke into your flat and raided your personal files. While he was there, he also planted a few sachets of cocaine – more of that later. Can you continue the story, Pete?'

I related a summary of the flashback about my visit to the bank and the fraudulent use of my credit card. 'What I can't figure out is how he hacked into my bank account? I know I've never written down my login details.'

'Even Sebastian admitted that was a tough one,' Andy said. 'He first tried to bypass the security on your home PC, but failed. He reckoned he could, had he been able to take it back to his office, but in the end he didn't have too. The information he needed was on your PC at work. The account number and sort code were easy; he found a copy of an e-mail to our parents which contained the details so they could transfer money to you. Then Sebastian used those items as a key to search your PC for a previous login to your banking system. He found one, pointed home-grown deciphering software at it and he was in. By the end of his two-week assignment at Ferndown, he'd completed his objective.

'Did you recall how much was siphoned out of your account?'

I tried to picture myself waking up in Brian's studio after the flashback. 'I'm not sure. Around £21,000?'

'Does £21,619.85 ring a bell?' Andy asked.

'Yes, that was probably the figure. He was lucky though there was only just enough in the account to cover it.'

'I'm afraid luck didn't come into it. That exact figure had Sebastian drooling with pleasure. I don't suppose you know the significance.'

Charlotte gave me a pen and paper, and I wrote down the number and stared at it. 'Does it represent ... a date – 21/6/1985?'

'Well, you may have lost your memory, but your numeracy is still intact. Yes, it's a date. Of when?'

About fifteen years ago, I was at school, ten years old. 'The date of Barry's bank robbery?' I offered.

Andy nodded.

'But why?'

'He treated the whole exercise as a game and thought that would be his *coup de grâce* ... until you returned.'

'And then he killed Josh?'

'He didn't actually. Josh genuinely died of a drug overdose, if Sebastian is to be believed.

'Josh had told Sebastian you were due back on the Friday and to satisfy his morbid curiosity, Sebastian wanted to see how you reacted to the events he had set in motion for when you arrived home. Josh, under instruction from Sebastian, had already stirred up the situation with the landlord, saying you had lost your job and were penniless. Of course, this struck a chord with him since he knew by then you had defaulted on your rent, so he switched off your electricity to try to flush you out. Moreover, Sebastian had already checked your phone was no longer working and had made an anonymous call to Ferndown to verify you had been dismissed; and another to the police tipping them off you were a drug dealer. His plan was to install himself in Josh's flat before you got back and from there, observe your panic as the plot unfolded; but things went very wrong for him on Friday.

'He was delayed travelling to Harlow and arrived moments after you. He watched you enter the building and a short while after, saw you go to a phone box. It was only then he went up to Josh's flat and was puzzled there was no answer. That wasn't a problem since the Kent's were paying for the flat anyway, so Sebastian let himself in with a spare key. Now you have to draw your own conclusion about the next part. Josh was sprawled on his bed and dead as a dodo. It appeared he had recently injected himself with heroin by the drug paraphernalia at his side.'

'So how did I become a suspect?' I asked.

'I'm coming to that,' Andy said. 'Sebastian had a theory about Josh's death. He reckons a couple of unfortunate events came together. Josh had been disturbed by the conspiracy against you and had recently been entrusted with a stash of pure heroin to open up a new distribution channel. Josh was strictly a crackhead and Sebastian thought he had probably sampled the heroin and had got the dosage wrong.'

'Plausible, but unlikely,' I commented.

'Whatever you believe, Sebastian panicked. He knew he had been seen entering Josh's flat and might become a suspect. Besides, Josh's flat and van were full of valuable narcotics and incriminating documents, and he wanted to ensure they weren't confiscated. So, he gathered the stuff together, took Josh's keys and made off in Josh's van just before you returned to your flat. He hid the van in a quiet part of town, walked back to pick up his own car and later transferred everything from the van. He was very disappointed to miss acting as voyeur to your troubles, but consoled himself by turning his attention to inflicting the same financial penalty on me, which he had decided to set in motion on the Sunday morning. Sebastian made a slight miscalculation though. He had assumed that by then the police would have arrested you for possession of drugs.'

'Which they did of course on Saturday afternoon only to release me the following morning,' I chipped in.

'Exactly, so of course your arrival at Nazeing Tye on Sunday was quite unexpected; Sebastian was in the process of searching my cottage.'

'Where were you and Kylie?'

'I was ... um ... abroad. I had to go away at short notice on the Friday. Kylie had gone to stay with her sister. I did try to leave a message on your answerphone, but your number was unobtainable. I now know why.'

From the little I knew about my brother, quizzing him further about where and why he had gone abroad was pointless and probably privy only to Her Majesty's Government.

'Did Sebastian brag to you about hitting me with a jack handle?'

'He didn't actually. Despite being a Kent or Tremlett, he abhors violence. He prefers intellectual destruction and leaves the heavy stuff to Ronnie and his disciples. He had acquired my address from your flat and had broken into my cottage that Sunday morning with a view to obtaining personal information about me. As you know ... or may know ... because of my position, I have to be very careful about such matters and all such information is hidden in a secret safe. Sebastian said he panicked when he saw you entering the garage and only hit you hard enough to knock you out. He assumed you had seen your attacker and concluded it was best to deliver you to Ronnie so that he could take over the physical part of your destruction. He trussed you up, dragged you into his car and set out to London. He was almost at BQC when apparently you cried out, coughed and then went still. That panicked him even more. Convinced you were dead he stopped the car, and dumped ... your body.'

At that point, Andy stuttered to a halt as he recalled the emotion he felt with the knowledge his brother was dead. He suddenly looked tired and older. I noticed dark rings under his eyes for the first time. Charlotte stood up and went to the other side of the bed. She bade Andy to stand up too, and he did so, albeit shakily. Then she put her arms around him, and he slumped into her body almost toppling her over.

'Sorry,' Andy said, 'the last few days are catching up with me.'

It was second time I had seen Andy drop his cold-hearted guard. First, he had hugged me, now he was hugging Charlotte.

Charlotte gave Andy a friendly shake. 'I think we need a break. Why don't we get some fresh air? There's a bakery opposite the hospital that sells the most delicious bagels. We'll bring some back with coffee and have a party.'

I think Charlotte was embarrassed by Andy's reaction and was attempting to make light of the situation, but it had the desired effect. Andy stood upright and, now obviously in control, said: 'Bagels? With cream cheese? Let's go.'

Chapter 50

THIRD SUNDAY – 11:20 a.m.

The bagels and coffee did the trick. While we ate and drank, there was a kind of party atmosphere. I felt like the proverbial gooseberry because Andy and Charlotte somehow got onto the subject of student pranks during rag weeks. I was jealous that my memories couldn't contribute, but my loved ones had enough stories to cover for me. We laughed to excess, no doubt in an attempt to stall Andy's return to the troubles of recent events. But with a final swig of coffee from a plastic cup, Andy became serious once more, and calmly resumed his reportage from where he had left off.

'Ronnie went crazy when Sebastian told him he had killed you because he had been deprived of slowly mutilating your body, which unsurprisingly he had planned would start with a disfiguring wound to your left cheek. So Ronnie decided to accelerate my own abduction and immediately sent a couple of heavies to stake out the cottage to await my return. Frustratingly they had to wait over a week until I got back home from … my trip, on Monday afternoon.

'With two of them, both twice my size, they easily overpowered me and on instructions from Ronnie, chloroformed me into unconsciousness. The next thing I knew, I was chained to a bed and locked inside the cellar where you saw me at BQC. My initial assumption was that I had been taken as a hostage for negotiations relating to my recent activities for … my employers. I was restrained, yet treated civilly, but nobody would tell me why I was there.

'On Tuesday morning, I had a visit from the ponytailed man who introduced himself as Sebastian Tate, but qualified I might know him as Trevor Tremlett. The surname rung a vague bell, but I didn't make the connection until he announced he was Victor Tremlett's youngest son. Still I had no idea what this was about and then Sebastian started to tell me the story I related earlier.

'When he got to the part about you and Ferndown he became very excited. Here he was in his element, bragging about how easy it was to hack into

Ferndown's computers and how smart he'd been in financially crippling you right down to the detail of the bank robbery date matching the amount he had stolen. Then his tone completely changed. Suddenly he became nervous, like he was trying to unburden himself of a great sense of guilt, and he attempted to portray himself as an unwilling partner in the conspiracy against the Shadwells. I started to worry because I knew there was a bottom line coming. That's when he confessed about your *murder*. I've been trained to suppress my emotions, but dealing impassively about the death of a brother had never been covered in the script. I went about as crazy as I could, bearing in mind I was shackled to a bed. Worried I would eventually break free, Tate fetched two of his apes to secure me more tightly and quieten me down. Then it dawned on me there was no way I would be set free. You had been killed, so why not me too. There was no way Tate would have given me the background unless he already knew the knowledge would go no further.

'After a couple of hours Tate plucked up the courage to approach me again, and this time I stayed calm, reasoning the more information I could extract from him, the better chance I stood of getting out of my predicament. I was to remain where I was until Ronnie returned on Thursday morning. He was abroad for a few days setting up a drug deal and Ronnie was to decide my fate. So, for the next few days there was little I could do but hope that by Kylie reporting me missing, there would have been some evidence to lead the authorities to find me at BQC. But I knew that notion was so remote it wasn't worth seriously considering.'

'Your ... employers ... obviously took action,' I said. 'I called the cottage on Thursday morning and somebody I recognized answered the phone. Who was that?'

'I've since found out a great deal about what happened. Phil, an office-based colleague took up residence at the cottage after I disappeared. He had spoken to you on the Friday you returned from the Lake District. When he also spoke to you last Thursday, the strange way you reacted led him to believe you might be involved somehow. It didn't take much research to discover the police wanted you for various crimes, and a DI Bradley was trying to find you in the Stepney Green area. Our men leaned on Bradley and he revealed the arrangement he had made with you. They put a trace on his mobile phone and when you called on Friday morning, they sourced the call to come from a phone box in the Broadgate area. A number of men were immediately despatched to the location to keep a lookout for you. Eventually you were spotted being bundled out of a silver Merc and taken into a house. There wasn't enough time to organize a tail on the Merc and it was discovered from the Police National Computer that the registration number was false. Later, things really became interesting when another man arrived at the house and he was identified as a known thug. The assembled surveillance teams guessed something was brewing, but decided not to act until you made a move.'

There was a gap in Andy's personal fate. 'What happened when Ronnie got back from abroad?'

'There was a significant event before then. On Thursday morning Tate came rushing into the cellar to show me a report from that day's *East London Gazette*. There you were, picture and all, on the run, but *alive*; Tate was almost as relieved as me. The news gave me respite that maybe there was a way out after all. Such comfort was short lived when Kent arrived that afternoon and revealed your alter ego Robin Forest was already known to the Kent organization, and he was confident of picking you up within the next 24 hours. I found out from Superintendent Dixon yesterday that courtesy of Bradley's duplicity, you were found in Charing Cross.'

I knew this contentious point would arrive some time. 'Bradley's duplicity!' I said angrily. 'Don't tell me you of all people have been suckered by Dixon.'

Andy was shocked by my outburst and was about to argue, but Charlotte interrupted. 'Let Andy finish, we'll get to that later.'

Andy continued. 'Thereafter I gleaned no further information about what was happening until the strict briefing I had from Tate, of what to say and what not to say, before you appeared in the cellar with Kent. The reason for the meeting between us was a complete mystery and then I didn't see another soul until shortly after seven o'clock that evening, when all hell broke loose.

'I heard many sets of rapid footsteps overhead and the sound of heavy trucks manoeuvring outside. Suddenly an army of people descended into the basement and a chain was set up to convey boxes to the waiting trucks. It was like a military operation: disciplined, swift and accurate. Within ten minutes, the contents of the basement were almost gutted. A few people noticed, but ignored me, and five minutes later, the place was in silence. But they need not have rushed; it took another quarter of an hour before a cacophony of police sirens arrived for a raid. Dixon reckoned there must have been another of Kent's men keeping watch at the hospital, and as soon as your assassination attempt failed, Kent was notified to set the evacuation in progress.'

'Dixon *would* say that. I'm convinced *he* made the phone call.'

'Hey Pete, saying things like that will get you into deep trouble. Dixon's an obnoxious bastard, but he's a clever copper.'

'Yeh, clever enough to frame Bradley for collusion with Kent.'

'If you stick with your accusations, you better have some evidence.'

I thought I had enough, so I bounced my theories off Andy with corroboration when necessary from Charlotte. In my opinion, Bradley had acted with integrity throughout my dealings with him. He was genuinely determined to put Ronnie Kent away. Why would he have briefed me so well on Kent's organization if he was part of it? My original suspicions against him were based on a weak theory of poisoned asparagus sandwiches; and Charlotte's on his unhealthy, albeit excusable, interest in being the first to know what Kathy had to say. Haynes was demonstrably on the right side of the law and he had ultimate faith in Bradley. Then there was Dixon. Maybe a clever copper, but I wasn't convinced about his Chad versus Brad theory, and he was the obvious person to have given the warning to Kent. Andy was thoughtful while Charlotte and I hit him with Bradley's defence. When we had finished, his mind was still mulling over the information. I decided to let him dwell on what I had said and asked him to relate what had happened since the raid.

When the police found Andy, he was detained as a potential suspect until his colleagues and Dixon arrived to verify who he was. Dixon explained I had been shot, but not life threateningly, and then he set up an operations centre in Kent's offices. A senior member of Andy's agency arrived (Andy just referred to him as K) and took control, much to Dixon's displeasure. K needed to establish Andy's kidnapping hadn't been connected with any National security matter, and he was soon satisfied when Andy revealed Kent and Tate's motives. Dixon was pleased when K departed, and positively relieved when he succeeded in getting K to agree Andy should be placed temporarily under his command, until the initial investigation was over. Dixon apparently had the stamina of a marathon runner. He was personally involved in everything that went on: interviewing Andy's surveillance teams and the BQC staff; organising the SOCOs; liaising with computer forensics; and disappearing a couple of times to interview me and other staff at the hospital.

The BQC staff had claimed they knew nothing about the business being conducted from the physically separate and secure offices being used by Kent and Tate. A search at Companies House showed BQC was wholly owned by a parent company called Abbeydale Holdings, whose declared owners were Victor, Alan and Trevor Tremlett with addresses in the Cayman Islands. Abbeydale also owned a number of other companies: bookmakers, furniture warehouses, chemical manufacturers, all of which were now being investigated in case they were fronts for illegal operations.

The evacuation team hadn't managed to rid the building of all evidence. There were still some boxes in the cellar area where Andy had been held and these contained porn videos and counterfeit software CDs. In a separate concealed basement area, there were traces of substances and pills believed to include heroin, cocaine, crack and cannabis.

Most of the computer equipment seemed to have been abandoned intact, although a closer examination had shown the hard disks had been removed or erased. The cybercrime unit had confirmed that the Internet sites believed to be operated by the Kent and Tate, had gone down around seven o'clock on

Friday night; only to be resurrected by ten o'clock the following morning, presumably via mirrored sites.

A separate raid at BioRemedy on Saturday morning had unearthed an enormous cache of drugs underneath a false floor in one of the laboratories. This of course was no surprise to Charlotte; she wished the previous search had been as thorough.

Kent and Tate had vanished. Their mother had provided an expected response. She hadn't seen Ronnie for a few days and thought he was away on business somewhere. She had denied knowing anyone called Sebastian Tate. A computer and paperwork had been removed from her house for analysis.

Andy had been kept at BQC for over thirty hours at the behest of Dixon, supposedly as a key witness, and he was re-interviewed each time that new information became known. Eventually he had been released at one o'clock this morning and taken home by a government car. He had spent an hour with Kylie, slept for two hours, showered and then had immediately returned to London to see me.

'That's it. Brain dump accomplished,' Andy said light heartedly, relieved his tale had been told.

'What's the situation regarding the charges against me?'

'Dixon's dropped them all – for the moment. My statement clears you of Josh's murder and the drugs offence. The poisoning of a beggar was a trumped up charge conceived by Bradley to get you arrested. The rape won't be pursued because of your own statement about Stella being at BQC. As for Santori, Dixon is pleased there is one less villain on the streets. He is content to let his death be ascribed to you as self defence, despite knowing how Santori was really killed.'

There was a gasp from Charlotte. I looked at her and then back to Andy. Dixon's remark had been strangely ambiguous. 'What did he mean by that?'

'I'm not sure. I thought perhaps you might be able to qualify,' Andy said to me.

'I know … what he meant,' Charlotte said nervously, 'Kathy … killed Santori.' Dixon had already hinted about a second shot from Santori's gun and I had assumed, but not wanted to say, that it had been fired by Charlotte. 'Kathy recognized him. He was one of the men that came to BioRemedy. He injected the drugs into her.'

'But Kathy said she didn't remember?'

'Not initially. When Santori came into her room, seeing him triggered the memory. Your shot only stunned him for a moment. While he was recovering, Kathy picked up the gun he had dropped and fired at his head. I wiped the gun and put it back into Santori's hand.'

'My God. How does she feel about what she did?'

'Justifiable homicide. A self-defensive action to save our lives and probably the lives of others he would have taken in the future. She has already flushed the event from her mind and never wants to discuss it again. What she hasn't forgotten though, is that the shooting has stimulated the recollection of more details of the night she was drugged. She is adamant Kent talked to "Chad" from BioRemedy. Furthermore, she has recalled the moment when Santori injected her. He said to Kent: "... you're sure this is the way Dixon wants it?"'

'Bloody hell, Charlotte, why did you wait until now to tell us?' It was the first time I had shouted at Charlotte and she looked hurt by my outburst.

'I was hoping I wouldn't have to tell you at all, so that I didn't implicate Kathy. But as Dixon has worked it out and with Andy still on his side, it had to be said.'

'I'm not on his side Charlotte. I'm merely trying to play judge and jury if we make this information official. From what I've heard there is no definitive evidence that can be used against Dixon. No disrespect to Kathy, but her memories could easily be dismissed as the rantings of a sick woman, particularly if Dixon used the killing of Santori to discredit her. Pete's support of Bradley could be twisted to show him as an accomplice. Measure that against the documents Dixon presumably has to incriminate Bradley and where would your guilty vote go?'

Andy was right of course. We debated the issue a little longer and I persuaded Andy to use his influence to make background enquiries about Dixon and Bradley, although he wasn't hopeful. We consoled ourselves that maybe it was best to forget the past, and I joked that I had forgotten most of mine anyway. Soon it would be time to think of the future. For Andy that was easy, for me less so, and for Kathy and Charlotte, the future looked bleak. We could have started to make plans then, but my concentration was beginning to fade. I felt feverish; the early morning exercise of body and brain had perhaps taken its toll.

'You're looking deadbeat little brother. It's probably best if we let you rest for a while,' Andy said.

Charlotte reluctantly agreed. 'But we'll come back this afternoon?' she asked Andy.

'Yes. I'll escort you back to Kathy, then I'll take a cab to the office to make a few enquiries on our behalf.'

'But it's Sunday, isn't it?' I said slightly uncertainly.

'True, but *my* department never sleeps,' Andy replied teasingly.

As departing gestures, Andy touched my arm and Charlotte pecked me on the forehead, then the door burst open.

'You can't stay here. Shadwell's not allowed visitors,' said the man in the doorway.

I shifted my position to see Sergeant Underwood standing there looking harassed. I thought Andy would put him in his place with a flash of his government ID, but for once, he was momentarily speechless. His assuredness returned: 'No problem. Give us thirty seconds to say goodbye then we'll be on our way.' He grabbed the door and closed it, forcing Underwood to retreat.

'Who is that?' Andy asked with an odd urgency.

'Sergeant Underwood, one of Dixon's fellow conspirators,' I said accusingly. 'Why?'

'I've seen him before – recently – although he wasn't enforcing law and order at the time. In fact, quite the opposite.'

Chapter 51

NINTH SATURDAY – 11:00 a.m.

We were all knackered, especially Kathy. The badminton game had been billed as friendly, but everyone had a point to prove: Andy that he was the practiced expert; Kathy – his playing partner – that her body was now in good shape; Charlotte, in her first ever game – that she could quickly adapt her tennis skills; and me – that the long gone stitches in my head and side, and my thigh muscle were no longer impediments to physical activity. In deference to Kathy's exhaustion, we declared the contest a draw despite Andy single-handedly dominating the last set. The girls adjourned to the single changing room adjacent to the badminton court; Andy and I took the short path across the snow-bedecked garden back to the house.

We entered the conservatory and slumped into the canvas chairs positioned in front of a small oil heater. Considering the outside temperature and the expanse of glass around us the heater did an adequate job to steal the chill from the room. Kylie had heard us come in and presented us with glasses of a cold spicy non-alcoholic drink, before disappearing back to the kitchen complaining she was behind schedule with her preparations for lunch.

'Will Kathy be alright?' Andy asked.

'I'm sure she will.' Every time I looked at Kathy, I recalled the image of when I first saw her in hospital, her comatose life sustained by electronic apparatus. The transformation from nine weeks ago had been remarkable, not just to me, but also to the doctors that had attended her. She was still painfully thin, but day-by-day her constitution had become stronger and with a few extra pounds on her frame and more smiles on her face, she would be as stunningly attractive as her sister.

'Isn't it strange, to my knowledge she's never mentioned anything about the Santori incident.'

It was an insensitive statement to make. I lowered my angry voice: 'Is that *really* surprising? He almost killed her and she killed him. I can't think of anything so traumatic. If you had killed someone, wouldn't you want to suppress that knowledge from your brain?'

Andy avoided my eyes and took a long swig from his drink.

'Andy?' I prompted, but I knew he wouldn't answer. I'd touched on the forbidden territory of his profession again. This latest revelation didn't bear thinking about – I changed the subject back to Kathy.

'She's so grateful to you for providing a roof over her head; and Charlotte, and me come to that.'

'As I've said before, thank the government for thinking enough of one of its employees to want him secure in a safe house.'

He was referring to himself of course. As the extent of Kent and Tate's notoriety reached the ears of his bosses, they had suggested to Andy that perhaps he ought to move away temporarily from his home. While he was thinking about the idea, only three days after the raid at BQC, a lethal parcel bomb was successfully intercepted on its way to his cottage in Nazeing Tye. The event had persuaded him, and he and Kylie had moved immediately into this extensively renovated Georgian house on the Finchley Road in Hampstead, North London. They were sad to leave their countryside idyll, but excited by the space and sports facilities. Two hundred years ago, the house had been part of a farm and the previous owner, a crook and badminton fanatic, had converted a surviving barn into a badminton arena for his private use. Twenty years ago the owner had been arrested and his property had been sequestrated for government use. Now the spacious house was a temporary home for three Shadwells and two Rensbergs.

'At the rate you're earning money, I expect you'll be buying your own place soon. Not that I want you to leave, but K wants the house back after Christmas and Kylie has at last found a place in Epping she likes.' Andy said.

'It's a bit premature to think about buying. I'm earning enough to afford renting a property, but acquiring the capital for a deposit would take longer. I don't suppose I'll ever see the savings that Tate stole, so I'll wait until dad's promise to help us out financially next year, when another of his investments matures. In fact, I inspected a flat last night not far from here. It's clean and tidy, with a one year lease and big enough for two.'

'Two?'

'I haven't told Charlotte about it yet, so please don't say anything. I'm going to ask her if she'll move in with me.'

'Forgone conclusion, isn't it?'

'Not entirely. She's very protective towards Kathy, but the job Kathy originally wanted in Boston is still available to her, and if she decides to accept, then I think Charlotte might be interested in my idea.'

We had all lived together compatibly now for seven weeks and the house had been big enough for us not to get in each other's way. We came together on the ground floor for meals and the occasional social evening, but otherwise we had been like three separate families. Andy and Kylie lived on the first floor; Charlotte and I on the second floor, albeit with separate bedrooms; Kathy in the loft converted bedroom; and each floor had its own bathroom facilities. We weren't unsociable, but I suspected we feared being together in a group, in case conversation drifted back to the traumatic days of two months earlier. Besides, we had each been busy reconstructing our working lives.

Luther had reminded me that Howard Winston's offer of a job still stood and blindly I had accepted. I had briefly considered Ferndown's offer to reinstate my employment, but the burdensome journey from Hampstead to Harlow dissuaded me and I wanted a fresh start. Fortunately, it hadn't taken too long to justify Howard's faith in me. I was now a trusted and productive investment statistician, earning far more than I would have at Ferndown, and commuting to an office only eight stations away on the underground.

Charlotte had been able to secure a late enrolment for her final year at medical school. She was two months behind on her studies, but was working like a Trojan to catch up. Andy had loaned her the money to fund her tuition fees, and she had volunteered to take an evening and weekend job to pay him back. I had insisted otherwise, and unbeknown to Charlotte, I had been re-paying Andy myself from my generous income. Every morning and most evenings Charlotte and I shared travelling arrangements.

At first, Kathy didn't do much at all, but on advice we left her alone, to allow her physical and mental healing to take effect naturally; and it worked. For the last four weeks, she had been immersed in books and the Internet, to research the latest developments in genetic engineering, and had recently reinstituted her contacts at University College and an American biotech company in Boston. It only remained for her to convince the doting Charlotte she was well enough to start her career, and then she would be on the next available flight to the USA.

I was reviewing these facts and how Kathy's apparent badminton exhaustion would affect the situation, when Kathy and Charlotte appeared in dressing gowns in the conservatory.

'Hey you lazy boys, get showered. Our guests will be here soon,' Kathy said with a big smile on her face.

'You're in good spirits,' I said. 'Minutes ago you were absolutely drained.'

'Perhaps you hadn't noticed Robin Forest, I was trying harder than anyone else on court.' It had become a habit that whenever someone in the house wanted to tease or admonish me, I was referred to as Robin Forest. I suppose it was used to moderate what was said by addressing my past alter ego. 'I had to prove to myself that my body could stand such punishment.'

'And did you?'

'I met and exceeded expectations so much that I have an announcement. I've decided to take the job in Boston.'

I couldn't see Andy, but I could feel his wide grin burning a hole in my back. 'That's wonderful news – I think.' I looked at Charlotte to gauge her reaction. She gave a slight nod and smiled to indicate her agreement.

Like a mind reader Kathy added: 'Anyway, I think my role as gooseberry has gone on for long enough. It's time you two love birds starting cooing to each other properly. Come on Charlotte, let's dress for the party.'

Kathy strode away with a definite bounce to her step. Charlotte blew me a kiss and followed.

After my shower, I went through the ritual of examining my body. It was a vain inspection to establish that the signs of my own injuries were fading. I suppose, with thoughts of living with Charlotte, I wanted my disfigured body to be worthy of her intimate inspection. The appendectomy incision was barely discernable, but the bullet wound had left a white scar about two inches long. Grazes and cuts had long healed, but even now, I was still conscious of the slight baldness around the stitched areas on my head. My left ear was noticeably misshapen, and I had let my hair grow uncontrollably to cover the damage. The blondeness of my hair had faded and reverted to its dark brown, but a haircut was overdue. I would have to choose a hairstyle that considered my narcissistic requirements.

As I descended the stairs, I heard the doorbell ring. 'I'll get it,' I shouted and went to answer the door. Luther stood there awkwardly holding a bunch of flowers. 'Happy Saturday,' he said.

'Are they for me?' I asked, indicating his bouquet.

'Are you cooking the lunch?'

'No.'

'Then I'd ought to come in and present them to Mr. or Mrs. Chef. I have a different present for you.' He tapped a slight bulge in his jacket pocket.

We headed towards the lounge, but I stopped him short of the door. 'Are the flowers kosher Luther?'

He laughed. 'Of course, I nicked them from a Jewish florist outside Swiss Cottage station.' Even the normally saturnine Luther was in good spirits these days.

Only Andy was in the lounge, fiddling with a hi-fi system that never functioned for more than five minutes at a time. I could hear female giggles coming from the kitchen. Andy and Luther hadn't met before, but the information Luther had been able to supply to Andy had significantly contributed to today's celebration. I made the introductions and went to fetch the chefs. The happy threesome followed me back to the lounge. Kathy and Charlotte ran to Luther and hugged him, much to his embarrassment. I introduced Kylie, and Luther formally offered to shake her hand, but she followed the other girls' example and hugged him too. With a straight face, I prompted Luther to present his flowers and teased him that he had a problem since there was a Mrs. Chef and two Miss Chefs. My explanation quickly followed, and giggling once again, the cooks returned to their duties in the kitchen.

We chatted about the cold weather, hi-fi systems, the multi-cultural life on Finchley Road, how I was progressing at Winston Investments, subjects instigated by Andy and me to prevent Luther from raising the unspeakable subject, which he often alluded to.

I enquired about the status of Luther's aspiration to become a pop impresario, but his dogmatic stand as a Fourth Man had seen his comeuppance. He had secured increasingly prestigious gigs for Millennia; scruffy pubs, up-market pubs, lowly nightclubs and eventually a well-known nightclub in the west end. There, an existing pop manager of some note had approached the group, and talked with authority about concerts, tours and recording contracts. Millennia had been swayed by the man's status, and when he offered to manage the Liverpudlians for a 20 percent stake of their earnings, the deal was done. Millennia had since vacated the Jubilee and much to Luther's chagrin were currently on tour as the warm-up band for a chart-topping girl group.

The doorbell rang again and we assumed it announced the arrival of our guests of honour. Andy went to welcome them, but returned with just a bundle of mail.

'Delivery from Nazeing Tye,' Andy said, glancing through the pile in his hand. Once a week one of Andy's colleagues checked out his cottage and dropped in the mail on his way back to London. 'Here's one for you. From Darlington?'

'That will be from Adrian,' I said.

I took the letter from Andy, opened it and read it out aloud. Adrian had settled comfortably into a modern grammar school, where discipline and standards were high, and sexual preferences were tolerated and understood. He was living on a small out-of-town housing estate; had made lots of new friends and was genuinely happy with life. He had followed the emerging story of police corruption and drugs in East London on the TV and in the press, and hoped all his old friends were well and re-homed. Finally came a request. His novel was progressing well and he wanted to make significant progress over the Christmas break, but he was stuck on realistically portraying the true feelings and emotions of a young person mysteriously finding himself homeless. Was there a possibility I could help and if so, how could he proceed?

'You could help the old fag, couldn't you?' Luther said.

I gave Luther my best disapproving stare. 'Yes, but I think you should be less offensive Luther. Gay is more acceptable. Adrian was a good friend to me at the Jubilee.' Normally Luther would have argued the point, but on foreign territory he conceded with a subdued 'Sorry'.

'Adrian's request reminds me I never did retrieve my homeless duffle bag. It didn't contain anything of value except my makeshift diary in which I recorded the kind of thoughts that Adrian needs. I'd like to get that back and send it to him.'

'Well, bugger me, if that ain't a coincidence,' Luther exclaimed. He withdrew a brown paper bag from his jacket and passed it to me. 'Here's the present I have for you.'

I opened the bag and smiled at its contents. I took the blue beret and put it on my head. Andy laughed and Luther made a disparaging comment. 'You still look a prat in it, but I thought it would be an interesting memento of your vagrant days.'

'You must have got this from George and Jessie's, which is where I left my duffle bag. What happened to the two of them?' I asked Luther.

'I went to see George a few days after your shooting. The police had questioned him on the Saturday morning about his involvement, but they couldn't stick anything on him. As George said, it's not a crime to have two guests around for afternoon tea. He told the police he had no idea one was a known assassin and the other was an assassin in waiting; and it wasn't illegal to dye someone's hair. The police searched his place, but found nothing – not even my stack of video recorders; he'd taken those to a friend of his, fearing the police would come snooping. He owed me £200 for those, but refused to pay because he said you – *my friend* – had promised him £1,000 for services rendered, and he would offset the £200 as a deposit. I didn't argue. Based on what you had already told me Pete, I didn't want to deal with George any more, despite his adamant declaration he was no longer a stooge for the Kents. He gave me the beret to give to you as a reminder of what you owed him and said you could have the rest of your things when you coughed up the balance.'

'Isn't that the couple that live in Grace Street?' Andy asked, but the front door knocker rapped loudly and stopped our conversation dead. We glanced at each other looking apprehensive and then the doorbell rang.

'That must be them,' I said and went to the front door.

'Don, how are you? And this must be Vanessa. Come in out of the cold.'

'Sorry about the knocker, Pete. Force of habit from visiting the homes of criminals. Scare's the shit out of them.'

'You mind your language in other people's houses,' Vanessa said sternly.

I took Vanessa's coat, shook off the newly fallen snow, and hung it on the coat rack. Don declined, saying he had to fetch something from his car and we watched as his big frame brought back an enormous box, which he deposited in the hallway. 'For later,' he said.

There was a mysterious lack of noise at we entered the lounge; then the room erupted with cheers, paper streamers and the sound of party poppers exploding. As the excitement abated, Kylie came forward to greet the final guests.

I said: 'You know everyone, but for Kylie – Andy's wife. Kylie this is Detective Inspector Don Bradley and his wife Vanessa.' Kylie shook hands and kissed them both on the cheek.

'Actually, Pete, your introduction wasn't quite right. Don is now Chief Inspector,' Vanessa said proudly. A new round of cheers broke out and Don gave an exaggerated bow to the audience.

Lunch was a jovial affair. How we maintained such a humorous and entertaining flow without once mentioning the events that had brought us together was an enigma, but aided considerably by Luther's streetwise tales. The meal was a joint effort by the ladies of the house. Kathy had prepared a smoked mackerel mousse for a starter; Kylie, chicken breasts cooked in wine and cream with croquette potatoes and vegetables. Charlotte announced she had laboured long and hard in the kitchen to produce *Asperge avec Pain* for the dessert, which puzzled everyone until I translated it as asparagus sandwiches. A ten-minute interlude was then necessary for the party to control their laughter, before Charlotte actually delivered a chocolate-rich tiramisu. Don then revealed the secrets of his box, and poured champagne as a prelude to his celebratory toast to thank everyone for their efforts in bringing Superintendent Dixon to justice.

While the champagne was still flowing, Andy took the opportunity to announce that he and Kylie would be moving to Epping, and Kathy confirmed her intent to go to Boston. That left unanswered questions about the coming homelessness of Charlotte and me so, presumptuously, I declared that we too would be sharing a flat very soon. Everyone looked at Charlotte, who smiled and didn't contradict, so I took that as a yes, and the champagne flowed again.

As the women had become tipsy, Andy volunteered the men to take control of the washing-up and we gathered in the kitchen. With tongues loosened by champagne, when Luther – who was the most incognisant of us about Dixon and Kent's outcome – started asking questions about the detailed downfall of Dixon, we each contributed to the story.

Andy's recognition of Underwood at the hospital had started the process, so he spoke first. He knew he had seen him during the evacuation of BQC and spurred on by the revelation, he had debriefed to K. K had discreet words with the Metropolitan Police Commissioner and Andy was given freedom to pursue his enquiries.

It was confirmed that Dixon and Underwood had left Stratford police station together around the time they received the call from Bethnal Green regarding BQC. Dixon had arrived alone at the hospital twenty-five minutes later. Normally the journey would have taken ten minutes and the extra fifteen minutes was sufficient time to detour via BQC to drop off Underwood. The telephone records were checked at BQC and there was an incoming call from a mobile phone one minute after the Bethnal Green call. The mobile phone was registered to a D. Green at an address in Hackney. The residents there denied all knowledge of a D. Green, but a Land Registry search showed the house belonged to Barry Kent. And of course, the name associated with the phone itself was a clue. A colleague of Andy's close to retirement, who was a TV addict, recalled an old police drama series called Dixon of Dock Green. Andy had called the mobile number several times from phone boxes, but every time the mobile switched into auto-answer mode, with an anonymous pre-recorded voice requesting the caller to leave a message. That seemed to indicate the phone was usually left switched off and maybe only used for outgoing calls. To prove the phone was used by Dixon, it had to be found in his possession, but confronting Dixon directly would have brought a denial and aroused suspicion. Indeed, to prove anything about Dixon's complicity, hardcore evidence was required, evidence that couldn't be intercepted or tainted by Dixon's preferential position.

Andy had obtained a personal profile of Dixon: divorced, but rumoured to be consorting with a young female PC; 48 years old; exemplary career to-date except for one unproven incident of sexual harassment of a police secretary; living alone in a disproportionately palatial detached house in Croydon.

I had acted as an intermediary to enlist Luther's help for an idea from Andy. Luther in turn passed on the scheme to a number of his *wealth distribution* contacts.

Despite the security of Dixon's property: razor-wired high walls, intruder lights and alarm system, it had been easily penetrated by one of Luther's burglary-biased acolytes, Luther not wishing to make the foray himself for such a high profile hit. Nothing incriminating was discovered – least of all a mobile phone – unless it had been concealed inside the impregnable safe built into a cupboard. While the house was being burgled, Dixon's movements were being tracked in East London. When he arrived at BQC to check on forensic progress (or we assume lack of progress), his Ford Mondeo was undetectably broken into and searched by a Lutherian agent – still nothing. All that remained was a body search and that took a few days to organize. It had been noted that when Dixon spent the day at Bethnal Green police station, at lunchtime he often used to visit a sandwich shop about a ten-minute walk away. The streets were usually busy with pedestrians at this time of day, and on route to and from the shop on one occasion, Dixon had to manoeuvre between a group of youths that had assembled on the pavement. Unbeknown to Dixon, on his way out his mobile phone was skilfully lifted from his coat and on his return, skilfully replaced. By the time he returned to the station, his possession of the critical phone had been established, and there was a Superintendent from another Borough waiting to arrest him. That single piece of damning evidence, together with the unsubstantiated rumours circulating about Dixon's behaviour, was sufficient to provoke a more detailed investigation. Within three days, Dixon was sunk with a host of corruption charges against him, and Bradley was re-instated to clean up the mess Dixon had left in his wake.

My contribution centred on attempting to trace Sebastian Tate's activities at Ferndown. Andy had conned the Ferndown management that on a matter of National Security, a government computer expert and I needed to access its Internet logs. They might have queried the demand had I not been involved, but they were wooing me to resume my old job; particularly since the financial press had reassured investors that Ferndown was not in trouble, and all previous rumours had been maliciously spread by an undiscovered third-party. We employed the same method used to disclose the porn sites I had supposedly visited before my dismissal – ironically a trick that Tate had imparted to the Ferndown IT staff. We concentrated on identifying the websites accessed by Tate during the evenings he had been contracting for Ferndown. Numerous visits had been made to risqué sites registered to Ironen Limited, which was a known shell company for the Kent's Internet operations. However, one password-protected site broke the mould and led to a new name of Basanites Limited. Surprisingly, the obvious anagrammatic links of Ronnie/Ironen and Sebastian/Basanites were not noticed until later. From the hierarchy of companies connected to Basanites, a list of office addresses was produced. All but one was an accommodation address or a solicitor's office. The odd one was a disused warehouse near West India Dock. The building was kept under observation, and for somewhere apparently disused, there were a great deal of comings and goings. At one peak period of activity, the local police were commissioned for a raid, and they stumbled upon staff and a complete mirror of the computer systems found at BQC. However, this time the computer files and records were inviolate, and the storage areas well stocked with illegal goods and substances. There were eight direct arrests, and the street value of items seized was estimated to exceed £8 million, but that had just been the start. Don Bradley had then brought us up to date.

The tentacles of the Kent syndicate had spread far and wide, and raids, arrests, seizures and the closing of supply lines were still on-going, recently under the direction of Chief Inspector Bradley. He viewed that as far as East London was concerned, major organized crime, particularly involving drugs, had come to a sudden and rapid halt – until the next time, he added cynically. He forecast it wouldn't be too long before new mobsters took advantage of the nefarious gap in the market, and the detection and eradication process would have to start again. It was even possible that Kent and Tate, who still hadn't been apprehended, would lay low for a while before attempting to rebuild their empire. Don said he had his doubts though. Ma Kent had moved away and was rumoured to be living in Spain, and Don had expected her sons to have done the same, no doubt with ample family proceeds from their ten years of terror.

With the history of the dark days finally revealed, the rest of the evening turned to happier times. The champagne fortified positive talk, and when the bottles were empty, the carefree momentum continued with alcohol-free optimism about the future. There was no need for Panglossism.

Chapter 52

NINTH SUNDAY – 10:30 a.m.

I phoned Adrian the next morning, thanked him for his positive letter and said I would be in touch soon about his request. I had considered attempting to re-write my early homeless and nameless thoughts, but realised I couldn't possibly re-summon the emotions of that period, nor did I want to. Giving Adrian my beggar's diary, if it still existed, was my preferred solution. Over breakfast I told Andy what I intended to do.

'Sounds like an unnecessary risk to me. Ring Adrian back and make an excuse,' Andy said – almost demanded.

'No, I've made up my mind. George doesn't bother me and besides, in a constructive sort of way, I'd like to read my diary before I send it to Adrian. It will be a final reminder that when you're down and out, things can only and will, get better.'

'Then I'm coming with you as your minder – just in case,' Andy insisted.

I didn't object, it would be company and, after a ten-minute delay while Andy made a strangely covert phone call, we were on our way.

We decided to travel by Underground. The snow had continued to fall over night, and recalling the pushing we had had to apply to Don's car the previous evening to free it from the drive, Andy was reluctant to go by road.

We wrapped up warmly with many layers: jumper, jacket, anorak for me and overcoat for Andy; donned waterproof boots and took the tube to Liverpool Street station. It was a memorable journey. I recall that for the first and only time, I asked Andy to relate some of our university days together.

At the station, I spied two beggars huddled in doorways and without a second thought dropped loose change into their begging bowls. For such a cold and damp day, the streets were busy, people no doubt taking the opportunity to visit London for a final burst of retail therapy to purchase Christmas presents. Festive lights, decorations and trees were abundant on the main street, but had disappeared by the time we reached the gloominess and slushy pavements of our destination, Grace Street. I recognized the phone box and newsagent I had used two months earlier, and then there was number 17. A familiar silver Mercedes was parked outside, but neither of us chose to mention it.

I knocked on the door. I heard movement inside, saw the grimy net curtains twitch in the front room and then the house was still again. I knocked a second time and waited. Eventually the door opened and George stood there.

'Hello George, long time, no see,' I said in a casual, friendly manner.

His reaction was completely unexpected. His mouth gaped open in total amazement. He looked over his shoulder into the house, then back again, his face now contorted with fear. Suddenly his expression changed: his mouth closed, his face relaxed and the convexity of mouth rapidly transformed to the concavity of a broad smile. It was as though I'd said his mother had died and followed through immediately with the news she had left him a million pounds. Andy and I looked at each other, puzzled.

'Well, if it ain't the Eyetie killer who's come to call. Luther gave you my message then. And this must be the infamous brother. Just been talking about you. You better come in.'

George stepped aside, beckoned us to enter and closed the door firmly. I expected us to be guided to the front sitting room, but George passed it by and I caught a glimpse of Jessie chatting to another woman, who from age and appearance could have been a twin sister. George paused at the back room, pushed the door ajar and stood back. Andy led the way and I followed.

Andy showed no sign of reaction when he saw a bearded Ronnie Kent standing by the window, but I visibly jumped with shock. The door closed behind us and I sensed it had been shut from the inside; I quickly turned around and facing me was Sebastian Tate, distinguishable even with closely cropped hair instead of a ponytail. For the first time in ages, I felt a tingling from the healed head wound that Sebastian had inflicted on me. I knew it was a psychosomatic reaction, but nonetheless raised my hand to touch the source of irritation. Sebastian took the movement as a threat and raised his concealed hand nervously to reveal a gun.

'Don't get too twitchy – yet,' Ronnie said to his younger brother.

I turned back to Andy. He glanced at Sebastian and seemed totally unconcerned by the confrontation. He just stood there casually with his hands thrust deep into his overcoat pockets – a pose he had adopted outside to keep warm, but strangely maintained now that we were inside.

'A fraternal meeting at last,' Andy said.

'None of your smart talk. Sit down, you prick,' Ronnie shouted.

'Why?' Andy responded.

What was my brother doing? Goading Ronnie like that wasn't a smart move.

'Because, I fucking said so, that's why.'

'You'd better sit down, Pete. Ronnie says so.' This time Andy shouted. His voice had an intimidating, evil tone to it. I was suddenly more scared of him than Ronnie and I sat down on the settee.

Ronnie looked rattled too by Andy's fearless stance and diverted his frustration to Sebastian. 'Tie up the young cunt – tight.'

Sebastian placed his gun into his belt at the small of his back, and bent down to pick up electrical cabling from the floor. This seemed an ideal opportunity to use the defensive lapse to take our captors by surprise, and I looked to Andy for a signal, but he just smiled – an eerie, knowing smile. The moment passed.

Ronnie had been trying to be the laid back hard man, but now exposed, he restored the arms advantage. He reached behind him, picked up a similar gun from the window shelf, and pointed it at Andy. 'You move and the old cunt gets plugged,' he said to me.

Sebastian put my hands together and began to wind the electrical cord around my wrists.

'Did you know "cunt" is derived from the Swedish dialect form of "kunta"?' Andy said to an invisible person in the corner.

Actions stopped for a few seconds, while everyone looked at Andy disbelievingly.

'Shut up, fruitcake,' Ronnie spat.

Now I was worried. I had no idea if Andy was being totally cool or had completely flipped. Whatever the answer, the situation now looked doomed. Already my hands had been immobilized; Andy was senseless, and we were trapped by two maniacs, whose intent was undoubtedly to inflict torture, pain and ultimately death. Retribution for a minor incident of fifteen years ago was about to be enacted.

What the hell was wrong with me? If I was going to die, I might as well go out fighting. And wasn't there the slimmest chance that Ronnie and Sebastian wouldn't have the courage to carry out their execution? I brought nauseating images to mind: Santori injecting Kathy; Tate hitting me with a jack handle; Kent kicking the shit out of my brother all those years ago, all aimed at making me boil with rage. Sebastian was now at my feet, about to tie my ankles together. I braced my legs ready to kick Sebastian's head like a stationary football.

'Did you know ...' Andy had turned towards Ronnie and was talking like he was drunk. His head twitched with each spoken word like he was having a fit. I was certain I heard a high-pitched beep, but it was drowned out as Andy continued his ranting.

'... there's ... only ...'

Ronnie and Sebastian gawped at Andy incredulously as if he was a bomb about to explode. I stiffened as I saw Ronnie's finger tense on the trigger of his gun. Sebastian stayed crouching, but reached behind him to draw his gun.

'... one ... cunt ... in ...'

Andy's arms, still buried in his overcoat pocket, were convulsing in rapid vertical movements. His voice was screeching like an injured animal. I heard the door open; someone had been attracted by the hideous noise.

'... Scunthorpe.'

With that final word, the world around me went crazy.

The window behind Ronnie's head shattered – an attack I discovered later that had been signalled by the radio in Andy's pocket. The surprise was transmitted to Ronnie's hand and thunder erupted from his gun.

On his Lincolnshire town amen, Andy had one final convulsion and had thrown himself backwards. At the same time, his right hand emerged from his pocket, holding what looked like a miniature water pistol. But when he fired, it wasn't water that hit Ronnie in the middle of his chest – unless it was of the red and sticky variety.

Whoever had opened the door had been diverted to the crashing sounds that came from the front of the house.

I turned away from the bloody sight and focused on Sebastian. His eyes were transfixed on his brother and then moved to Andy. As Sebastian raised his gun, I lunged upwards with my bound legs, but before they made contact, another report echoed around the room and Sebastian fell backwards with a neat hole drilled left of centre on his forehead.

Chapter 53

NINTH SUNDAY – 11:45 a.m.

Andy had to physically usher me from the room. I had been struck rigid by the sight of two dead bodies lying on the linoleum-covered floor. There were two armed and masked men in the hallway, and another two standing guard over George and the women in the front room. Andy nodded to one of the men who urged us into the street and a waiting army Land Rover. We climbed into the back, the canvas sides shielding us from sight. The vehicle took off at speed and we travelled in silence, Andy not wishing to speak and me unable to. Minutes later the Land Rover pulled over and Andy bundled me out. The Land Rover turned left and vanished. We were in London Wall, near Moorgate station. Andy dragged me to sit down on a bench seat adjacent to a war monument in a small ornamental garden. The seat was clear of snow, as though someone had used it earlier.

The shock had worn off, but I was still shaking. I lashed out at Andy. 'You knew all along that Ronnie and Sebastian were in hiding at Grace Street … didn't you?'

Andy was calm and collected. 'No, not absolutely. It had been a possibility since Bradley discovered Jessie's maiden name was Warburton, the same as Doreen Kent's or rather Doreen Tremlett's. They are sisters.'

'Then what was all that crap from Don about Ma Kent and her sons going to Spain?'

'It was disinformation propagated generally by him. He was worried by potential leaks about the police search for Kent and Tate, so he spread the Spain story hoping to put them off their guard.'

'So why did you let us go there?' I was screaming now.

'Keep your voice down. If you remember, I tried hard to dissuade you.'

'That's not an answer. Why didn't you tell me truth?' I thought I had guessed the reason, but I wanted Andy to tell me himself. Andy paused longer than necessary and I knew a lie was coming.

'It was a good opportunity to test Bradley's theory.'

'Bollocks, Andy. Put ourselves at risk to test a theory?'

'I phoned K and Bradley before we left so we had cover.'

'That's little consolation. And they sanctioned our visit?'

Andy nodded.

'I can't believe I'm having this conversation with my own brother. You deliberately endangered our lives to get at Kent and Tate. For Chrissake, Andy, what sort of fucking automaton are you? Haven't you any feelings in that robot brain of yours? You're a complete nutcase, do you know? I can't possibly be your brother. I don't even want to be your brother.'

I stood up and began to stride away shaking with anger. I stopped and looked back. Andy had risen to follow me. 'I'm going to call Charlotte and tell her everything – and Kylie. She'll want to know she's married to a cold-blooded killer.'

'You can't do that, Pete. This is between you, me and the Official Secrets Act. Say one word to anyone and you'll be arrested.'

'So now you're threatening me.'

'Not me, Pete. It's the law.'

'And you are a law-abiding citizen, are you?'

'Come back and sit down, Pete. For better or worse, I'll tell you everything.'

'No crap, just the truth?'

'Yes, but the confidentiality clause remains.'

Andy had adopted what I now regarded as his killing pose. Very upright, cool, hands thrust deep inside his overcoat. I shuddered, wondering whether his gun was still in his pocket. We sat down.

'A couple of weeks ago, word began circulating in the underworld that Ronnie Kent had offered a lucrative contract for the capture or killing of Andy and Pete Shadwell – £200,000 each for delivery of our live bodies, or £100,000 for dead. Clearly, despite the crumbling of the Kent Empire, there was sufficient money left in the kitty to take out the two key protagonists in its downfall. Sure, we had a significant role, but the true reason was Ronnie, and to a lesser extent Sebastian, had been deprived of satisfying the dying wish of their father. Bradley tipped me off, and fearful someone, even in my department, would be tempted to sell out for such a high figure, I began making plans for us to relocate at short notice.'

'Relocate?'

'We were terribly exposed. You working in London, Charlotte at college; it would have been a matter of only days before we were found. I chose Canada for our escape route. As an interim measure, bodyguards were assigned and for the last week we've had shadows wherever we've been.'

'But Kylie's been pursuing a house in Epping, and I'm on the verge of renting a flat.'

'I couldn't say anything. I didn't want to worry anyone in case the plans changed. And they did, when we picked up speculative intelligence that maybe our adversaries were lodging in Grace Street. We put the house under surveillance, but there was no sign of Ronnie or Sebastian. We assumed it was false information. But when Luther mentioned last night that George was looking forward to your visit, I became convinced there had to be another motive. To me it meant *Kent and Tate* were looking forward to your visit.'

'Then why didn't Bradley just charge in and take them – alive?'

'While they were alive, the contracts on us would have stayed active. I had no intention of looking over my shoulder for the rest of my life, and couldn't face having a phone call one day to say you had disappeared or been killed. Bradley and I decided the problem had to be terminated at source. Kill before being killed. It was the perfect solution. And, we would save the taxpayers a bundle of money by not having to bother with costly trials.'

'Taxpayers? Jesus, stick to the first excuse, at least it's more credible. But how were you going to get away with it?'

'It had to be me to kill them. Whenever the police shoot someone, irrespective of the circumstances, the event becomes public property. Committees are formed, inquiries held, and the Press suddenly becomes holier than thou before starting to protest about Human Rights and firearm restrictions. Whereas, if the operation was under the umbrella of my department, we could legitimately – or rather had the mandate to – hush the event up as a National Security matter.'

'And that's what happening now … at Grace Street. Your commandos are sweeping clean?'

'Yes. The reign of Kent and Tate really is over, for the last time. You can sleep easy now little brother.'

I gasped in disbelief at his statement. 'Sleep easy? With a crazy hoodlum for a brother? *Are* you crazy? You acted like a bloody schizophrenic at Grace Street. Do you remember? Twitching and talking like someone possessed.'

'Pete, I assure you, I'm perfectly sane. What you witnessed there was part of my training. There's nothing more unnerving and distracting for the enemy to see manic behaviour. Mad gestures and mumblings – they make him uneasy and vulnerable. It's an effective technique. Try it some time.'

I had no intention of trying it – anytime, I just wanted to go home to Charlotte. I could trust her, but I would never trust my brother again.

Chapter 54

CHRISTMAS DAY – 2:45 p.m.

Christmas day was the last full gathering of the two Rensbergs and five Shadwells. At short notice, my parents had arrived nominally for a festive stay, but Andy and I knew that despite the government cloaking of our exploits, certain facts had leaked across the Atlantic, and parental concern had been the prime reason for their visit. They were returning to Canada after the New Year, but kept hinting they could come back *anytime* for the wedding of their younger son, which Charlotte's innuendos had planted in their minds. Kathy was due to fly to the States in two days time, and Charlotte and I were moving out to our flat the day after.

Andy and I were sitting in the conservatory after lunch, both browsing silently through the books we had received as Christmas presents. Out of necessity for our parents' peace of mind and the household's stability, we had been civil to each other since the Grace Street *visit*. Kylie had detected the ensuing chill between us, but I dismissed her concerns as sibling friction, which sometimes occurs following periods of family stress. I had kept my promise to Andy and not revealed what had happened at Grace Street. Nor did Kylie discover the truth any other way; the event had been clinically covered up by Andy's agency. I had to lie about returning without the diary; *there was nobody at home and I pushed a note through the door requesting that it was sent to me*. The diary did appear a few days later courtesy of Andy's never-ending influence, and I forwarded it immediately to Adrian without giving it a glance.

Andy looked up from his book as if prompted by something he had just read. 'I can't possibly imagine how it feels to not remember your past. Does it worry you?' He suddenly asked.

This had been the norm recently. Andy would periodically attempt to start a conversation rather than the other way round. Often I would just grunt or offer a curt reply, but distractedly absorbed in my book, I answered without thinking.

'Indeed, history is nothing more than a tableau of crimes and misfortunes.' I said, reading from the copy of *L'Ingénu* in front of me.

'Is that an answer or a quote?'

'Both, though whether it applies to me, I'd rather not know.' Somehow, I was reminded of my first recollection in the Royal London hospital. 'Did I ever tell you about my most distant memory?'

'No.'

'It's from the afternoon I came back from convalescing in the Lake District. I'd called in at the local library to return some books I had read while I was away. I ended up having a row with the librarian because the name and address details on my library record were blank. It was weird considering Peter Shadwell ceased to exist – temporarily – a few days later.'

Andy didn't reply. He was staring at me thoughtfully and mouth slightly agape.

'Something wrong?'

'Um ... No. Not really.'

'Andy, we may not communicate much these days, but I'd be extremely pissed off if you were still keeping things from me.'

'You won't like it.'

'I'm beyond shocks these days, particularly if it's anything to do with you.'

Andy adjusted his spectacles and ran his fingers through his hair. These gestures, I had recognized, were the only signs my iron-hearted brother ever exhibited of nervousness.

'Months ago, I had a bet with a German colleague at work. He worked in the systems department and was always bragging how technically inferior the British were, particularly when it concerned computer security. He boasted that he could hack into any system in the UK and alter or remove data. I was determined to call his bluff and gave him a task, which I thought would be impossible. I thought of you and a library ...'

Epilogue

I received a small parcel in the post a year later. I opened it excitedly, since I was expecting delivery of a rare book that Charlotte had located for me in a bookshop near her college. I tore off the wrapper and there on the rear jacket of a hardback book was a photograph and resume of Adrian Perry. At least I recognized it as Adrian, but he had used the pseudonym of Robin Forest. I turned to the front cover and there artistically blurred, like looking through frosted glass, was a photograph of a squatting homeless man. Remove the blur and it could have been me. I looked at the unusual title and smiled in recognition. There was a dedication on the seventh page.

To the real Robin Forest.
A friend, a source of inspiration, and the original Panglossian.

THE END

Author's Postscript

I hope that you have enjoyed reading *Panglossian*.

Pete Shadwell may appear to be settled in his new life, but expect the secret life of his brother, Andy, to return to haunt him in an industrial espionage sequel provisionally entitled *Downfall or Destiny?*

Meanwhile, the following pages are the first chapter of my third novel *Schoolfrenz*, a psychological thriller, which was published in November 2005.

Visit my website http://ray-crowther.me.uk for news and updates.

Schoolfrenz

Chapter 1

Prison life had reformed the newly named Richard Bard, until he passed a slim and fit looking Patrick Bonnett strolling along Roscoe Street.

He had last seen him twenty-one years ago, but he recognized three unmistakable features. The most obvious was the birthmark on his left cheek. About two inches by one inch, it was oval shaped and had earned Patrick the nickname of Egghead at school. To image-conscious teenagers it would have been the bane of their lives (and Bard was well aware of the effect of physical deformities), but Patrick had been thick-skinned, and had treated his distinguishing mark as a trophy rather than a disfigurement. Then there was his shocking blonde hair; even at 35 years old, it still shone like a beacon and he styled it in exactly the same way as before, long and curly. Lastly, it was his bouncing gait. He walked like he had rubber legs and, all those years ago, the motion had been likened to the Goons from a Popeye cartoon. Goon had been Bard's alternative nickname for him.

There was a cool wind blowing down the street, but beads of sweat formed on Bard's forehead as he fought the anger building up inside him. He had not felt this way since he had been buggered on his first day in Berrima. His counsellor in Berrima Correctional Centre had supposedly trained him to control his emotions, but with this crucial test of its effectiveness, the good work had been undone.

It had only been a month since Bard had been released having spent five years inside for aggravated robbery. He really thought that this time he was on his way to true rehabilitation. He had a job. Admittedly, only a temporary position Stefan Tate had arranged for him at his cousin's plumbing firm but, strangely, he was enjoying his closeted apprenticeship mucking about with pipes and radiators. Stefan had owed him after all. Stefan had been smart and worn gloves; not that *his* fingerprints or DNA would have shown up on police records, because for all the blags he had been involved in, he'd never been caught or even implicated. Superficially, Stefan was the model of respectability running his own car repair workshop, particularly as his best customer was the Sydney police department. Underneath he was the mastermind behind a good proportion of the major robberies and burglaries in New South Wales during the last ten years; yet, he lived modestly and was an honourable man. When the eventually-to-be Richard Bard was caught he knew the score: say nothing about his accomplice, be a model prisoner, return the stolen money and be patient. He'd be out in a few years, and then Stefan would see him right.

Stefan had kept to his word.

The robbery of a substantial residence in Wollongong had netted $50,000 and Bard's share was $10,000, which luckily for him was approximately the amount the victim had declared he had lost. Since there had apparently been a full recovery of money, the police had not pursued the issue of accomplices once Bard had been indicted. The victim had been Joe Prosho – a notorious villain – who could have been criminally compromised to reveal a greater loss. Less fortunate was that Joe held grudges, and through the frequent beatings, forced buggery and threatening notes, Bard had often been reminded there was the small matter of an additional $40,000 to be refunded when he rejoined the outside world. This was the major reason why Bard had resigned himself to a reformed life. He'd had enough of living on the edge and the thought of pursuit and retribution by Prosho had made even him shudder. Besides, through an intermediary prison visitor, Stefan had promised him $20,000 and a new identity for his silence, and that would set him up nicely for a fresh start; in Perth was the plan, far enough away from the Prosho influence.

From a covert release, he had been spirited to the security of Bret's – Stefan's cousin – house in Bondi, and was repaying his hospitality by helping to recondition heating systems. According to Stefan, the false documents in the name of Richard Bard should be ready tomorrow and that meant Stefan could then deposit the twenty grand in a new bank account. In theory, the flight to Perth and the fresh start were just a few days away, time enough to find out what that bastard Patrick Bonnett was doing in Australia.

Bard stopped to look into the shop window of a gift store. His reflection confirmed why Egghead had not recognized him. The long black coat he wore failed to conceal the hirsute and gangly appearance that was different to the last time Egghead had seen him. An ageing of twenty-one years had helped, but Bard's short hair, beginnings of a beard and rakish frame bore little resemblance to his school-day exterior; and even the stubbly chin could not completely cover the scarred evidence of the prison beatings. He glanced right and followed Egghead as he bounced his way towards the beachfront.

Within an hour, Bard had obtained a working profile of Patrick Bonnett.

One fact was easily discernible when Egghead had entered the changing rooms of Bondi Pavilion and had emerged five minutes later adorned in red shorts and yellow top, and carrying a similarly coloured holdall emblazoned with the title of Bondi Surf Bathers' Life Saving Club.

For the last week the sky had been cloudless and the temperature abnormally warm, yet Bard was still amazed that even in mid-winter Bondi beach attracted hoards of people intent on enjoying sea, surf and sand.

Egghead headed towards a lifeguard tower – a canopied platform raised about four metres above beach level – some fifty metres before the current tidemark. On his way, he stopped to chat with hardy sunbathers who presumably were regulars. Then he had an animated conversation with the lifeguard he was relieving, who pointed out to sea and at a group of teenage boys gambolling near the water's edge. The contrast between the patrolmen was significant. Heights were similar, but Egghead was a thin, white individual, while his colleague was muscled and tanned. By girth, they were a David and Goliath. A lifeguard was such an unlikely occupation to Bard; Egghead was a timid, weedy and water-shy person at school.

Bard watched from a distance. The second lifeguard finished his debriefing and went to change. Egghead studied the playful group and when the members ventured into the sea, he grabbed a white rescue surfboard and strode out purposefully to the sea edge to oversee their actions. Bard took the opportunity to approach one of the male sun worshippers Egghead had spoken to earlier.

'G'day,' Bard said. His years in Australia had trained him to use a near native accent such that few now questioned his English heritage. 'Is that my old cobber Patrick over there?' Bard waved in the direction of Egghead, who now appeared to be lecturing the teenage swimmers.

'Pat Bonnett?' the man asked.

'Yeh, that's him. Haven't seen him for years. Does he live near here?'

The man sat up and eyed Bard suspiciously. 'Who's asking?'

Bard caught his distrust and quickly added: 'Richard Bard. I'm in a rush and thought I'd call on him tonight.'

'He lives in Ocean Street. Swanky white-boarded duplex, called ... Surf something ... Surfhaven, that's it.'

'Well, thanks for that mate,' Bard said, and strode quickly away to emphasize his haste.

He headed back to Campbell Parade – the main promenade – with the seeds of a plan in his mind. As he mingled with the crowds, he adjusted his hat to conceal as much of his face as possible. He didn't think any of Prosho's heavies would be looking for him in Bondi, but he still needed to be careful. While staying with Bret for two weeks, and under advice from Stefan, other than a trip to his mother's he had not ventured further than the workshop in his backyard. At first, the minor improvement in space and freedom over the confines of Berrima had been a joy, but today, with Bret away on business for the next 24 hours and the winter sunshine streaming through the workshop fanlight, the temptation to explore had been too great.

In a stationery store, he browsed a local map and found Ocean Street. Follow the promenade into Bondi Road, and turn left in about half a mile.

Twenty minutes later, he had located "Surfhaven", though not without having to ask a postwoman on her rounds. All the properties in Ocean Street were swanky dwellings, and most of them were white. Surfhaven had fooled him with its front wall name plaque being concealed behind the purple flowers of an overflowing rhododendron bush. The building was impressive; the width and depth suggested multiple bedrooms and reception rooms and in front of a double garage were two cars: a large Ford and a small BMW. The front plot comprised, but for the small patch of ground which accommodated the bushes, an expensively tessellated parking area. Details of the rear were hidden from view by a fence and trees, though by reference to adjacent properties it probably extended over sixty metres to open parkland.

As Bard scrutinized the property from the opposite side of the road, another rush of anger consumed him as he made a comparison between his own life and his vision of Egghead's. *I bet he's got a gorgeous wife too* was passing through his mind when the front door of Surfhaven opened and he saw the head and shoulders of a brunette woman emerge. From a distance, she looked no more than mid-twenties and Bard uttered *gorgeous* to himself as she waddled rather than walked towards the cars. She stopped at the Ford and retrieved something from inside, and then Bard saw that her tummy bulge showed she was pregnant. He sniggered and whispered to himself *fuckable too*.

On past nefarious dealings with married couples, Bard had found he had a flair for ingratiating himself with women. He wasn't particularly good-looking – not that he had ever found looks were important to a woman – rather it was a combination of his slightly rough, rugged appearance and the verbal gift he seemed to have to make women feel at ease in his presence. Flirting had always been out of the question, since this riled the husband, but make a relaxing impression with the wife and guards were dropped. Time to test whether he still had the knack. He strolled across the road and stopped at the driveway entrance.

'Mrs Bonnett?'

The woman looked puzzled and said gently: 'Do I know you?' Then something clicked and she raised her voice: 'If you're from that bloody insurance company …'

The change in voice had revealed her origins. The softer introduction had the lazy drawl of an acquired Australian accent. The outburst had signalled that her origin was in the northeast of England. Quite naturally, Bard's brain switched to a comforting Geordie accent. He took a few steps onto the driveway.

'Nay, lass, but I know your husband – Patrick. We both went to Dovedale Secondary School in Hebburn.'

'Really? What's your name?'

'Um … Colin Peterson,' he conjured from the name of a fellow inmate, not wanting to reveal his original or new identity.

She thought for a moment. 'Pat's told me a lot about his old school friends. I don't recall a Colin Peterson.'

The former *was* interesting. Did it mean he was still in contact with them? The latter he expected, but he had already prepared an answer. 'We weren't exactly friends. I was two years above him, but Patrick was renowned throughout the school for his academic abilities.' True – flattery hurt no one.

Moving to the front door she said: 'Pat's at work at the moment; I'll tell him you called.'

A put-off. He wanted to keep the conversation going. Play dumb. 'I expect he's a captain of industry now. Wheeling and dealing in corporate finance?'

The suspicion continued. 'How did you know we lived here?'

'I was at the first floor window of a café in town and saw Patrick stop in the street below to speak to someone. By the time I reached the street, he had disappeared, but I asked the man he had spoken to. He confirmed it was Patrick and told me where he lived.' Another prepared answer delivered with the most endearing narrow-mouth smile he could muster, but she was still unconvinced.

'Leave me your phone number. I'll ask him to call you.'

Not a good idea. Bard was angry that he hadn't won through. His hand began to shake. Had the time inside moderated his charm? He calmed himself and persisted. 'If you don't mind I'll call back later. What time does Patrick get home?'

An answer to the final question would leave the door open for his return. She appeared relieved the conversation was ending and replied: 'Some time after four o'clock …'

'Okay. Thanks,' he replied and quickly strode away before she had the opportunity to add a qualification.

The Nearest FarAway Place

For the last ten years, Carl Denham has immersed himself totally in establishing and running a successful business. Inexplicably his company is suddenly taken over and he finds himself unemployed, but two million pounds richer. With unexpected freedom, his mind turns to finding Sarah Zurek, the girl he loved who drove him to his workaholic exile all those years ago.

Carl embarks upon a search for Sarah and uncovers a web of deceit perpetrated by his ex-wife, his business partner, and Sarah's family. Officially, Sarah committed suicide, but his alarming discoveries suggest she was murdered instead.

A car bombing, an arson, a murder and a trial later, Carl is alone again, ready to start another new life. Now someone is trying to kill him ...

ISBN: 0-9541110-0-1